the Festival by the Sea

June Loves is the author of over one hundred
non-fiction books for both children and adults,
and she has been a newspaper journalist,
freelance writer and teacher librarian. She lives
near the beach in Victoria with her husband.

MICHAEL JOSEPH
an imprint of
PENGUIN BOOKS

JUNE LOVES

the Festival by the Sea

MICHAEL JOSEPH

Published by the Penguin Group
Penguin Group (Australia)
250 Camberwell Road, Camberwell, Victoria 3124, Australia
(a division of Pearson Australia Group Pty Ltd)
Penguin Group (USA) Inc.
375 Hudson Street, New York, New York 10014, USA
Penguin Group (Canada)
90 Eglinton Avenue East, Suite 700, Toronto, Canada ON M4P 2Y3
(a division of Pearson Penguin Canada Inc.)
Penguin Books Ltd
80 Strand, London WC2R 0RL, England
Penguin Ireland
25 St Stephen's Green, Dublin 2, Ireland
(a division of Penguin Books Ltd)
Penguin Books India Pvt Ltd
11 Community Centre, Panchsheel Park, New Delhi – 110 017, India
Penguin Group (NZ)
67 Apollo Drive, Rosedale, North Shore 0632, New Zealand
(a division of Pearson New Zealand Ltd)
Penguin Books (South Africa) (Pty) Ltd
24 Sturdee Avenue, Rosebank, Johannesburg 2196, South Africa
Penguin (Beijing) Ltd
7F, Tower B, Jiaming Center, 27 East Third Ring Road North, Chaoyang District,
Beijing 100020, China
Penguin Books Ltd, Registered Offices: 80 Strand, London WC2R 0RL, England

First published by Penguin Group (Australia), 2012

1 3 5 7 9 10 8 6 4 2

Text copyright © June Loves 2012

Cover and text design and illustration by Allison Colpoys © Penguin Group (Australia)
Typeset in 12/17 pt Fairfield by Post Pre-press Group, Brisbane, Queensland
Printed and bound in Australia by McPherson's Printing Group, Maryborough, Victoria

National Library of Australia
Cataloguing-in-Publication data:

Loves, June, 1938–
The festival by the sea / June Loves
9780670076444 (pbk.)
A823.3

penguin.com.au

For my brother Ron,
the consummate
small-town librarian.

FOUR WEEKS

TO GO

Monday

I took a second cup of strong, very strong, black coffee on to the balcony with the 180-degree view. The sky was grey and threatening. Shelly Beach bay was a swirl of washing-machine waves with an extra measure of washing detergent added to them. I watched the foam flying in the air as the waves crashed on the rocks below.

The Dog had followed me. Formerly known as Hugo, the Dog and I have been cohabiting for a year and a half. I've grown rather fond of him, and he's reconciled himself to me. He recently considered adding an extra 'g' to his name. He's into mid-life name changing. I convinced him not to – at least not until he brings out a hip-hop album.

A bedraggled seagull landed on the balcony rail. The Dog did his guard-dog thing and chased it off.

'That was mean. It was a juvenile. Didn't you see its grey legs?' The Dog didn't care.

'Our absentee owner says I can extend our house-sitting contract.' The Dog and I had been house-sitting for six months – we were renting our own place before, but had quickly vacated it at the prospect of a rent-free stay. 'She needs more time to organise a

3

loan so she can demolish this house. Build a to-die-for mansion on a much sought-after cliff top. Then she'll sell the to-die-for mansion with the cliff-top view and become very rich.'

The Dog looked out to sea.

I arrived in Shelly Beach a year and a half ago with my life packed in two Louis Vuitton suitcases. I'd pared back. Not through choice. As a new member of the back-to-basics movement I'd become an earnest minimalist. I'd been a barely fifty-something who'd quit the rat race to launch a brilliant writing career – I even had a publishing contract – when my publisher went broke, my marriage went kaput and I lost virtually everything. Note to self: Do not leave finances to King Rat ex-husband. A lucky break brought me to Shelly Beach, and I'd been here ever since.

Over the last year and a half, the Dog and I have happily consolidated our philosophy of living with less. We've celebrated the ordinary things in life. A kettle that boils! A coffee percolator that percolates! A Vespa with an engine that turns over with a twist! My MacBook Air that lights up with a zing! A portfolio of three jobs that provide enough to live by. And most importantly, a shower that emits hot water in the early morning *and* late at night, unlike others I have known.

The reliable hot-water system at White Sands came with compliments from a friend's friend's daughter at Sea Haven Real Estate. The friend's friend's daughter negotiated a new system from my absentee landlord and I baked my award-winning flourless chocolate cake for her. And that's just about how good things happen in Shelly Beach.

According to locals, White Sands beach house was a popular holiday boarding house in the 1950s. The Dog and I only have access to the top floor: one bedroom, one bathroom and a roomy kitchen/living room that leads onto the balcony with the unbelievable view of the bay. And there's only a short walk down a sandy track to the rocky part at the end of beach.

'What do you think, Dog? Should I renew the house-sitter contract? Or should I wait until I know if I'll be moving to the city?' I pushed a wayward red curl behind my left ear. I'd let my natural colour and curls make a comeback recently, but still wasn't convinced by either.

The Dog ignored me. He knew I had a job interview coming up in the city, and he wasn't happy about it.

I finished my coffee, taking big gulps of icy sea air. 'If the weather's like this the, writers' festival will be a flop.'

The Dog went back to the kitchen to complete his hoovering for double-chocolate muffin crumbs. I picked up the last shard of a blue-and-white striped mug from the floor, placing it in the bin and closing the lid with a flourish. The Dog raised one hairy eyebrow.

'That was my favourite mug.'

The news I'd been trying so hard to forget came back to me. I looked at the stack of folders and papers labelled *The Shelly Beach Writers' Festival* strewn across the kitchen table. I scooped up the jar of Brazilian coffee beans and deposited it in the pantry, giving the pantry door a satisfying double-slam.

Adrian (former lover, now friend) had called in for coffee that morning. For the last year he's been organising a writers' festival in Shelly Beach. He'd convinced authors to come, raised funds through charity events, persuaded the local council to chip in, and advertised the festival far and wide. And now, with a month to go, he's gone and got himself a job in the city. So guess who's running the festival now? No choice in the matter. It's a *fait accompli*.

The Dog wasn't fluent in French but he got the drift. He dodged as I lifted the two kitchen chairs upright and placed them back at the kitchen table.

'Bloody hell! And he's supposed to have retired. Doesn't that mean you don't accept job offers?'

The Dog wasn't sure.

'He's got a twelve-month contract with the National Curriculum Authority and taken a lease out on a city apartment. Prime position with a river view!'

The Dog had an inkling that Adrian might be making a move.

'Typical! Adrian's got his career back on track, without a thought for me and my career. No matter that I have a job interview next week and might be leaving Shelly Beach myself. A fresh start *is* possible.'

The Dog agreed. He'd had about five fresh starts. And he knew how I felt about the state of the job market for women over forty-five. 'Covert discrimination' didn't even begin to cover it.

'Adrian's already spoken to the festival committee and got the go-ahead for me to take over as director. *I'm* on the committee! Adrian didn't speak to me until this morning!'

The Dog knew that I knew I could easily manage the role. In a former life I·managed conferences and events without so much as breaking a fingernail. But it was the *assumption* that I would do it that got under my skin. Typical Adrian! And he leaves tomorrow to take up his new job, so we're back to email communication. Here we go again. Endless email streaming. And it'll be my fault if I don't check my inbox.

'Adrian claims he's got everything locked in – that the festival will go like clockwork.' I straightened the writers' festival paperwork into neat stacks on the kitchen table. 'But I need time to get my head around *my* major job interview. I don't need a local writers' festival to worry about. I'm ready to get myself back on track, Dog.'

The Dog pointed out that I haven't exactly been off the track during the year and a half I've been living in Shelly Beach.

True. But it depends what you call successful. Does a part-time position as Children's Services librarian and Acquisitions Officer at the Sea Haven library, barista shifts at Piece of Cake bookshop cafe, and taking food orders at Rosa's pub on Saturday nights (thus preventing mortal combat between Rosa and her chef Lorenzo) equate to a portfolio of plum jobs?

The Dog reminded me that my multiple jobs provide enough cash to keep the wolf from the door – not that he's ever seen a wolf in Shelly Beach. A renegade fox, maybe.

'But can you believe Adrian could hand over his writers' festival so easily? I couldn't sense a smidgen of regret. He could hardly even spare the time to go over the festival's two-day schedule with me. He was jubilant. *Jubilant!* Couldn't wait to drive away in his car-that-goes-with-the-job and leave Shelly Beach.'

The Dog wasn't all that surprised. What could you expect from a cat-lover?

In a former life the Dog lived with Adrian in Shelly Beach. This was before I arrived with my life packed in two Louis Vuitton suitcases and took over the Dog's care as Adrian's house-slash-dog-sitter for six months. In the meantime, Adrian had become the owner of a prize Siamese cat, Princess. When Adrian moved back to Shelly Beach, I moved out – and the Dog came with me (although we haven't signed permanent pet ownership papers yet).

The Dog pattered onto the balcony again and I joined him. We watched the waves crashing below as they devoured our stretch of sand. When I was still a newcomer to Shelly Beach and hadn't learnt how to say no, I'd been caught in a net of extensive and intensive fundraising events to pay for Adrian's writers' festival. International celebrity authors don't come cheap, but we managed to secure two. Adrian decided to rely on local authors to take the rest of the sessions in our program.

Why had Adrian organised the festival at all? During one phil-
osophical discussion with locals after a fundraising meeting at
Rosa's pub, we pondered this question. Maybe Adrian, taking early
retirement and thinking that most of his life goals were accomplished, wanted to give something back to the small seaside town
he'd been born and bred in? Perhaps he was left with unaccus-
tomed hours to fill since he'd settled again in Shelly Beach. Was it
egotism or altruism that drove him? We'd agreed it was altruism.
Adrian genuinely wanted to bring money back into Shelly Beach,
and he had the charisma to make it happen.

The Shelly Beach locals were more than happy to take on
Adrian's plan of holding a writers' festival to bring back some spar-
kle and life to their small seaside town. Maybe the festival would
be the first step to revive Shelly Beach as a tourist haven? But do
Shelly Beach locals want their small seaside town to change from
a speck on the map to a sizeable dot?

'Did you think I sounded polite but in control when I talked to
Adrian?'

The Dog thought I sounded purposeful. He wasn't sure about
polite and in control. He glanced towards the bin and its shards of
broken mug.

Some of my tension *might* have come from the fact that my
'just friends' relationship with Adrian was very new, prompted by
a disastrous recent holiday together. The Dog told me I needed to
have a good talk to Adrian. He might be right. I hadn't talked to
Adrian about his new role in our 'just friends' relationship. In fact,
I hadn't even got my own head around it. And the Dog thought I
had a lot of balls in the air. I had to choose which balls to catch and
which to let fall to the ground. When I make up my mind which
balls to catch, he'll decide what he'll do.

'What do you think, Dog? Will you come with me to the city?'

The Dog announced he felt like a walk on the beach, even if it was blowing a gale and about to rain. He was so over my non-decision-making.

Tuesday: Festival committee meeting at Rosa's pub

I recovered sufficiently from my new festival-director status to convene festival committee members for an extraordinary dinner meeting at Rosa's. I took a few deep breaths before heading out the door. I needed to get a handle on the festival organisation and find out just how bad it was.

The Shelly Beach Writers' Festival committee consists of nine members. However, locals who are not on the committee are likely to be called on to help in any way needed. Actually, there's no such thing as a 'no' option in Shelly Beach. If you're asked to do something, you do it. (If not with passion and energy – with energy minus the passion.)

Rosa greeted us when the Dog and I arrived. Rosa's pub is Shelly Beach's main watering hole and meeting place. The Dog quickly slipped under the table, his favourite spot. He likes to rest his head on my foot.

Rosa, owner of Rosa's pub, is a member of our committee and has supported Adrian's writers' festival from its inception. Her enthusiasm is unstoppable.

'Gina! So good that you're taking over the festival. It will put Shelly Beach on the tourist map. We'll make a heap of money. Customers can drink lots of wine at Rosa's. Look at the sea. Talk about books and writing.'

Hopefully.

According to Adrian, Rosa has been invaluable, coming up with one entrepreneurial idea after another for our festival umbrella events. (Apparently that's the terminology for the events *around* the main event.) Rosa has an unending list of cousins and exes to assist her with any umbrella event she wants to run.

Rosa called from the bar, 'No need to use the billiard room, Gina. We can hold the meeting in the dining area. Not many members coming tonight – too cold, too wet. Violet texted me. She's bringing the apologies. But not to worry, everyone is very happy for you to be big boss of the festival.'

Everyone except me, that was. I smiled a tight smile.

While we were waiting for the others to arrive, Rosa made me admire her new paint job. 'Cousins finish painting. What do you think? All you have to do is slap on the paint and you have a beaut-i-ful pub.'

I smiled and agreed.

'My cousins are very quick painters. They give you a good price if you need painting, Gina. I tell them they have to use whitewash paint and the egg-blue colour Adrian tell everyone on Beach Road to use for doors.'

'Duck-egg blue.'

'Exactly.'

Rosa was ecstatic when it was suggested we set up the meet and greet table for the festival in the pub foyer. It gave her an excuse to paint it. 'Cousins used buckets of paint. I took up the old carpet. Polished the floorboards.'

'You've done a brilliant job, Rosa. It looks fantastic. Stylishly casual.'

Rosa beamed. 'Upstairs bedrooms are painted whitewash and egg-blue colour too. I give very reasonable bed and breakfast offers to people who come to festival. Whitewash and egg-blue bathrooms at the end of the corridors. What more do you want? And Lorenzo cooks pasta all day long. Come and see my new veteran furniture in my backyard.'

'Vintage furniture.'

'Exactly. I buy it from a city pub. Owner going down the plug-hole. Had to sell everything. Palm trees thrown in too.'

I gathered the Dog under my arm and we made a quick trip through the pub to admire Rosa's backyard (rebranded 'beer garden'). It was looking upmarket and stylishly casual thanks to the bankrupted city pub. The palm trees looked a little sad bending in the strong sea wind but you could see the potential – if the sun ever came out.

The Dog and I went back inside and sat down at a dining table to check Adrian's list of committee members and the corresponding jobs they were handling. The names all looked very familiar from my time as ad-hoc convener of the Shelly Beach Writers' Group – another job I was roped into in Adrian's absence. The writers' group had essentially morphed into the Shelly Beach Writers' Festival committee for the duration of the festival. Adrian had clearly purloined – sweet-talked – members into various festival roles. Too bad about their unfinished novels.

Rosa called over from the bar. 'Pandora's just texted. She's not coming tonight. She's gone to the city to see her photographer boyfriend again. She'll be back tomorrow but says not to worry, she's got everything covered. You can talk to her tomorrow.'

My friend Pandora, owner of the Writers' Retreat – one of Shelly Beach's two B&Bs – is a former high-profile spin-doctor. Naturally, she's in charge of marketing and publicity for our festival. She's also a man-eater with a figure to die for, and an enviable ability to jog along Shelly Beach without getting instantly red and sweaty. She was holding down a high-pressure job as a media consultant in the city until her father died a couple of years ago. She decided to undertake a Shelly Beach sea change, renovate her father's old home and transform it into a snazzy B&B. Locals have been impressed with the excellent PR Pandora has delivered thus far for our festival. We have a great website thanks to her, and we've already had a heap of hits. According to Adrian, most of our 150 tickets have been sold.

I called a 'thank you' to Rosa and ticked *Marketing and Publicity* on my checklist.

Alf and Beryl arrived and the Dog emerged from under the table. The Dog is very fond of Alf and Beryl. They're a salt-of-the-earth local couple who look after the Dog if I need to go to the city and visit my daughter and grandson. Tanned and fit sixty-something-year-olds, Alf and Beryl have lived in Shelly Beach all their lives.

'Sorry I can't stay long, Gina,' said Beryl. 'I've a Poetry Group meeting. Alf will fill me in on anything I need to know. But catering's under control – nothing to worry about at the moment.'

I smiled and ticked *Catering* off my list.

Potholer and sundry sons arrived. After lots of handshakes and 'Good on you, Gina's, they headed to the bar to order drinks. Potholer and sons are Shelly Beach's resident builders. They run a profitable building company and also fix whatever needs fixing around Shelly Beach. They charge very reasonable prices and frequently give their services without asking for payment. But I still get confused between Potholer's sons. When I arrived at Shelly Beach I thought I was seeing double. Rosa set me straight. 'You're not seeing double, Gina. It happens to everyone when they arrive at Shelly Beach. Potholer's wife, Aphrodite, had three sets of twins. She tell me she finally get the hang of twins when the third set arrived. She tied labels around each little ankle so she knew which twin she fed last.'

Looking now at the lifesaver-sized Potholer sons, I'd say Aphrodite did an excellent job rearing her boys. Alf, Potholer and sons are in charge of health and safety for the festival.

'No problem, Gina! Everything's under control.'

Health and Safety off the list.

Rosa called from the bar. 'Violet's texted again. She's almost here. Just getting the cats inside for the night.'

Violet is Shelly Beach's eccentric cat woman. She keeps a herd of cats and is constantly rescuing stray tabbies and finding homes for them. She's also Shelly Beach's resident cosy-crime fiction writer. She writes her novels in the Piece of Cake bookshop cafe where I work the occasional shift. She's had her first cosy-crime novel featuring Red Blaze, her amateur detective, published, with another due for publication this year. Violet has embraced the writers' festival, as you'd expect.

At that moment Violet arrived and gave a general wave to locals in the dining room. While she divested herself of layers of clothing, she started talking. 'Perishing weather outside. Hope it's not like this for the festival. Adrian told me you're taking over as director, Gina. You'll be able to handle the role with no bother. Just be ready for a few curlies if they're thrown your way. Adrian's done the main organising anyway, and if I know Adrian everything will be set in concrete.'

I gave Violet one of my mean smiles.

She sat down and unpacked a basket of soft toys she'd brought with her – quirky cats holding *Do Not Disturb: Writer at Work* signs. 'What do you think about these? Writers can hang their cats on the doors of their writing places: sheds, cars, attics, whatever. Adrian thought they were an excellent added-value product to sell at the festival.'

How could I disagree?

'Beryl and the Shelly Beach craft group are sewing oven mitts and making Serious Seville marmalade,' Violet continued.

I wasn't surprised to hear this. Producing added-value products to sell at the festival has consumed every group in Shelly

Beach this year and stretched our talents – perhaps too far? I cast a raised-eyebrow glance at Violet's cat toys.

'Digby sends his apologies, and I suppose you've heard from the others,' Violet said. 'I don't know why you bothered to hold an extraordinary meeting, Gina. Fortnightly meetings were all we needed when Adrian was director.'

'I realise that, Violet. I just thought I'd try to find out where we're at with the organisation. Check everyone is happy with their roles and so on.'

'Whatever you think best, dear. Oh, before I forget, Matt Galinsky, Dimity Honeysuckle's manager, is arriving tomorrow morning. If you're working at the library, I can meet Mr Galinsky and settle him into the Sea Crest B&B.'

Matt Galinsky is the manager of Dimity Honeysuckle, one of our two celebrity authors for the festival. Dimity's an international children's author-slash-illustrator-slash-entertainer who's famous for her bestselling series of children's picture storybooks featuring Atticus the mouse.

'No need, Violet. I'm not working at the library tomorrow. I'll be at the Sea Crest to meet him.'

While the Dog and I walked home, I let off some steam. 'What a pointless meeting! There are only four weeks until the festival and I still have no idea what's going on.'

The Dog agreed that I needed to know what was happening. He knew I liked to tick off my dot-point to-do lists.

I'd begun to resign myself to the festival – I didn't really have a choice – and even to convince myself it *would* be a fantastic opportunity to gain real-life experience to bolster my CV. If I was going to do it, I was going to do it well – even if that meant jumping tall buildings in single bounds.

The Dog suggested I reconsider my jumping-tall-buildings-in-one-bound attitude. He wasn't prepared to be a super-dog and he was sceptical as to the benefits of wearing your underwear over your clothes.

I ignored the Dog. 'I'm glad I'm not working tomorrow. I don't want Violet to be the first Shelly Beach local Matt Galinsky meets.'

The Dog agreed. Sometimes Violet can give you the idea that she's one sandwich short of a picnic. Locals know this is not true. But if Violet was in her wild cat-woman persona (in contrast to her new published-author-of-cosy-whodunits persona) Matt Galinsky would wonder what had hit him. He might think twice about bringing his celeb children's author–illustrator Dimity Honeysuckle to our festival.

Wednesday: Meet Matt Galinsky

The Dog pattered into the bedroom. Time for breakfast. I fed the Dog and took my coffee on to the balcony. Another dull overcast day. Medium-level waves. Not very cheery weather to greet Mr Galinsky.

It was a freak piece of luck landing Dimity for the festival. Adrian was seriously challenged trying to find two international celebrity authors willing to come to Shelly Beach, and the GFC didn't help. Adrian booked one US crime fiction author who suddenly decided he'd better stay at home to finish his novel in order to keep food on the table for his children. And Jessica Hart, well-known UK romantic fiction writer, fell down the mahogany staircase in her London home and broke her leg in two places. Obviously she couldn't travel to Shelly Beach.

Adrian was becoming desperate by the time he met Matt Galinsky at a writers' festival in the UK last year. Dimity was booked to do a series of sell-out concerts in all our capital cities already, and Adrian pitched Shelly Beach as a great place for Dimity to start her national tour – a secluded out-of-the way seaside town where it's easy to avoid the paparazzi; a place where Dimity could relax, prepare and ease her way into her national tour. (Evidently Dimity's concerts are excellent platforms to market her CDs and merchandise, pitched around her picture storybooks. Pandora said Dimity Honeysuckle must be a biz-savvy young woman or has a very clever manager. Committee members are keen to meet Matt Galinsky and form their own opinions.)

I'd blu-tacked Adrian's schedule to the kitchen wall and consulted it now. 'Matt will be here a week before Dimity and her assistant, Sandy, who arrive next Monday. My big interview's the day after. It's all a bit too close for comfort, Dog.'

The Dog knew how I felt, but he had confidence in my organisational abilities. After all, he gets a daily walk – even if I sometimes need prompting on the 'When can we go?' window-of-opportunity question.

I decided on smart casual to meet Matt: designer jeans, a white linen shirt, red cashmere sweater, ballet flats and a denim jacket. All came from my friend Daphne's charity shop. I gave myself and the Dog a quick brush, and we raced off to the Sea Crest B&B.

Geraldine and husband Claude (relative newcomers to Shelly Beach) are the owners of the five-star Sea Crest B&B. We'd hardly seen them since they moved into Shelly Beach last year. They'd spent months and months on the renovations in order for the place to be ready and open for festival bookings.

I remembered Geraldine and Claude celebrating at Rosa's a while back, thinking they'd hit the jackpot when they received the lucrative bookings from Dimity's team. It was a great start to their B&B business. Matt Galinsky booked the whole place for a month. Geraldine and Claude were planning to store the excess furniture in their shed so Dimity's team could use two bedrooms as private lounge rooms.

Geraldine, Claude and I were waiting at the reception desk when Matt Galinsky pulled up outside in a two-door Audi.

Geraldine whispered, 'He's hot! Smoking hot!'

We watched from behind the blinds as a tall and extremely good-looking fifty-something male collected his baggage from the Audi and made his way to the reception.

The Dog and I went to greet him. Matt immediately dropped his baggage and bent down to pat the Dog. The Dog lapped up the attention. One heart already won.

I greeted Matt, explaining I was taking over Adrian's role as festival director. He already knew. Adrian had emailed him. Would there be an email for me from Adrian? Don't think about it. Move on, Gina.

I introduced Matt to Geraldine and Claude and we went to check out the rooms for Matt and his party. Matt was impressed, which impressed Geraldine and Claude. Their B&B does have superb bay views, and they planned their renovations well. After excellent coffee and muffins in the Sea Crest dining room the Dog and I left Matt to settle in.

Walking down the hill from Sea Crest we bumped into Violet coming up. 'Have you met Matt Galinsky yet? He's a bit of all right, isn't he?'

(I'm constantly amazed at Violet's ability to know what happens in Shelly Beach before it happens.)

No time to reply. Violet continued without a trace of breathlessness – for a seventy-something-year-old she's extremely fit. 'I met Matt at Rosa's pub earlier. He wanted directions. I introduced myself and told him I'd be looking after the rooms at Sea Crest. Incidentally, he was interested in the flyer for our poker school. He's going to eat at Rosa's tonight and check it out.'

'Right.' I let mention of Violet's poker school pass. Note to self:

Remind her to go easy on Matt if he joins. Violet has a reputation as a nifty player. I don't want her taking Dimity Honeysuckle's manager down – not a good look. 'You're working at Sea Crest during the festival, Violet?'

'Didn't you know? Geraldine's employed me to service the rooms and do the breakfasts while Matt and his team are staying there. Geraldine has to work in the city up until the festival opens and Claude's not much use. Always a dodgy idea, marrying an older man.'

The Dog and I let this comment pass. We smiled our goodbyes and continued our walk home.

As soon as I returned to White Sands I couldn't help myself – I opened my inbox. Bingo!

From: Adrian <bookstreet@network.com.au>
To: Gina <glaurel@peninsula.com.au>
Subject: New pad
Hello Gina,
You'll be pleased to know I've settled in quickly. Daughter and son-in-law came and helped me unpack. You'd love the city and river views from the bedroom.
Have you meet Matt Galinsky? He's a great guy.
Hope you're over your post-holiday blues. How's your spider bite healing?
xx Adrian

From: Gina <glaurel@peninsula.com.au>
To: Adrian <bookstreet@network.com.au>
Subject: Re: New pad
Delighted you're settling in well.
Yes, Matt Galinsky arrived safe and sound, and is more than happy with Sea Crest accommodation. No, I'm not over post-holiday

blues!! I still need antibiotics and cortisone for spider bite, not to mention rash, which keeps recurring. The doctor says rashes like mine can keep recurring for years.
Gina

I made a cup of very strong coffee and the Dog and I went out on to the balcony. 'Bloody hell! Adrian hasn't a clue. He. Just. Doesn't. Understand.'

The Dog understood that Adrian didn't understand. The Dog generally doesn't understand either.

I acknowledge I have a heap of stuff to sort through. Was I going to accept a corporate job again if I was offered one? Would I leave Shelly Beach to take up city living again? It would be nice to be closer to my daughter, Julia, and grandson, Barney. And what was I going to do about Adrian?

The Dog was staring at me with his beady eyes.

'Deciding to do something often makes things worse. Deciding to do nothing can be good . . . but also bad. Often you don't get a solution. Just a trade-off.'

The Dog kept staring at me.

'Don't say a thing. We're going for another walk.'

Beach Road, Shelly Beach, is a single-sided shopping strip. On the opposite side is the foreshore with our new rotunda, toilets, children's playground and a community hall in need of repair. In a seagull's squawk you're at the beach, and then there's a pier stretching into Shelly Beach bay.

The shopping strip used to consist of three working shops – Jenkins' General Store, Scissors Salon and Rupert's

Butchery – book-ended by Rosa's pub and Piece of Cake book-shop cafe. The remaining four shops had been boarded up for years, existing in a state of benign neglect.

Last year it wouldn't have taken a Shelly Beach visitor a minute to realise that what was once a thriving small seaside town was barely surviving. Sea Haven to the north had enticed the tourists away with its glam infrastructure and boutique services. Kingston, the commuter town to the south, had gobbled up Shelly Beach's resources, cash and services.

But with the Shelly Beach Writers' Festival looming on the horizon, Beach Road has had a complete turn-around. All the premises have been smartened up, following Adrian's suggestion of creating a harmonious streetscape. He recommended whitewash paint and duck-egg blue trims, and adding new 'vintage' signage. Result: a picture-postcard small seaside town. A brilliant place to hold a two-day writers' festival.

Dr Digby Prentice-Hill (a literary, not medical doctor), my friend and festival committee member – a charismatic force to be reckoned with – is now the proud owner of Pages Gallery, in what was once the drapery store. Locals weren't surprised when Digby announced last year that he'd purchased the shop and would turn it into a gallery. Coincidentally, it was located right next door to Piece of Cake – the thriving bookshop cafe set up a year and a half ago by Adrian. Digby and Adrian grew up in Shelly Beach, and they've competed all their lives. They both returned to Shelly Beach after taking early retirement, and they're still competing.

'Typical males. Can't help it,' Violet often says. She's known Shelly Beach's two alpha males since they were boys. She'd maintained that Digby's property purchase was not quite the use-less move it seemed at first. Alf and Potholer had inspected the boarded-up drapery and told Digby it needed to be completely gutted, re-roofed, restumped and rewired. For a start. But Digby wasn't fazed with the renovating costs and gave the go ahead.

According to local goss Digby's swimming in money – he inherited his 'castle' and quite a bit of money after wife number two died. And of course Digby's had a prestigious university career and probably invested wisely. From my limited experience of Digby's lifestyle, I'd say local goss is accurate. Digby's loaded. Now, nine months later, Pages Gallery is amazingly completed and will open in time for the festival.

The Dog and I were headed there now. I knew Digby would bring me up to date on the festival organisation. He's a smooth operator, and had volunteered to organise lots of events for the festival. His contacts with publishers and the general literary literati have impressed our committee. (Not Adrian.) The most important event is a red-carpet cocktail do to be held at Digby's castle (aka heritage homestead with beautiful views) on the festival's opening night. The red-carpet do would be followed by a gala barbecue and barn dance at Henry Shepherd's property. Henry, who died last year, was a beloved member of the Shelly Beach community, and his family are happy for the gala to continue on his property.

The gala was the biggest event in Shelly Beach each year, and according to locals it had been held on Australia Day for decades. But at a writers' festival committee meeting, Digby, using his consummate negotiating skills, persuaded members to move the barbecue and barn dance on the Shelly Beach calendar. 'Only for one year! We'll add it to our writers' festival program.'

'Pushing the goal posts,' was one of the many grumbled comments heard at the meeting.

Nonetheless Digby's powers of persuasion won out. He convinced locals that the barbecue and barn dance, with high-priced tickets, would bring in more funds for the festival.

Digby and Tiffany were both in the gallery when the Dog and I arrived. Digby had employed Tiffany, a former student of his, to oversee the renovation and conversion of the drapery. Tiffany has been quickly accepted in the Shelly Beach community. Digby decided it would be better if Tiffany took up residence at his castle during the renovations – 'More convenient. Saves her travelling up and down to the city' – and locals never blinked an eye when Tiffany moved into – and then out of – Digby's castle. She's now renting a room at Rosa's pub.

Digby came over to greet me wearing his charismatic smile, which is impossible to resist. I received a sexy hug and kisses on both cheeks as I inhaled his Armani cologne.

'Congratulations, Gina. Heard you're the new festival director. Too much on my plate at the moment to help Adrian out and do the director bit – but I'm here whenever you need me.'

I acknowledged Digby's congratulations with a wry smile. I knew Digby had been caught up with the publication of his book to be launched at our festival, but I was also sure Adrian never offered the position of director to him.

Tiffany joined us, a slim twenty-something figure in black. 'Hi, Gina. What do you think of our reception table?'

'Stunning.' I admired the Italian glass-topped table balanced on its swirly metal stand. 'Whitewash on the walls works well. Love the polished concrete floor. You've done a brilliant job, Tiffany.'

She accepted my compliments with a modest smile. 'Digby's spared no expense to make Pages Gallery a must-see destination. We're waiting for the lighting to be installed, then we can start hanging artwork and we're ready to open. I met Matt Galinsky this morning at the pub. He was looking for the Sea Crest B&B. Charming man. I'm so pleased he's agreed to let us show Dimity's original artwork during the festival. We'll start hanging it next week.'

The Dog was getting twitchy. I took the hint and turned to Digby. 'Have you got the list of the events you're organising for the festival, Digby?'

'Tiff's in charge of events, Gina.'

Tiffany smiled and instantly launched into her efficient event-coordinator role. She consulted the leather-bound appointment book placed strategically on the imported glass-topped table. 'There's Digby's book launch for *War and Wool 1938–1958*. His publishers are going halves with us for the grog and nibbles.

'The red-carpet cocktail do at the castle on opening night is under control. We've got locally donated wine, and Digby's covering the cost of the catering. The barbecue and barn dance that will follow is not our problem – not sure who's organising that. But the two sessions of nibbles and drinks here in Pages are covered. Sponsored by publishing houses. Local catering.'

Tiffany was still working from her appointment book. 'And there's a buffet dinner at Digby's castle sponsored by Singing Bird, Dimity Honeysuckle's UK publishers, on day two of the festival.'

I smiled, reigning my panic in. 'Well done, Tiffany. Everything seems under control.' The Dog was really getting twitchy. Two seagulls were standing a fraction inside the gallery, encroaching on his territory. Time to go.

Digby put an arm around my back and walked me to the door. Another very close hug and cheek kiss. 'I've some excellent wine I want you to help me taste and select for the festival events. Are you free tomorrow night?'

I was put on the spot and didn't have a quick lie ready. '. . . Yes.'

'Marvellous. Say about seven?' And then came that knowing wink, which I chose to ignore.

On the way home I wallowed in the guilts. Since I started my friends-only relationship with Adrian I'd tried a more-than-friends relationship with Digby. If you could call it that.

'I'm well aware a love triangle can get very messy. All right – tricky! Anyhow, it was only a one-night stand. I blame the Moët. Adrian and I were over. *Are* over. And Tiffany had already moved to the pub.'

The Dog ignored me. I'd ignored his advice in the past about crossing the boundary between friendship and a sexual relationship. And I'd lived to regret it.

Conversation was very limited on the way home.

~

That afternoon, the Dog and I were checking supplies in the Piece of Cake kitchen when Pandora burst in, looking alarmingly fit and glam with her signature red lipstick and winged eyeliner.

'Congrats, festival director!' I received a cheek kiss and a hug. 'I'll fill you in on the stuff I've been doing but first I want to hear what you've been up to. I haven't seen you for weeks! I have to hear about your holiday-from-hell.'

I finished checking supplies and made a note for Gail who was on Piece of Cake duty tomorrow. Pandora made coffee and we sat down for a catch-up. 'Well . . .' I stirred my coffee and stalled for time, but I knew from experience that Pandora was an excellent keeper of secrets. 'Adrian pitched our holiday-from-hell to me as five wildly romantic sexy days. Five days when we could slip away from everything and everybody to a glam tropical island. You know he's been so busy these last few months, staying at his daughter's place in town heaps – now I know why, of course. But he knew that we hadn't spent much quality time together, and he said he'd make it up to me.' I ignored the slight smile on Pandora's mouth. 'So of course I agreed to go.'

'And . . .'

'He didn't tell me he was getting a bargain deal! The island resort was closed to paying guests due to major renovations, but his friend Greg operates a cargo flight company and regularly flies supplies to the tropical island from hell. Greg offered Adrian free seats on his plane – he owed Adrian a long-time favour – and organised free DIY accommodation for us. Otherwise known as a tent. We'd have the whole place to ourselves, he promised. Not difficult due to the island being closed to normal, sensible, fee-paying guests who did not want accommodation on a building site!'

'It could have been romantic . . .'

I ignored Pandora. I was on a roll. 'It wasn't. Adrian likes to travel light. *Very* light. He never told me I could only take carry-on luggage. He knows I'm a kitchen-sink traveller. *Gina's a kitchen-sink traveller* should be embedded in his brain.'

'But it was only for five days. All you needed was a couple of bikinis, sarongs and sunscreen.'

I ignored Pandora.

'It was *so* embarrassing at the airport. And it wasn't even a proper airport. Certainly not the big international one. It was a tin-pot airstrip with a corrugated-iron shed-office where Greg tethers his plane. Don't laugh. This is serious break-up-a-relationship stuff.'

'I'm sorry.'

'Before I was allowed to board Greg's ridiculous little plane I had to transfer minimum gear into a disgusting backpack Greg loaned me. Adrian and Greg supervised and advised while I unpacked and repacked essential clothes to last the five days – right down to the number of pairs of knickers I could take with me!'

25

I took the last sip of my coffee. 'And my Louis Vuitton suitcase containing my Armani trench coat is still stored in Adrian's friend's tin-shed office at the tin-pot airport.'

'Do you want another coffee?'

I shook my head. 'Can you believe there are still airplanes made of paper and sticks that fly unprepared passengers to dodgy tropical islands? If I'd known we were going to fly in such a tiny aeroplane I would have taken anti-nausea tablets. Consequently . . . consequently, I was sick the whole flight – there and back. Adrian and Greg were really annoyed with me. I realise it's unpleasant to fly in a small plane when someone has divested themselves of their last meal. But not – my – fault!'

Pandora nodded. 'And the days in between?'

'Hideous. Nothing but one disaster after another. I got food poisoning from dodgy seafood on the second day. Did Adrian, who lived on nothing but seafood the whole five days, get food poisoning? No. And after the cyclone on day four – it could have been a tropical hurricane, I suppose – I decided to venture out of my leaky tent. I fought my way in driving rain and wind through a tropical rainforest to join Adrian and Greg and sundry suntanned young building crew at the semi-renovated tiki bar. This was when I must have come in contact with a deadly tropical plant. That night I was covered in a head-to-toe rash.'

'You can hardly blame Adrian for your medical problems, Gina.'

I ignored Pandora. 'And I was bitten by an unidentified poisonous spider.'

'No time for any romance?' Pandora's mouth was twitching.

'Don't you dare laugh, Pandora! No! I was either sick or zonked out to stop me from scratching myself to death. In the meantime Adrian snorkelled, scuba-dived, swam and had great fun with his pilot friend Greg and the bunch of tanned Gen Ys who were sup-posed to be working on the renovations.'

Pandora was stifling a smile. 'I know you've had a nightmare experience, Gina, but you can't blame Adrian.'

I gave Pandora a grudging smile. 'You don't think so?'

'I can remember you telling a group of us at Rosa's one night that you thought Adrian could be your Mr Darcy.'

'I would never have said that.'

'No. It was probably Bianca talking about you and Adrian.'

'It might have been okay if we'd had a chance to talk when we got home, but we'd only been back a day when Adrian raced into town again to sort out stuff for the festival. The festival that *I* am now running. And he *still* hasn't retrieved my Louis Vuitton suit-case from Greg's tin-pot airport office. It's obvious that I'm better to stay single and be happy on my own terms.'

Pandora didn't say anything, just gave me a funny look. She knew better than to argue with me, and skilfully changed the topic. 'Here, have a look at the festival's website. A friend just updated a few things for me.' Pandora opened her laptop and clicked on the Shelly Beach Writers' Festival site.

'The line-up looks brilliant! Can we *really* deliver this?'

'With a bit of luck I think you can, Gina.'

I ignored the emphasis on *you*. 'Let's check our rosters for the next two weeks.'

Walking home later I didn't get a smidgen of sympathy from the Dog. He told me not to go on my five-day tropical island holiday with Adrian (now friend, former lover). The Dog knows I'm lost without my iPhone and my dot-point lists. His sixth sense told him I'd go stir-crazy on a tropical island – especially if a cyclone hit – and he could feel in his bones a cyclone was looming on the horizon.

I ignored the Dog.

Thursday: Ambassador Dog and blue marquee

Mid-morning, the Dog and I were relaxing at White Sands when Terri called in to see us. The Dog gave her his over-the-top welcome. Terri, a thirteen-year-old going on thirty, is a friend of mine. She lived next door with her family when the Dog and I were house-sitting Adrian's home in Sea Spray Street. I used to call Terri Bossy Child, but she will no longer answer to the name – apparently she's no longer a child. Terri is the Dog's only exception to his dislike of the younger breed of people.

'Don't you look gorgeous, Dog?' Terri heaped pats and cuddles on the Dog. Terri, her young brother Sam and accountant mother Joan were excellent neighbours. To be honest (and at this stage in my life I think I'm finally approaching honesty) I have to admit the annoying Q&A sessions I used to have with Terri played a large part in keeping me on track when I first settled in Shelly Beach.

Now was the time for reciprocal support. She wasn't happy. Her dad died two years ago after a lengthy battle with cancer and her mother hadn't seen anyone else since. She, Joan and Sam are a tight-knit family. But romance has loomed on the horizon for Joan and huge changes might be about to take place in the family.

When Terri turned thirteen earlier this year, she'd announced, 'I'm never smiling again – not until I'm twenty. And I'm not eating anything with eyes!'

The Dog and I avoided the 'not eating anything with eyes' statement but we knew what had prompted the not-smiling decision. Joan had found a boyfriend – an accountant called Paul who worked with her. But Paul wasn't the problem. It was his son.

Terri dumped her bag of Ambassador Dog gear on the floor and came to help me make coffee, hot chocolate and cut a few slices of cake.

'Toby's driving me nuts, Gina.'

'Toby?'

'I've told you! Paul's son.'

'Right.'

'He's a week-about kid.'

'A week-about kid?'

'Well, you know that his parents are divorced. Toby spends one week with Paul, and then one week with his mum. His mum stayed in their original house but Paul is just renting. If my mum and Paul decide to live together, Paul is going to move into our house. Mum says that makes sense.' Terri rolled her eyes while she cut the chocolate cake.

'And . . .'

'Toby's sixteen next month. His parents have told him that once he's sixteen he can choose to live permanently with either of his parents if he wants to. He hates the week-about stuff. He says living out of a suitcase sucks.'

'Right . . .'

'So if Toby chooses to live with Paul full-time, and Paul moves into our house, I'm moving in with you.'

Bloody hell! 'Have you talked about this with your mum?'

'No.'

'Right. Can we talk about this after the festival? I've got an interview for a job in the city next week. I'm not even sure if I'll be staying in Shelly Beach.'

'Everyone knows about your interview, Gina. I've decided that if you get it, and Paul and Toby move into our place, I'll go for a scholarship for a city school and move in with you . . .' She looked at the Dog. 'And the Dog.'

The Dog pattered out on to the balcony. I knew he was glad he had more independence than Terri. He has control of his life. If he doesn't like his owner he can escape and hit the road. Find a new owner. And he has the security of a microchip implant – although the implant does say he's Adrian's pet.

'I promise I'll talk to your mum, Terri. I'm sure it won't be as bad as you think it will be.'

I received a cross-eyed plus rolled-eye look.

'Let's look at the gear you've made for the Dog.'

Terri came up with the idea of making the Dog resident pooch at our festival. Apparently resident pooches are a hit in a chain of Canadian luxury hotels. The dogs reside in the foyers of the hotels, sitting beside the concierges. Guests can pat them or take them for walks.

The Dog has agreed to be patted under sufferance but not to be taken for walks by festival attendees. We called him inside so we could fasten a blue-and-yellow Shelly Beach Ambassador rosette to the Dog's collar. He was surprisingly tolerant.

Terri showed him the sign she'd made to go on his basket, which read *Shelly Beach Writers' Festival Canine Ambassador*.

'Great, Terri!' I quickly checked Adrian's blu-tacked list. 'Do you want to come with me to Rosa's? I need to measure the beer garden to make sure the blue marquee will fit.'

'Cool.'

The festival committee had worked long and hard to raise funds to hire the blue marquee from Sea Haven Party Hire. According to the hire company's catalogue and Adrian's info, the blue marquee is a very attractive 150-seat marquee, one that should fit perfectly in the backyard of Rosa's pub. A perfect marquee for a boutique writers' festival being held in a small – *very* small – seaside town.

The committee plan to use the blue marquee as our major facility for keynotes, sessions and workshops. We also plan to use the community hall, even though it's a little dodgy, and borrow tents from the lifesavers' club for extra sessions and workshops – big tents, not the type you might encounter on a tropical island holiday-from-hell.

Rosa greeted us when we arrived at her pub equipped with a tape measure, notebook and pencil.

'No problem, Gina! Adrian measured. I measured. Blue marquee will fit. I hired it for cousin's wedding. I gave them good price for sit-down meal. I can give you a good price if you want to have a wedding here.'

'Thank you, Rosa. I just want to check again.'

'Go ahead. Free coffee when you and Terri finish.'

Terri and the Dog helped me measure precisely. My measurements agreed with both Adrian's and Rosa's measurements. The blue marquee would be fine.

Terri watched as I ticked off the blue marquee from my list. She's smart. She didn't make an 'I told you so' comment. The Dog was not talking. Point taken.

Rosa made us coffee. 'Not too strong for the girl. Coffee keep you awake, Terri. Young girls need plenty of sleep to keep looking so beaut-i-ful.'

We drank our coffee. I promised again to help Terri sort out her unsortable problem. Not that I'm an expert.

I received a cross-eyed look in agreement.

The Dog was supercilious. He'd sort out his own problems.

Friday: Meet Bill Kerr

I worked my shift at the library and then headed to Rosa's afterwards. I'd arranged to meet Bill Kerr for coffee. Bill is Shelly Beach's much-loved short-listed local writer. Two books published and well received; a third with a deadline to be met by Christmas.

Bill is also the tutor for the Shelly Beach Writers' Group. We all know Bill's a brilliant writer and tutor, but he hates talking about himself or his writing. He considers publicity and marketing a necessary evil. Violet says, 'Bill will become famous for hating fame. It worked for J D Salinger.' Apparently Bill had agreed to do a session for the festival, but I wanted to make sure he was still okay with it.

'If he can't do it, who can? We need locals to fill our program.'

The Dog said not to worry.

I collected a coffee from the bar and told Rosa I was waiting for Bill.

'Bill's had a blockage.'

'Excuse me?'

'Bill's been talking to me. He's sad. He says he has writer's blockage.'

'Writer's block.'

'Exactly. I tell Bill to sit at a table. Write in Rosa's pub! Drink plenty of red wine! Blockage will go in no time. He'll be able to write pages and pages and pages of his new book.'

Locals knew Bill was struggling with his third novel – but then again, he struggled with his second . . . and his first, too. Partner Deb had returned to teaching to help pay the mortgage. Looking after Hunter, their three-year-old son, has caused a serious halt to Bill's creative flow.

The Dog empathised with Bill. He thought it would be impossible to write with a three-year-old roaming the house. If you put Hunter on a long lead it might work.

'That's an excellent idea, Rosa. We'll see if we can arrange someone to babysit Hunter. Bill can bring his laptop and work at a window table.'

'Maybe Sophia could do it? She's Lorenzo's cousin. She's arriving here next week to help out for the festival. You can ask Lorenzo if she'll do babysitting. I'm not talking to him. Pig-hearted man.'

It's common knowledge in Shelly Beach that Rosa and her chef,

Lorenzo, have a love–hate relationship, conducted exclusively in Italian. My tourist Italian has helped overcome near-death incidents between Rosa and Lorenzo. Fortunately Lorenzo's English is improving. I look forward to mediating more effectively in English.

'A pig-headed man.'

'That too. I'm only writing sticky messages for him – I can't talk to him. When you see him, Gina, ask him what's he going to do about the mices in the kitchen. Do we need to lend Violet's cat?'

Fortunately Bill's arrival put a stop to me playing intermediary again between Rosa and Lorenzo.

'Congratulations, Gina! Adrian told me that you were going to take over as festival director. You'll do a great job!'

I smiled my thank-you. Apparently Adrian told every Shelly Beach local that I was taking on his festival director's role before he told me.

'Anyway, I'm fine to do my session. Looking forward to it, in fact. But Siobhan called me yesterday. She's taking leave from work for a bit.'

Siobhan O'Reilly is Bill's editor at a publishing house in the city. She'd offered to take a session for the festival. Mentally I checked the festival program. 'Is she all right? Not ill?'

'Not to worry. She's still coming to the festival and taking her session. And she should still be able to work on my next novel.'

I got the guilts. All I'd really cared about was how I could find another editor to fill Siobhan's spot in the festival program at this late stage. Not a thought for Siobhan, taking leave, or for Bill, stranded on a sandbank, halfway through his novel . . . and with a possible change of editors.

Walking home along the beach I thought about my future while the Dog searched for a rotting pelican carcass – or seagull, he wasn't picky. Would I have a glass-walled corner office again? An office with a 'verdant' view? A view overlooking a city park would be lovely.

I looked out to the horizon of an endless grey-blue Shelly Beach bay. No wonder some early sea explorers thought ships would tip over the edge if they sailed as far as they could see.

The Dog returned to my side. He smelt disgusting. He'd found what he was looking for.

'What do you think, Dog, will I be a top exec again? I once had a black belt in time management, and I'm sure I can reach that level again.'

The Dog didn't care – just as long as he knew either way soon.

When I returned home, I couldn't help myself. I turned on the computer and started typing.

From: Gina <glaurel@peninsula.com.au>
To: Adrian <bookstreet@network.com.au>
Subject: Violet's poker school
What do you know about Violet's poker school? She's inviting Matt Galinsky to join her school while he's staying at Shelly Beach.
Gina

From: Adrian <bookstreet@network.com.au>
To: Gina <glaurel@peninsula.com.au>
Subject: Re: Violet's poker school
I think it's okay. They don't play for high stakes, but you'll have to talk to Violet. If she carpets Matt Galinsky it won't look good.
Hoping to get to Shelly Beach to be with you on the weekend.
xxx Adrian

• Wine-tasting for festival events

It had been two days since my hasty response to Digby's wine-tasting invitation. Yesterday I'd come up with a plan. I'd suggested Digby extend the invitation to all the festival committee. He took the tactful rebuff in his stride.

'Great idea, Gina. I've got some advance copies of *War and Wool* I can show the committee.'

Of course he has. *War and Wool 1938–1958* is Digby's book, fortuitously completed in time to be launched at the festival.

I was still embarrased about ending up in a one-night stand with Digby. It had been awkward for the last few weeks, but with this latest invitation I was hopeful he would get the message. I nearly stuffed up an interesting friendship with an intelligent male. Note to self: One-night stands are out! The beat-up I gave myself the next day was not worth it.

From intimate experience I can now verify that the renovations to Digby's tower room are complete. To gain access to Digby's tower room you have to ascend a magnificent circular mahogany staircase. It's designed for seduction. A lion's den? More like a friendly dragon's lair that comfortably accommodates captured princesses. Bookshelves are built under the window seats with their 360-degree views of Shelly Beach. The bookshelves are crammed with books, some valuable and old, some must-read titles selected because of the reviews. A Persian rug woven in jewel colours covers the floor. Lighting, heating and cooling systems, a hidden TV and sound system are easily accessed at the press of buttons. A kitchen nook hidden behind screen doors completes this idyllic escape from the real world.

Note to self: Do not walk up Digby's mahogany circular staircase again. Well, definitely not under the influence of Moët. And I'm refusing any further syrupy invitations to hear a Puccini opera.

35

I can buy my own Puccini CDs and I've decided never to drink champagne ever again.

Digby's castle was lit up like a liner when I arrived. Digby, his silver mane caught in an academic ponytail, was at the entrance of his castle to give committee members his traditional open-house welcome.

His 'wine-tasting' had turned into an OTT extravaganza. Local growers had been enlisted to the cause, and tables were beautifully set with gleaming glasses and interesting bottles of wine in what was once the ballroom. I was introduced to the owners of several of our local vineyards, who were waiting at the ready to offer us glasses of wine to taste.

Digby whispered, 'Daphne's out the back on the verandah. Settling in Bluey. The Dog can go there too.'

Bluey is Daphne's grown son's dog, a retired sheepdog. Daphne's son was travelling overseas and Bluey had moved in with Daphne and her husband Charles. Daphne is my amazing yoga-teaching friend, a tanned attractive sixty-something. She's my sometime stylist as well as the proprietor of the Sea Haven charity shop, aka Sea Haven Vintage. According to local goss Daphne was a tree-hugger, an environmental warrior in her youth.

'Gina!' Daphne hugged me, her bangles jangling. 'You'll have to call in on the weekend and pick up a jazzy little suit I've found for you. It'll be perfect for your interview. Throw your Armani trench around your shoulders and you'll look the bees' knees.'

'Problem, Daphne. My Armani trench is in a suitcase in the office of Adrian's friend at a tin-pot airport.'

'Oh, right . . .' Attuned to mood as a good yoga instructor should be, Daphne avoided enquiring further into the whereabouts of my much-prized Armani trench from my previous life. 'Not a problem. You can borrow my trench. It's not Armani – it's a copy of a copy – but you'd never know.'

I'm very fortunate to have made such good friends since I've been living at Shelly Beach. Daphne is not only tactful, but incredibly generous with her styling advice, always helping me find an appropriate wardrobe at a minimum cost.

The Dog enjoys Bluey's company. We left the dogs and went back to the wine-tasting.

Most of the committee members had fronted up, minus Pandora, who was back in the city tonight, and Rosa. Digby received a message from Rosa on his iPhone. 'She's on her way as soon as she can close the bar.'

'Digby's do's are always fun! Doesn't his hair look cool?' Bianca, our local hairdresser, asked.

I grudgingly agreed with bubbly, chatty Bianca, twenty-something owner of Scissors Salon on Beach Road. Great reader and writer of romance fiction and committed Jane Austenite, Bianca finally got her happy ending last year when she married Josh, her high school sweetheart (and the local primary school teacher). 'We've been growing Digby's hair this year. And we've got his goatee shaping beautifully.'

Locals are indebted to Bianca's salon for our stylish hairdos. I provide cooked meals for Bianca and her husband Josh twice a week on the evenings they have lifesaver club training. In return I'm given free appointments to tidy my split ends, for foils to colour my life, for manicures, pedicures, and the occasional massage. Bianca's also the trusted confidante of half the town. 'You wouldn't believe some of the stuff clients tell me, Gina,' Bianca says. But she only listens. Never offers advice. 'Not my job!'

True. Bianca is well aware of the importance of confidentiality and of not getting involved in a client's personal issues – the good stuff or the not-so-good stuff. She plucked at one of my corkscrew curls. 'Your hair is looking brill! If you run out of that new product I gave you just call in at the salon. I told you it would look good going *au naturale* colourwise, and letting your curls go wild.'

Violet arrived with a cat in her arms. 'Look at Sylvester! Poor boy. He's like a piece of limp seaweed.'

True. Sadly, Sylvester was bitten by a black snake. 'Snakes are out early this year,' Violet continued. 'Because of the rain. Sylvester was missing for twenty-four hours. He was in the garden all the time but he could barely even meow. The Sea Haven vet just managed to save him. If Sylvester had been a dog it would have been the end for him.'

Violet accepted heaps of consolation from pet-owning committee members before taking Sylvester to sleep off his anti-venom in one of the castle's numerous bathrooms. Hopefully not in the en suite of the master bedroom, where Digby's second wife, former owner of the castle, tumbled to her death from the bedroom balcony into the bed of petunias below. According to Shelly Beach goss it's taken Digby a few years to recover from his wife's tragic death, but he has completed the castle renovations and is in control of his life now.

Digby now turned his attention to showing captive local wine growers advance copies of his book *War and Wool 1938–1958*. Correction. *War and Wool 1938–1958* is not Digby's book, but an edited compilation of dear old Henry Shepherd's wonderful diaries. Prior to Henry's passing, he'd asked Digby to help him put his twenty years' worth of diaries into book form. These diaries were edited by Digby into an impressive collection of Australian history dating from the Second World War and the subsequent years, when Henry Shepherd earned a living as a local sheep farmer.

Bianca joined Daphne and me as I watched Digby pitch advance copies of his new book. 'Apparently Digby still has another twenty or more of Henry's diaries to edit. He's saving them for the next book. Henry wrote in his diary every day of his life from the age of ten. Awesome!' She tucked her perfectly blow-dried hair behind her ear. 'It's not really Digby's book, though. The copyright belongs to Henry's estate, doesn't it?'

I nodded. Bianca was correct. She has an innate ability to spot the stray elephant in the room at Shelly Beach. And she has the uncanny ability to tell the truth without getting people offside.

Feeling a smidge guilty, I thought I should add some support for Digby. After all, I'd been helping Digby with the editing . . . which was what led to the one-night-stand-we-don't-talk-about. 'Digby's a talented editor. Editing is hard work.' The Dog and I knew that Digby spent weeks, months, well over a year, editing the diaries – turning them into an engrossing and entertaining memoir.

'I don't doubt it,' said Bianca. 'Digby's name's on the title page, along with Henry's. But Digby's given Henry's family most of the publishers' advance. *And* he's made arrangements for all future royalties to go to the family. They could really do with the money. The drought has knocked their farm about these past few years.'

Daphne and I agreed Digby was very generous.

'If Henry hadn't died, he'd be launching his book at the festival. He would've been so chuffed! I'm going to see if I can buy a copy and get Digby to sign it.'

Daphne and I watched Bianca join Digby and the wine growers, grateful Bianca had brought stuff into the open that lesser mortals like us avoided. Digby was at the ready to sign copies of his book, Mont Blanc pen in his hand.

Making our way home later that evening, the Dog brought me up to date with Bluey's news. Bluey attended a doggy daycare centre in the city when he was living with Daphne's son. Sadly, Bluey was asked to leave because he kept rounding up the other dogs.

Although Bluey is in his older dog years he still has a hankering to round up sheep.

We agreed it's hard to let go of something you've done well. I ventured to ask the Dog if he might like to go to doggy daycare if I got a job in the city.

The Dog would not commit to an answer. He'd have to trial it before he could reach a decision.

Saturday: Check Crow's Nest Flat

I was woken at an ungodly hour by a knock on my door. Two minutes later I was left with a fruit basket from the Sea Haven Florists with a handwritten note attached.

> *Sorry, Gina, my love. I can't make it this weekend. I promise I'll make it up to you. xx Adrian*
> *P.S. Would you mind checking the plumbing and lights at Crow's Nest Flat? Anton Brandt and his lion-killer wife Stephanie are due to arrive any day now.*

I was still thinking about the note when Pandora called.

'How about meeting at Rosa's for a meal tonight?'

'Love to. Something to look forward to after I finish my tasks for Adrian. Can you believe he sent me a fruit basket with a to-do list?'

Pandora laughed. 'So what do you have to do?'

'I have to check out the Crow's Nest Flat – plumbing and lighting – before our celeb author Anton Brandt and his wife arrive next week. Apparently their accommodation has to be five-star perfect.'

'It won't take you long. Why don't I meet you there about six? When you're finished we'll head downstairs to Piece of Cake and we can cook a meal in the kitchen. If I know Gail she'll be out the door at five past five and we'll have the place to ourselves. Oh, and you haven't forgotten we're both working there tomorrow?'

'No, I haven't forgotten.' Pandora and I generally fill in at Piece of Cake when it's Gail's day off. Gail's the manager and owner-to-be of Adrian's bookshop cafe, as well as Bianca's mum. Pandora takes casual shifts at Piece of Cake to combat boredom when custom is slow at her B&B. I work at Piece of Cake in order to keep my bank account in the black. But Pandora and I both take great pride in pulling really good coffees. And we're experts at coffee art!

Once I'd hung up the phone I turned to the Dog. 'It'll be nice to catch up with Pandora.' The Dog is fond of Pandora. She's a dog person without a dog.

The fruit basket caught my eye again. 'Adrian's definitely freeing himself of his ties in Shelly Beach. First it was all about having retirement plans – Piece of Cake, for example. But now . . . talk about executing a U-turn. Amazing! Once Piece of Cake was up and running he sold it.'

No comment from the Dog.

Piece of Cake is Shelly Beach's only coffee shop. It's as stylish as any city coffee shop and loved and frequented by locals – especially the Shelly Beach Writers' Group members. When I was house-sitting for Adrian, I set it up. Well, that's not quite accurate. All I had to do was follow the detailed manual of instructions Adrian left behind. The cafe and flat were half-finished when I arrived in Shelly Beach.

The flat was quickly christened Crow's Nest for its spectacular view, and is an expensively furnished modern – minimalist – apartment. Adrian managed to secure our second big-name international author for the festival, the crime fiction author Anton Brandt, using the flat as bait. Anton and his wife, Stephanie, get gratis accommodation in our paparazzi-free, picturesque seaside town.

A place where Anton and Stephanie can relax before Anton begins his major publicity tour with his Australian publisher. Adrian had planned to rent Crow's Nest Flat to fund his retirement. I can only assume it will be on the market soon.

Pandora looked bright and beautiful when I met her outside Piece of Cake soon after six. 'You look like you've been having European-movie sex.'

'You guessed it. You should try it sometime, Gina. I had a brilliant time in the city last night. And my new guy is minus a wife, girlfriend, any other attachment and – wait for it . . . he's into commitment!'

'I don't believe it!'

Pandora laughed. 'Let's do Crow's Nest. Then we can have a meal, relax and catch up with the goss.'

Everything was perfect in the flat. Crow's Nest, with its selection of down pillows, ample fluffy towels, high-thread-count linen and a balcony to watch sunrises and sunsets across the bay, would be hard to beat anywhere in the world.

'Stunning view. The Brandts can't find fault with this place.'

I agreed with Pandora. And the plumbing and lighting were fine.

Pandora was checking the evening sky. 'I hope the weather picks up for the festival.'

'Alf and Potholer have been checking the long-term forecast. It's looking good for the festival weekend.'

Pandora had brought her laptop and opened it on the kitchen table. The Shelly Beach Writers' Festival's website popped onto the screen. 'Check this out, Gina! Read *About the director*.'

I read the short but imaginative bio and took note of the quite appealing photo of myself. 'Where did you get this stuff?'

'I wrote it. Thought you'd like it. Updated the website as soon as Adrian gave me the go-ahead.'

'Adrian gave you the go-ahead? When?'

'Don't go there, Gina. *After* he'd spoken to you, I promise.'

'I'm just not in a good place at the moment. I've got this festival to worry about while I'm trying to prepare for my job interview on Monday. Plus Adrian and I are back as "good friends".'

'I know it was the holiday that broke the camel's back, but you're crazy, Gina. He's obviously in love with you. You are so good together.'

'Well, we're not at the moment.'

'Is it the job stuff?'

'His job? That's part of it. He didn't even tell me he was applying for it! Did he expect me to just follow him to the city? Or pine away in Shelly Beach instead? But it's more than just that. I'm mad as hell with myself!'

'What have you done?'

'I slept with Digby.'

Pandora's mouth dropped open. 'You didn't!'

'I did. It was *after* the holiday, mind you. Digby hasn't referred to it since. I'm hoping it'll all just go away.'

'Don't worry, Gina. Digby's memory is notoriously fallible. Just as well he didn't write a memoir. He'll move on if he doesn't get a reciprocal signal when he tries it on again. Has he hit on you since?'

'Yes, but I deflected it and I think he got the message.'

'Digby will move on, and I think he'll keep it to himself. He'll find another female – charming Digby can be very persuasive. As Violet says, he has a sweet tooth. He likes to keep a jar of jam in the cupboard.'

And Pandora, being a sensitive friend, moved the conversation on. We went downstairs to Piece of Cake where I made a quick pasta dish with ingredients from the coffee shop's fridge. Over a post-dinner coffee Pandora and I checked the rest of the festival's website.

'We've sold just about all the tickets. And I have to admit the schedule looks fantastic. We've got the sizzle. Can we deliver the steak? Will the festival work in real time?'

'The festival *will* work, Gina. Stop worrying about it and focus on your job interview instead. Remember you're not the sum of the dot points of your CV! You still have an excellent reputation in the industry.'

I kept repeating Pandora's comforting words in my head as I settled the Dog in his basket on the back of my Vespa and we made the short journey home to White Sands. 'I'm nervous, Dog. Change is in the air. And if Adrian's sent me another feel-good fruit basket I'm going to scream.'

The Dog didn't hear. When you travel with the wind in your ears it's hard to keep up a conversation.

Sunday: Outfit for interview and boxed lunches

One day to go until my job interview. The Dog and I went to collect the 'interview' suit Daphne had found for me. I left the Dog to sit in the sun with Bluey outside Daphne's charity shop.

'It's a fantastic suit with a soft edge. And it's a perfect fit, Gina,' Daphne said while I checked myself out in her fitting-room mirror.

'I love the colour.' The suit was a smoky plum, and when I looked at the label I was impressed. 'Bloody hell!'

Daphne smiled. 'This is a suit that says all the right things about you.' She enjoys hunting for vintage and pre-loved fashion – aka second-hand clothes – for a cash-poor friend needing armour for battle. 'I did well snaffling this little beauty. It's professional but with a smidgen of sex in the cut, don't you think?'

I thought Daphne's description was a bit over the top but I loved the suit. 'I have that pair of plum-coloured patent heels I can wear with it. But I'll wear my comfortable loafers and carry the heels in my bag.'

'Sensible move. The suit will double for the official stuff you have to do in your new role as festival director.'

Bloody hell!

'I'll fetch my trench for you – it's out the back. Then would you like a cup of herbal tea?'

Again Daphne tactfully avoided any talk of my Armani trench still trapped in my suitcase at the tin-pot airport.

With my wardrobe sorted I relaxed. I could have done with a good strong cup of black coffee, but as a yoga instructor and believer in all things natural Daphne is definitely a herbal tea girl. I accepted my peppermint tea with a smile. Maybe if I get this job I'll swap strong blacks for peppermint tea.

I hadn't had a chance to properly talk to Daphne since her big decision to take a break from her husband, Charles. It is general knowledge in Shelly Beach that Daphne and Charles have a complex relationship. They've actually been divorced and remarried already. Now they're sharing the same house but not living together.

Most of what I know of it comes from Bluey via the Dog. The good news for Bluey is that he frequently gets fed twice. The bad news is that sometimes both Daphne and Charles forget to feed him and he has to scrounge his own food. Nonetheless, it's been much calmer at Daphne and Charles's since the decision to divorce, and Bluey expects it to continue when Charles leaves. (Daphne and Charles's house suits a dog getting on in years. Far superior to living with a Gen Y with Lady Gaga blasting out at top decibels all hours of the day and night.)

'I love Charles, but I'm not in *love* with him,' Daphne explained after I tentatively broached the subject.

'Right.' I wasn't sure what to say next. My soft-spoken friend usually is the receiver of news – not the deliverer.

Daphne continued in her calm voice. 'I'm content living in Shelly Beach. I have the shop and my yoga classes. Charles wants to keep running around the country with his camera. He still enjoys joining every environmental action campaign he can find, or else he's off on one of his eternal bird safaris. Likes living rough. I'm just not into active campaigning any more. Social media is far more effective.'

'I absolutely agree. I so hate camping – and any two-star accommodation with the bathroom at the end of the hall.'

Daphne looked at me. Was I too trivial?

'Anyway,' she continued, her bangles tinkling, 'we just don't click like we used to – he'll move out after the festival. I wanted a trial separation, and Charles has agreed. What about you, Gina? Where to from here?'

(An intrusive question from anyone but Daphne.)

'Relationship-wise, Adrian and I are in a bad place at the moment. In fact we're not in any place at all. You know my marriage was not the stuff of fairy tales. I'm not sure I'm ready for a committed relationship again. The kind I think Adrian wants.'

Daphne nodded and offered me a bran and raisin cookie. A conversation with Daphne leaves silences you feel obligated to fill. As a person who likes to leave silences in conversations for other persons to fill, I find this discomforting.

The Dog says it's to do with Daphne's aura. He's been hanging around Daphne's yoga on the beach or in the less picturesque community hall if the weather is inclement. He particularly likes attending yoga now that Bluey accompanies Daphne to her classes.

'And then there's the job thing. Did I tell you Sea Haven library have offered me a full-time position? I want to resurrect my high-flying position in the city again, but I'm not sure I can.'

'I wouldn't worry, Gina. Get this interview over. See if you're offered the job. Take time deciding how you want your life to be, and who you want to spend it with.'

Daphne's reflective words floated around me. She was still talking, and I tuned in again. 'Serendipity plays as much a part in careers as planning. Life is riddled with chance events. You'll find you have many options. Take some walks along the beach. Making lists helps. For-and-against or needs-and-wants lists clarify things. And don't worry about the festival, really. It'll be fine. Two days and it will be over. It will float out of Shelly Beach bay on the tide.'

True.

I gave Daphne a hug, and strapped the Dog in his basket on the back of the Vespa. I balanced my professional suit (with its smid-gen of sex) in front of me, wrapped in its protective cover, and we were off. 'I already knew all that stuff Daphne was telling me. But it was good to hear it anyway.'

The Dog ignored me. Wind in his ears again.

'We'll call in and see the boys at Beach Eatery du Jour.'

The Dog heard me this time.

Harold and Gary greeted us with big smiles when we arrived at their shop, previously Rupert's Butchery, now Beach Eatery du Jour, a gourmet produce store. Harold's dad owned the original Rupert's Butchery, with its constant smell of raw meat in the air. It was the Dog's favourite Shelly Beach shop. Now it's been rebadged and had a refit, the Dog wasn't so sure.

Potholer was just leaving with a bundle of sausages under his arm as we arrived. He told the Dog, 'You're as fit as a butcher's dog,' and gave him a comforting pat, which set the Dog up for the day. The Dog likes hearing the stories Potholer tells about the old butchery at Rosa's pub. 'Customers would ask for sixpenn'orth of meat for the cat and say, "Don't drop it in the sawdust because it gets in my father's teeth."'

And the Dog's favourite: when Potholer was a little boy, he was sent to buy a pound of steak for his dad, and a shilling's worth of meat for the cat. When he reached the butchery his mum rang and said, 'Cancel the steak, the cat's just caught a mouse.'

Harold, the beaming proprietor, runs the Beach Eatery du Jour (with accompanying stylish signage) with his partner Gary. Gary is an ideas man. When they did the refit, they lost the raw-meat smell but kept the black-and-white tiles, the butcher's chopping table and the sawdust on the floor. They started stocking locally made prosciutto and importing *jamon iberico*. Shelves were stacked with sweet 'made-here' chilli, fig and cherry jam, and deli products sourced from locals. Long-stemmed foliage and flowers in recycled milk bottles added 'oomph'. Harold, like his dad, is practised in whole-carcass butchery. He and Gary are thinking they'll go with a line-up of dry-aged certified organic steaks plus their crowd-pleasing sausages to complement a range of local wines.

'Adrian told us he'd left the festival in good hands.'

'I accept the compliment, guys.'

Harold and Gary had bravely put their hands up to supply festival guests with boxed lunches. As part of the set ticket price, the 150 attendees could choose to receive a boxed lunch both days of the festival as well as a choice of continental or cooked breakfasts. Evening meals were to be funded by attendees themselves at Rosa's pub or they could take a shuttle bus to upmarket Sea Haven with its many cafes and restaurants.

Result: we were able to ask a bit more for tickets, and had already covered our festival costs. We might even make a profit.

A profit to kickstart Adrian's dream for an Information and Community Centre for Shelly Beach.

I checked Adrian's notes. 'So, you're right to organise 150 boxed lunches two days in a row? And you're catering for seventy continental breakfasts on both days too!'

'It's cool, Gina,' reassured Harold. 'We've got a team of friends coming down from the city to help. Thought you like to try a sample.' He passed over a beautifully presented brown cardboard box.

I took a peek inside. Nestled in duck-egg blue tissue paper were sourdough sandwiches, a slice of carrot cake, an apple, a cheese slice and a mini bottle of organic fruit juice.

'Looks fantastic!'

Gary and Harold smiled.

I ticked *Boxed lunches & continental breakfasts* off my list. Rosa had organised her cousins to do the cooked breakfasts out of catering vans on the foreshore.

Harold and his mum had operated Rupert's Butchery for years after his dad died. Harold enjoyed being a butcher, but he was desperate to tell his mum that he was gay. Eventually he'd asked for Shelly Beach locals to help him come out of the closet. Most of Shelly Beach had known Harold was gay before his mother did. He'd tried to talk to her about it but she refused to listen. He always used to say that his mum never stayed still long enough to listen.

True. Harold's mum was commonly known in Shelly Beach as a live wire. She'd been the driver of the success of Rupert's Butchery. Customers travelled miles to buy her sausages.

Finally Daphne came to the rescue and held a dinner party so Harold could announce to his mum that he was gay. Shelly Beach Writers' Group members rose to the occasion to support Harold (Harold was thinking about joining, but at that time he wasn't an official member). Besides the food, the dinner party turned out to be a night to remember.

Between the first and second courses Digby clinked his fork on one of Daphne's crystal goblets, and introduced Harold 'with something important to say'. (Daphne and I were guarding the door to stop his mum escaping.) Harold took a deep breath and announced to dinner guests that he was gay and proud of it.

Guests clapped, whistled and cheered. Harold's mum cried all through the third course (my oozy chocolate puddings) but cheered up considerably by the time the cheese and biscuits were passed around the table. After several glasses of dessert wine she seemed fully recovered, and the next day she left on a fifty-two-day cruise of the Pacific. Harold's not seen her since, but things are good.

'How's your mum, Harold?'

'She's good. We text and email. We're thinking about using Skype. You know Mum met a New Zealand farmer on her cruise? Mum says it's a case of last love for both of them. She's settled on his farm on the North Island. Working on lamb sausage recipes!'

Gary chipped in. 'She's actually switched the title deeds for this place to Harold's name. How good is that?'

True.

So Harold is now the official owner of the former Rupert's Butchery plus the recipe holder for Rupert's Butchery beef and pork sausages – but not lamb.

Gary, Harold's partner, has been absorbed into the Shelly Beach community. The blokey bar consensus from Rosa's pub was, 'Definitely a city bloke – but definitely not your blow-in type.'

As I left the shop, I smiled at the Dog. 'Well, that was a very satisfactory meeting! The boys have the lunches and the continental breakfasts under control.'

The Dog wasn't happy. He doesn't like sourdough bread. Too upmarket for his taste.

- **Panic about interview**
'Let's start.'

Later that evening Pandora met me at White Sands to help me with a practice run for my interview.

'All you can do is your best, Gina. You've got the right experience and you have the qualifications.'

'I know.'

'And don't forget this is the third round of interviews. You've already survived two. If I know anything about companies, your boss will have either checked you out thoroughly or hired head-hunters to do it. Stop worrying. They wouldn't be interviewing you a third time if they didn't like what they saw.'

Neither of us was very hungry so I made sandwiches while Pandora made some coffee. We sat down at the kitchen table and I opened up my laptop to show Pandora my CV on screen.

Her eyes widened. 'This is hopeless, Gina. Why didn't you run it past me before you sent it? I'm amazed you've had two interviews. Your CV has to *ooze* flair. It has to be as attractive as possible – like a blog. It has to pop out at the reader and be instantly engaging.'

Bloody hell!

'And don't forget to add your new title.' I watched Pandora key in a dot point at the top of my CV. *Director of the Shelly Beach Writers' Festival*.

'Shelly Beach Writers' Festival is hardly big-time.'

'It looks impressive if you check out the website. Let them know tomorrow about the new role. The festival will look great as a current example of stuff you're tackling.'

In a former life I was the one doing the hiring, not sitting in the interview chair. The rest of the evening Pandora asked me interview questions on the projects I'd accomplished in the past. We ignored barista duty but we decided we could talk about my Children's Services and Acquisitions Officer appointment at the Sea Haven library. I told Pandora about being asked to go full-time.

'Well done, Gina! What did you say?'

'I haven't said anything yet. I'm taking a wait-and-see approach.'

After we'd cleaned the kitchen, Pandora turned to me with a smile. 'I forgot to ask, Gina. How's your tropical rash healing? And your spider bite?'

'Don't laugh. The rash keeps returning but the spider bite is healing.'

'I'm glad to hear. Catch up with you soon, okay?' We exchanged hugs at the door.

I turned to the Dog after she left. 'I don't know why I have friends who never get sick. They *so* lack compassion.'

No comment from the Dog. He'd stopped to scratch.

'It would be nice if one of my friends got sick sometime so I could look after them.'

In the bathroom I checked the unidentified tropical spider's bite. 'It's just about healed, thank goodness.'

The Dog was having another serious scratch. His back leg was going like a frantic little machine.

'We'll have to go to the Sea Haven vet and get a new prescription for your anti-itch medication. If I'd died from a poisonous spider bite on the holiday-from-hell and my body was shipped back to be buried at Shelly Beach, would you have come to my funeral?'

The Dog wasn't sure. If he'd read about it in the *Sea Haven Sentinel*'s hatch and dispatch notices he probably would have, but

I was not to expect he'd do the Greyfriars Bobby stuff, i.e. live in the cemetery for years after my death.

Fair enough.

From: Gina <glaurel@peninsula.com.au>
To: Adrian <bookstreet@network.com.au>
Subject: Plumbing
As per your request, I have checked the plumbing and lighting at Crow's Nest Flat. All good and ready for Anton Brandt and wife Stephanie's arrival on Wednesday.
I'm thinking I'll need another visit to the doctor for treatment of my tropical rash. If you happen to be passing your friend's office at the airport could you possibly retrieve my Louis Vuitton suitcase?

From: Adrian <bookstreet@network.com.au>
To: Gina <glaurel@peninsula.com.au>
Subject: Poisonous rash
Do get your rash checked at the doctor's again. I've heard those sorts of things can keep reappearing for months – years, even.
Love you. Be back soon.

THREE WEEKS TO GO

Monday: Job interview

I was floating on air, staring out the window of a city tram. It looked like a fantastic position was mine for the taking. I could already feel the excitement of once more being in charge of a team of people, working together to achieve goals and projects. And if I was honest, I could understand why Adrian might chase after jobs that offered exciting, worthwhile challenges.

I thought about my successful interview with Rod Lidner, one partner of the two-partner firm I've been invited to join. I'll be working as a social media chief, training teams to train other companies' staff to stay out of online trouble. Train-the-trainer stuff. 'Huge business opportunity opening up here, Gina,' Rod, my potential boss, had said. 'The net is creating professional and personal issues for companies that can make or break them if they're not wary.'

I could only agree with him.

He was delighted to welcome me to the company, with an extra incentive based on my experience. If I can make the Shelly Beach Writers' Festival a success, I'll be in a position to negotiate a substantial salary increase. No more minimalist lifestyle.

I couldn't quite believe that my reputation still stood. Then

again, I had been the hard-working CEO of an information management company with loyal staff.

Rod Lidner and I had even discussed the time almost three
years ago when I had the unenviable task of telling my staff that,
despite our best efforts, our company was going into voluntary
administration. I supported them as best as I could until they
found new placements, and many of my talented staff are still
working in the industry. Maybe that's how my reputation lives on?

Why didn't I find myself another job straightaway? Because I
planned to launch my writing career. For a year I lived in a dressing-
gown as a trapped-in-the-attic writer writing a go-nowhere novel.
And my marriage collapsed at the end of that writerly year. Don't
go there, Gina. Move on.

I shook myself out of my job-interview euphoria just in time to
alight from the tram and make the short trip to my daughter Julia's
home.

I was greeted with open arms. 'You look fantastic, Mum! How
did it go? Oh, by the way, Digby dropped your case in.'

Digby had offered me a 'friendly' ride to the city this morning.
He was coming up for a meeting with the publicity and marketing
department at his publisher's. I accepted. Fool not too. Listening to Sibelius' Symphony No.1 and Symphony No. 4 (seventy-six
minutes playing time x two) in the luxurious air-conditioned comfort of his Alfa didn't compare with an ungodly early start and a
very lengthy journey on the bus and train from Shelly Beach. (I
chose to ignore that Violet says Digby's the 'kind of man mothers
warn you about'. We worked on renewing a friendly relationship.)

'I can see by your face, Mum – you've got the job!'

I broke into an enormous grin, pushing a wayward curl behind
my ear. 'I've clinched it! In fact, the company partner is coming
to Shelly Beach the weekend of the festival to check out the Sea

Haven Resort as a venue for conferences. He'll meet me on the Sunday when the festival finishes and he'll be bringing my contract with him.'

'This is amazing news! Congratulations!'

My daughter Julia and I have come a long way in the past year and a half. Once she would never have called me Mum – it was always Gina. Our relationship suffered for years due to my work commitments, but I've worked hard to regain her love and respect. Supporting her after the birth of my adorable grandson Barney and during the recent break-up of her marriage has played a considerable part. I have a lot of years as a hands-off mother to make up for.

(Julia's marriage was short-lived. I tried to console her: 'People put up with an awful lot before they admit their marriage is a failure. You've decided early.' Julia and Simon, her ex, started a business together, and the marriage didn't survive. They're still working on the break-up of finances.)

'As soon as you decide where you're going to live in the city, Mum, I'll be happy to move near you. Seriously!'

Julia had joined the queue of people waiting for me to make a decision: when to move, where to live, who with. I'd already said that I'd help babysit my adorable grandson if I moved to the city, in order to support Julia in her single-parent role. (Well, almost single-parent – Simon's moving interstate.)

At that moment Barney woke up and Julia brought him to me. I love holding this energetic young toddler but already I was envisioning how tricky it was going to be managing support time for Julia while I tackled a challenging new job. Maybe I could just look after Barney every Saturday or Sunday to give her a break? And of course I'd be able to babysit at night.

'Did you talk about a salary package, Mum?'

'It's an alarmingly enticing amount. There's a car, laptop and iPad included. And best of all, I can negotiate even more if I manage to pull off the writers' festival.'

'Wasn't Adrian organising the festival?'

I grimaced. 'It's a long story. I'm doing it now – as the director. But I'm pleased there might be something in it for me after all.'

'Will you buy or rent?'

'I guess I'll have to look at apartment rentals. I doubt there are any house-sitting arrangements available for city apartments with a river view.'

Julia smiled. 'Now, I've invited Eva and Hester for dinner tonight. It's the nanny's night off so Eva's bringing little Godfrey. I thought it was a great opportunity to meet up with your friends.'

'That's a lovely thing to do, Julia.'

Eva and Hester are my long-time, long-term friends. We've been friends since college days. Eva is now an 'older' mum with a young son, Godfrey. 'We're not cooking dinner, are we?'

'No. I'm ordering takeaway.'

'Good!' I was still on a high. I didn't feel like returning to earth to cook dinner. In the past when I met with Eva or Hester, we'd go to the latest must-visit restaurant to catch up with news. However, finding time to eat out has been fraught since Eva had her child.

'And there's another thing I need to talk to you about . . .'

I caught a distressed look on Julia's face.

'What's wrong?'

'Kenneth wants to talk to you. I mentioned you were staying with me tonight. He asked if he could come here for coffee in the morning.'

'Bloody hell!'

'I know. But it seemed a reasonable request.'

Kenneth is Julia's father, aka my ex-husband. Secretly I was pleased Julia was still calling her father Kenneth. He hadn't earned his stripes yet. Leaving your wife of many years for your pregnant PA, who happens to be the same age as your daughter, can rattle a father–daughter relationship.

'I told Kenneth you only had a short window of time. I said I was taking you to catch an early train to Shelly Beach – which is true.'

'True. I have to be back in Shelly Beach tomorrow. One of our keynote authors and her assistant is arriving. And our other celeb author and his wife are arriving the day after.'

Julia waited while I considered what I'd do. Meet Kenneth or tell him to go to hell?

I sighed. 'If I have to, I have to.'

I looked at the relief on my daughter's face. It wasn't fair to put her in the middle, and it wasn't my daughter's fault that her father was a King Rat ex-husband.

I played with Barney while Julia quickly tidied the lounge before my smart, successful, long-time friends and baby Godfrey arrived.

The second Eva arrived she was apologising. 'Godfrey's not at his best, Gina. He's teething and fretful. Thank God we're ordering takeaway.'

I made all the right calls about cute baby Godfrey, cooing over him, and he finally settled as Eva calmed down. We caught up with our goss over Chinese. I accepted my friends' congratulations on my new appointment and apologies in advance for their non-attendance at the festival. 'Not to worry. We'll catch up when I move back to the city to start the job.'

Turned out Eva had a new man in her life. 'He loves Godfrey. Has kids of his own from a previous marriage.'

As did Hester: 'Mine's the same. But thankfully his kids have left home!'

And of course Eva and Hester were interested in the progress of my love life. They'd met Adrian when they'd visited Shelly Beach – when we were still lovers and not 'just friends'. 'Still having fun with your sexy Adrian at Shelly Beach?' asked Hester.

I smiled and nodded, moving the conversation on. Not going there. The evening came to an early end due to Godfrey waking up. Teething!

Tossing and turning in Julia's uncomfortable guest bed (Julia will have to get a better guest bed if I'm to do my share of overnight babysitting) I thought about my friends' congratulations. Eva had said, 'You've landed the job because you're the best qualified person. And now you're in a perfect position for a seat on a board. Twenty years of experience in senior management is more than enough. Many companies are looking to recruit more women to their boards in order to meet their quota. It's that whole leaky pipeline theory – women drop out at senior levels in disproportionate numbers.'

Hester had added, 'We'll keep our networking contacts open for board appointments. You can apply as soon as you take up your new job.'

Exciting times ahead. I heard Barney give a little cry in his sleep then settle. Maybe I hadn't missed the boat after all? But I did feel a smidgen of anguish . . . guilt? . . . regret? . . . when Eva and Hester had asked me what was happening with my novel-that-got-cancelled. My year spent in the attic wasn't totally in vain – I got a publishing contract out of it. But after my publishing house went bust I put the manuscript aside. I'd answered, 'It's not. I've been too busy.'

Hester understood. She quoted me her thought-for-the-day from her iPhone app: *Everything in its time, and a time for everything*. 'I'm sure that applies to writing a novel, Gina.'

Tuesday

Over breakfast, Barney and I were playing games when we heard a car pull up outside Julia's house. We watched King Rat ex-husband (Barney's grandpa) as he parked his car. Kenneth, hiding behind rock-star aviator sunglasses and now with carefully designed stubble, walked to Julia's front door and rang the buzzer.

I handed Barney to Julia, took a deep breath and prepared myself to greet Kenneth. When I opened the door my ex gave me his white-teeth smile. He removed his sunglasses. 'Permission to enter, Gina?'

I nodded and held the door open.

'You look fantastic. Love the hair.'

'I feel fantastic. What do you want, Kenneth?'

Julia shot me a look and gave Kenneth a hug. 'Mum, will you make coffee? I have to bath Barney.' And she disappeared up the stairs, leaving me alone with Kenneth. He followed me in to the kitchen while I percolated the coffee. His cologne was overpowering.

'How was the job interview?' Kenneth asked.

'It went well. Julia tells me your young son Griffin is a charmer.'

(Now Kenneth knew I could play the I-know-what-you're-doing game too.)

Kenneth nodded. 'He's a bit of a handful at the moment. But we have an excellent nanny.'

'Good.' I watched Kenneth adding sugar to his coffee. He'd put on a few extra kilos since he left me. Clever Angela, former PA and now wife and mother of his child, would have to put him on a diet. Good. Kenneth hates dieting.

'Julia tells me you're enjoying living at Shelly Beach.'

'I am. How are you?'

Kenneth played his usual game, ignoring difficult questions

and adding another sugar to his coffee. 'Do you miss your old life, Gina?'

I took a nanosecond to reply. 'No!'

'I'm still trying to figure stuff out. Attempting closure.'

'Are you referring to our marriage, which came to an abrupt finish? The marriage you decided to end?'

'I've been doing a lot of work on myself. I've been attending guys' workshops. I've been lost in the wilderness, but I'm emerging.'

I suppressed a smile. 'I'm glad.'

'Angela's been having sessions with a therapist too. Luckily, she's over her post-natal depression. Not so moody. She's back at work developing her designer maternity and children's wear company. She's loving it.'

I looked at my watch. 'I have to leave in a few minutes, Kenneth, to catch the train back to Shelly Beach.' And I couldn't resist the next sentence. 'It's a huge amount of work being festival director.'

'Ah, well, it's good that you should mention the festival. There's something I wanted to tell you.'

'Really?'

'Angela said you mightn't have realised we've booked to attend. We're staying in a four-room apartment at the Sea Haven Resort for the weekend. Taking the nanny and our fitness trainer. Angela's particularly interested in Dimity Honeysuckle's sessions because she's thinking of writing children's picture storybooks too. They're a good fit with her maternity and children's wear brand.'

Bloody hell!

'Angela thought you should know. It might have given you a surprise to see us in your territory.'

Smart girl, Angela. I stood up and smiled my professional woman's smile. 'Thanks for the heads-up, Kenneth. I'll look forward to meeting you, Angela and Griffin, and Griffin's nanny, and your fitness trainer at the festival.' I took Kenneth's unfinished cup of coffee from his hand and shepherded him to the door.

'Sorry to rush you, but I have to catch my train. See you at the festival.'

Julia came downstairs with Barney when she heard the front door slam. 'Kenneth's gone already?'

'Yes. Did you know he and Angela and little Griffin are booked to attend the festival? Oh . . . I forgot . . . and the nanny and their fitness trainer.'

Julia laughed. 'I did, Mum. I'm glad he told you, though. You have to see the funny side of things.'

'I suppose it is funny, in a weird kind of way. At least I know I'm in control when I'm in Shelly Beach.'

'And Martha will be there too.'

'*What?*' Kenneth didn't tell me my ex-mother-in-law was going to be there too. 'I thought Martha was blissfully happy with her Italian count in Tuscany.'

'No. Her husband died earlier this year and she's back for a few months. As far as I know she's staying with Kenneth, Angela and Griffin. She emailed me, saying she wants to meet up with you at the festival.'

'Bloody hell!'

Julia smiled. 'Martha's thinking of exporting a line of Italian beauty products and selling them in exclusive retail outlets. She's planning to pitch the idea to the Sea Haven Resort while she's spending time with Kenneth, Angela and her new grandson. But she definitely wanted to see you too.'

Bloody hell! My former mother-in-law had morphed into a high-end saleswoman.

'You'll be relieved to hear, Mum, Barney and I have decided

not to come to your festival. We thought we'd see one of Dimity Honeysuckle's performances when she does her city gigs. I realised the last thing you needed was us there during the festival – you'll be too busy coping with your exes.'

I grabbed my daughter in a bear hug. 'That's one of the loveliest things you could have said to me. Thank you, Julia. I don't think I'll have a minute free during the festival weekend. I'd feel miserable if I couldn't find time to spend with you and Barney. Let's make a date for after the festival. Now can we leave for the train?'

Julia grabbed her keys and picked up Barney. I followed, pulling Pandora's Gucci overnight case behind me like my shadow.

• Official meet and greet for Dimity's team

Once I got off the bus in Shelly Beach I walked to Pandora's to collect the Dog. He wasn't happy. Pandora had taken him for a walk that morning but he was *so* against joggers walking dogs. He thought there should be a law against humans jogging when they were 'walking' a dog. Jogging breaks almost every known dog-walking convention. Next time I leave him he requested to stay with Alf and Beryl, who 'walk' dogs at a respectable pace.

'How do you feel about being an inner-city dog?'

No comment.

'The city job is mine. I'm meeting the company partner at Sea Haven Resort at the end of the festival to sign my contract.'

Still no comment from the Dog.

'The interview dredged up depressing three-year-old memories I thought were well and truly buried. It was a terrible time back then. One day I was CEO, leader of a talented workforce, secure in their jobs. The next day I was told the company was bankrupt.'

The Dog understood. One day he was secure in his role as a family pet. The next he was in a lost dogs' shelter.

'Can you believe I still have an excellent reputation in the industry?'

The Dog wasn't surprised. Reputations are like shadows. They're always attached to you. He never underestimates the value of his reputation – it worked well for him when he was in the shelter looking for a new owner.

Later that evening I unpacked my smoky plum interview suit with great care and hung it up in readiness for official festival functions, when a professional suit with a smidgen of sex might be needed.

I had the job in the bag, with a sizeable salary – plus a festival bonus – on the table. I looked out the window of White Sands to the spectacular view beyond, and imagined what it would be like to live in the city again. No time for view-gazing, that's for sure.

The Dog was getting twitchy. I pushed my thoughts away and we headed to Rosa's pub to meet Dimity Honeysuckle.

When I arrived neither Dimity, her assistant Sandy nor Matt Galinsky were there, but everyone else was.

Violet filled me in with Matt's integration into Shelly Beach. 'He's become a regular at Rosa's. Loves Lorenzo's food. And plays a cool hand of poker.' (Translation: he's not ripping off Shelly Beach poker players.) Evidently Matt Galinsky's elastic charm has stretched around Shelly Beach and smoothed the way for his star client and her assistant.

Violet continued, 'Matt's bought a wetsuit and has started meeting up with the local surfers at the back beach whenever the swell is up. Swims in the bay with the Icebergers too.'

'Don't you just love his dishy Hugh Grant voice?' Bianca joined us. 'He's *so* funny and lovely.'

We agreed with Bianca. Matt Galinsky does have more than his fair share of intelligence and charm. He uses it well.

Before we could continue, the door of Rosa's opened and Dimity Honeysuckle arrived. In 'real life', Dimity was all her website, marketing and publicity hype-and-spin predicted she'd be. Pretty, pleasant, glowing with a tan she'd picked up during her stopover in Honolulu, Dimity Honeysuckle was the 'must-have' client in every agent's dream; a client to reel in blockbuster sales.

Sandy, Dimity's assistant, was close behind, wearing a giant mouse suit. We could only presume it was Atticus, the main character in Dimity's storybooks. A giant mouse asking for a Writers' Block daiquiri caused an instant halt to surfing and fishing conversations. Not an easy thing to do in Rosa's.

Sandy and Dimity worked the room all evening. Sandy, with her mouse head tucked under her arm (an attractive young woman, I'd guess, if we ever see more than her head) and pretty, boppy Dimity were an instant hit with locals. Best of all, Dimity's team have decided they love their accommodation. Love Shelly Beach. Love us – the local inhabitants. Hopefully they'll love being part of our festival.

'What a huge relief!' I yelled to the Dog as we rode home on the Vespa.

He didn't answer. Wind in his ears.

Wednesday: Welcome Anton Brandt and wife Stephanie
Before lunch Violet was at White Sands to accompany me to Crow's Nest Flat. Anton Brandt's publicist had texted me Anton's arrival time, and Violet and I were the welcoming committee for our second celeb author and his wife. I was surprised to learn that Violet had promised Adrian she'd do the Crow's Nest cleaning and look after the Brandts' breakfasts and sundry requests.

'Are you sure you haven't too much on your plate, Violet? You're doing all the breakfasts for Sea Crest, too, aren't you? Plus you're taking a session on writing cosy whodunits for the festival.'

'I'm fine, Gina, don't worry. I can call on my friend Scarlett if I need extra help. I'll sub-contract. You've met Scarlett. She works in the Sea Haven pharmacy.'

'Right,' I said sceptically. I had met Scarlett, but she didn't exactly inspire confidence.

I observed Violet running a finger down a list of instructions. Obviously Adrian had left Violet one of his lists for Crow's Nest. Adrian's good with lists.

'Anyway,' continued Violet, 'I'm only doing the rooms and break-fasts at Sea Crest until the festival starts. Geraldine's decided to take holiday leave for the festival. She wants to be around to sort out any problems for Matt and the girls. Just as well, considering Claude's so useless.'

I winced. Before we could continue, we heard a car approaching. It stopped outside Crow's Nest and three people got out – one smiling and two not. The younger of the three walked briskly over to me.

'Gina Laurel? Holly Hart.' The neatly dressed woman handed me her business card with a smile. She was Anton Brandt's publicist. 'And this is Anton and Stephanie.'

'Gina Laurel and Violet Harris.' Violet and I smiled politely at our celeb author and wife, who smiled tightly in return.

We watched Holly leave a card with Stephanie. 'Contact me if you have any queries, Mrs Brandt. I'll be back for the festival and I'll drive you to your city hotel at the conclusion. Have a fabulous stay, won't you?' And with that Holly executed an Olympic high jump into her car, did a screechy U-turn in Beach Road and sped off.

Violet and I exchanged raised-eyebrow looks and turned our attention to our celeb author Anton and wife Stephanie.

Anton Brandt matched his publicity photos perfectly: a handsome, grey-haired seventy-year-old (who once could have been classified as dishy), a respected author with a remarkable publishing reputation. In the millionaire category, if you believe the sales figures for his thirty-one novels.

Stephanie, meanwhile, towered above us all, Anton included. She was a slim-figured forty-something with long, blonde hair and icy-blue eyes, which were fixed on us coldly. 'Anton's exhausted. He needs to rest. The flight here was unbearably long and tedious.'

I joked that when you live in the Antipodes you are a long way from civilisation. No smiles. I accepted a firm handshake from wife Stephanie. Anton gave me a practised smile with his handshake. I quickly guided them to the Crow's Nest Flat.

Violet and I waited while Stephanie walked through the rooms, her towering stiletto heels clinking on the turquoise tiled floor. After a few tense moments we received a nod of approval. The excellent view was appreciated. Thank heavens there was a gentle Shelly Beach sea breeze flowing through the apartment.

'We'll need a hire car by this afternoon,' said Stephanie. 'Adrian said he'd leave a list of five-star restaurants we can eat at in Sea Haven. Sea Haven's not far away?'

'Only a fifteen-minute drive. And I'll see to the hire car.'

'Excellent.' Stephanie finally graced us with a smile. 'Everything looks fine. Anton needs peace and quiet. Privacy. He's had a hectic European book tour.'

All we could see was the back of Anton in his Italian bespoke suit, gazing out at Shelly Beach bay.

'Violet will be servicing your rooms and doing the breakfasts,' I explained.

'Excellent. I'll have bircher muesli soaked in apple juice – bio-dynamic, if possible – with poached rhubarb, and buck rarebit. Anton will have a full English.' And we were dismissed.

Violet and I went downstairs to Piece of Cake. 'I need a strong cup of Earl Grey, Gina.'

I agreed. I needed a very strong black.

We sat at Violet's usual table, where she normally taps away on her laptop, writing her cosy whodunits with the bay view in front of her, fruit toast and a pot of tea on hand.

We'd expected 'riders' – conditions celebrities require in order to be your celebrity author, speaker or entertainer – but we'd expected a word or two of thanks in return. Dimity's team was easy: a room for Dimity, Sandy and Matt and two extra private rooms available for relaxing.

Violet read Stephanie's breakfast order again. 'Can you buy these supplies in the fancy Sea Haven deli, Gina, on your way to work?' I nodded. Violet read the list aloud. 'Bircher muesli with poached rhubarb. Rhubarb's out of season. You might be able to buy it frozen. If you can't, buy frozen raspberries. Buck rarebit? I'll do a fancy roll covered with melted cheese and mustard, topped with a poached egg? And Anton just wants a full English. He mustn't have a cholesterol problem. It's a wonder the Ice Queen didn't request rose petals in their loo.'

'Are you sure you'll be okay with all this, Violet? Dealing with her?'

I could see Violet was steaming up. 'Don't worry. I can keep the Brandts happy. I can make a tasty rarebit. I just need to add the egg.'

I nodded and quickly changed the subject. 'Do you know of a hire-car place in Sea Haven?'

'You won't have to go to Sea Haven. I happen to know that Pot-holer just shelled out a ridiculous amount of money for a Porsche.

Aphrodite is furious. She thinks it's ridiculous to spend all that money on a two-seater when Potholer needs a new truck. Why don't you ask him if he'll hire his Porsche out? If he's smart he'll use the money to buy some jewellery to soften Aphrodite up. Actually, I must tell him she'd prefer a laptop for her poetry writing. She's joined Beryl's poetry group.'

I nodded. The unstoppable Violet continued. 'I'll give Potholer a call. He'll need insurance cover for a second driver. I'm sure Stephanie or Anton will have their international drivers' licences.'

I listened while high finance, conditions and bribery were negotiated over Violet's mobile. She hung up. 'Not a problem, Gina. Potholer's fixing up the insurance at this moment. He'll have the Porsche parked in the Crow's Nest garage in an hour.'

So, amazingly, the Brandts' hire car problem was sorted.

From: Gina <glaurel@peninsula.com.au>
To: Adrian <bookstreet@network.com.au>
Subject: Meets and greets
Dimity Honeysuckle and her team are 'loving' Shelly Beach. Only been here five minutes, so I hope enthusiasm lasts for the next two weeks. Anton Brandt and Stephanie are another ball game. You can definitely take over the Brandts during the festival. Earlier, if you can possibly make it.
Can I expect to see my suitcase anytime soon?

From: Adrian <bookstreet@network.com.au>
To: Gina <glaurel@peninsula.com.au>
Subject: Meets and greets
A thousand thanks! I will do my best to collect your suitcase.
Congratulations! Julia emailed me to say you nailed the job.
Can't wait to be with you on the weekend.

Thursday: Deal with monumental booking glitch

I woke up in a contemplative mood. All the thoughts about my future I'd successfully banished came rushing back. The Dog recommended I stay in the moment. Concentrate on my lists. He always lives in the moment. The Dog was absolutely confident that my personal and professional decision-making would fall into place naturally if I stopped thinking about them for five seconds.

I called Violet and Geraldine to make sure our celeb guests were comfortable and happy. Violet had quickly become very anti-Brandt. 'This morning the Ice Queen changed her entire breakfast order! Now she wants a macrobiotic vegan breakfast. Oatmeal with soymilk and berries. At least it will be easier than doing one of her fancy-schmancy breakfasts.'

True.

'Anton's no problem so far. Seems like an early riser. Sits and writes at his computer all day. And he's a teetotaller. In bed by nine.'

Geraldine was happy with Dimity's team. 'They're no problem, Gina. Matt's the loveliest person. So are the girls. So easy to get along with!'

In the afternoon I called at Bianca's Scissors Salon to deliver two lasagne dinners and to book an appointment for a trim and colour before the festival. Geraldine and Pandora were there. I went to the back room to make a pot of herbal tea, returning to find Stephanie Brandt the main topic of conversation.

Bianca had googled Anton Brandt and was a treasure trove of information. 'Stephanie is his fourth wife but Anton is Stephanie's first husband. I'm sure Stephanie was a model in a former life. She has those classic features and beautiful bone structure. And have you seen her legs? Like a giraffe!'

We considered Bianca's description of Stephanie.

'She has to be at least twenty years younger than Anton,' chipped in Geraldine.

We acknowledged Geraldine's superior knowledge in this matter. Geraldine was also a member of the much-younger-wives club.

'Have you noticed Stephanie finds it hard *not* to pose?' said Pandora. 'She can't stop herself tilting her head and giving that pouty forced smile whenever a camera lens is in sight.'

Who could disagree with Pandora, deliverer of spin and hype, who'd taken publicity photos of Anton and Stephanie that morning?

'Stephanie's had her eyebrows done by a top eyebrow stylist in London. And she's best friends with Jimmy Choo. He personally fits all her shoes for her in London.'

Silence while we took on board Bianca's info. The fact that Stephanie had beautifully arched eyebrows and to-die-for shoes – albeit with heels that could actually kill – shouldn't change our opinion of her, should it?

'How did you find all this out? From the internet?'

Stupid question to ask Bianca. Stephanie had been in that morning to get her hair styled ahead of her publicity photos. We all knew clients told Bianca the most intimate stuff when they were getting their hair styled or when they were naked and vulnerable on the massage table.

'Stephanie says she works very hard at keeping fit. And she's had work done. Some surgical tweaks, apparently minor. And she's botoxed.'

'Really?'

Bianca's older clients took comfort from this information.

'Once you start getting work done you're on a slippery slope. There's no stopping. You have to keep tweaking.'

Then Violet – an unusually rattled and puffed Violet – burst into Scissors. 'Gina! Glad I've found you. I think we have a problem with the festival booking software.'

Instantly all attention was on Violet. As committee members we knew Adrian had left the festival bookings in Violet's supposedly capable hands.

Guilt! Guilt! Guilt! I'd been meaning to check in with Violet and see how she was going with the bookings. It was next on my to-do list. 'It'll be all right, Violet. Whatever it is. Don't worry.'

Bianca sat Violet down. 'I'll make you a strong cup of tea.'

'Earl Grey, thank you. Well, Gina. . . . it looks like there's a glitch in our booking software. When you look at the bookings, we seem to have 300 attendees, not 150. And when I checked the festival's bank account, we seem to have received funds for an extra 150 attendees.'

I swallowed. 'Right.'

Violet took a sip of her Earl Grey. 'So it looks like we have 300 attendees for the festival.'

I took a deep breath and pushed a curl behind my ear. 'Not to worry, Violet. Finish your tea. We'll go to your place and double-check the booking software. I'm sure we'll be able to do something about the stuff-up.'

Inside I was seething. In a previous meeting I'd told Adrian it was a dodgy move to leave the booking software to Violet. He'd disagreed. 'Violet's competent with computers, Gina. I've given her a day's training. The festival application software is very similar to the software she operates for the Cat Club show ticketing system.'

Wrong, Adrian!

A check of the software at Violet's place confirmed my worst fears. Back home at White Sands the Dog watched me as I took calming deep breaths before I called Adrian. No answer. I left a short official message and sent an email.

From: Gina <glaurel@peninsula.com.au>

To: Adrian <bookstreet@network.com.au>

Subject: Panic

I suggest you return as soon as possible. Violet has double-booked the festival.

We now are holding a festival for 300 attendees with seating and accommodation for 150.

Don't forget my suitcase.

From: Adrian <bookstreet@network.com.au>

To: Gina <glaurel@peninsula.com.au>

Subject: Panic

Returning late tomorrow for the weekend as promised.

Confident I can help sort out the problem.

Can't wait to see you again. x

Friday: Festival jitters

Violet's nerves were no better the next day, so Pandora and I took her to Rosa's for a five o'clock G & T. Pandora had checked the festival booking software as well, and the stuff-up was confirmed. Our bookings were doubled due to a computer glitch . . . technical issues . . . gremlins . . . whatever.

Shelly Beach locals at Rosa's put forth their own theories. Alf blamed the stuff-up on the fat-finger syndrome. 'I read that an IT person with a fat finger had stuffed up the New York stock exchange. One fat finger caused huge global effects on the economy.'

Violet shook her head vehemently. 'I'm thin. So are my fingers. And I'm a competent computer operator.'

No one dared to disagree. Violet's president of the State Cat Club. She successfully manages all the Cat Club online communication – including bookings for their visit to the UK Cat Club show. (Apparently the Cat Club overseas trip was disappointing. A blizzard caused airport shutdowns and delays for days. Violet keeps reminding members, 'The weather is outside my control.')

'Maybe it was a power outage?' I said.

Shelly Beach committee members with fat fingers liked the power-outage theory. No way did the festival committee contemplate cancelling the tickets.

'The cash is all good, Gina,' Alf said. 'It's a great start for our Information and Community Centre fund.'

True. And I couldn't consider a messy cancellation for 150 paid-up attendees. It'd be all over the papers. Our reputation would be trash. I didn't like the thought of meeting my new boss as director of a non-existent or partly trashed festival. Calm and generous-spirited Daphne thought it would be disastrous for Shelly Beach locals' morale. Committee members agreed we needed to locate a second marquee to accommodate the extra attendees. It could go nicely on the foreshore.

Finding accommodation and food for an extra 150 attendees, however, was another problem. Not to mention doubling the festival program.

When we left Rosa's the atmosphere was upbeat. Locals were convinced that I would come through with a Plan B. We agreed on a committee meeting for Sunday lunch at Rosa's.

The Dog and I returned to White Sands. The Dog mumbled something about the number of balls I have in the air at the moment. He understood, however, that if you are a festival director, you need a festival.

I started preparing *boeuf bourguignon*, a certain former lover's favourite dish (it's one of my favourites too). Many a night Adrian's postponed returning to Shelly Beach at the last minute. The Dog quite enjoys sitting at the table and dining with me on a tasty plate of *boeuf bourguignon*. He usually passes on the tossed French salad.

The dish was in the oven. The smell was infiltrating the kitchen and floating out on to the balcony where I was having a glass of wine with the Dog. We were enjoying a brilliant sunset that made the Shelly Beach sky a swirl of pinks and reds when we heard the key in the door.

Adrian had arrived.

I walked out to meet him. He looked good – a comforting silver fox with those delicious eyes. He dropped his overnight bag and my Louis Vuitton suitcase in the hall. He wrapped his arms around me. And then he kissed me. I felt him run his hand under my shirt and up my back. An electric tingle went down my spine.

'I've missed you, Gina.'

I was losing my balance again. Crossing the line between a professional friendship and a romantic relationship. What the hell!

The Dog watched me with his beady eyes. He wasn't happy. No dining on *boeuf bourguignon* until leftover time tomorrow, and he suspected he'd be sleeping on the day bed in the living room tonight.

I did my best to reinstitute a just-friends atmosphere over dinner, but the candlelight didn't help. Over the meal and then wine and coffee on the balcony Adrian explained his rescue operation for the festival. I knew he wouldn't be able to let the (once his, now my) festival flounder and sink to the bottom of Shelly Beach bay.

'I rang a few contacts and spent a serious couple of hours negotiating.'

Of course he did. As a result, the Shelly Beach Writers' Festival has gained the cost-free loan of a 300-seat marquee complete with the latest bells-and-whistles-IT equipment, plus portable bathroom facilities.

'Well done. Will it fit on the foreshore?'

'No problem.'

'What colour?'

'Yellow.'

'Good. No confusion for attendees. We can use the yellow marquee for our keynote sessions, and then hold dual sessions concurrently in the blue marquee and the yellow marquee. We'll need to work out a new schedule for our presenters. Maybe double sessions?'

Adrian reached out and took hold of my hand. He was staring at me again with those delicious blue eyes. I moved the conversation along. 'Where on earth did you find another marquee?'

'It's a loan from the National Curriculum Authority. We can have it for the Friday and the weekend of the festival. We were lucky to get it. It's booked for a city event on the Monday after the festival. We have to pack it up and get it on the truck Sunday night.'

'We can do that!'

A smile and another hand squeeze.

'Thank you, Adrian. Now we have to think about accommodation and food for 150 extra attendees.'

'We can talk about that tomorrow. Let's go to bed.'

And somehow, that's exactly what happened. I stood up to take the wine glasses inside and before I knew it, Adrian had wrapped his arms around me and was kissing me. And then he was leading me into the bedroom. I blame the moonlight and the wine.

But the next morning it felt like a dream. Adrian was up early, sipping a coffee while he packed his bag.

'Weren't you staying for the weekend?' I asked.

'So sorry, Gina. I have to get back to the office – this new job is taking all of my time. I hate leaving you with the accommodation and food to sort for the extra attendees. And there's the Schools Day to manage too. Did I mention that I promised we'd add the Friday before the festival as a Schools Day to get the marquee?'

Had Adrian mentioned a Schools Day? I would not panic. 'No. Right.'

I watched Adrian as he slipped on his jacket. I couldn't help feeling a pang at the thought of him leaving.

'You just need to find a few schools in the peninsula area to invite for the Schools Day,' he continued. 'And some speakers to do a few sessions – for kids as well as adults. I can find funding. Ask the committee members for a hand – Beryl, Violet —' He laughed. 'No, probably not Violet. Beryl and Daphne should be able to help. Email me as soon as you work out what's happening.'

Before I could say a word, Adrian took a last sip of his coffee, gave me a lingering kiss and was gone.

The Dog watched me stagger into the kitchen and make myself a strong black. 'Don't say a thing! I refuse to get stressed. Adrian knows that I know a successful festival is the first step in obtaining funding for Shelly Beach's desperately needed Information and Community Centre.'

The Dog stared at me with his small eyes.

'And Adrian knows that I know I can handle a new Day One. I'll go big-picture, then I'll go back and fill in the detail. I'm relieved Shelly Beach still has its festival – albeit with a new unplanned Day One. The bad news is that we're still short of accommodation and food for 150 attendees. I'm going to make another cup of very strong coffee. Then it will be time for a walk.'

I'd lost the Dog with my Adrian-knows-that-I-know explanation, but he was up for the walk.

Sunday: Extraordinary lunch meeting at Rosa's

I spent most of Saturday in a state of numbed panic, but had mostly recovered when Pandora called in the following morning.

'I thought I'd walk with you to Rosa's for the meeting. I've done a ring around and made sure committee members know to come to Rosa's. Where's Adrian?'

'Been and gone.'

'What? What happened? Did he help with a Plan B?'

'Well, a Part One of a Plan B.' I grimaced. 'We need to come up with Part Two today.'

'How do you feel? You look ... fantastic, actually. You haven't ... ?'

I nodded. 'We did.'

'You're absolutely hopeless, Gina. Worse than a teenager.'

'I know. Don't talk to me. I'm mad at myself again. Can't think about it now. Not only do I have to sort out the festival bookings – accommodation and food – but we've got a new Day One.'

'A new Day One?' Pandora smiled. 'You're enjoying this, aren't you?'

'I most certainly am not!'

(But I do love a challenge.)

I continued, 'Adrian and Digby have found a new state-of-the-art 300-seat marquee we can erect on the foreshore. We can use this marquee for the keynotes but we'll have to change our weekend program to work across two marquees. You won't have to change much on the website. There's just one proviso. We have to make the Friday before the festival a new Day One – a Schools Day for students and teachers in our area.'

'What!'

'It's not a problem, Pandora.'

Pandora looked unconvinced. Children and Pandora are not a good mix.

'I'm more worried about the accommodation and food for the extra 150 attendees. I haven't a clue how we can sort this out.'

'You'll think of something.'

As we approached Rosa's we could hear the committee having pre-lunch drinks on the deck. Shelly Beach Sunday mornings are all about church and lifesaver club training, but loyal committee members had fronted up for my extraordinary meeting at Rosa's.

Over lunch, committee members listened to Part One of Plan B.

Of course the committee voted yes to add a third day to our festival. And of course they unanimously voted for me to organise the new Day One. Then we moved on to Part Two of our Plan B. Where could we find accommodation and food for an extra 150 attendees?

'I've already contacted the council, Gina,' piped up Alf. 'They said we could extend the camping area for another fifty campsites and open up the north ablutions block.'

'Brilliant, Alf.' Fifty down, one hundred to go.

'And I'll help you sort out the kids' program, Gina,' said Josh.

I shot a grateful look at Josh, local teacher and Bianca's much-adored husband.

The meeting ended without any more suggestions, but with a promise from all to think long and hard ahead of our next meeting.

Pandora gave me an amused smile and a warm kiss on the cheek as she left me outside Rosa's. 'I've no doubt you'll organise our new Day One brilliantly, Gina. Call me when you need to update the festival website. And let me know what I need to do publicity-wise. I hate to admit it, but cute pics of kids will make for good media coverage.'

I groaned.

Pandora laughed. 'Think of this as practice for your new exec position. Get the adrenaline flowing. And don't forget to send Adrian my regards when you email him next.' She winked.

Beryl caught me just as the Dog and I were leaving. 'Gina! Great news – Blythe Blodnik thinks she can solve your accommodation problem.'

'Blythe Blodnik?'

'You've met her before, I'm sure. Forty-something woman, slim, with long brown hair? She's in our poetry group.'

'Right . . .'

'Last night I put pen to paper and wrote a poem called "Festival Fiasco", about 150 extra festival-goers and not a hotel in sight. I posted it on our group's website and Blythe got in contact.'

'Well done, Beryl!'

No local has been more astounded at Beryl blossoming into a talented poet than husband Alf. Beryl is now convenor of the Shelly Beach Poetry Group. (Alf's not into poetry. He's happy with the birdwatchers' and lifesavers' club, and his boat-building projects. He and Potholer are building a boat in the Potholers' front room, a topic that's widely avoided whenever Potholer's wife, Aphrodite, is within hearing distance.)

'Blythe's the marketing director at Sea Haven Resort, Gina, and says the new building has been completed earlier than expected. It's got 144 rooms in total. She's going to talk to the resort manager about opening it for the festival weekend. A win-win arrangement for everyone concerned. It'll give the resort a chance to iron out any accommodation wrinkles before the official opening of their new conference centre.'

'I'm stunned, Beryl. I don't know what to say.'

'I've always believed events happen even if you don't do anything to make them happen.' And with that Beryl left with Alf to walk home along the beach in the early spring sunshine.

The Dog and I walked in the other direction. 'Can you believe it? I think our accommodation problem is about to be solved. But there are still a lot of loose ends to be tied up.'

The Dog told me to relax.

TWO WEEKS

TO GO

Monday

I woke feeling good. 'Early breakfast today, Dog. Then we're going for a brisk walk. When we get back I have to email Adrian to get our Day One program happening.

'I'm over throwing pity parties for myself. We're going to enjoy ourselves with this. After all, it's only two more weeks of my life.'

Walking into the kitchen, I stopped to read some notes I'd written at the magical writing hour of three a.m. I could hardly read them but remembered the notes were for a book idea.

The Dog wagged his tail. He was pleased with my new positive attitude. And he was glad I was thinking about writing again.

'It's not the novel. It's an idea I had for a picture storybook. Could be dog lit. It's about a dog who thinks he's human.'

The Dog was of the opinion that the 'dog lit' market was saturated – but I shouldn't give up. It was a good niche. I could sell my book at vets, pet shops and lost dog shelters. Maybe it would make a film? But I shouldn't count on him to help with the sales and marketing.

I decided last night that as director of this festival, I would steer it home. And I was not going to beat myself up about the on-again-off-again Adrian thing. I'm a modern woman who understands no-strings-attached sex. I found the Dog's lead. 'Let's go.'

We walked briskly past Daphne who was taking yoga on the beach and gave her a wave. 'No time to stop and chat with Bluey, sorry, Dog.'

Back home I topped up the Dog's water bowl. 'I'm working at the library today, but then we're meeting Josh at Piece of Cake for coffee.'

The Dog eyed the pencilled addition *meet Josh* to today's date on the calendar. My work schedule, aka three-pronged attack against poverty, leaves him confused at times. And he was already having second thoughts re: my new positive attitude. He doesn't approve of 'brisk' as an adjective when it's used before the noun 'walk'.

There was barely time for a second coffee before I had to go to the library for Mother Goose reading time. If I don't get there before the borrowers, the library is a wreck and my biscuits are already gone, gobbled up by young children and desperate parents and carers.

- **Brainstorming with Josh**

I sat opposite Josh, our local primary school teacher with surf-bleached hair, sipping a coffee.

'Only two weeks to the festival, Gina.'

'I know. It's like a volcano has erupted. We're going to make it by the skin of our teeth.' I looked at frantic scribbles in my notebook. 'Okay. I'm thinking a pirates theme for the Schools Day. Pirate workshops for young writers. And we don't want too many students. Definitely not 300.'

Josh nodded. 'Great idea. And we'll dress up?'

I sighed and nodded. I'd accepted dressing-up goes with my

position as children's librarian. I'd already been a bear at the teddy bears' picnic, the wicked witch from the west, and a compost bin for our Enviro Day. Another potentially embarrassing gig was neither here or there. And pirates are more fun than compost bins, witches or bears.

'I'm thinking thirty young wannabe writers each from four local schools will do – 120 students plus their teachers.' I checked my calculations again. 'One hundred and twenty kids divided into four groups sounds manageable. What do you think?'

Josh agreed. 'Easy. I can take some workshops on the beach. Kids can dig for treasure, learn to tie reef knots and walk the plank.'

I smiled. 'You'll need treasure. I'll ask the Jenkins if they'd like to contribute gold-covered chocolate coins.'

Like all locals, the Jenkins family had enthusiastically supported the festival. Jenkins' General Store was now refitted and rebadged as Jenkins Produce (no apostrophe). The missing apostrophe took a considerable allocation of general business at one of our war-cabinet festival meetings.

Josh warmed to the theme. 'I'll tell bloodthirsty pirate stories and make crafty stuff with the kids – you know, things like eye patches, pirate hats, shoe buckles and spy glasses.

'And surely Dimity Honeysuckle would be cool to take a few workshops.'

'It'd be brilliant if she would. But we'll still need one more person to help with workshops.'

'What about Alex Dessaix?' Josh asked.

Alex is a Shelly Beach lifesaver, and a children's author and illustrator. The Dog and I had met Alex through my work at the library. Alex is an archetypal Gen X, and works in the accounts and administration department of the library. He's had one picture storybook published and is working on another.

'Genius, Josh!' I wrote Alex's name in my notebook. 'I'll see if I can organise time off for Alex so he can do the workshops. It'll be an excellent opportunity for him to promote his writing.'

Josh was on a roll. 'And we can use our young gofers to help too. It'll work.'

'I think it will.' I made a note to talk to Terri, head gopher. Josh's enthusiasm was catching. 'If it doesn't, I'll take great delight in making Adrian walk the plank. And I'll make sure sharks are circling below.'

No comment from the tactful Josh.

As the Dog and I walked home along the beach, we passed the community hall. Boppy, poppy sounds were blaring out into our clear Shelly Beach sea air and we couldn't help but investigate. I stuck my head around the door and saw Dimity Honeysuckle and a huge mouse dancing together. The Dog and I were a little disconcerted when Atticus removed his head and a smiling-faced Sandy was revealed.

'Hi, Gina,' said Dimity, flushed and breathless from rehearsing.

'Hello, Dimity.' I decided to take the bull by the horns. 'How would you feel about moving your opening performance from the Saturday of the festival to the Friday? And . . .' (I gave my most winning smile) 'maybe taking a workshop or four for a small group of young writers?'

I went with my tell-it-like-it-is strategy and explained to Dimity the new changes in our festival program due to a computer glitch.

The pretty young author-slash-illustrator paused for thought and then her face cracked into a grin. 'I don't mind at all. It'll be fun! Matt's been working on a *How to write a picture storybook* presentation for me to do when we get back to the UK. This will be an excellent dry run. And your pirate theme fits *so* well with my latest Atticus book.'

Sandy, mouse head under her arm, agreed. 'It'll be cool!'

I ignored the Dog's beady-eyed look and tried not to look smug. Dimity's latest children's book is *Atticus's Pi-Rat-I-Cal Adventure*.

I continued with the caring-but-frazzled director persona. 'Should I talk to Matt about the changes in your program?'

'Don't worry. I'll sort it,' replied Dimity. 'Matt's happy to go along with whatever I want to do.'

I thanked the girls profusely and left them to the rest of their rehearsal. When I was sure we were past the pier and out of sight, I executed a mad piratical dance.

'I've only got to talk to Alex Dessaix tomorrow at the library, to see if he can be released from work for the day. The admin people will have to agree, and then we've got the morning session for Day One practically in the bag.'

Tuesday: Accommodation issues

During my lunch break at the library the next day I raced down to the Sea Haven Resort. Blythe Blodnik, poet and marketing manager of the five-star hotel, wanted to meet me.

Blythe and I met with our notebooks at the ready. Hers electronic, mine manual.

'Happy to put up your extra attendees, Gina. But we'd like a sandwich board reading *Sea Haven Resort supports the Shelly Beach community* in our foyer.'

'Not an issue.'

'And we'll put a bit of PR on our website about the Shelly Beach Writers' Festival and attendees staying at our resort.'

'Great. Contact Pandora Papadopoulos. She'll have content and pics you can use. She'll make sure the resort gets a pitch on our website too.'

Blythe smiled and checked her iPad. 'Now, if you're happy we can use our own minibuses to get attendees to the festival from the resort if they don't have their own transport. Or you could contact Hamish at McPherson's buses. They don't use their school buses on the weekend. Tell Hamish we'll mention him in our promotion.'

I made another dot point in my notebook.

'We're offering a basic package – accommodation and continental breakfast – but only for festival attendees and only for the two nights of the festival.

'That's fantastic! Thank you so much, Blythe.'

'Have you a minute? Bring your coffee and I'll give you a quick walk-through the resort.'

Basically sprinting around the Sea Haven Resort (Blythe was clearly very fit), I was given a mini-tour to fit into my lunch break. It was as glam as I had imagined.

'I'm amazed you've never been here before, Gina.'

'Been under the pump 24/7. Busy, busy, busy.'

Sea Haven Resort definitely earns its five-star rating. I was shown through one of the four-bedroom stand-alone apartments complete with a sea-view plunge pool. A similar apartment to the one I presume King Rat ex-husband plus entourage will be staying in during the festival. We quickly walked through Waves restaurant with its blue-and-silver colour scheme and breathtaking sea views.

'Of course anytime you and your partner are free we'd be pleased to welcome you to dine at Waves as our guests,' Blythe said as I sneaked a glance at my watch. 'It's Adrian, isn't it?'

Bloody hell! I nodded and smiled.

We checked the sumptuous spa and beauty salon where Bianca works occasionally and where guests can receive relaxing massages and treatments – complete with stunning sea views. And I was given a quick walk-through the nearly completed conference centre with – you guessed it – incredible sea views.

'The resort's been upgraded for multiple conferences,' Blythe explained. 'I'm taking conference bookings starting in October but I've been offering weekend taste tests for prospective clients.'

Like Rod Lidner, my soon-to-be boss.

We'd arrived back at our starting point, the impressive entrance. I thanked Blythe but she wasn't ready to let me leave yet. 'The poetry group is indebted to you, Gina, for the help you've given us with the website. It's been *fab*-ulous getting to know other poets. And our group find your poetry tips and ideas really useful.'

I'd forgotten I've been writing regular tips for the poetry group. Blythe continued, 'Once I have an idea, a title, or even the first line for a poem, it niggles in my mind for weeks. I'm only happy when I can get it down, post it on our website or read it aloud to the group. It's been a fab way of exorcising personal ghosts.'

'I'm glad.' I checked my watch again. 'Have to get back to the library.'

We exchanged a brief hug and I fast-paced it back to the library, thinking about the stunning environmentally friendly resort and Waves restaurant.

The committee was delighted when I emailed them with our accommodation problem solved. Daphne, Violet and I put in time that evening to email confirmation info to our extra paid-up attendees who now have somewhere to sleep – either in their own tents on the foreshore with an ablutions block nearby, or in the Sea Haven Resort's indulgent rooms with cosy white doonas, plenty of pillows and comfort to match.

From: Gina <glaurel@peninsula.com.au>

To: Adrian <bookstreet@network.com.au>

Subject: Festival bookings confirmed

Have clinched deal for accommodation for most attendees at Sea
Haven Resort. Remaining attendees have camping sites.

Are you free to dine at Waves sometime soon?

From: Adrian <bookstreet@network.com.au>

To: Gina <glaurel@peninsula.com.au>

Subject: Dinner for two

Congratulations – never doubted you could sort our
accommodation issue.

How does this weekend sound for Waves?

Wednesday: Meet with volunteer gofers

After school I sat with Terri and her nerdy friends at Piece of Cake.
They'd offered their services as festival guides, aka gofers.

At an early committee meeting, members voted to invite young
locals to participate in the festival as gofers. The idea was that the
teenagers would help people find festival sessions, coffee, toilets,
and generally assist with the organisation. We'd put the word out
and got a group of volunteers together, and I'd already contacted
their parents to ask permission for our young locals to participate
in the festival.

Terri watched me make a dot-point in my notebook. She was
serving hot chocolate and cupcakes.

'Toby with-the-fringe is really charming, Terri.' The Dog and I'd
had several chats with Toby with-the-fringe when we bumped into
him at the beach.

Wide-eyed stare from Terri. 'Are you for real? He's such a *pain*!
Mum said I have to include him in festival stuff with me.'

'I don't know why you complain about Toby. He's a well-groomed sixteen-year-old. Plays the violin, and he's a prefect. Your mum says he's polite and good with Sam. She told me he's won the science prize for the second time and he played the lead role in *Under Milkwood* with a perfect Welsh accent.'

Terri gave me her newly honed icy teenage stare and a shrug.

'And . . . he likes writing.'

A chilly two-minute silence.

Walking home later, the Dog thought the meeting went well. Best of all, the volunteer festival gofers were happy to help out with the Schools Day and wear token pirate gear: neckerchiefs and eye-patches.

Thursday: Catering panic

Somehow in all the excitement of securing accommodation for the extra attendees, I'd forgotten that I'd have to feed them as well. On Thursday I called a meeting of the catering committee – i.e. Beryl and Rosa – at Rosa's. The Dog was catching panic vibes from me. I wasn't exactly panicking, just stressed. I'd never had to get my head around the logistics needed to feed and provide tea and coffee for an extra 150 people over two days.

Rosa helped solve the food problem by announcing she had miraculously conjured up more cousins with 'cooking vans'.

'Catering vans.'

'Exactly. You are breaking into me when I'm on a roll, Gina.'

'I'm sorry.'

'Sorry accepted.' Rosa eyeballed Beryl to press her point, as you do in a biz presentation, and continued. 'Some cousins can cook all-day breakfasts, some can cook hot dogs, some can cook sausage in a sandwich, some can cook healthy sandwiches. All in their cooking vans.'

The catering committee gave their approval. Both Beryl and I tried to ignore Rosa's last comment: 'I tell cousins I'll kill them if they don't front up and cook in their vans for the weekend.'

Beryl reported that Harold and Gary were also happy to help out with the extra numbers. Apparently they'd subcontracted foodie friends in Sea Haven to prepare the extra boxed lunches we needed.

Tea and coffee stations for the festival breaks provided an unexpected hiccup. Providing 300 attendees with coffee, tea or herbal tea and a biscuit in a fifteen-minute break *was* tricky.

'We need to keep the friendly small-town feel, Gina,' said Beryl. 'No way can we provide store-bought biscuits to go with the tea and coffee.'

The catering committee agreed that Piece of Cake, Rosa's pub, and Beach Eatery du Jour (aka Rupert's Butchery) deliver excellent coffee and tea daily but couldn't cover 300 cups of tea or coffee in fifteen minutes.

Then Beryl had one of her eureka moments. 'We'll extend the breaks, and make them thirty minutes!'

We were on a roll again. The committee decided to conclude the meeting. Lorenzo was closing the kitchen and we needed to put our meal orders in.

'I'm not panicking, Dog. But I'm finding it hard to get in my calm zone.'

No comment.

Friday

I was staring at my wardrobe, thinking about what to wear. After yesterday's catering committee meeting I'd come home and rediscovered my calm zone with the help of a glass of red. Now it was in danger of going AWOL again. At that moment Bianca, my bubbly beautician, drove into the driveway. As soon as I let her in, she collapsed at the kitchen table. She was in meltdown.

'Herbal tea?'

'No! Coffee. Black and strong.'

'Right. What's happened?'

'I've stuffed up my interview with Anton. Stephanie's furious with me.'

I found the tissues. 'Take some deep breaths.'

Bianca counted as she took four deep breaths in and exhaled four times. Then she launched into her story. 'You know Stephanie said it was fine for me to do an interview with Anton?'

'Yes.'

Bianca took some crumpled, double-spaced A4 sheets of typed copy from her handbag and handed her profile piece to me. 'Over a thousand words of copy! I was hoping to submit my piece to the *Sea Haven Sentinel* or post it on the writers' festival blog.'

'Right.' I scanned Bianca's profile.

Bianca continued with her story at her usual rapid pace. 'It was such a gorgeous interview. Anton gave me some brilliant quotes like . . .' She scanned her copy over my shoulder. 'Like, "Authors are allowed to be temperamental. If they weren't they'd be bus drivers or dentists."

'Anton writes for two four-hour sessions every day and has for thirty years. He uses Staedler pencils and notebooks. Stephanie does the keying in for him. And . . .' Bianca checked her copy again, 'Anton told me when he first saw Stephanie it was love at first sight across a crowded room.' She started to tear up again. I offered her another tissue.

'Apparently when he shook hands with Stephanie at their first meeting, it felt like an electric shock through his body. He knew he'd found his soul mate.'

I nodded sympathetically. Bianca would have been rapt with the interview – it made for a catchy romantic piece from a charismatic famous author.

I waited for Bianca to blow her nose. 'But when I showed Stephanie my interview before sending it to the *Sentinel*, she told me to kill it! She accused me of making up the quotes, said I'd read about Anton's life on the internet and made up info to fit. As if I would *do* that!'

I waited while Bianca coped with another flood of tears.

'Exactly. You never would. She's being irrational.'

Bianca gave me a grateful look. 'She said the stuff I had about Anton meeting her for the first time was lies, and that's how she knew I'd made it up. Apparently that "love at first sight" thing was with Anton's *first* wife – Stephanie is his *fourth* wife. But it's not my problem if Anton can't remember which wife he's with now!' Bianca dabbed her puffy eyes again with a tissue. 'Stephanie said Anton's first wife would sue if she read my profile piece.'

'I doubt that.' But Violet had told me that Stephanie had told her that Anton's first wife contacts the mainstream media at the drop of a hat. Gives out felicitous and mean soundbites about Stephanie and Anton.

'Put it down as experience, Bianca. You've had a journalist's down day. And it's not your fault.'

I received a weak smile. 'After Stephanie bullied me into not publishing, she was very nice. She said I could have an interview with her tomorrow to write about her lifestyle – the benefits of eating raw vegetables, having early nights and drinking five litres of water a day. But no photos. She'll supply the photos.'

'Well, there you are.' I smiled wryly.

Bianca made a face. 'It'll make boring copy, Gina!'

'You'll think of an angle. Ask her about her clothes and shoes.'

'Good idea. And I could ask her about their houses. Anton said they've a penthouse apartment in London with sensational views across the Thames, a villa in the Languedoc, and a mini modern castle in Vancouver.' Bianca lovingly smoothed her A4 double-spaced copy again. 'I should've known. Violet warned me. Apparently Stephanie makes sure she's in attendance whenever anyone wants to talk to Anton. She monitors everything he says. Stephanie uses excuses when Anton starts losing the plot, like she has to get him a double macchiato – or he needs his tablets.'

'Let's hope he doesn't lose his plot during our keynote address.'

'Anton will be cool if Stephanie's on hand. He's a lovely man – we were getting on really well. He has that sense of entitlement you expect men like him to have.' Bianca gave me her writerly smile. 'I'll use that sentence in my Jane Austen fan fiction.

'Apparently Stephanie's very touchy about the whole Anton thing,' she continued. 'Anton is her meal ticket. What will happen if he can't keep up his brilliant career?

'Violet thinks that Anton's not functioning at one hundred per cent. Not even fifty per cent.' Bianca took a sip of her coffee. 'I don't know what you see in strong blacks, Gina.' She put her cup down and gave me a hug. 'Thanks for listening. I think I'll give Stephanie's interview a miss. I'll concentrate on my Jane Austen fan fiction instead.'

'Good idea. Speaking of Jane Austen, why don't you list your Jane Austenites meeting under *Umbrella Events* on the festival schedule? You could hold it during one of the festival lunchtime breaks.'

'Really? I'd love to!'

The Dog and I watched Bianca give us her usual happy wave and beep on the horn as she drove off into the Shelly Beach afternoon and into the comforting arms of husband Josh.

'She'll be fine. Keep your paws crossed, Dog, that Anton is okay to deliver his keynote and his two sessions. What Anton Brandt does after the festival is not my problem.'

The Dog approved of my sentiments.

- **Day One organisation**

I watched the clock on the kitchen wall tick over to six p.m. A Shelly Beach pink-and-gold sunset had lit up the sky. I was fretting about my wardrobe. The Dog was disconsolate. He knew I was going out and he wouldn't get any leftovers. I warned him, 'You'll be sleeping on the day bed tonight.'

I'd decided to go for my 'clean and elegant' look to wear to Waves: tailored black pants, a red silk shirt and my ballet flats. I was just taking a last check around the tidy kitchen when I heard the key in the door. Adrian had arrived.

Adrian was wearing his 'city look', his smart wheeling-and-dealing outfit – a bespoke suit but with a pastel-blue shirt, open at the neck. The tie I'd helped him choose was sticking out from his pocket. Adrian with-the-friendly-blue-eyes looked hot.

He dumped his overnight bag, briefcase and a clutch of shopping bags on the floor, scooped me up in a gigantic hug and delivered one of his excellent kisses. 'Ridiculously difficult day! Working with politicians is a bloody nightmare. I'm so glad to see you, Gina.'

I found myself a little lost for words.

His face softened. 'I hope you didn't mind, but I cancelled our dinner reservation at Waves. Shopped at a deli on the way down. I'm cooking a romantic dinner for two. Oh, and I thought we could spend the evening sorting out the Day One program.'

Typical!

Adrian gave me another excellent kiss. 'If you don't mind, that is . . . and we can work out a schedule for new sessions for the rest of the festival tomorrow morning. I have to be back in the city tomorrow afternoon to catch a flight to Perth. You'd better put the oysters in the fridge, by the way.' He smiled and headed to the bathroom.

The Dog heard the shower start and gave me his beady-eyed stare.

'I'm not letting it get to me. He *is* going to cook! I'm channelling no-strings-attached casual romance.'

No comment.

I sniffed the oysters and put them in the fridge. 'Heaven. They smell of the sea. My favourite. And he's brought yellow roses!'

The Dog checked the remainder of Adrian's deli purchases while I arranged the flowers in a jug. 'I love yellow roses.'

No comment.

'I'll bet he's going to make us that pasta dish with the farfalle, prosciutto, parmesan and cream. He's even bought a bunch of parsley. And my favourite Greek pastries.' This was a no-strings-attached seduction *par excellence*.

The Dog sulked in the corner.

Once we'd eaten, Adrian announced he'd settled the teachers' afternoon session for Day One.

'You haven't?'

Adrian had. The teachers' afternoon session would consist of a thirty-minute presentation on the new maths curriculum followed by group workshops on how to implement said curriculum.

'A maths curriculum hardly fits a writers' festival. Couldn't you find a speaker to give a presentation on the literacy curriculum?'

'I tried. But I did get excellent funding for food at the afternoon break and a drink voucher for teachers to use at Rosa's if they want to stay for networking after the workshops.'

'That's more like it. But I'm not looking forward to telling the festival committee that we're having a maths presentation and workshops to implement a maths curriculum.'

We'd taken our coffee and Greek pastries on to the balcony. Adrian found my jacket and draped it gently round my shoulders, his face brushing close to mine.

We listened to the gentle lap of waves beneath us. 'Plenty of stars. Not too cold, thank goodness. I'm keeping my fingers crossed we'll have reasonable weather for the festival weekend,' I said.

'You worry too much, Gina.'

'That could be construed as *rather* condescending. Especially given that most of my worries revolve around a festival a person has dumped in my lap.'

'Point taken. My apologies.'

There was a brief silence filled only with the sound of the waves.

'When we've finished our coffee, we can start looking at the changes we'll need to cover the new numbers for the festival program.'

Adrian moved closer, pushed a curl off my face and gave me a long kiss. 'Let's not. Let's have some fun. We deserve some fun.'

And we did have fun.

Saturday: New two-day schedule to organise

I woke up to the smell of pancakes floating into the bedroom. The Dog slid off my bed, pattered out to the kitchen and reported back. Adrian had been for a swim with the Shelly Beach Icebergers and was now making my favourite breakfast.

The Dog wasn't impressed. He doesn't like pasta leftovers or pancakes. He fancies leftover Thai curry, even if it does play hell with his digestive system.

I showered, dressed and ambled out to the kitchen. Adrian gave me a kiss as he tousled my wet curls. I sat down to an impeccably set table (including one of my roses with the stem shortened to fit in an eggcup). 'Help yourself to fruit, Gina. I used the strawberries we didn't eat last night.'

I smiled my thanks. Adrian's motivations were transparent: we were having an early breakfast because he had to leave soon. Then again, part of me loved his new drive, his man-in-a-hurry ambition – not to mention the new skills he'd acquired (i.e. cooking and cleaning up).

Adrian poured the coffee and we took it on to the balcony. It was a gorgeous day, the bluest of skies decorated with fluffy clouds. Shelly Beach bay, stretching out to the horizon, was a matching sky-blue.

'So . . . obviously you can't stay. I understand – it's cool,' I said. 'I can do the program rescheduling for Day Two and Day Three. And I can sort out the logistics of Day One. Email me the name of the maths presenter so I can get it onto our program.'

Adrian looked relieved. 'Are you sure, Gina?'

'I'm sure I'm sure. Handling anything that's thrown at me is good practice for my new job.'

Once we'd finished our breakfast, Adrian collected his bag, briefcase and suit bag. 'Anything you need – anything at all – just email me.'

I received another excellent kiss and a hug. The Dog and I walked Adrian to the front door and watched him turn his zappy new goes-with-the-job car around. And then he was gone.

The Dog was still sulking when I gave him his breakfast.

'It's the new Fun Me, Dog. No questions asked and no strings attached. I'm definitely not going to be a martyr again.'

The Dog wasn't a huge fan of the new martyr-free me.

There was hardly any time to breathe before there was a knock at the door. Terri and Toby had come for a visit. Toby paid the Dog his due attention and Terri followed me to the kitchen.

'It's Toby's weekend with Paul, and Mum said I had to look after him,' she whispered. A rolled-eyed look. 'I hope it's okay to call in like this. I didn't know what else to do with him.'

'Of course it is. I like Toby. He's a nice young man.'

I received another rolled-eyed look. 'Any pancakes left?'

'No, but there's batter left in the jug. You can make pancakes for yourself and Toby. Actually, you might be just the people I need to run some ideas past for the new schedule for our festival.'

And Toby and Terri proved excellent sounding boards – full of practical ideas for the new schedule. Twenty minutes later, Toby had designed a grid for the schedule on my computer. 'The keynote addresses will be held from nine to ten each morning in the yellow marquee. You were going to have four sessions on each day of the original program. Now your presenters will have to double up. They'll each present their session in the yellow marquee on Saturday, and repeat their session in the blue marquee on Sunday. Simple.'

Toby received a cross-eyed look behind his back. I sent a cross-eyed look back to Terri. 'That's brilliant, Toby. I can see it will work. Thank you!'

'You'll need to ask the presenters to repeat their sessions,' chipped in Terri.

'I'm aware of this fact, thank you. Dimity Honeysuckle has already said she's happy to do two sessions – as well as the keynote for the Schools Day and a young writers' workshop.'

Terri raised her eyebrows, impressed. 'But don't give the schedule to Pandora to put on the website until you've checked all the presenters are happy to double up on their sessions.'

'Of course I won't.'

Terri responded with a teenage shrug and once she and Toby had finished the pancakes, they left to head back to her home along the beach. The Dog and I watched from the balcony as my helpful but angsty teenage friends walked along the waters' edge like two strangers.

'They're really making things difficult for themselves.'

The Dog thought this was common practice among humans. He's found the majority of humans enjoy making things difficult for themselves.

I ignored the Dog and went to get ready for the festival committee meeting at Rosa's pub.

~

Beryl had accomplished miracles.

'I've sourced tea and coffee urns from the Sea Haven Lions and Rotary clubs and enlisted the combined efforts of the Sea Haven and Shelly Beach catering corps to make one hundred dozen biscuits: fifty dozen shortbread, fifty dozen chocolate chip. And we're doing muffins for the meet and greet table for the morning sessions.'

Beryl must have caught the look of awe on my face.

'We've got ample time, Gina. We'll bake and freeze. It's for such a good cause!'

Adrian's vision for an Information and Community Centre for Shelly Beach has enthused every local living on this end of the peninsula.

'You're a genius, Beryl!'

Our catering queen blushed. 'We couldn't do this without you, Gina. We need you to keep an eye on the big picture – like a jellyfish using its tentacles to keep everything together. My volunteers have coped with fire and flood. We can do this easily.' She began to pull statistics from her head. 'We'll need six tea and coffee stations each serving fifty attendees – give or take a few.' She listed five stations on her hand. 'Yellow marquee, Rosa's pub foyer, band pavilion, foreshore shelter and here at the community hall. We were one station short but Digby's come to the rescue.'

'How?'

Daphne took over. 'He gave the committee permission to use the small marquee he's installing in the yard of Pages Gallery. He plans to use the marquee for spill-over guests from the two drinks-and-nibbles parties publishers are throwing in his gallery.'

Beryl said she'd enlist helpers to serve the tea and coffee. The committee decided on colour coding to help attendees find their designated tea and coffee station.

'Attendees can head to their colour-coded watering place for their thirty-minute breaks. We can stick coloured library dots on attendees' programs so they know what colour they are,' said Beryl. (The committee ignored Potholer's query about colour-blind attendees.)

I'm back in my calm zone.

From: Gina <glaurel@peninsula.com.au>
To: Adrian <bookstreet@network.com.au>
Subject: Action
1. Catering sorted
2. Tea and coffee stations sorted
I need to know your contacts and schedule for Day One immediately!

From: Adrian <bookstreet@network.com.au>
To: Gina <glaurel@peninsula.com.au>
Subject: Only you
I'll email afternoon session program asap.
Missing you madly.
xx Adrian

Sunday

Gentle waves lapped along Shelly Beach as the Dog and I went for our morning walk. We decided to drop in and see Rosa, and were stopped in our tracks as we entered the pub.

'Gina! What do you think?' Rosa beamed as she came over to us. 'My ex – the one who found my veteran furniture for me – came to visit last night. We had a beaut-i-ful time. We might even get back together again . . . maybe after the festival. He gave me fantastic new ideas for my pub.'

'It certainly looks different, Rosa.'

'Ex and I spend all night moving furniture around. He says communal-table dining is the new thing in the city. I think it will be excellent. Two people keep taking tables for four people, and you don't have a table for four people ready when four people want a table. Customers get angry if you make them shift to other tables. This way problem is solved! Ex says to go with no bookings for meals during the festival. And forget the entree-main-dessert menu. We will have an "open food" menu at Rosa's. An earth approach to food.'

'An organic approach?'

'Exactly. Best way to keep people happy and make money. I have a new goal. I'm getting Rosa's pub on hottest fifty pubs list! I make Rosa's pub an exciting eating-out destination!'

'Sounds like a great goal, Rosa.'

'One problem. I have to tell Lorenzo about new menu. He will be the one big sticky fly in the honey. My ex says we should include orphan fish species like mullet and leatherjacket, and serve sea and shoreline vegetables. Lorenzo doesn't like to cook orphan fish species. And I don't think he knows what are sea and shoreline vegetables.'

'Right!' Neither did I.

'But we don't go there until after the festival, Gina.'

Another after-the-festival decision to be made.

'Come and see my other fantastic idea. I make you a meeting place – a puboffice. Ex says cafoffices are big in the city – people are using tables in cafes like offices. They use their own phones and computers. But if people come to cafoffices to work and meet, they have to order food and not take up too much space.'

I didn't want to discourage Rosa, but I wasn't sure I needed a puboffice.

'Hurry up, Gina. Have a look at your new puboffice.' Rosa had taken me to a corner of her pub where there was one table with a chalkboard hanging on the wall above. *Gina's Writers' Festival Puboffice. Gina will be here each day. Call her for appointment.*

'What do you think?' Rosa asked, a smile on her face.

'I think it'll work. Thank you, Rosa.' I smiled back in what I hoped was a convincing manner.

'Good. But I have a warning. People have to buy drink and food if they want to tell you stuff about the festival and stay long time. My pub is a business. I have to make money.'

'I understand, Rosa. We'll give it a trial.'

Rosa clapped her hands in delight. 'I give you a complimentary glass of best sauv blanc from a local grower.'

Why not? It was almost lunch time, after all. The Dog and I returned to my puboffice with an excellent glass of locally grown wine (which can be purchased by festival attendees at a very reasonable price). I don't have a corner office yet, but from my new puboffice I do have a view over my favourite beach in the world.

The Dog settled himself under the table, dozing with his head resting on my shoes. I looked at the time. Shelly Beach's one and only church service would have finished. Committee members would soon be ambling into the pub for a drink and chat before they set off for lifesaving training, boat building, poetry writing, rockpool rambles, foreshore weed-busting or any of the multitude of activities one can do in sleepy Shelly Beach.

I took a sip of my wine. When I was a mere festival committee member and Adrian was festival director, our committee meetings frequently resembled war-cabinet meetings. Huge chunks of time were spent in deciding such essential items as what fonts to use on our brochures. And of course there was the meeting taken over by the discussion of the use or non-use of an apostrophe on Jenkins Produce's new signage.

Another controversial committee meeting was spent deciding on the greeting we'd use at the festival. 'Have a nice day!' 'Enjoy!' 'G'day, mate!' 'You're welcome' – were all suggested and abandoned. Finally, committee members voted to wear *Hello I'm* _____ stick-on name tags. And we would wear superglue smiles and say, 'Can I help you?' if any attendee looked puzzled or in trouble. 'Smiling is vital,' Bianca had said.

Members ignored Violet's 'Why?'

It was during the last meeting with Adrian that the enormity of what we were doing dawned on members. Adrian was talking us through our most recent bank statement (the hefty total we had in hand came from 150 paid-up attendees and two years' worth of fundraising). There was enough money to cover the festival but not nearly enough for our proposed Information and Community Centre.

By this time the committee was knowledgeable about other writers' festivals (national and international) through the magic of Google. Bianca had even found a festival for sale in the UK. 'It's been going for five years. You can't buy the town or the buildings it's held in, but you can buy the festival program and use the buildings.'

'Maybe we could sell the Shelly Beach Writers' Festival after we've had the festival?' asked Alf. 'That way we could make enough to build the centre.'

Maybe.

What promised to be another lengthy discussion was interrupted by our spin-doctor Pandora. 'Umbrella events. We need umbrella events. Events and activities that can be held before, between and after the festival. Think fun stuff – drinks and nibbles, extra workshops, pitch sessions, guided tours . . .'

So after another long, long meeting we'd arrived at a list of umbrella events for attendees that used the talents of Shelly Beach locals, requiring a small extra fee to attend.

I took my eyes away from calming Shelly Beach bay. Rosa had kindly lent me her laptop, and I clicked on our festival website. Under the heading *Umbrella Events* we had a good selection of early-morning keep-fit activities for disgustingly fit attendees who want to keep disgustingly fit during the festival. Daphne was taking yoga on the beach, soon-to-be ex-husband Charles was taking tai-chi on the beach, and Pandora was leading a team of early-morning joggers each day. Icebergers were on their own. Hopefully the bay would be shark-free. Note to self: Ask Alf about shark danger.

As usual Rosa had a bottomless pit of ideas for umbrella events. The website listed early-morning fishing trips with Rosa's cousins and a book launch for Rosa's nephew, Sergio.

'I get my famous soccer-playing nephew to launch his cookbook in my pub for Saturday lunchtime,' she'd explained. 'He cooks something beaut-i-ful from his own book and everyone will buy a copy.'

Yesterday Bianca called to tell me she'd set up a meeting of her Jane Austenites for during the Sunday lunchtime break. 'Any other Jane Austen devotees are welcome to attend. No cost.'

And then there was Breakfast with the Birds. Alf would take all interested parties to the back beach for birdwatching early in the morning. Not for me, but definitely for someone.

The door of the pub opened and the first of the Shelly Beach Sunday-lunchers walked in. One of them was Bianca, who waved and joined me at my puboffice. She watched while I scrolled through our festival website. 'Our umbrella events look brill! Josh has got the literary quiz at Rosa's under control. You'll have to check with Beryl about her Poetry Slam, though. She's a bit wobbly. Her poetry group has never held an official slam.' She paused. 'Josh saw Adrian's car drive out of Shelly Beach yesterday morning when he was jogging on the beach.'

Bianca knew about my decision to try just-friends with Adrian. Let's face it, by now so did everyone who lived in Shelly Beach.

'Are you two back on again?' Before their marriage, Bianca and Josh had a teetering romance that could have gone one way or the other. Fortunately it went the other way. 'I hated the on-again, off-again thing. Your head is constantly full of questions. If you go out with another man you're always asking yourself, Is this a fling? Or the real thing? If it's a fling and it turns out to be a flop, will there be more chances for flings?' Bianca looked at me. 'Not that I mean you, Gina. You'll have plenty of chances.'

I smiled gratefully and took my wise young friend's words of wisdom on board. 'Adrian and I are back on. Sort of. I'm going with the flow.'

'Good.'

'And would you believe, I'm actually cool with things as they are.'

'Oh, good!' Just then Bianca's face lit up. She'd seen Josh enter the pub. 'I'm going up to order, Gina. Do you want a crab salad or a pasta dish?'

I chose a crab salad. The Dog stirred at my feet. He was exhausted from disturbed nights due to me waking to update my lists and write notes to myself. It's a bad habit of mine. I know there's only so much we can do to control our own lives, but somehow writing notes gives me the illusion that I can do more. Over our crab salads, Bianca filled me in on her Jane Austenites' group. 'Can we change the name on the website? We're calling it Bonnets and Ruffles now.'

Early this year, inspired by DVDs (and then later by the books) Bianca (erstwhile chick lit writer) and her friends decided to form a Jane Austen appreciation society. Austenites meet to discuss Jane Austen's novels, drink tea, eat cake and become immersed in the Regency world.

'We just love the stories, Gina. Jane's novels are full of smart women and maladjusted men. Makes a nice change from death and vampires. We started with *Pride and Prejudice*. Then moved on to *Emma* – and *Clueless*, the modern film version. Now we've gone back to Jane's first book, *Sense and Sensibility*. Can you also post *BYO lunch* on the website for our meeting? Attendees can buy their food or collect their boxed lunches and bring them to the meeting.'

Josh walked across the room from the bar to the lifesavers' communal table, and Bianca followed her handsome young husband with adoring eyes. 'Did you hear Geraldine's giving a presentation at our meeting? It was serendipitous. I was chatting about the

Austenites and Geraldine told me she'd actually been to Jane Austen's house when she visited the UK last year. I instantly snaffled her up to talk at the meeting.'

'That should be good.'

'Geraldine attended a workshop given by a writer-in-residence at Jane Austen's house, which is now a museum, and it was the highlight of her and Claude's UK tour. Worth every cent of the entrance fee.' Bianca took a mouthful of her crab salad. 'Geraldine doesn't want to write a Jane Austen-type novel, she just likes reading them. But she said that it was *so* meaningful seeing the table Jane actually wrote at, and two pages in Jane's gorgeous handwriting. Can you imagine writing six novels over 80 000 words long by hand? Do you think Jane would start all over again when she wrote the next draft or could she just do cross-outs on the original? How many drafts do you think Jane wrote?'

I couldn't answer these questions. Maybe Geraldine would be able to.

'If I become famous do you think anyone would want to keep the laptop I've been writing on when I die? Put it on display in Scissors Salon?'

Again I was unsure.

'Did you know Jane Austen's novels are considered realist novels? The plots are your classic boy-meets-girl, girl-gets-boy; Jane put the real-life bits in everywhere else. And she used to write at the table in the living room and cover her writing when she had visitors.'

Jane Austen's writing process sounds familiar. I know the Dog thinks I'm paranoid about my privacy, and especially about my writing. I instantly close down my laptop if anyone comes in sight. And I don't talk about the novel I'm resurrecting, or the picture storybook I'm thinking of. I've tried to explain to the Dog that all writers tackle their writing in different ways. If I talked about the novel too much it would feel as though I'd already written it, and that's not a good thing.

The Dog couldn't relate to my writerly rationalisation. He doesn't mind talking about a hole he's thinking of digging. And if he's in the process of digging said hole he doesn't care who stands around and watches.

Bianca and I finished our meal and Josh came up to our table. 'Hey, Gina. We're off to do some weed-busting on the foreshore. Tidy it up for the festival.'

I watched Bianca and Josh leave with a bunch of sun-bleached lifesavers for their weed-busting. Shelly Beach locals never cease to astound me with their willing attitude to work.

Terri and family entered the pub as Josh and Bianca left. Terri made a beeline for me, giving me her discreet rolled-eye look. 'We're having a family Sunday lunch with Paul and Toby. How's the festival going?'

'Looks like we've got a maths literacy session for teachers on the afternoon of Day One. And pirates in the morning.'

'Maths! I don't think committee members will be happy about a maths session for teachers.'

'I don't think it'll cause a fuss, Terri, because if we don't have a Schools Day we can't have the new marquee for our extra attend-ees. That's what life's about – give and take. Compromise.'

I received another rolled-eyed look and a teenage shrug before Terri sloped off to join her expanding family.

The Dog thought I'd made a good attempt at trying to slip some wisdom under Terri's radar, but he didn't think it got to her.

- **Day One maths presentation and workshop**

The Dog and I dropped back into White Sands after lunch to check our email. According to Adrian, all the teachers coming for Day One will now be attending Digby's red-carpet do that evening too. And the barn dance. And the barbecue. My newfound enthusiasm dipped slightly. Pandora had texted earlier to ask me to drop round, saying she wanted me to see a video clip she'd made before she posted it on the festival website. As we walked along the beach on the way to Pandora's we paused to watch Dimity and Atticus (aka Sandy) practising their routines in the sunshine outside the community hall.

Our celeb children's author and her two-man (well, one man and a human mouse) team have melted into our community. According to Violet, Dimity, Sandy and Matt are revelling in our spring weather. Matt's surfing on the back beach or swimming in the bay most days. He seems to have found an unending number of females he can impress with his ruggedly handsome good looks and Hugh Grant voice. And there's an endless list of Shelly Beach lifesavers willing to take Dimity and Sandy under their wings and give them free surfing tuition. As we ambled along the beach, the Dog and I mused over the surprising information we'd acquired via Bianca about Matt Galinsky. Turns out Matt is Dimity's father! Dimity told Bianca when – you guessed it – she was having a beauty treatment.

'This is really confidential info, Gina,' Bianca had said over our crab salads. 'You won't tell anyone?'

I swore secrecy.

'Dimity said her mum was furious when Matt turned up a few years ago. Dimity's mum had always told her that her dad died just before she was born. Dimity's mum – who was in a semi-famous singing group back in the nineties – went back to her parents'

115

home when she had Dimity. After the birth her mum ran a music shop and gave singing lessons. Dimity's very close to her mum, who's worked hard to give her a good life.'

Bianca looked at my nails. 'Come in tomorrow – I'll redo that colour for you.' She refocused on her story in hand. 'Dimity's mum and Matt had got together when she was in the singing group and he had a band. Matt discovered he had a daughter when he saw a photo of Dimity and her mum in a glossy.' Bianca sighed. 'Isn't it amazing how people find each other?'

She didn't wait for my reply. 'But the sworn-to-secrecy bit is for real, Gina. Dimity and Matt have decided to keep their relationship a secret. Better for business. Matt can present an entirely professional front as her manager. Dimity said everything's been cool biz-wise since Matt's been managing.'

When we arrived at Pandora's, I hugged my friend and sat down in front of her computer.

'Ready?' Pandora asked, before pressing play on a short video clip. Three agonising minutes passed.

'Well, what do you think?' she asked, her eyes lit with excitement. 'I'm rapt. It's worked out better than I thought. I'm posting it on our website immediately – if you agree.'

I remembered a painful afternoon that seemed to last for days until Pandora was happy she'd captured what she wanted on video. At least I didn't have to stand in the freezing cold on the pier again.

I watched myself as the video clip played once more. There I was, the Shelly Beach Writers' Festival director. I was wearing a simple white silk shirt, the skirt from my smoky plum suit and I was showing an ample amount of leg. I must admit Pandora's red stilettos (which at the last moment she insisted I wear) were a clever touch. Despite the fact that I could hardly walk in them.

Pandora had ended up using the footage she shot in her lounge with the deep-seated sofa, the background lit with low-wattage lights. I was standing in my faux director pose, pretending to take a call; a close-at-hand table held an open laptop and a small jar of local wildflowers. I looked the epitome of a calm, dedicated director of a boutique writers' festival.

'Well? What do you think?'

'It doesn't look like me.'

Pandora smiled. 'It *is* you. Have I your permission to post the clip on our website?'

How could I say no? I looked really, really good. 'Of course. If you think it'll make good publicity for the festival.'

I received an amused smile from Pandora. Once she'd packed up her gear we drove to Rosa's for a meal-slash-committee meeting. Eating at Rosa's while also sorting out the festival saves time and money. The Dog was pleased we went in Pandora's car. He refused to walk another step.

Amazingly, committee members were still maintaining a high level of enthusiasm and energy. They liked the video clip, which I used to soften them before I gave them the bad news. I explained very carefully that in order to gain the new upmarket marquee to house our extra 150 attendees, we were holding a session to promote the new maths curriculum. As I'd anticipated, the committee was initially resistant, but recognised that using our festival as a platform to push a maths curriculum was a necessary move. Yes, a maths curriculum was hardly literary, but . . .

Committee members, stifling their cynicism, were consoled by the considerable funds added to our festival coffers. The Department of Education is paying for relief teachers and transport.

'It's just moving money circuitously.' *Circuitously* is Bianca's word-of-the-week. She used her manicured hands with their yellow nail polish to demonstrate her argument. 'The money we gain from the Department of Education will go towards our Information and Community Centre, which will become part of another state government department, which is linked to the education department.'

The evening concluded with my brief explanation of the second part of the afternoon session – a workshop for teachers after the presentation. I read the last note on my list: 'After the workshops, teachers will attend the red-carpet do, barbecue and barn dance, but they will also have time for networking, to be held in Rosa's pub. Teachers will be given a free drink voucher.'

The meeting ended with cheers and clapping.

ONE WEEK

TO GO

Monday: Source pirate gear

Daphne had promised she would find me pirate gear to wear for the new students' session on Day One. Bright and early on Monday morning, she met me at her charity shop – rebranded Sea Haven Vintage – with a calming cup of chamomile tea. 'It's tricky, Gina. You're the festival director and you'll be doing official introductory stuff. We need to keep you looking cool, professional and connected with children and teachers – whom I presume will be dressed up as well?'

I nodded.

Daphne fished clothes from her immaculately ordered racks. 'This is a great skirt. Check the tattered hemline. Hang on – wait a minute.' She raced out to the back of her shop and returned with a black velvet buccaneer's jacket with gold buttons and cuffed sleeves. 'I found this when I was in the city last week. And this' – she produced a red satin corset – 'will look brilliant underneath the jacket. Wear the knee-high boots I got you last winter. And wait a minute . . .' Daphne raced out the back again and returned with a tricorn hat. She plonked it on top of my birds'-nest curls. 'And of course you'll need hoop earrings to finish the look.' Daphne grabbed a pair from her jewellery stand. 'Go and try your pirate gear on. Remember we're going for a *classy* piratical look.'

I did as I was bid. Daphne knows her stuff when it comes to styling.

I emerged to an intake of breath from Daphne.

'Brilliant!' We checked my image in the mirror. 'You can add a spotted bandana if you like, but don't do anything stupid like drawing a moustache on your face, Gina. You can change in the lunchbreak into your smoky plum suit for the afternoon.'

'The designer suit with a smidgen of sex in the cut?'

Daphne smiled. 'That's the one. Stick with your signature style for the rest of the festival: skinny jeans, classic linen shirts and loafers. If you feel natural and comfortable it'll help you last the distance. Oh, and I've sourced two blazers if the weather chills up. There you go.' She deposited them into my hands.

'Right.' I accepted the burnt-orange and ink-blue linen blazers and gave Daphne a hug. Not for the last time my cool, calm and fashionable friend had come to the rescue. 'Thank you so much.'

'One last thing! You can't go yet. You need a dress befitting a festival director to wear to Digby's red-carpet do.' I watched as Daphne pulled a breathtaking black lace sheath from a rack.

I slowly took the dress out of its protective covering and looked at the label. 'Wow! It's incredible!'

Daphne smiled. 'It's definitely a "wow!" dress. Try it on. But be careful. There's a nude full-length slip that goes with it.' She tossed me a pair of gloves. 'Wear these when you're putting it on. The lace is gossamer-thin.'

I headed back into one of Daphne's fitting rooms. With great care I passed the dress's flesh-coloured satin slip over my head. Then I manoeuvred myself into the black lace sheath, threading my arms into the long lacy sleeves that clung to cover half my hands. I checked the mirror and my eyes widened. This was a dress with amazing powers.

Once Daphne had admired the dress, I hugged her again, gingerly this time. 'I love it. How much do I owe you?'

'Forget it, Gina. It was a vintage bargain. I knew it would be perfect for you. You've done hours of work helping me prepare marine environmental grants.' We hugged each other again. Teared up a bit.

'Leave the clothes here,' Daphne continued. 'I'll bring them to your place on my way home.'

The Dog and I sped along the road from Sea Haven to Shelly Beach at Vespa top speed. I made conversation over my shoulder. 'Daphne says clothes should enrich who we are. I'll go with that. Don't you just love that black lace dress? I'm not sure about the pirate gear though. I'll need to dredge up buckets of courage to wear it. You don't think I'll look too OTT?' I didn't give the Dog time to reply. 'I don't give a damn. I'm wearing it.'

No reply from the Dog. He had trouble hearing. Wind in his ears.

From: Adrian <bookstreet@network.com.au>

To: Gina <glaurel@peninsula.com.au>

Subject: Can't wait

How are you progressing with the program schedule for the festival?

How did the committee go with the idea of a maths curriculum presentation?

I'll be back in Shelly Beach on Friday night. Can't wait until I'm with you. Got to go. My flight is being called.

xx Adrian

From: Gina <glaurel@peninsula.com.au>

To: Adrian <bookstreet@network.com.au>

Subject: If you're lucky

Committee fine with the maths curriculum – we want the big marquee. No progression on schedule – too busy sourcing pirate gear for Day One.

Gina

- **Sort out festival schedule**

The Dog and I had finished lunch and were standing on the balcony, staring across an endless blue sea to the horizon. 'We'll miss this view when we leave here.'

The Dog agreed.

'But I've always had my doubts about a house built on the side of a cliff. You can never be sure about the foundations. We could slide into the sea at any moment.'

No comment.

We moved inside and I poured myself another black coffee. Strong. I looked at the festival schedule with huge blank spaces to fill, thanks to our new marquee. I could barely bring myself to start. I wanted a free week or two ahead of my new job in the city . . . my last chance to relax before rejoining the rat race. My dot-point to-do list stared back at me accusingly. 'I *have* to sort out the weekend schedule. Gina, you have to get this festival on the road.'

The Dog hates it when I do the self-talk thing. It confuses him.

I sat down at the kitchen table. 'Right. I have to check whether our presenters will repeat their sessions. We're relying on their generosity of spirit, or their hardwired ambition to sell their books and make a fortune.'

The Dog thought ambition or generosity of spirit both ended

up in the same place – the bottom line: 'Where is your next bone coming from?'

'Okay.' I found the list of session presenters from the pile of papers Adrian had left me and opened my laptop. 'Serious organisation starting . . . *now*. Dimity and Sandy are fine to repeat their session. Anton Brandt? He's down for our keynote on Saturday and he's also taking a session called *Tips for Series Writing*. Violet says Anton Brandt's not fit to lift the skin off a rice pudding, but hopefully he can do a second take of his *Tips for Series Writing*.'

No comment.

I continued down my list. 'Bill Kruger, our short-listed local author, has said he's cool to repeat his session *A Writer's Journey*.' Tick. Bill had changed his presentation from *A Writer's Day*. He felt it was hypocritical to talk about his writing day when his day involves looking after a three-year old and not much else.

'Siobhan O'Reilly, Bill's editor, is doing a session called *Self-editing secrets*. I'm going to see her this afternoon so I'll check if she's okay with doing a second presentation. Did you know she just broke up with Piers, her boss, who's also taking part in the festival? I'm betting Siobhan's going to deliver a feisty presentation.'

No comment.

'Next is Violet.' I gave Violet's session a pre-emptive tick. Our resident writer of cosy murders will delight in repeating her presentation. 'Violet's been part of successful workshops all around the state. Digby attended one and said it was entertaining and informative. Not sure why Digby would have gone to one of Violet's workshops, though . . .' Could Digby be thinking of writing crime fiction now he's finished his memoir? Murder in a university's staffroom . . .'

I continued down my list. 'Dr Lionel James. Presentation: *The*

Hero's Quest.' Lionel James is a nice man. A writerly friend I met through Digby and Adrian. He lectures at the same university as Digby and is an expert on myths and legends. 'I'm not sure if his presentation will wow the audience, but beggars can't be choosers. He arrives Thursday – I'll catch up with him then.'

The Dog was feigning sleep.

'Last is April Somers, who writes romance novels. According to her bio she's had two books published by an online publisher and is writing another.'

I remembered a particularly robust festival meeting when a volatile Rosa arrived brimming with excitement and a sense of accomplishment. She tossed two paperbacks on the table. She'd found an author to take a session at our festival: April Somers, romance novelist.

The books were passed around the committee. Bianca read the blurb on the back of one and gave her summary. 'Girl meets boy, boy is haunted by a dark secret, boy can never love another, but girl heals his broken heart, girl gets boy. Cool!'

I could see by the look on Adrian's face that he was immensely relieved and didn't care who got who. We had found another local author. The committee breathed a reciprocal sigh of relief. Finding authors who were prepared to give their time to talk about their writing and carry their own costs had not been easy.

I'd spoken to Rosa earlier about April doing two sessions, and Rosa was confident it wouldn't be a problem. 'No worries, Gina. I talk to April when I get my teeth fixed on Tuesday. She'll love to do two sessions.'

I queried the connection between April Somers and Rosa's teeth. 'April's my dental hygienist. Lives in Sea Haven.' Of course.

I added a tick to our final sessional presenter, Dr Digby Prentice-Hill. His session is called *Writing the Truth.* 'Now that will be a fascinating presentation,' I muttered to the Dog. Digby has been heard to say that the truth is frequently underrated.

No comment.

My mobile rang. It was Pandora. 'Gina, help! I'm doing an extra shift at Piece of Cake, and Siobhan O'Reilly has arrived early to book in at my B&B. She's a total mess. Can you come down? Talk to her while I close up.'

'Do I need to bring anything?'

'Have you got one of your chocolate cakes on hand? Stocks are low here. Only a few muffins left.'

'Actually, you're in luck. I was making a double-chocolate one as a thank-you to Daphne.'

'Make another for Daphne. She'll understand. And you'd better make it a triple chocolate cake if you can. Add another layer of chocolate. Mousse? Fudge? Siobhan's very distressed. The bastard she just broke up with was trying to change their booking for him and the new light of his life. I sent him to Sea Haven and kept the room for Siobhan. Can you believe the man would do that?'

'I can.' I checked my festival schedule, my director persona taking over. 'Did Siobhan happen to say anything to you about her ex still being happy to take part in the discussion panel on Sunday?'

'Gina! You're hopeless. I hear where you're coming from, but the poor woman is an absolute mess. If Siobhan's ex is staying at Sea Haven Resort with the new light of his life I'd presume he's still going to appear on the panel. You can ask Siobhan . . . when you get here.'

'I'll see you in thirty mins.'

It was just what I needed – something to galvanise me into action. 'Okay, Dog. Let's go.' The Dog watched as I added a layer of chocolate fudge icing to Daphne's former cake. 'Voila. A super-comforting chocolate cake for a woman who's just split with her boyfriend. Now we're going to walk along the beach to Piece of Cake. Are you ready?'

The Dog wasn't happy.

'I promise I won't make you walk up or down McIntosh Hill.'

- **Salvage Siobhan's presentation**

Siobhan, Bill's editor, had become a familiar figure around Shelly Beach during the time I'd been living here. She'd decided that visiting Shelly Beach to work with Bill, our reclusive short-listed novelist, was the best way to work with him during the editing of his two books.

As such, Siobhan's been a regular guest at the Writers' Retreat, Pandora's B&B. Siobhan frequently used to extend her stay over the weekend so her partner, Piers, publisher at their publishing house, joined her.

Pandora and I had become friendly with Siobhan, and admitted to each other that it was partly for networking purposes. We have a nose for contacts who could be useful in the future, and Siobhan's an excellent editor. But we're not as calculating as Digby with his blatant networking. Pandora and I have treated our relationship with Siobhan with respect. Now I found myself thinking about how Siobhan's sad situation might work out well for us (and her). If she was looking for a new job, I might be able to employ Siobhan to extract my novel (and picture storybook) from me – guide me through the process of getting to the finishing line again . . .

I remembered our first meeting with Siobhan at Piece of Cake. Pandora and I were on barista duty. Siobhan came in, had a flat white and pronounced it 'excellent coffee'. Professional bonding took place quickly after that.

The policy at Piece of Cake is to use only premium-grade beans. We serve cappuccinos and lattes in glasses, and flat whites in ceramic cups. We avoid using shots of caramel or vanilla and we only recently sourced soy milk. The Jenkins family who run the general store (now Jenkins Produce, without an apostrophe) had trouble sourcing 'fancy schmancy' milk.

During that first meeting with Siobhan, over a second flat white the conversation came around to office romances. I was still full of angst then about my King Rat ex-husband getting off with his PA, and Pandora shared the tale of her office romance that turned sour. She'd explained to Siobhan that to avoid potential media fall-out she abandoned her career and fled to Shelly Beach.

Siobhan was starry-eyed at this time, madly in love with her boss Piers, and sharing a work-and-home-life in his 'gorgeous' apartment. Life was rosy. Back then.

As soon as the Dog and I arrived at Piece of Cake I could see it was time to banish our calculating – there, I've admitted it – relationship with Siobhan and offer her good down-to-earth comfort. She was in a bad way. Pandora shut Piece of Cake early and we walked Siobhan back to her B&B. 'If people want coffee they can go to Rosa's,' rationalised Pandora.

I agreed.

After a double serve of my triple chocolate cake Siobhan opened up. 'Piers and I have been together for two years. I thought we were in a good place – thinking the same way, feeling the same way . . . we were even finishing each other's sentences. Then I suggested we might consider having a child. I'm almost thirty.' More tears. 'That remark was the end of our two-year relationship. The next morning Piers basically asked me to leave. He didn't feel he was ready to commit. He felt our relationship had run its course. He's forty-something and he's not ready to commit! What's he waiting for?'

We offered our sympathy and more cake.

'This is *so* typical of me,' Siobhan continued, wiping away her tears. 'My relationships only seem to last two years. The magical two-year mark. I thought Piers and I would last forever.'

More sympathetic noises.

'And to add insult to injury' – here Siobhan paused with a hic-cupping sob – 'I found out he's been having it off with the trainee editor. She can't even tell the difference between "there", "they're" and "their"! I resigned from work the day after I knew. How could I work with Piers knowing all the time I'd been jilted for a trainee editor with big boobs, great legs and a hopeless understanding of semi-colons?'

Another flood of tears, and a huge amount of sympathy from us.

'I've moved my stuff into Mum's, and now I'm here. In your beautiful, healing Shelly Beach. If you don't mind having only one guest in your gorgeous five-star double room, Pandora.'

'Don't be silly.' Pandora was giving Siobhan a comforting back rub.

Siobhan smiled through her tears. She took a deep breath. 'I know I've masses of choices and opportunities to start a new life.'

We agreed.

'I thought it was best to leave the company before my work started to slip. People only tend to remember the tragic or brilliant stuff you do – not your consistent hard work. I'm thinking of set-ting up my own business as a freelance editor. Maybe I'll do some agenting for clients with novels I can believe in.'

Pandora found an interesting bottle of riesling in her cellar. We relaxed over the wine and affirmed Siobhan's career choices, mak-ing a list of office romance Don'ts. Don't do it, if you can help it. But if you can't . . . Don't forget you're at work. Don't flaunt it. And avoid PDAs (public displays of affection) at all times.

'And don't think colleagues don't know!' Of course Siobhan's colleagues knew she was with Piers, but her colleagues were also well aware her partner was having it off with the trainee editor.

Ouch.

'And don't take your eye off the ball at work if it gets ugly,' Pandora added.

I smiled sympathetically. 'And *do* remember it is possible to get your career back on track again.' I gave her shoulders a squeeze.

Siobhan gave us a watery smile. After all she was young and talented, with her whole life ahead of her. We sat in contemplative wine-filled silence for a few minutes, before Siobhan turned her attention to me. 'I'm looking forward to the festival, Gina. It's been getting great publicity.'

'The excellent PR is all due to Pandora.'

Pandora smiled her acknowledgement. Siobhan blew her nose and continued, 'And Adrian gave you the director's role too. Clearly he trusts you. He's a gorgeous man, your Adrian. You're *so* lucky. You two are *so* good together.'

Pandora gave me her raised-eyebrow look.

I gave her my embarrassed smile.

Then Siobhan segued back to her own dilemma. 'Why do older men have this thing for younger women?'

It was a question without an answer.

Later, when I was carrying the Dog down McIntosh Hill (and he couldn't feign deafness) I picked up my director's role niggles. 'Do you think Siobhan will handle her session okay? Should I have asked if she was willing to take two sessions?'

The Dog thought Siobhan would handle her session brilliantly. And as for my second question: no! It wasn't the right time to ask Siobhan to take two sessions.

• Check real-estate op

After the Dog woke from his late afternoon snooze I popped him into his basket on the back of the Vespa. Alf and Potholer had alerted me to a really good real-estate opportunity they'd found. A chance remark in Rosa's pub ('I'd like to own a little house') had resulted in them going on the lookout for a reasonable property with a nice price.

'Have a look at this place,' Alf had said. 'When you start your city job you could pay it off and you'd have a nice little investment to come back to in your retirement.'

True. Am I old enough to be thinking of retirement? Adrian and Digby tried it and have become un-retired. Perhaps I'll have to keep working until I'm ninety, considering my budget.

As an intelligent businesswoman I'm still finding it hard to come to terms with how I left all my personal finances to my King Rat ex-husband. In the aftermath of divorce and near-bankruptcy I am well aware this has cost me. I should have been more savvy, but instead I was too consumed by my own career and too tired to argue with King Rat. I may have made more money than Kenneth, but he channelled my salary and my father's inheritance success-fully into his disastrous business deals . . . and I allowed him to do it. Result: zero cash in my bank account and no home post-divorce.

The Dog reminded me to live in the moment and not look back. Your tail always gets in the way.

Alf and Potholer keep telling me to 'move on. Keep moving on, Gina.' And I am, and my bank account has grown since I've been in Shelly Beach.

The Dog and I followed Alf's map to the property. We regarded it in silence. It ticked quite a few boxes: a good-sized block of land; room to build one or two studio-type residences on it; water connected; stand-alone plumbed bathroom. (Although the stand-alone plumbed bathroom barely rated a tick. It was made from galvanised iron and was basic. *Basic*.) The 'house' was ready to go: a caravan. A place where you could cook, sleep and sit at a table with a laptop and write a novel. Or a picture storybook.

Talking to the Dog on the way home I summed up our mixed first impressions. It didn't have a view – but then again, the Dog and I are over houses built on the side of the cliff. The accommodation was really basic – but Alf and Potholer said they could build me a neat little studio at a very good price: polished wood floor, walls of windows and a wrap-around verandah. But they'd be building my studio in between other jobs and it could take forever. Then again, I wouldn't be saddled with an Everest-like mortgage. And there was no rush, anyway – I'd be working in the city until I was ninety.

The Dog thought there were a lot of pluses and minuses involved with my Shelly Beach real estate idea.

'I'm going to be paid a very respectable salary for my city job, but I'll have to budget carefully. I'll have a hefty rent, or if I decide to buy an apartment I'll be saddled with a mortgage. Just as well a car and a fuel allowance comes with the job. Cabs cost heaps. And I'll have to look good. Clothes, shoes and hair will probably cost a fortune. I'll ask Daphne to look out for respectable suits and shoes.

'And I'll have to consider the cost of doggy daycare for you. I don't want you to go all psycho locked up in an apartment all day – that is, if you decide to live with me. And I'm not getting you a doggy friend, sorry. But I think I'll buy or hire a treadmill machine, and you can walk beside me on a lead. I can work out and catch up with the news on the TV, or listen to the sound of waves on my iPod. I might even buy you a little pair of headphones so you can hear the sound of the waves.'

No comment.

'I'll have to watch I don't contact the too-tired-to-cook disease and buy takeaways. You'll be fine – you'll still have your packets of vitamin-enhanced pellets. But I don't think landlords approve of dogs having fun with bones in rented apartments. In fact I think we'll have an issue locating a pet-friendly rental. Maybe we could share a house with Julia and Barney? That would be fun. We'd look for a house with a garden. Barney could have a sandpit to play in and you could have your own little patch of garden where you could dig holes and bury bones.'

No comment.

'Did I tell you about the trendy design of the building I'll be working in in the city?'

I hadn't.

'It's all about open-plan collaborative zones to encourage ABW – activity-based work. Apparently this creates a non-territorial environment – i.e. no fixed desks – with lots of flexible space. You can't personalise it like a normal office, but you get your own laptop and a locker. And I can have family snaps of Barney and Julia and you as screensavers.

'There are one or two beautiful corner offices with great views and lots of windows, but I won't have one full-time for myself. I think Rod said the offices with windows were available for anyone who needed a quiet space to work. Then there are cafe-type spaces to meet for strategy team meetings. For everyday work, you can choose to work at a desk in a larger space. Or maybe from home?'

The Dog thought working at home sounded the best. The non-territorial environment sounded like the workspace I have as festival director at Shelly Beach. The Dog likes being territorial. He likes personalising his environment, marking his territory. It's a basic need. But he refuses to enter into the pluses or minuses of city living and new work environments. He just wants to know when it's all going to happen, and how.

• Put together goodie bags

The Dog and I went straight to Rosa's pub. Violet's poker club – minus Matt Galinksy – graciously forfeited their poker night to help assemble goodie bags for our attendees. Aphrodite, Potholer's wife, was our chief product controller. She pointed to the three stacks of products donated by God-knows-who to be distributed into the three types of goodie bags. 'We've got children's bags, official admin material for teachers and 300 bags of the feel-good stuff for our festival attendees.'

This was serious product control. I collected some products for myself and divided them into stacks for distribution. A mindless production-line process was set up with good humour and lots of goss. Not hot goss – just medium-level.

Violet and I decided we'd do the children's and teachers' bags. Dimity's publishers donated copies of her picture storybooks, and Alex Dessaix had conned his publisher into donating copies of his picture storybook too.

The rakish young man grinned. 'It was a win-win, Gina. Good publicity for my publisher and excellent promo for me.'

Violet was very amused with the title of my new job. 'Social media consultant?'

'What's so funny? I'll train teams to go into companies and advise them on managing their social media: Facebook, YouTube, Twitter, any blogs. Wrongly or inefficiently managed, a company's social media profile can cause immense harm.'

I received an I-don't-believe-it look from Violet.

'All you need is to tell clients, "Don't do, say, or post anything on the internet you wouldn't say to your mother – or want your mother to see you do!"'

I gave Violet my mean smile. She quickly segued and moved on to her new favourite topic – Stephanie Brandt.

'Ice in her veins, that woman. But she's warming up. My secret is lemons, spring posies and hanging her smalls on the line.'

I looked puzzled.

Violet elaborated. 'I've been bringing Stephanie lemons from my tree for her G & Ts, and posies from my garden to freshen the apartment. And I've been taking their smalls downstairs and hanging them in the courtyard of Piece of Cake. Nothing like a sea breeze to make your laundry smell fresh.'

'You're very kind, Violet.'

'I think Stephanie's very lonely. Must be tough looking after Anton all the time. Imagine waiting until three wives were knocked off their perches before you flew in to roost.'

'You'd need great perseverance.' Note to self: Do not become a fourth wife.'

'Can't help but feel sorry for the woman. We've been having cosy chats. She was a model, you know, before she was personal assistant to Anton. A bit worn around the edges now, of course. Planet Stephanie takes a good deal of maintenance. She couldn't last ten minutes without a hairdryer. I'd say she and Anton have logged up a power-plant-sized carbon footprint with their jetsetting lifestyle. Stephanie'll hate it if she ever has to give up her swanky hotels and globetrotting lifestyle. Since she's been married to Anton she'd have developed the instinctive habit of turning left when she boards a plane.'

Silence while I contemplated the never-to-be-enjoyed-again joys of travelling first class on a plane. We went back to filling the young writers' goodie bags.

'Stephanie's passionate about cats. Waxes lyrical about them. She has two Siamese at home. Misses them. I've lent her Marmalade until she and Anton leave. He's a smart cat. He sits on her lap at every opportunity.'

I counted the children's goodie bags I'd filled with educational tools, a jazzy pen, a notebook, and the picture storybooks of Dimity and Alex.

'Don't forget these.' Violet passed me several boxes of health bars to distribute. 'They're from Jenkins Produce.' She gave a slight harrumph. She still hasn't got over the lack of apostrophe.

'You had better check on the goodie bags for the attendees too, Gina. We've got a pen and a notebook to slip in their bags. I think Sea Haven newsagency donated them. Required a little twisting of arms, but they eventually coughed up. They even managed to get the festival name on the pens. The rest of the stuff to go into the bags is just brochures and advertising rubbish.' Violet gave her cynical laugh. 'Amazing how lucky people feel if they think they're getting something for nothing.'

I went to check our sorting and packing production line. Hours passed. The pub closed, and still the bags kept coming. Filling 300 took time, but my focused and hardworking team didn't let up until the last *Shelly Beach Writers' Festival* pen was placed into the last goodie bag.

Rosa yelled from behind the bar, 'I'm opening the bar. Don't tell a soul and try to have the correct money.'

Thank you, Rosa.

Tuesday: Organise raffle

From: Adrian <bookstreet@network.com.au>

To: Gina <glaurel@peninsula.com.au>

Subject: Festival schedule priority

How's that finalised schedule coming along?

Pity we didn't have it ready to put into attendees' goodie bags.

xx Adrian

From: Gina <glaurel@peninsula.com.au>
To: Adrian <bookstreet@network.com.au>
Subject: Nothing but work
If you had *any* idea how long those goodie bags took . . .
I'll get to the festival schedule soon. I've got a big-ticket issue to
tackle after I work a full day at the library.

From: Adrian <bookstreet@network.com.au>
To: Gina <glaurel@peninsula.com.au>
Subject: Work and play
I thought you only worked a half day at the library on Tuesdays.

From: Gina <glaurel@peninsula.com.au>
To: Adrian <bookstreet@network.com.au>
Subject: In sickness and in health
I do, but everyone's down with the flu. I'm filling in. Just like another
job I said yes to – or rather, had foisted upon me.

From: Adrian <bookstreet@network.com.au>
To: Gina <glaurel@peninsula.com.au>
Subject: Look after yourself
You don't need to do this, Gina. You have enough on your plate.

From: Gina <glaurel@peninsula.com.au>
To: Adrian <bookstreet@network.com.au>
Subject: Worked to the bone
And who put it all on my plate?!
I think I can hear you being called for your flight.

I would never call a raffle a 'big-ticket issue' anywhere else but
in Shelly Beach. You simply cannot run any event or function here

without a raffle ticket being given out at the door. It doesn't really matter what the prize is (it's never a sheep station) as long as a Shelly Beach inhabitant can yell, 'It's me! It's me!' Then everyone else checks their ticket number (and colour) to see if they've won the runner-up prize. The owner of the lucky ticket collects their prize to applause.

If it's the weekly lifesavers' club raffle at Rosa's, the prize is usually a fruit and vegie basket or a meat tray. We have the occasional chook raffle if a local has the heart to donate a beloved but past-its-laying-time chicken – preferably one that hasn't dropped off its perch.

Geraldine, seconded festival committee member, had offered to be in charge of the raffle for the writers' festival. Members were relieved to put the organisation into Geraldine's stylish and competent hands. As Bianca said, Geraldine's a woman who knows how to get things done – and in style. Arriving home from a full day at the library the worse for wear, the Dog and I decided to trek up the hill to Geraldine's B&B and collect the raffle prize. Rosa had said she had room to store it out the back of the pub. The committee planned to have the prize displayed on the meet and greet table in Rosa's foyer.

The Dog wasn't remotely interested in the raffle even though winning the occasional fruit and vegie basket or meat tray has helped our constricted budget at times. The Dog was in one of his grumpy moods. He was constantly disturbed from his naps today by classes of noisy schoolchildren invading the library. When they were sent to wash their hands in the bathroom they'd stick their heads in the office to see if he was asleep or just faking it.

The Dog is over being taken to work. He thinks Take Your Dog to Work day should be struck off the calendar. The Dog has never heard of a Take Your Cat to Work day. Cats are smart. They don't get caught up in the work life of their owners except to doze in a sunny shop window when it suits them.

I moved the conversation on. 'The Vespa is sounding a bit sick. I'll have to get it serviced after the festival – get it ready to sell. I can hardly see myself zooming around the city in a helmet, suit skirt stretched to the limit and heels barely resting onto the pedals.'

The Dog wasn't happy at the thought of riding in the basket on the back of the Vespa in peak-hour traffic. One dodgy move on my part, or a heel slipping off the pedal, and he'd land on his head in the middle of the road. Worse still, he could get bounced out of his basket if I stopped suddenly at a traffic light. Then some criminal type would dognap him. He'd heard there was big money in dognapping and reselling cute friendly dogs.

I ignored the Dog. 'We'll take the Vespa to Geraldine's, but if it doesn't make it to the top of the hill and I have to push, it'll be your fault.'

When we arrived on sunset, we found Matt Galinksy and Geraldine sitting in the secluded indigenous garden, drinking champagne with the awesome view of Shelly Beach bay. One empty bottle was on the ground, another bottle was open on the garden table. A brilliant platter of oysters and prawns occupied the remaining space on the table in the Sea Crest cliff-top garden, along with a finger bowl of water with slices of lemon floating in it. Geraldine was looking flushed and very pretty. Husband Claude, Dimity and Sandy were nowhere to be seen.

The Dog and I had broken up an intimate tête à tête.

'Do join us, Gina.' Geraldine smiled thinly.

This was not a genuine invitation; we were intruders. 'I can't stay, Geraldine. We've just come to collect the raffle prize so we can store it at Rosa's.'

Geraldine visibly relaxed. 'No problems. I'll just go and grab it for you.'

She raced off and Matt immediately switched on his charming professional side, discarding his seducer persona like a lizard discards its winter skin. 'The organisation for the festival seems to be going well, doesn't it? Dimity and Sandy are very happy here.'

'Good to hear.' I wondered how he felt about his hidden relationship with Dimity. 'Dimity doesn't mind the changes and extra sessions she's agreed to take?'

'Not at all.'

I accepted the juicy Shelly Beach oyster Matt offered me. I watched a flushed Geraldine return with an elaborately decorated hamper. Our raffle prize.

'It looks great. Thank you again, Geraldine. You've done an awesome job.' I peeked inside and saw a bottle of choc body sauce nestled amid other less controversial treats. Don't ask, Gina. I swallowed another oyster and rinsed my fingers quickly in the finger bowl. Then we realised the hamper wouldn't fit on the Vespa.

'Don't worry, I'll drop it into Rosa's tomorrow,' Matt said. I thanked the accommodating Matt Galinsky. The Dog and I tootled home on the Vespa.

'Did you get that hardly subtle vibe between Matt and Geraldine?' The Dog hadn't. 'Geraldine's clearly besotted with the man. Just as well he's only staying in Shelly Beach until the festival is over. Otherwise Geraldine could find herself in a nice little mess.' It didn't bear thinking about.

I was brushing my teeth, getting ready for bed, when Pandora rang. 'Gina, we need to finalise the festival schedule. I have to get it to the Sea Haven printers asap.'

'Okay.' I paused to rinse my mouth. 'Can you ask Siobhan if she'll do a repeat session on Day Three? I'm meeting April Somers,

our chick-lit author, at Rosa's tomorrow night to get official confirmation that she can present two sessions. I know Rosa said
April was willing to do as many sessions as we need but I don't
trust Rosa's negotiating tactics. She keeps threatening people with
death if they don't comply.'

Pandora laughed. 'Okay, but we're right down to the wire. This
is serious – I need to have the festival session ready to go by Thursday night.'

'I promise it'll be done.'

Wednesday: Confirm April Somers' sessions

'Why am I doing this, Dog? Am I procrastinating with the festival
schedule just to annoy Adrian?'

No comment from the Dog. He knew I was.

After another hectic day at the library the Dog and I were glad
to retreat to my puboffice, have a glass of wine and enjoy a meal
before meeting April Somers.

The young romance writer burst into Rosa's pub with a smile
on her face and a spring in her step, as you do when you're a young
romance novelist. She went straight to the bar to talk to Rosa.
They were laughing and talking – I assume about dental hygiene.
Then Rosa pointed to my table and yelled over the noise of the
dining crowd, 'April's here to see you, Gina. I'm sending her over
to your puboffice.'

Bloody hell! The Dog stirred at my feet. I lent down to pat him
and whispered, 'It's only Rosa doing her PA thing for me.' The Dog
went back to sleep.

April is a beautiful young lady with the dazzling dentist's
smile. She's actually written five (not two) romance novels for a
UK publisher who does print-on-demand publishing – e-books
and hard copies. (I tucked this comforting fact away for desperate

want-to-get-published-before-they-die Shelly Beach Writers' Group members contemplating self-publishing.)

I looked at the copies of April's books she'd so generously donated to our festival (maybe they'll tuck into the hamper?) and at our festival schedule with the blank spaces. I got straight to the nitty-gritty. 'Could you possibly take another session on the Sunday? We'd love to have you in the big marquee.'

A dazzling smile. 'Don't worry, Gina. I'm happy to do two. It will be great publicity for me. Can I do back-of-the-room sales after my presentations?'

'Of course you can!' I was eternally grateful to the lovely dental hygienist.

Bianca came over to interrupt my heartfelt thanks. 'Hello, April. I'm Bianca. It's so lovely to meet you. I just love your books!'

(Had Bianca read April's books?) Note to self: Remind members we promised faithfully to read at least one book by a contributing festival author. Bloody hell, Adrian! You should have kept pushing this all year. Second note to self: Remind Adrian he'd forgotten.

Bianca raced on about the thrill of doing the intro for April's sessions. The two romance writers were able to exchange a writerly chat about April's last book. Clearly Bianca *had* read it – thank heavens for that. 'It's an absolute page-turner, April. Couldn't put it down. I just loved the URST!'

Thank you, Bianca, for knowing romance acronyms like Unresolved Sexual Tension.

Finally April stood to leave, tossing her blonde locks behind her shoulder. 'I'm sorry. I must get home and write my thousand words for the day.' She flashed her caring dental-hygienist charm on me once again. 'Thank you *so* much for inviting me to the festival, Gina. I usually spend my weekends in my PJs working on my novels. Your festival is a wonderful opportunity to introduce my books to new readers. I'm so looking forward to it.'

'How long do you think it will take her to write a thousand words?' Bianca asked after April had left.

'Could take all night, but I hope not, considering she's working with dental patients tomorrow.'

'Isn't she gorgeous? You recognise her in a nanosecond from her photo on the back of her books.'

True. No need for this young author to use a salad-day photo. (Yet.) I wondered if April had been hired as a dental hygienist because of her dazzling smile, or was the dazzling smile one of the perks of her job? There'd be plenty of perks for a writer, too: collecting love-lorn tales from patients waiting in a dental chair until their mouths went numb, ready to mumble about anything to hide their fear.

Bianca idly picked up April's latest novel and read the blurb on the back. 'It's about a dental nurse having a will-it-won't-it-last affair with her boss. It sounds awesome. Can I take it home?'

'Of course you can.' I filled in April Somers' name and her presentation *Romance Your Reader* in a blank block on our festival grid. A quick check of my phone revealed a text message from Pandora. *Siobhan will do 2 sessions.*

I texted back, *So will April Somers. 2 down, 1 to go. Looking for Lionel James tomorrow.*

From: Gina <glaurel@peninsula.com.au>
To: Adrian <bookstreet@network.com.au>
Subject: Missing presenter
Everyone has said yes to two sessions except Lionel James. I can't get in contact with him.

From: Adrian <bookstreet@network.com.au>

To: Gina <glaurel@peninsula.com.au>

Subject: Re: Missing presenter

Sorry, Gina, should've told you. Lionel has been camping at my place.

xx Adrian

Thursday: Nail down Lionel James

It was another of those magical mornings in Shelly Beach: still sea air, a blue, flat-mirror bay. The Dog and I decided the best time to catch Lionel James was early in the morning. But what did Adrian mean when he wrote 'camping' at his place? You definitely didn't need camping equipment to stay at Sea View Cottage . . . any more.

When the Dog and I house-sat Sea View Cottage, Adrian's house barely rated as one-star accommodation. Now Sea View has been renovated to the enth degree. State-of-the-art everything. You'd never know it was the same cottage.

'What irritates me is that Adrian waited until we moved out to do all the renos. And his swanky bathroom has unlimited hot water now!'

No comment from the Dog. Wind in his ears.

As we drove to Sea View Cottage on the Vespa I thought about my new work space. This whole open-plan thing was worrying me. I had a vision of myself unable to work due to the noise and lack of privacy. And what if there were unisex toilets?

The Dog thought this could be true. He imagined that I'd have to work at a desk (if one was even vacant) in a huge, dark, stuffy room crowded with miserable colleagues slaving away at desks they'd had to fight for. The Dog was definitely not prepared to sit under or near a desk in a gloomy windowless office.

I ignored the Dog and carefully extracted him from his basket on the back of the Vespa. 'There you go. Safe and sound.'

Sea Spray Street is famous for its potholes. Travelling around Shelly Beach's unmade roads is hazardous – but locals never complain. As Beryl tells all and sundry, 'We love our dirt roads.' (And we are aware of potholes and know when to avoid them.) You can usually keep up with the development of the more dramatic potholes through goss at Rosa's. If the potholes get too bad Daphne or I take turns in ringing and emailing the council. Result: Hazardous potholes are sometimes filled in.

The Dog stood patiently beside me while I hammered on the door of Sea View Cottage. We walked around to the back garden while I yelled at the top of my voice, 'Lionel? Lionel?'

We peered into the windows of the three bungalows around the back. They used to be decrepit but thanks to Alf and Potholer, they were now ready to rent as holiday accommodation. The only trouble is that Shelly Beach is not your top-of-the-list tourist destination. Our dollar having parity with overseas currency had put the brakes on Adrian's plans to retire comfortably.

I checked my watch. 'It looks like the elusive Lionel James is not a resident of Sea View Cottage or the bungalows. We'll give one more hammer on the door and then we're leaving. I'll have to find another speculative fiction expert to fill in the blank spaces on the festival program.'

On my last knock, a very dishevelled Lionel appeared at the door clutching a blanket around him. 'Oh, it's you, Gina. Hello. I wasn't expecting visitors.'

'Oh my God, are you all right?'

'I'm fine. Fine. Come in and we'll have a cup of coffee. Maybe tea. Not sure I've got coffee.'

The Dog and I followed Lionel inside. I'd first met Lionel at a function Digby held at his castle last year. As fellow writers we instantly bonded. We agreed we were hardwired to write. We felt miserable if we didn't write. We felt miserable when we did write. (Will I ever have time to write again when I take up my new job? Move on, Gina . . .)

For a while Lionel and I kept in touch, emailing pieces of our writing to each other. We were a two-man online writers' group. But over the last few months our writerly communication had vanished into the ether. We'd both been too caught up with jobs, family responsibilities, love-lives, whatever, to find any time to write.

Now I watched Lionel, unshaven, bleary-eyed, clutching a blanket like a cape around his shoulders, shuffling around the kitchen to make us coffee. The Dog and I exchanged looks. Adrian's sleek kitchen had been turned into a nightmare. I estimated that there wasn't one clean cup to drink from, or one clean plate to eat off. The benches were piled high with washing up, covered with bits of food, and there was a powerful odour coming from the bin. Lionel continued his shuffle around the kitchen, collecting dirty mugs, and scraping uneaten food from the plates into the bin to clear space.

'Stop, Lionel. Stop! Go and have a shower. I'll make the tea. Have you had breakfast yet?'

A weary-looking Lionel checked the clock. 'No. No. I haven't. What day is it?

'It's Thursday.'

'Shit!'

I looked startled. I'd never heard my writerly friend swear before.

'I'm sorry, Gina.' He picked up his mobile from the bench and checked it. 'Shit. Sorry. Just as well you called in. The wife and the boys are arriving on Saturday. I would have kept self-editing.' He clutched the blanket around him.

'Has the heating broken, Lionel?'

'No. No. I forgot to turn it on.'

'Right. Have a shower and I'll sort out a cuppa. I'd shave as well, unless you're planning on growing a beard.'

'Right. Right. Don't. Touch. My. Laptop.'

'I promise. Go.'

The Dog and I started loading Adrian's state-of-the-art dishwasher. Then I tackled the benches and table, but I left Lionel's laptop exactly as it was. I took a brief glance at the screen. 'It's his novel. It looks like he's actually finished! Four years in the writing, if I remember correctly.'

The Dog was vacuuming the tiled floor.

'I wouldn't do that. You'll probably get food poisoning and we'll have to go to the vet.'

The Dog gave up and slipped under the table.

Thirty minutes later, the Lionel James I was familiar with emerged. He smelt of high-end cologne and was dressed in smart casual.

'What have you been up to, Lionel?' Silly question to ask since the answer was on the table.

'My wife told me to take two weeks off and finish my novel. She said she and the boys couldn't stand me complaining about not getting the time to write.'

'Your spec-fic novel?'

Lionel nodded. 'I'm owed heaps of leave, and it was a term break. Adrian offered me the rental of his cottage and I took him up on it.' Lionel looked at the date on his watch. 'It's been nearly two weeks, and the family's going to stay with me until the festival.'

'That sounds lovely. Have you been outside much in your two weeks?'

A victorious smile was spreading across Lionel's stubble-free shiny face. 'No. But I've finished my novel. Nailed the ending!'

'Congratulations!' I smiled as I poured the tea. 'Not much food left, otherwise I would have served biscuits too. You'll have to go shopping.'

'I know. The wife packed DIY catering to last the two weeks so I wouldn't have to interrupt my chain of thought for my novel.'

Clever wife. I smiled. 'You've done well, Lionel.'

'I'm a bit obsessive. It's over 600 pages.'

'I understand. It's a writerly thing.' Six hundred-plus pages! Bloody hell! I found my notebook in my bag. 'By the way, we've had to make changes to the festival. We now have two marquees to work our sessions across. Are you happy to repeat your session on the Sunday?'

My smiling, writerly friend, who has at last completed his novel, nodded.

'Excellent, thank you.' I finished my cup of tea. 'Well, the Dog and I have to be on our way.'

'Thanks for dropping by, Gina. It'll be a great little festival.'

The Dog and I left a beaming Lionel, about to enter the real world again, standing on Adrian's jazzed up verandah.

'Hang on!' I yelled to the Dog while I did a few zappy swerves to avoid the potholes. 'You know Lionel did his doctoral thesis on the archetypal structure of the hero's journey in classic literature?'

The Dog was familiar with this fact.

Lionel's sessions could be dry . . . then again, at least we have a full festival program.

- **Festival schedule online**

We headed straight to Pandora's B&B. She practically snatched my completed festival schedule out of my hand. 'Did you speak to Lionel James?'

I nodded smugly.

'Well done, Gina!'

'He's been hiding out at Adrian's cottage for the last two weeks. He's finished his novel. Six hundred-plus bloody pages!'

'You're kidding!'

Pandora and I contemplated this enormous achievement.

'And he's lecturing full-time, and he's got a wife and kids.'

'He's the guy I met at Digby's function last year? The one who'd actually *handwritten* one third of his spec-fic novel?'

I nodded.

'The guy who took his handwritten novel with him in his brief-case when the family went on holiday? The same guy who left his briefcase in the taxi when they were going to the airport?'

'That's the guy!'

'Thank God for honest taxi drivers!'

I nodded.

Pandora was checking the festival schedule. 'It's looking good. Spreading the sessions over two days across the two marquees gives attendees the chance to pick and choose what they want to do. And there will be time for umbrella events and networking. I'll post the schedule on our website now and deliver it to the printers tonight.'

Siobhan emerged from her five-star room and smiled at us. She was looking decidedly better.

'Good morning, Siobhan. It's so good of you to do a second session.'

'Not a problem, Gina. Does anyone else want a coffee? You

150

don't mind if I use your coffee machine, Pandora?'

'Feel free.' We watched as Siobhan went to the kitchen.

Pandora beckoned me on to her sea-view balcony. 'Her bastard of an ex has been on the phone complaining he can't get a booking at Sea Haven for himself and his trainee editor. I gave him the number for the Seagull's Rest.'

'The one that Scarlett runs?'

'That's it.'

'But it's only a two-star B&B and Scarlett never stops talking.'

'I know.'

We smiled.

'I've been talking to Alf and Potholer,' said Pandora. 'I'm thinking of making a brand change for my B&B – from a writers' retreat to a wellness retreat.'

I raised my eyebrows. 'Not one of those horrible boot camps where you eat nothing but clear broth and grainy rice?'

Pandora laughed. 'No. I'm thinking of building an extension with a treatment room, plunge pool, sauna and jacuzzi. Make my place a "destination" spa. I'd enrol in a few courses too – massage, macrobiotic cooking, stuff like that. Are you interested in joining me?'

I shook my head. 'I refuse to contemplate another thing that will complicate my life. Besides, I'll be in the city.'

'Pity. We could have fun. I was thinking of going to Thailand for my training.'

Siobhan returned with our coffee. The Dog and I stayed for a respectable amount of time and then we left, zooming down McIntosh Hill.

'Nothing wrong with this Vespa when it goes downhill.'

The Dog didn't look reassured.

From: Gina <glaurel@peninsula.com.au>
To: Adrian <bookstreet@network.com.au>
Subject: Completed program
Found Lionel. Festival schedule now locked in. Pandora's posting it
on our website and taking it to the printer's tonight.
Told you not to worry. Wherever you are, sleep well.

From: Adrian <bookstreet@network.com.au>
To: Gina <glaurel@peninsula.com.au>
Subject: Woman of my dreams
I'm in Perth. How can I sleep well if you're not next to me?
Can't wait until I'm with you on Saturday. Thank you, festival director.
xx Adrian

Back home, the Dog and I were taking deep breaths and doing
yoga stretches on the balcony. Our purposeful, reflective states of
mind were soon shattered by the doorbell.

'Oh my God!'

Atticus was standing on the doorstep. Toby with-the-fringe was
standing beside Atticus and stepped forward. 'I'm sorry if we gave
you a fright. I told Terri it was a bad idea.'

Atticus removed his head and Terri came into view. 'It's me,
Gina!'

'I can see that. You're lucky you haven't a fifty-something dead
female on your hands, pulling a stunt like that. What on earth are
you two doing off school?'

Terri walked into my kitchen, holding her tail with one paw and
keeping Atticus's head tucked under her other paw. 'It's a pupil-
free day. We're supposed to be doing community conservation
stuff. Can we have hot chocolate and something to eat? It's really,
really hard work wearing a mouse suit.'

'I can imagine. You'll have to make yourselves sandwiches. I haven't had time to bake lately.'

A rolled-eye look from Terri. She waved her paws at me and I could see her point. Mice can't make sandwiches. Toby took the initiative and went to my kitchen.

'There should be salad stuff in the fridge,' I called before turning back to Terri. 'How on earth did you get permission to wear the Atticus suit?'

'Dimity and Sandy have two suits. They didn't mind me wearing their second one. Having two mouse suits allows them to employ someone else so Atticus can do promotional stuff in two different locations. Did you know it's got a personal fan built into it? And before I put it on, Sandy sprayed me all over with hospital-grade disinfectant to stop bacteria hanging around and multiplying inside.'

I screwed up my nose. 'Moving on . . .'

Terri insisted on showing me the personal fan inside the suit to prevent the wearer dying of asphyxiation. I took the opportunity to ask her *sotto voce* about Toby. 'So you two seem to be getting along?'

A teenage shrug. 'It could be worse.'

Over hot chocolate and salad sandwiches Terri, Toby and I discussed the psychological implications of inhabiting a mouse suit.

'Sandy says that being inside a mouse suit is a lonely place to be. You see life from a different perspective. People don't know how to react to you.' Terri looked at me. 'Except some people, who scream as if they've come face-to-face with a serial murderer!'

I gave Terri my mean smile. Toby and I agreed that Terri would gain valuable life experience as a wearer of a mouse suit.

'Violet met us on the way to your place,' said Terri. 'She thought it was a cool idea for me to wear Atticus's suit. She said you never really understand a person until you're stepped inside their skin and walked around in it.'

'Violet got that quote from *To Kill a Mockingbird*,' said Toby (he's studying *To Kill a Mockingbird* – 'awesome book' – for English lit and he should know).

'I've got a note for you, Gina. It's here somewhere.' Terri was in bossy mode. Her two front paws unzipped the top half of her mouse suit and scrabbled around until they emerged with a scrunched-up note. She smoothed it out. 'Mum said to remind you that you're on seal-watch from 6 p.m. to 8 p.m. tonight —'

'Bloody hell!'

'— but Mum says she'll do it. The ranger thinks the seal is looking good and should return to the bay tonight.'

'Excellent. I accept your mother's generous offer. Please thank her for me.'

Terri hadn't finished reading her list. 'And you have to come with us to collect the pirate flags Mum's handicraft group made.' Terri lost her teenage disdain for a moment. 'You should see them – they're so cool!'

Toby nodded. 'Joan's craft group invented a clever way to stiffen the flags. They look like they're flying in a breeze.'

I noticed Toby was referring to his prospective stepmother as Joan. It's tightrope-walking for kids today entering blended families. I wonder if my beautiful grandson Barney will become a member of a blended family. It could happen – if Julia meets a new partner with a family. I stored this potential challenge in the too-far-down-the-track basket to worry about.

Terri still hadn't finished delivering her message. 'Gee-naah!'

'I'm all ears!'

'When you've collected the flags, take them back to Rosa's. She's agreed to store them because Mum told her we had to get them out of our house before Sam destroyed them.'

I understood. Terri's young brother Sam is renowned for his

alarming talent to accidentally wreck whatever he happens to be near. The Dog is constantly on the alert when young Sam enters the premises.

'Right! No rest for the wicked. Come on, Dog, we're off. If you're too tired, Toby can carry you to Terri's place, but you'll have to walk back to Rosa's.'

Walking to Sea Spray Road took twice as long as usual because Atticus's scamper had lost its zing. I suggested that Atticus could perhaps shed his skin.

'I can't take the suit off. I'm only wearing my undies.'

Point taken. Toby and I exchanged looks and continued on our painstaking journey. When we made it to Terri's place, Joan wasn't there but had left all the pirate stuff for me. The flags had white skulls and crossbones beautifully hand-stitched on to a black background. I noted how the flags were ingeniously stiffened.

'They look fantastic, Terri. Tell your mother to thank her craft group. They'll make great markers for our young writers' workshop stations on Day One.'

Terri and Toby left to return Atticus's suit as the Dog and I headed to Rosa's.

'Don't forget to take your clothes! You don't want to scare folks if you have to walk back from the Sea Crest B&B in your underwear.' My warning was met with a practised disdainful stare.

The Dog and I made it to Rosa's, flags and all. We carefully propped the pirate paraphernalia against the wall in her storeroom and decided to have coffee in my puboffice until we regained our strength to return home.

As the Dog and I sat and contemplated Shelly Beach bay, Violet, our cosy-crime writer, entered the bar and joined us with a G & T.

'Hello, Violet. How are our celeb guests?'

'Don't get me started. I'm managing to keep Stephanie and Anton happy finally. Stephanie's growing on me. Must be tough living with Anton. It's hard work keeping him happy for a few weeks.' Then came one of Violet's thunderbolt segues. 'Did you know Dimity and Sandy are an item?'

'Excuse me?'

'An item. The girls are gay. They've been together for two years now but they're keeping it quiet. They're planning to get hitched when they do their US tour. They would have got married here, but it's not legal.'

'Well, that's interesting to hear.' Why on earth would Dimity and Sandy confide in Violet? Stupid question, Gina. Violet's been looking after them, servicing their rooms, making their breakfasts, and fussing over them as only Violet can do. I wondered how Dimity and Sandy must feel with so many secrets in their lives. First Dimity's relationship with Matt, and then Dimity's relationship with Sandy.

A group of hunky Shelly Beach lifesavers entered the pub. Violet looked over at their rowdy table. 'Those boys have been wasting their time giving Dimity and Sandy free surfing lessons.' She finished her G & T. 'Don't mention a thing about Dimity or Sandy. They're planning on coming out when they get to the US. Matt's managing the publicity deals – they'll sell their story and photos to magazines.' And with that, Violet left to go home to her cats.

The Dog and I sat in silence, contemplating the stuff you hear and learn in Shelly Beach. Information you're bound *not* to repeat. You get told stuff in strictest confidence but eventually – somewhere down the track – you find out that everyone knows what you've been told in confidence. I wondered how much stuff Adrian knows that he's never told me.

The Dog was becoming tetchy. It's hard being a canine

therapist, always radiating warmth in an uncomplicated, direct, unconditional way to a stressed owner.

I checked my messages and saw there was one from my daughter Julia. *Do u mind if we come for the weekend? Arriving tomorrow afternoon? x*

I smiled and texted my reply. *U and Barney R very welcome to stay here. Can't wait to C U. x*

'We may be a bit crowded for sleeping space this weekend, Dog. Julia and Barney can have my bedroom. It's better for them to be near the bathroom.'

The Dog hates it when I give up my bedroom for Julia and Barney. He dislikes sleeping in the corner of the living room while I sleep on the day bed.

'And if Adrian's stay overlaps with Julia's and Barney's, Adrian and I will have to sleep on the day bed.'

The Dog knew that I knew that Adrian's sleepover *would* overlap with Julia and Barney's stay. I was delighting in making things difficult. Sleeping on the day bed is like sleeping on concrete. The Dog knows Adrian hates sleeping on the day bed. Adrian's feet hang over the end and there's no room to turn.

'Knowing Adrian, he won't even turn up. He could miss his plane. Get stuck at the airport. His flight could be cancelled due to a volcanic ash-cloud sweeping over Australia from some exotic part of the world.'

No comment.

Friday: Rosa's mice problem
The day was off to a good start until Rosa left a message on my mobile. 'Ish-oo, Gina! Big problem with mices and Lorenzo. Please call at pub as early as poss.'

I will be *so* relieved when this festival is over.

'Come on, Dog, finish your breakfast and we'll call on Rosa. Julia will be here about midday. God knows what time Adrian will turn up. Let's hope we can solve Rosa's ish-oo without too much effort.'

We'd had a minor mouse plague in Shelly Beach this year but not as drastic as the mouse plague in inland country areas. According to locals, we were very lucky. Long-time locals like Alf and Potholer tell gruesome tales of past mice plagues. 'Lines of mice would run up the legs of your bed, across you when you were trying to get to sleep and then go down the other side of your bed. They ate everything. Books, clothes, food. You name it – they ate it. Mice drove some people insane. We ran out of poison to kill the little buggers off.'

Newcomers shuddered and counted our blessings that our mouse plague was minute compared to the country areas. Rosa has long been a fan of total extermination: 'Squash! Spray! Poison! If one doesn't work, another will rid pub of horrible pests.'

Obviously her methods weren't working.

The Dog and I arrived before the pub was open for business. Rosa ushered us into her office, ashen-faced and trembling. 'It's Lorenzo. He's off his head. He sat on a stool all night and shot at mices.'

My jaw dropped. 'What! Why?'

'Lorenzo's very sad. And very angry. He's still in love with me and he hated me having ex here last week. He found big gun he brought from Sicily and he started popping off mices like crazy.' Rosa smiled at me nervously. 'Lorenzo likes you. You can do something about this, Gina. Next thing he'll be popping me off planet!'

Bloody hell! I could just see the headlines: *Multiple deaths at seaside writers' festival.* Not quite the PR we'd hoped for.

'Where's Lorenzo now, Rosa?'

'He's still in kitchen. He went crazy after shooting mices. He went to beach to shoot at stars. Then he came back to the kitchen, sitting on stool. He still has gun.'

'Right! Make me a mug of good strong coffee and start saying your prayers.'

Rosa revels in her long-time lovers' feud with Lorenzo, but Lorenzo with a gun was not good news.

I collected a mug of black coffee from Rosa and cautiously pushed the swing door into the kitchen. Lorenzo was sitting on a stool in the middle of the room. No gun in sight. I gave Lorenzo the coffee and we sat in silence for a few moments.

'Rosa's a difficult woman, but I'm sure you can talk things out with her.'

'Rosa breaks my heart, Gina. She tells me I'm the one for her but then she talks about ex all the time. I've just killed little mice. No harm done. I put my gun in the car boot.' And Lorenzo started to cry.

The kitchen floor was splattered with a few dead mice. I gave Lorenzo a hug and his big body heaved with sobs. We stood like that for a few moments. Then Lorenzo reached into his pocket and gave me his car keys. 'You keep my gun, Gina, until I get a licence.'

I left him drinking his coffee.

'Lorenzo's locked his gun in the boot of his car,' I said to Rosa. I'm going to take it back to White Sands. I'll return Lorenzo's keys to him. You're right – he was upset about your ex being here.' I gave her a pointed look. 'He loves you very much, Rosa.'

Rosa ignored the reference to her city ex-lover. 'I go and be nice to Lorenzo, Gina. Don't you worry. We'll clean up dead mices and I make him happy again. You're a fearless woman, Gina. You want coffee before you go home?'

'No, I'm fine, Rosa.'

'Lorenzo will need more coffee. Make him feel sparky again.'

Rosa poured two mugs of black coffee and the Dog and I watched her carrying them while she pushed the kitchen swing door open with one slim hip.

'Come on, Dog. We're collecting a gun from a car boot, and hiding it at White Sands before Julia and Barney arrive.'

~

The Dog and I had just finished changing the sheets on my bed and making up the portable cot for Barney when Julia drove into the driveway. Lots of hugs and kisses. I'm truly grateful that after years of gross neglect, my relationship with my daughter and gorgeous grandson is well and truly back on track. I have a family I cherish.

Adrian, with his precision timing, drove his car-that-goes-with-the-job into my driveway ten minutes later. He wasn't stuck in Perth airport after all. 'Didn't think you'd mind if I just turned up,' he said with a boyish grin.

Another hug – and a really good kiss. Adrian released me quickly as Julia entered the room came carrying Barney.

If I was really back together with Adrian, there would only be a few blended-family complications to negotiate. Adrian has known my daughter Julia since she was a child. Julia and his daughter have been best-friends-forever. In fact, it was when Adrian and his daughter were visiting Julia that I met Adrian for the first time. (Actually it was the first time I *remember* meeting Adrian. Julia insisted I'd met Adrian twice before – once with his first wife, who left him because he belonged to the too-boring school of husbands, and the second time at a school function, when Adrian and wife no. 2 executed a stunning tango. Sadly wife no. 2 died of cancer about seven or eight years ago.)

Adrian engulfed me in a firm, sexy hold. 'I've booked lunch for two at Waves restaurant.'

I raised my eyebrow as Adrian picked up Barney in his arms. Two know-it-all males exchanged conspiratorial smiles. 'But we can always cancel. Can't we, Barney?'

Bloody hell!

'We can have a picnic on the beach all together. That'll be fun.'

Tactful daughter Julia stepped in. 'Don't worry about us, Adrian. Barney and I are grabbing a meal at Piece of Cake. I want to go and visit Joan and ask her about setting up a one-woman accountancy business.'

I smiled gratefully. Julia and Barney would be fine – everyone knows them from their frequent visits.

'Well. If you're sure.' I checked the time. 'I'll have to change.' Adrian looked so good in his casual clothes. I would look chic too – thanks to Daphne.

'I'll make coffee while you get changed. The Dog is scratching again, Gina. You need to get him to the vet in Sea Haven.'

'I've made an appointment.' (Lie.) 'And in case you're interested, my rash is still causing me hell.'

The Dog padded after me. He always guards the bathroom door when I'm having a shower. I whispered to him, 'Do you think Adrian didn't hear me – or did he choose to ignore me?'

Saturday

Adrian at his charming best is hard to resist as a dining companion. And Waves is the latest hotspot on the peninsula, with good reason. After we'd ordered, Adrian focused his friendly blue eyes with the crinkles around them on me. He took off his watch and placed it on the table.

'Thirty minutes where I fill you in with the Day One afternoon session, and thirty minutes where you tell me where you're at with the rest.' He took my hands and held them tightly in his. 'Agreed?'

I nodded. And from oysters *au naturale* to our entrée, Adrian detailed the running order of the Schools Day afternoon. By the time we'd finished our main course, I'd brought him up to the moment with the details of the festival.

'It sounds fantastic – you've done a brilliant job. Now you can sit back and relax – coast through the next few days until the festival is over and you launch into your new career.'

I doubted Adrian's summary of the next few days, but didn't say anything. He reached to take my hand again but I rescued it when our dessert arrived – oozy chocolate pudding flavoured with cinnamon and orange.

'Have I told you how wonderful you look? Shelly Beach air gives you a glow.'

'Nice food, isn't it?'

Adrian smiled wryly. 'Excellent food. Waves deserves the reputation it's building. We should come here more often.'

Over coffee Adrian entertained me with his current work stories. It was impossible not to be caught in his whirlwind of energy and city-life adrenaline. And then he carried the same level of enthusiasm into a conversation about the Shelly Beach Information and Community Centre – still a dream. I had to admit his passion was infectious.

'Shelly Beach needs a focus or else we'll just become a small set of pop-in shops selling shelly souvenirs.'

'Maybe Shelly Beach locals are happy to be a bypass on the way to Sea Haven or Kingston.'

'I don't believe that, Gina. The older generation, maybe. But we need to build a vital Shelly Beach for the next generation. Kids like Terri, or your daughter and Barney.'

I watched Adrian. He lights up when he talks about his plans for Shelly Beach. I was going to offer my counter-argument, delivered in a strong calm tone, but decided to let it be. And Adrian was on the wrong track with Julia. With any luck, she would soon be looking for a place to live somewhere near me – or with me – in the city. A sub-urb within not-too-difficult commuting distance to my company.

After lunch we strolled through the grounds of the stunning resort with its spectacular landscaping. (Seascaping?) We kept stopping to soak in the breathtaking views. Relaxation 'stations' had been designed to make even the most stressed-out guest focus on the view – vast ocean on one side and the contained bay on the other.

'What do you think of an open-plan working environment?' I asked. This question had been keeping me awake at nights. In my getting-back-on-track career I'd envisaged myself sitting at a big, tidy desk in a corner office with a verdant view. I wasn't so sure my dream was going to materialise.

'Is this your new job?'

I nodded. 'I thought I'd have a corner office with a park view, but looks like I'll be grabbing any desk I can.'

'Your new company's using ABW?'

'You know the jargon too. Yes, it's an activity-based workplace. I've never worked in one before.'

'You'll cope brilliantly. Just think of how you work in Shelly Beach – constant interruptions. ABWs are just the latest trend. They'll work well in some companies. Not in others.' Adrian smiled at me and took my hand. 'You'll just have to ride it out.'

Note to self: Let go of the corner office. You'll be working wher-ever you can find a space.

'And what about the actual job? How are you feeling about moving to the city?' asked Adrian, gazing at the view.

'I know I'll love it. Once I get back into the pace. I'll miss the view, though.' And a few other things.

'I have my own office at the university. Travelling for the face-to-face meetings gets tedious. I'll reconsider my workload when my contract is finished. Spend more time with you. Maybe we could work on projects together?'

I took Adrian's comment on board, but no way was I changing my course now.

It was an early spring day, blue sky and the smell of sea in the air. 'Let's detour and walk on the back beach,' Adrian said. He needed an ocean wind to clear his head.

We spent the remainder of the afternoon carrying our shoes in our hands and sloshing through the ocean waves as they lapped over our feet. We exchanged a companionable mix of the profound and trivial that two people who know each other well can discuss: books, music, politics . . . but we didn't touch on the dodgy topics of love, the future and us.

Sunday: Entertainment for Plus Ones

A bleary-eyed Adrian left Shelly Beach after a quick breakfast. He gave me a last hug. On his face there was the disarming twist of his mouth that came with yet another apology for leaving the festival in my competent hands. 'Have to catch a flight to Sydney, Gina. You're cool with everything?'

'I am.' I smiled.

Adrian quickly checked his iPad. 'Only five days until it all kicks off. I'm flying back on Thursday afternoon. I should be here at about seven.'

'Well, I'll see you then.' I gave Adrian's back a comforting rub. I felt and looked a much chirpier human being than he did. The day bed is hugely uncomfortable for two people, and Barney was fretful, waking on and off the whole night. Note to self: Buy new comfy day bed for new house.

'Now the schedule is locked in I feel like a new woman. I can relax. Have fun.' (Lie!) I showed Adrian my new resolution in the notes section of my iPhone. *I will only do the things on my list that sound fun.* He was impressed.

'I'm going to have to start thinking about packing after the festival.'

Adrian turned to me. 'There are things I want to talk to you about, Gina. About us and Shelly Beach. Wouldn't you like somewhere we could call our own?'

I wasn't ready for this line of discussion. I accepted another really delicious kiss as Adrian prepared to slip into his zappy car, and cleverly avoided commenting.

Julia, Barney and I waved as Adrian drove off. Unfortunately last night didn't provide the greatest opportunity for a fun-filled night of sex. Tactful Julia gave us ample warning before she invaded our territory to either get stuff for Barney or make herself – and later us – cups of tea. 'Sorry, guys. Barney's either teething or he's coming down with a cold.'

We surrendered any dreams of a stormy sexual encounter on the dodgy day bed and joined Julia for midnight toasted sandwiches and tea in the kitchen.

Amazingly once Adrian had done his usual retreat – driving off into the distance – Barney's temperature came down and a pleasant day at the beach stretched in front of us.

Paddling and making sandcastles is not top of my list of fave activities but Barney loves both. Julia and I were just placing the last piece of seaweed on top of the castle in preparation for Barney to knock it down when Toby and Terri jogged in sight.

'We've been trying to find you everywhere, Gina!' Terri said, out of breath.

'Sorry.'

'You didn't bring your phone?'

'Not to the beach when I intended to build sandcastles and paddle in the water with a grandchild. I decided world-shattering messages could wait until we returned home.'

I received a disdainful stare from Terri. Toby was much more polite. He smiled before he burst into his rapid-fire request. 'We need you, Julia and Barney to be our audience. Rosa's employing us to entertain kids in her pub on Saturday and Sunday lunch breaks during the festival. Maybe during early dinnertime.'

Terri added, 'Rosa doesn't want kids racing around her dining room.'

'Right! Why do we need entertainment? I wouldn't think we'll get many children coming to the festival.'

'Rosa thinks they'll be in the Plus One category.'

I remembered Rosa discussing a unit called Plus Ones when she was taking her online hoteliers course. Plus Ones are usually the partners who accompany the conference attendee. Clearly Rosa had extended this definition to mean children too – Plus Two? Three?

I could remember being a Plus One at several conferences King Rat ex-husband and I attended when we were newly married. Then, as my career took off, I was quite content for Kenneth to go solo. Presumably he'd had a jolly good time. And if I remembered rightly, Kenneth accompanied me in a Plus One role too. He had 'fun' as well as making business contacts.

Amazingly, Kenneth and baby son Griffin would be Plus Ones (Twos?) at the Shelly Beach Writers' Festival while Angela was soaking up info on how to write a blockbuster children's storybook.

'Gee-naah!'

'Sorry, guys. I'm all ears.'

'Can we come to your place this afternoon about three?' asked Terri. 'We'll bring Sam to be part of our audience too. Rosa says you have to give our entertainment a thumbs-up or she'll hire her magician cousin to fill our slot.'

'We don't want that!'

I could see Toby was a little lost with the political machinations: how to grab a money-making job in Shelly Beach before it goes to one of Rosa's cousins. 'I'll make sure you have a captive audience.'

Barney and I watched Toby and Terri, deep in conversation, leave to walk along the beach. 'At least they're communicating, Barney. This could be a good or bad thing. You never know with teenagers.'

We went back to our sandcastle-stomping.

Later that afternoon, Julia, Barney, Terri's little brother Sam and I were seated at White Sands watching the show. Toby and Terri had perfected a neat little performance. They were dressed as clowns – not scary clowns, but child-friendly clowns wearing straw hats and wigs, big red noses and patchwork jackets. Their *pièce de résistance* was a stellar display of balloon animals, aided by a pump. The pump was a genius idea. No exhausting puffing or blowing was required to turn the balloons into animals, flowers and insects.

Our applause subsided. 'Excellent, guys! Tell Rosa I give my full approval. And you deserve top pay rates.'

Toby was sincere about needing feedback. 'Do you think we make enough different balloons to give to the children? We're a bit short of sea stuff. We can only make an octopus that sits on a kid's head.'

'I wouldn't worry. It'll work, and keep kids happy for their average ten-minute-max attention span.'

Toby and Terri didn't know about the ten-minute-max attention span. As a Mother Goose reader to young library guests, my expertise is known and valued.

'Do you think our act is funny enough?' Toby asked.

'It's superb.'

'We can move around to each table separately if there are lots of kids. I checked the meal breaks. We only have an hour at lunchtime, longer at dinner.' Terri looked anxious.

'I'm sure you'll be fine.'

Living in a single-parent family, Terri was concerned with the profit she and Toby would make. I overheard her saying to Toby as they left with Sam, 'We have to include the cost of the balloon giveaways.'

Smart girl.

~

Julia and I don't tear up when we say goodbye any more. We're more confident that our relationship as mother and daughter is on solid ground. Thank heavens! Barney cries when he leaves me, but then again, Barney's at that stage when he's quickly diverted. I produced a cute Atticus added-value soft toy that I'd purchased in grandmotherly anticipation of tears at leaving time. Barney was very happy chewing on Atticus's tail.

'Don't worry, Mum,' Julia said. 'I'll snaffle it off him when he goes to sleep.'

'Good.'

'And you're okay about us not being here for the festival?'

'Oh, yes! Not that it wouldn't be lovely to have you here, Julia . . . but I'd have so little time to spend with you.' I looked at my daughter. 'I'm not all that confident that everything is going to work to schedule.'

Julia laughed. 'If there's one thing I know about you, it's that you can be depended on to produce a brilliant event. An event that Shelly Beach locals will talk about for years to come.'

'That's a sweet thing to say, Julia.' More hugs and kisses. 'I'll see you soon anyway – not long until I start my new job.'

And Julia and Barney left.

'Let's go for a meal at Rosa's, Dog. It's a nice way to end a weekend. Stop scratching!'

The Dog's back leg was like a mini rotor machine. 'And this time you're taking every single antihistamine tablet. No pretending to take your tablets and then spitting them out and hiding them under the mat.'

The Dog ignored me.

Rosa was thrilled to see us. 'The kids have been to tell me you like my Plus Ones idea.' Rosa poured me a glass of wine and looked at the Dog over the top of her bar. 'Your dog's scratching again, Gina. Not a good look. People will think he's got fleas.'

'I know. We'll go to the vet's tomorrow.'

'Violet texted me to say that she's dropping by with her friend who has the parrots. Friend has good idea to take pictures of festival attendees with parrots on their head.'

I did a quick revue of Violet's friends in my head – the ones who had parrots. 'You mean Scarlett? She owns two sulphur-crested cockatoos. She takes photos of her birds sitting on people's heads?'

'Yes! Scarlett makes good money. She takes pictures quickly and returns with happy snaps of parrots on people's heads. People can take home photos to show to family.' Rosa adopted her diplomatic biz-woman persona. 'But I tell Violet and Scarlett even if I think it's a one hundred per cent brilliant idea, Gina has to give it go-ahead.'

'Thank you, Rosa. If committee members think we should do it then it's cool with me.' I had a sudden vision of festival attendees running screaming from Shelly Beach, sulphur-crested cockatoos attached to their hair.

As more and more people dropped by the pub, a small meeting of festival members took place. We quickly agreed to go ahead with the entertainment for Plus Ones and for Scarlett to take photos of attendees with her sulphur-crested cockatoos perched on their heads.

'Scarlett's birds are very tame. They haven't bitten anyone in years,' Alf said. This wasn't reassuring.

The meeting ended suddenly with Rosa's last call for meal orders. As the committee dispersed, Alf called, 'Don't forget my PowerPoint show on Tuesday night.' Alf is a renowned amateur marine biologist in Shelly Beach, and his PowerPoint shows on the local beach flora and fauna are always popular. 'It's a good chance to brush up on your local knowledge for the festival.'

'Are dogs welcome?' I asked.

'Of course. Especially ones that undertake marine exploration on Shelly Beach.'

Pandora, looking glam and sexy, left us to have drinks with Matt Galinsky. She winked at me. 'Talking shop, Gina.'

I hoped Pandora knew what she was doing. Last time I saw Matt he was charming the proverbials off Geraldine.

Violet watched Pandora leave. 'Matt's stretching his elastic charm again. One day it'll snap right back and get him.'

I gave Violet my mean smile.

'He's not a very sharp poker player, you know. When he's blinking too much you know he's bluffing, and when he starts tapping with his left middle finger you know he's got a good hand.' There was a good few minutes of silence while Violet considered Matt

Galinsky's poker tactics. 'He could be softening us up for the kill before he leaves.'

From: Gina <glaurel@peninsula.com.au>
To: Adrian <bookstreet@network.com.au>
Subject: Bird on the head
Committee have agreed for Scarlett to take photos of willing attendees with her cockatoos perched on their head. Forty per cent profit to festival, sixty per cent to Scarlett.

From: Adrian <bookstreet@network.com.au>
To: Gina <glaurel@peninsula.com.au>
Subject: Cock-a-hoop
I've met Scarlett and her cockatoos. They are magnificent. Have you seen Alfred Hitchcock's *The Birds*?
xx Adrian
P.S. How do you feel about me putting in a bid on White Sands? Alf and Potholer told me it's just been put on the market.

Monday: Solve scratching problem

Four days to go, and counting. Rising panic was not helped by thoughts of future city job minus corner office. Luckily I was distracted from my worries by the Dog's frantic scratching. A quick call to the vet and we had an appointment.

The Dog was given his usual diagnosis: seasonal dermatitis due to messing around in native grasses along the foreshore. Medication: antihistamine tablets.

'Did you hear what the vet said? You have to swallow your pills. If you spit them out you will *not* get better. And you need to exercise a little self-control – if you keep scratching you'll end up with lots of hairless, red-raw patches all over your body. You'll look a mess, and you'll have to wear a bucket collar again. And you know how you hate those.'

The Dog waited outside the Sea Haven pharmacy while I collected his anti-itch tablets. I was served by the cockatoo-owning Scarlett. She works part-time at the pharmacy, part-time at the post office, operates her two-star B&B and does the occasional bird photography gig. By my reckoning that makes about two-and-a-half full-time jobs.

'I'm looking forward to the festival, Gina. It should be great fun.'

'Hello, Scarlett. Are you enjoying having Piers stay with you?' I smiled to myself at the thought of Siobhan's sneaky ex and the new love of his life staying at Scarlett's seen-better-days B&B.

Scarlett rolled her eyes. 'Don't ask.' And then she proceeded to tell me. 'He decided to come early. Brought his assistant with him to help him get some work done in the P and Q. I wish they'd stayed back at the office. They want fresh towels every day, need the shower pressure fixed, and complain about my cockatoos squawking. His assistant can only eat gluten-free bread, and he wants undercover parking for his Mercedes . . .'

'How does he compare to Anton Brandt?'

Scarlett handed me my change. 'From what Violet says, it's Stephanie you've got to watch out for. But Violet's got her number.'

I collected the anti-itch tablets and smiled my confident and calm festival director's smile. 'See you soon, Scarlett. Good luck with Piers.'

'Remember not to drink grog when you're taking your tablets, dear. They can have a very nasty effect.'

I roused the Dog from his napping place outside the pharmacy and we walked back to the Vespa. I checked my to-do list. *1 p.m. Meet Shelly Beach food traders at Piece of Cake.*

'Pandora's working a shift today. We can get a good cup of coffee and a sandwich.'

I believe I'm the one and only Shelly Beach resident who actually appreciates the Shelly Beach seagulls. I love their pristine plumage in muted shades of grey and white. I love their orange-red beaks and legs, which add a touch of pizzazz. And thanks to Terri, I know that not all seagulls have orange-red beaks and legs. It depends on the age. The juveniles have grey beaks and legs.

The Dog and Barney love the chaseability of seagulls. The Dog finds it incredibly satisfying to do a bark-and-run attack on seagull squadrons stationed on the sand. You can see the joy on his hairy little face, his sharp teeth gleaming in the sunlight as the seagulls lift off their sandy runways and fly to another destination.

Grandson Barney loves feeding the seagulls with a trail of stale bread. Then he sets off on an eternal hero's quest to capture a seagull and bring it home, so I can bake a seagull pie.

Alf and his birdwatchers' club don't spare a thought for Shelly Beach seagulls, which, without any hiring fee, decorate Shelly Beach in their squadrons – on the sand or bouncing on the waves in the bay.

I remembered discussing my affection for seagulls with Terri. She'd responded with a face. 'You know seagulls are known as the rats of the ocean, Gina. They're ubiquitous scavengers. They hang around tips all over the world. They'll eat anything.'

I'd ignored Terri and her expanded vocabulary. 'I don't care. I still think seagulls are elegant and smart. They can smell a hot chip from miles away.'

This ability was the reason the Shelly Beach food traders had called a meeting to discuss the 'seagull ish-oo'. They were concerned that festival patrons enjoying al fresco dining would be terrorised by gangs of seagulls, whipped into a frenzy by their boxed lunches (or hot chips). Only a few weeks ago Rosa was threatening to shoot any seagull that put one leg on her new verandah with the expensive concertina glass doors, but since Lorenzo's episode with the mice I'd noticed Rosa hadn't mentioned shooting a seagull again.

Shelly Beach's food traders were already seated in Piece of Cake when the Dog and I arrived: Rosa, Harold and Gary from Beach Eatery du Jour and Jody from Jenkins Produce. Pandora, as the representative of Piece of Cake, was hovering, ready to take orders if required.

Coffee was served and Rosa spoke first. 'I know it's illegal to shoot or poison seagulls.' (I breathed a sigh of relief.) 'However, everyone knows I invest in hugely expensive renos to my pub – especially the beaut-i-ful bulletproof glass concertino doors to keep the inside in, and the outside out.'

Traders nodded. (We were already aware of the bulletproof nature of Rosa's glass doors. Alf and Potholer had wondered about Rosa's underworld connections . . . but we let that thought go.)

'If customers sit outside, it's their responsibility to shoo the seagulls away. And if evil seagulls steal customers' food, I want a policy of "no refund" to customers. If seagulls take food, customers can pay again for a new food order.'

Bloody hell!

Thankfully the less militant Shelly Beach food traders had a slightly different take. Gary assured Rosa that a great seagull heist during the festival was highly unlikely, and Harold gallantly offered to create *Do Not Feed Seagulls* signs in appropriate duck-egg blue lettering on white backgrounds for traders to post around their shops.

Satisfied with this outcome, Rosa left to return to duties at her pub. 'Your coffee is not as good as ours, Pandora! Tell Gail I give you the name of organic coffee bean supplier in the city.'

Remaining food traders relaxed as we watched Rosa exit Piece of Cake. Pandora took coffee and toasted sandwich orders and we all settled in to enjoy our lunch.

• Battle plan finalised

That evening the Dog and I were back at Rosa's for a final committee meeting to run through our schedule in detail. The idea was to nut any last-minute faults, but I was sceptical it would. The Dog disagreed with his owner-of-little-faith. He was just pleased because he knew he'd get the chance for an off-the-lead mad run round Shelly Beach foreshore and environs.

Bianca, hubby Josh and fellow lifesavers reported they'd already marked out the boundaries of the blue marquee in Rosa's beer garden, and those of our promised state-of-the-art yellow marquee with flags and ropes on the foreshore. Beryl and friends were well versed in their various tea and coffee stations. Pandora and I were seated at the meet and greet table, already set up in Rosa's foyer. The Dog was under the table, ready to go on his mad off-the-lead run as soon as Terri turned up to supervise him.

As each committee member arrived, Pandora and I presented them with our newly printed, colour-coded festival programs as if they were going on a scavenger hunt. Charming Matt Galinsky with the rugged jaw made an unexpected appearance with Dimity and Sandy (both wearing Atticus body suits). (Well, perhaps not so unexpected – for Pandora.) Dimity and Sandy had just finished a promotional gig at a bookstore at the Kingston shopping centre. I noticed the not-so-subtle wink Pandora received from Matt, and the equally not-so-subtle one she returned.

'You're absolutely incorrigible, Pandora!'

No comment.

When the meeting was over and there was the usual run on the bar, I sat with my head in my hands and closed my eyes for at least five minutes. My fun mood had blown out to sea.

'Pandora, do you think everyone realises how much money people have paid to attend our festival? It will not be funny if we have stuff-ups.'

'Relax, Gina. Everything's going to be fine.'

I groaned.

'I'm sorry I've got to leave. I'm going home to freshen up – Matt Galinsky's taking me to dinner tonight. Purely a business meeting. We're discussing when you need to create a small target strategy.'

'It sounds fascinating.'

Pandora smiled and gave me a hug before racing off. Potholer joined me, beer in hand, notebook in the other, to run over a few points from the meeting. It took my mind off my friend who enjoys living dangerously with charming men.

After Potholer had ticked off the items on his list, he closed the notebook with a flourish. 'Not one problem, Gina.'

'You think so?'

'You've done well, girl. You should do this sort of thing more often. You're a great little leader. Just what this town needed.'

I bathed in Potholer's genuine compliments. I could even live with the 'girl' and 'great little leader' tags.

'I hope so. It's difficult taking responsibility for another person's dreams and goals.'

'Adrian knew what he was doing when he handed the festival over to you. We all knew you were the person to do it. Never thought about achieving goals myself, so I've never had to think about a strategy to achieve them. Things haven't worked out too badly.'

I agreed. Potholer's no-goal strategy for life has worked extremely well. He has a loving wife and six sons, a successful building business, a boat he's nearly completed building in his front living room, and a nifty late-model Porsche, currently leased.

Potholer checked his watch. 'Got to leave you, I'm afraid. Aphrodite likes us all to eat at six thirty. Things are a bit touchy lately, what with me buying the Porsche and her being all caught up with her poetry.' Potholer finally found his keys down the bottom of his jacket pocket. 'Still . . .' He gave me a wink. 'Adds a spark or two to life.' And Potholer roared off in his utility, hopefully on time for dinner, and hopefully to find a spark or two after dinner.

From: Adrian <bookstreet@network.com.au>
To: Gina <glaurel@peninsula.com.au>
Subject: Real estate
Forgive me – I'd completely forgotten that Alf and Potholer had found a promising real estate deal in Shelly Beach for you. Forget about White Sands.
xx Adrian

From: Gina <glaurel@peninsula.com.au>
To: Adrian <bookstreet@network.com.au>
Subject: A home on the range
You're forgiven. I've put in an offer for a piece of Shelly Beach land with a stand-alone bathroom and a comfortable caravan. Great for overnight and weekend stays when I'm working in the city. It might fit two.

From: Adrian <bookstreet@network.com.au>
To: Gina <glaurel@peninsula.com.au>
Subject: Creature comforts
I'll start putting my small change aside for a good mattress and a jumbo-sized gas bottle to ensure hot showers.
xx Adrian

Tuesday: Start packing

The Dog and I were on the balcony in the morning sunshine, staring into the never-ending bay. I was feeling euphoric; my offer on the Shelly Beach block of land had been accepted. I was soon to be the owner of an excellent block of land (plus stand-alone bathroom and a liveable smallish caravan) within walking distance of Shelly Beach bay. It was the first major financial commitment I'd been able to make since I landed in Shelly Beach last year, flat broke and dumped from a disastrous marriage I should have ended myself. Moving on . . .

I'd only taken one sip of my coffee when Terri yahooed at my door. 'Gina? Are you there?'

'Why aren't you at school?'

'I told Mum I was coming down with flu. She let me stay at home. She's checking on me every hour.'

'Are you going to tell her you're visiting me?'

I was treated to one of Terri's cold stares. 'No. I'll just tell her I'm feeling better and will be able to go to school tomorrow.'

'You realise you've made me an accomplice in the criminal act of deceiving your mother.'

I was given another glare. 'Can I have a cup of coffee? Puh-lease?'

'Help yourself. You know coffee stunts the growth of teenagers?'

'Gee-nahh . . .'

'You're welcome to make yourself an omelette now that you find you're on the mend. How lucky you are to have escaped a severe attack of the flu.'

I watched Terri, my favourite teen spirit and competent cook, make a cheese omelette and pour herself a cup of coffee. The Dog and I joined her at the kitchen table. 'I'm glad you're here,' I said. 'You can give the Dog his tablet. He's being difficult.'

Terri groaned. 'It's easy, Gina. You're too soft. Just get it over with quickly. It's for the Dog's own good.'

'I know. I can do it – but as you've turned up you might as well do it.'

Terri sighed exasperatedly and checked the papers on my

kitchen table. 'You've bought the land! Excellent! You're staying. Good. I'll move in with you.'

'Yes, I will soon own a block of land complete with a stand-alone bathroom and a caravan. Well, own complete with an affordable mortgage I can manage to meet in the future.'

Terri fastened her eyes on me. 'And . . . ?

'I'm not staying in Shelly Beach. I'm due to sign the contract for my new job on Sunday. I'm starting to pack today.'

Terri was pensive. 'Okay. I won't be able to move in with you here. However . . .' Her needle-sharp brain was churning. 'I'll go ahead and sort stuff to action a move to a city school when you're settled in your job. I can sleep in your living room on a day bed. Go to school, of course, but also be a kind of au pair for you and the Dog. And you know I don't hog the bathroom.'

I knew this important piece of personal information would probably change as Terri advanced in teen years. But regardless of whether she hogged the bathroom or not, I had to remind her of the realities of life.

'Terri . . . How would your mum feel if you moved in with me?'

I could see Terri's calculating young mind working at a teen-age pace. 'I'll apply to sit for a scholarship to Trinity College.' She stopped to take a mouthful of omelette. 'Do you think you might house-share with Julia and Barney? And could I still live with you?'

I gave Terri a wide-eyed look.

'Julia told Mum she's thinking of buying a new house. She's got enough put aside for a deposit from her divorce settlement. She's just waiting until you make up your mind.'

That was news to me. How did Terri know this? No need to ask. My daughter clearly had no qualms talking about her plans with Joan while discussing her accountancy business.

'I'm not sure if I'm going to house-share with Julia and Barney. But —'

Terri was on a roll. 'If Julia buys a big enough house – say four bedrooms – I could board with you and babysit Barney. Take the pressure off. You'll be under the pump, Gina. It's going to kill you doing a high-flying job again.'

'Excuse me?'

'Or maybe you'll be sharing Adrian's apartment. He said he's renting a totally awesome apartment with a fantastic view over the river. That would be cool. I could be a weekly boarder at Trinity College and visit you and Adrian on weekends.'

Terri's mobile rang. I grabbed it first. 'Hi Joan, it's Gina. Terri's with me. No, she's fine. Feeling better now.' I gave Terri a meaningful look. 'She's just had an omelette and is on her way home to do her homework after she helps me give the Dog his tablet.'

I passed Terri's mobile to her.

'Is it okay if I help Gina with her packing? She's got heaps of stuff to sort out.' Clever girl. Silence while Terri listened. 'I promise I'll do my homework tonight. And go to school tomorrow.' Terri hung up. 'You're so *mean*, Gina.'

I grinned. 'I'm nothing of the sort. I refuse to be part of your devious machinations, that's all. Come on, lighten up. Help me start my packing.'

We started with my books: a collection that began at zero and has multiplied by tens, transforming me from a borrower of books to once more being an owner of a library of treasured books.

'So things with Toby are still bad?' I asked my now-silent teenage friend.

Terri sighed. 'No. They're not. He's fine. That's not the problem.'

'Well, what's the problem, then?' I asked, pulling books from the shelf.

'Everything's going to be different if Toby lives with us. I'll have to get used to living with other people.'

The perils of the blended family. 'They're not other people, they're just Toby and Paul.'

Another sigh.

My favourite teen spirit has been through a lot of upheaval for someone so young. 'Believe me, Terri, everything will work out. Just give it time. Don't expect it to be perfect in a week. Or a month.'

Terri was writing labels for the boxes: novels, reference, cooking. 'Are you going to marry Adrian, Gina?'

'Excuse me . . .'

'You and Adrian make a cool couple. After you've both finished with your careers you can grow old together.'

'And you could move in to our home to look after us in our old age?'

Terri pulled a face. 'Not going that far! I'll probably be living in Rome or London, doing my doctorate at university when you and Adrian need home help.'

'Right!'

I watched Terri writing the last label for my boxes of books. 'Let's start packing my clothes.'

'You're doing your stick-your-head-in-the-sand thing, Gina.'

'I'm not. I just want to be absolutely sure I'm making the right choice when I decide if I want to commit to somebody again.'

We were staring at my wardrobe, which was looking good thanks to Daphne. Daphne has an artist's eye, and a bowerbird instinct to spot new trends. And she's a good listener.

'Not bad,' I said, fingering the black lace sheath dress for Digby's red-carpet do. 'Daphne's helped me find my fashion edge.'

Terri also appreciated Daphne's flair in sourcing clothes for a difficult-to-please teenager. 'She's awesome. She always finds good stuff for me. Being tall and skinny is a help. It must have been easy to find clothes for you after you got skinny.'

When I first arrived in Shelly Beach I was a little larger. A writerly year in the attic subsisting on peanut-butter sandwiches had taken its toll.

'Actually, I've changed my mind. I don't think I'll pack my clothes until after the festival. What do you think of the suits Daphne's found for me?'

Terri was checking the high-end labels in my wardrobe, hung according to function.

'That first suit, the plum-coloured one, is the suit I'm planning to wear for official stuff at the festival. Otherwise I'm going to stick to my usual stylish casual gear for the rest of the festival – jeans and shirts. And flat shoes.'

Terri counted my new biz suits, freshly sourced from Daphne. 'Five.' She grinned. 'I'm guessing you asked Daphne to find you five suits to wear for your new job? You're going to wear the same suit on the same day each week. All your co-workers will know it's Monday because you'll be wearing your Monday suit.'

I acknowledged that I may have followed this schedule regarding my choice of clothes in a former control-freak life when my career was all-consuming. 'It won't be like that. I'll change the suits around. Mix and match shirts, shoes and scarves.'

In my former high-flying life I always decided what I'd wear the night before . . . and I admit I'm still doing this. 'Working out what you're going to wear the night before, checking your clothes are clean and ready to wear is an excellent way to save time. When you get older and wiser you'll realise that saving time is crucial in order to do the things you want to do.'

I glanced at Terri's blank face and waited for the

familiar 'Whatever'. I refused to give up delivering my useful life-management info. 'It's a good habit to get into. You can immediately focus on what you're going to do for the day – not waste time deciding what you're going to wear and then miss your bus.'

I received a rolled-eyed look from Terri.

'In my new position I'll be working off-site with management and teams from other companies. *They* won't know I'm wearing my Monday suit!'

Terri came across my pirate gear and took the hanger off the rack to check my outfit more closely. 'It's good, but it's too glam, Gina.'

'Excuse me? This is what I'm wearing for the young writers' sessions.'

Terri inspected my sexy red satin corset. '*This?* But the jacket's cool. I love the buttons and the sleeves. You'll have to keep it buttoned up.'

'The corset came with the outfit – and don't worry, I intend to wear the jacket buttoned up.'

Terri had found a notebook and pen and was intent on making a moving itinerary for me. 'I'll write down the heavy stuff you'll have to either take with you or store. Half the furniture was already here, wasn't it?'

'Yes. I'll only be taking my antique hat-stand, fridge and washing machine.' I looked at my sheer white curtains blowing in the sea breeze. 'And the curtains. They took days to make. I'm not sure about the Vespa. A car is included in my salary package.'

'I'll buy your Vespa!'

'I'm not sure that's a good idea . . . but I'll let you know if I put it up for sale.'

Terri was staring out into the wind-blown cliff-top garden. 'Are you going to take your dovecote?'

We looked at my blue and white three-storey dovecote with its sloping roof topped with a finial. It was a present from Alf's and Potholer's families when another of my fifty-something birthdays rolled around this year. My dovecote was standing firm against the elements but minus spotted turtledoves. No matter how much seed I put out I had not yet persuaded one single dove to move in.

'It didn't work, did it?'

I ignored Terri's reference to my attempt to inveigle Adrian's doves from Sea View Cottage. 'I've one seagull who likes being king of the castle. He flies in each day to balance on the very top of the finial. He likes having a seagull's-eye view of the cliff-top garden.'

'I doubt it's the same seagull.' Terri quickly gathered up the Dog. 'Let's give the Dog his tablet and get it over with.'

I passed Terri the packet and watched as she placed the tablet on the Dog's tongue, holding his jaws shut until he swallowed. She checked the packet. 'Only four left.'

'The vet gave me a short, strong course given the Dog's such a difficult patient.'

Terri put the Dog down and he ran off to sulk under the bed. I called after him, 'Don't think it will work if you make yourself sick and vomit the tablet up. Terri will just make you swallow it again.'

Terri's face was suddenly scrunched up. 'Soon I might not be able to help with the Dog. You'll be in the city, Gina. You've got a heap of choices to make.' She looked down and said in a wobbly voice, 'I better go home and start on my homework.'

'Can I help?' I looked at my much-loved teenage friend. 'Come here.'

Terri and I held each other in a gigantic bear hug. I heard her sniffle. 'I know life's tough at the moment. I promise I'll get permission for you to come and stay with me for as many holidays as you wish.'

Terri gave me a watery smile. 'Good.' She wiped her eyes and straightened her shoulders. 'Your lecture on clothes was very sensible. I'll probably follow your advice when I'm older.'

'Glad to hear it,' I said.

'And if I were you,' Terri continued, 'I wouldn't do the princess-and-the-pea thing much longer.'

'Excuse me?'

'Keep Adrian waiting for you. Violet says there are plenty of fish in the ocean.'

'I think you've got your fairytales mixed up. The princess-and-the-pea story was about a test to find a real princess.'

'But it was also about a grumpy princess who was never satisfied.'

'Thank you for your advice, Terri.' I gave my young friend another gigantic hug. 'I'll get started on making choices – quickly. And you'll be the first to know what I decide. I promise.'

The Dog returned when I called him to say goodbye to Terri. We received a wave, and watched Terri walking and waving backwards. She did her fancy twirl at the gate and then continued to walk home facing the right direction.

'I've never seen her fall over once when she does that.'

The Dog agreed.

From: Adrian <bookstreet@network.com.au>
To: Gina <glaurel@peninsula.com.au>
Subject: Welcome baskets
Hate to add to your to-do list, but do you mind checking if
Geraldine has delivered welcome baskets to the writers staying in
my bungalows?
Raining in Sydney.
Love you.
xx Adrian

Not long after Terri left, the Dog came to alert me that we had a visitor at the front door. It was Scarlett, cockatoo owner.

'Sorry to bother you, Gina. Violet asked me to pick up Stephanie and Anton's laundry from Sea Haven.' Scarlett handed me a parcel of laundry. 'Shirts! I'm short on time, so I wondered whether you could drop it in to the Brandts?'

I nodded and took the laundry package. Scarlett jumped into her car and was off. I'd guess she was running late for one of the multitude of jobs in her portfolio. The Dog, using his innate canine powers of deduction, guessed that Scarlett was running late for her work in the post office. She was wearing a postal uniform.

'We need a walk anyway. Come on, Dog, get your lead.'

The Dog obliged.

- **Laundry and welcome-basket mission**

I was standing tall, looking cool, confident and in control (as a boutique writers' festival director should) even though I was carrying celeb crime-writer Anton Brandt's freshly laundered shirts. The Dog and I knocked on the door of the Crows' Nest Flat.

Stephanie answered. She was doing her Grace Kelly impression. Immaculately dressed in designer jeans and a pastel to-die-for patterned shirt, she looked beautiful and serene. Her jeans alone would have cost many weeks of my three-pronged salary. The Dog and I actually received a cool smile, and an invitation to come inside.

'Would you care for coffee, Gina? I've just made a fresh brew. Or would you care for a drink?' Stephanie checked the watch on her slim, tanned wrist. 'It's just about time for cocktails.'

I went with the cup of coffee and the Dog was given a bowl of water.

'Darling little dog,' said Stephanie with a smile. 'Although I'm not really a dog person. I love cats. I'm *so* missing my cats.'

I concentrated on drinking my coffee and didn't look at the Dog.

'Thank you for delivering our laundry. The laundry in Sea Haven is doing a brilliant job with Anton's shirts. Anton's *so* particular about his shirts.'

I noticed the famous crime fiction author was nowhere in sight. Probably tapping out another bestselling novel on his laptop in the bedroom.

'And Violet's been looking after you?' I asked, not sure how to cope with friendly Stephanie.

'She's been a gem. She's an unbelievably helpful and kind woman.' An orange cat jumped onto Stephanie's lap. It started purring as soon as Stephanie began stroking its fur. 'Violet's lent me her Marmalade while we're staying here.'

An excellent move on Violet's part. I short-reined the Dog and brought him close to my leg, out of temptation. He has this perpetual love–hate thing with cats that can erupt at any moment.

'Anton's looking forward to the festival. We know everything will go like *clockwork*. Thank you for your daily email updates. The festival schedule looks brilliant – an *excellent* balance of presenters.'

I smiled and sipped my coffee. Note to self: Thank Violet for lending cat to Stephanie and send Pandora a bottle of champagne for sending festival updates to Stephanie and Anton.

'And I just adore young Dimity, and her charming friend Sandy. What wonderful choices for your festival. A fun contrast to Anton.'

I nodded. 'And once the festival's over, where will you be off to next?'

For a brief few seconds Stephanie lost her Grace Kelly serenity and looked tired and worn. 'We're off on another tour – author visits and festival events organised by Anton's Australian publishers. Huge festivals in capital cities.'

It's tough to be an author these days. It's not enough to just write – you've got to self-promote, tour, shake hands with fans and sign books until you're ready to sink under the table. I smiled and thanked Stephanie for the coffee. It was time to leave. It's difficult to know when the Dog will have one of his sudden I-hate-cats moments and enter in a mad chase. They usually result in a nasty fight that sees him coming off second best.

'I was very proud of you for ignoring Marmalade,' I said as we hurried down the stairs of Crow's Nest. 'I know he can be incredibly annoying.'

No comment.

'It's very hard to win in a fight with a cat. Especially one of Violet's cats. Sometimes a quick retreat is the best way to go.' When we were safely out of harm's way I put the Dog down. 'Now let's see if Adrian's writers have received their welcome baskets.'

With the arrival of Lionel's wife and boys, Sea View Cottage had lost its shambolic residence-for-obsessed-writer feel. When we arrived Lionel, wife and boys were halfway out the door.

'You've caught us just in time, Gina,' called Lionel. 'We're taking the boys for a surfing lesson.' I was introduced to Lionel's wife, who looked hugely relieved her husband had finally lost the albatross of a too-long-unfinished novel.

They had received Geraldine's welcome basket. 'It was delightful. Full of good things to eat. My mother is coming to pick up the boys this afternoon. We're so looking forward to the festival.'

I gave Geraldine a mental pat on the back for the choice of products for Lionel's basket. Did it contain choc body sauce? Maybe Lionel and his wife have put it aside for later use.

Lionel handed me the keys for Adrian's three bungalows. 'Adrian asked me to pass these on to you. Alice has arrived. She's in the first bungalow.'

'Alice who lost her novel when her computer was stolen? Who's made a fortune writing bestselling textbooks?'

'That's the one. Alice's hit the jackpot. Right textbook at the right time for the right students. She said she's thinking of joining our online writers' group. I told her I was having a break before I begin another novel. And I wasn't sure where you were at with your novel.'

'Giving it a break. Into kids' storybooks.'

'Dad!'

Lionel was needed. 'Have to go. Thanks for everything! See you at the festival.'

The Dog and I walked round the back of Sea View Cottage on our way to the bungalows. 'Lionel's a different man since he's finished his novel.'

The Dog agreed.

The first two bungalows were still occupant-free, so I opened up the windows and let a salty Shelly Beach breeze blow through them. We noted that Geraldine had left her Shelly Beach welcome baskets for Adrian's paying guests.

We then knocked on the door of bungalow three and Alice appeared, writer of bestselling textbooks. She pronounced herself delighted with her welcome basket. We didn't ask if it included choc body sauce.

'I'm doing the panel for the teachers' session in the afternoon and then I'm going to enjoy every minute of your festival,' she said with a smile. 'Indulge myself in the company of readers and writers. I'd love to join your writers' group, but I'll have to get back to you after the festival. Depends if I can find time to pick up my novel again.'

We smiled and farewelled Alice. I whispered, 'What do you think, Dog? Odds on Alice won't have time to get back to her novel.'

The Dog ignored me. He's not a betting dog, although if he was a greyhound he probably would be.

~

The Dog and I arrived back home a little worse for the wear. We'd detoured along Shelly Beach. I'd had a light-hearted paddle, the Dog a frantic dig, and he'd discovered a magnificent rotted pelican carcass. We both needed baths to freshen up.

From: Adrian <bookstreet@network.com.au>
To: Gina <glaurel@peninsula.com.au>
Subject: Truly, madly, deeply
This is a non-wedding marriage proposal.
Just you and me, in a registry office ceremony – no special clothes, no flowers, no cake, no rings, no friends or family. Just two people committing to be there for each other for the rest of their lives.
We'll have a crazy ride for the rest of this year – and beyond – while we pursue our respective careers, but we'll find time to be together. I can't contemplate a life without you.
xx Adrian

I stared at my computer, stunned.

I didn't know what to write back. My first reaction was to respond with a no. Who proposes via email, anyway?

But then I thought about how I feel when I'm with Adrian. How I feel when I think about him. How I feel when he looks at me with his blue eyes. How he gives me the space I need – for my career, for my sanity. How I trust him completely – well, in all matters not relating to holiday bookings. How he drives me crazy . . . in the best possible way.

From: Gina <glaurel@peninsula.com.au>
To: Adrian <bookstreet@network.com.au>
Subject: Time needed
Your proposal interests me. Can I ask you to wait until after the festival for an answer?
x Gina

It seems I've given myself another after-the-festival decision to make.

The Dog was amazed by Adrian's proposal. I did tell him that the only wedding I'd ever consider again was a no-fuss minimalist wedding – but I'm rethinking the no-ring part.

'I can't make a decision now.'

The Dog refused to comment. He'd find it very hard to devote himself to a cat lover.

'You understand, Dog, that this is strictly confidential. Adrian, you and I are the only ones who have access to the information about this possible non-wedding-to-be.'

We had quite a lengthy discussion about dog owners who talked to their dogs, and dog owners who didn't talk to their dogs. The Dog was pleased to inform me that many dogs were quite happy to live with an owner minus the in-depth, personal conversations. Saves pet burnout. Bluey, for example, didn't chat to Daphne. He was happy with a strictly professional relationship between himself and his owner. No intimate conversations to stress over. And he was cool to hang out with other working dogs and swap tales of herding a chicken into a tin can. No sleeping in an owner's bedroom for him. He preferred sleeping near the campfire.

A ping sounded from my computer. My heart rate quickened and then fell as I checked my inbox. It wasn't from Adrian.

From: Rosa <rosaspub@peninsula.com.au>
To: Gina <glaurel@peninsula.com.au>
Subject: Road blocks
Meet Alf, Potholer and me in thirty mins to check out new signs in Beach Road.
They're looking very cute.
Rosa

It wasn't difficult to locate Potholer, Alf or Rosa. They were standing at the corner of Sea View Street and Beach Road; the only humans in sight for miles.

'What do you think of our signs, Gina?' asked Alf. 'One here, one at the start of the lane.' Alf and Potholer were looking pleased with themselves. They were standing near a newly erected classy sign on the corner of Beach Road. The *Shortcut to Rosa's Pub* sign pointed up Sea Spray Street, with another sign reading *Shortcut Lane* a few metres further up the street, pointing to the lane that ran behind the Shelly Beach shops to Rosa's beer garden.

'Attendees will be able to take a shortcut from the yellow marquee to the blue marquee in my beer garden,' said Rosa proudly. Daphne had been behind the revamp of Shortcut Lane, a small addition to Shelly Beach's infrastructure. Locals came on board, giving weeks of willing labour. They shovelled out layers of sandy Shelly Beach soil to reveal old brick paving. In early settlement days the lane would have allowed horses and carts to make the necessary sanitary collections. Later when motor vehicles hit Shelly Beach, vans used the lane for pick-ups and deliveries.

Rosa was positively glowing with success. Not only did she have a new back lane, but now she had her personal sign for the festival.

I swivelled around and noticed the barriers placed across the start and end of Shelly Beach's small but essential shopping strip on Beach Road; detour signs directed traffic to the back streets around Beach Road to get to Sea Haven or to Kingston.

No wonder there wasn't a human or car in sight. 'How long have you had Beach Road blocked, Alf?'

'An hour or two. We're giving the roadblock a test run for the festival. It's working a treat. Closing Beach Road will keep visitors nice and safe, give a friendly feel to the town. Festival-goers will be able to stroll around and not worry about traffic.'

I nodded agreement and took a deep, deep breath. 'Can we legally block Beach Road, Alf? It *is* a main thoroughfare.'

'Not a problem. We've submitted an application to the council to close off Beach Road for the two days of the festival. Our application will get council approval – no worries. It just takes time for the wheels to turn.' Alf continued. 'By the time our application goes through the Finance and Administration Committee, the Infrastructure Services Committee, the Planning and Environment Committee, and the Peninsula Entertainment Precinct Committee —'

Potholer interrupted, 'You've forgotten the Sports, Art and Culture Committee, Alf, and the Water and Waste Committee.'

Alf said, 'You can see it's not worth worrying about.'

'Right! I'm still a little worried.'

'It's all good, Gina. The council actually gave us a loan of all the official road signs. If that isn't tacit approval I don't know what is. We'll get the signs back to the council on Monday morning and everything will be fine. If anyone starts to kick up a fuss, there'll be nothing to kick up a fuss about. The festival will be over and Beach Road will be open.'

'When you put it like that . . .'

'We closed Beach Road two years ago for the lifesaving carnival. And that was over two weekends.'

'You blocked off the main street for two weeks?'

'Two weekends. No one complained.'

'Well . . . if we have signs from the council . . . And you're confident there won't be any complaints . . .' I was the Shelly Beach Writers' Festival director and I was agreeing to my committee breaking the law.

'Got to get back to the pub, Gina,' said Rosa. 'See you soon for the PowerPoint display!' And Rosa raced off down the newly signed and named lane to her pub.

Potholer and Alf started to collect the road signs and unblock Beach Road – until the weekend. 'We'll shout you a coffee if you've time, Gina,' called Alf. 'Meet you in Piece of Cake? Can you ask Gail to pull two lattes and whatever you'd like to drink? You're not one of those skinny, fancy-milk coffee drinkers, are you?'

I assured the boys I was a strong-black type. As soon as we entered Piece of Cake the Dog escaped to the yard for a quick sniff of his territory while I refilled his water bowl. I gave the coffee orders to Gail and had a comforting chat with her before sitting down at my usual bay-view table.

When Potholer and Alf joined me I experienced a sudden urge to tell them about Adrian's proposal. My heart was racing. I realised I was going to have to live with a mix of stress and adrenaline buzzing around my body as the festival draws closer and closer – and until it's over.

Alf and Potholer were telling maddeningly worrying tales of the lifesaving carnival and everything that went wrong when a very flustered Violet burst into Piece of Cake. 'Thank heavens I found you, Gina. Stephanie and I are having a few problems over one of Anton's shirts.'

'What sort of problems?'

'Anton's lost the plot. Listen – he's still shouting at Stephanie.'

We stopped talking. It was true – you could hear Anton's angry voice spilling out of Crow's Nest Flat and down the stairs to Piece of Cake.

'Anton's been raving like this for more than half an hour!' Violet looked stressed.

'Over a shirt?'

'It's his white linen bespoke shirt. The one he planned to wear for his keynote speech. It's gone missing. Stephanie slipped him a sedative in his brandy to try and calm him down. She's worried about his blood pressure.'

As you would be.

'I've been on to Scarlett,' Violet continued. 'Stephanie and I think Anton's shirt was mixed up with the dirty bed linen and has been sent to the Sea Haven laundry.'

'I thought you were doing the Brandts laundry.'

'No!' Violet said, exasperated. 'Just their smalls.'

'Well, I'm sure it'll turn up. But I'm a bit concerned about Anton.'

Violet cocked her head. 'Wait. Listen.'

We listened. The yelling coming from upstairs had stopped.

'Stephanie says Anton's always like this before he does any public speaking. He gets very stressed. He says he feels like running away right up until he goes on stage. Of course he's fine once he gets up there.'

'Weird blokes, big-time authors.' I agreed with Alf and sipped my coffee in silence. I kept thinking about our star speaker wanting to escape until just before he goes on stage. With this sober thought tucked into my mind, I slipped into the cafe kitchen and made Violet a good strong cup of Earl Grey.

'Thank you, Gina. I need to soothe my nerves.'

'Absolutely. It's not your fault the shirt went missing. I'm sure it'll turn up.'

I made myself another strong black. I looked at Violet, Alf and Potholer. I knew I could do this. I could get this festival up and running, with the help of my team.

Alf finished his latte. 'You've got to hand it to Anton Brandt – he writes bloody good thrillers.'

True. I promised Violet I'd try to find Anton's shirt as soon as possible. Violet looked relieved. 'Thanks, Gina. I have to get home to my cats and make the supper for our poker school.'

The Dog and I were due back at Rosa's in an hour or so for Alf's PowerPoint show, but there was just enough time for a quick stroll along the beach in the sunset. 'Keep your paws crossed, Dog, that our keynote speaker can deliver a reasonable keynote speech and doesn't do a runner three minutes before his presentation. We need Anton Brandt to stay focused and in control until the festival is over.'

~

Daphne and Bluey were playing on the beach, where Bluey was doing his rounding-up-the-gulls act. After a good play, the four of us headed back to Rosa's via Shelly Beach's new infrastructure, Shortcut Lane. The dogs gave it five-star approval. Plenty of interesting smells to classify and analyse.

'I can't believe how fantastic it looks! It'll easily gain a heritage must-see-destination dot-point on the Shelly Beach brochure,' said Daphne, satisfied.

'And have you seen the new signs?'

'Perfect, aren't they? The festival gave me the perfect levering tool to get the lane fixed up.' Daphne smiled as we passed the tarted-up back entrances to Piece of Cake, Pages Gallery, Scissors Salon, Beach Eatery du Jour and Jenkins Produce, all with their stylish signage in duck-egg blue lettering on white backgrounds.

We stopped for a few minutes to admire the classy marquee that was already installed in Pages' backyard.

'I remember Digby telling me he'd purchased the marquee with the idea that it would become a semi-permanent structure.' I gave Daphne a wink. 'So he can avoid local council building restrictions.'

Daphne snorted. 'Digby never misses a trick.'

It was generally acknowledged in Shelly Beach that Digby and Daphne were formidable 'frenemies'. In my short time as a Shelly Beach resident I'd noticed that Digby always made a quick but smooth retreat when it looked like he could be going into battle with Daphne.

'Love the street art! It's all about Shelly Beach.' The once boring brick wall of the lane was covered with a creative tangle of seahorses, crabs, sea stars, seaweed and shells.

'Josh's done an excellent job with his students.'

We paused while the dogs sniffed Shelly Beach's vibrant street art. 'We didn't know what to do with this wall,' said Daphne. 'The owner won't sell his old factory, but he eventually gave permission for us to use the wall for artwork.' We waited at the back entrance of Rosa's pub until the dogs caught up with us.

'Hi, girls,' Rosa called when she saw us. 'I've reserved a table for you for dinner. Pandora's coming too. Lots of people are fronting up for Alf's Power Plug show on sea animals.'

I whispered to Rosa, 'PowerPoint.'

She whispered back, 'Exactly.'

'Where will the show be?'

'I've set up the billiard room.' Rosa served me a glass of wine. 'Chamomile tea for you coming up, Daphne! There's water for doggies in the foyer.'

I remembered a girls-only conversation I'd had with Bianca a while ago. We were watching Bianca's Josh and 'my' Adrian chatting to the female members of the Shelly Beach Surf Lifesaving Club.

'You know, Gina, your Adrian and my Josh have unaccountable appeal to women,' explained Bianca. 'They can't help but attract them. Loaded with sexy pheromones – but they don't act on the opportunities this presents. They're rare males. Actually Adrian and Josh have natural rapport with males *and* females. Don't you think?'

My bubbly young friend Bianca was equally blessed with the talent to get along with both men and women. Did she have this talent before she became a hairdresser and beautician, or has she polished her communication skills while pursuing her career?

Pandora with her signature red lips and winged eyeliner entered the pub. On cue every male in the bar fastened their eyes on her as she chatted to Rosa. The two of them came over to where Daphne and I were sitting.

'I've been telling Pandora not to get caught up with Matt Galinsky. He's a slippery ladies' man,' said Rosa. 'You're not going out with Matt tonight?'

'No.' Pandora smiled. 'He's playing poker in Violet's school. But he'll be here in time for Alf's show.' There was a flicker of anticipation in her eyes.

'You watch out! Matt is charming but you can't trust him.' Rosa put her hand on my arm. 'Not like your lovely Adrian.'

Pandora gave Rosa a kiss on the cheek. 'I promise I'll take care.'

I hoped Pandora could look after herself.

Rosa took our orders to the kitchen and it wasn't long before Lorenzo arrived with three steamy plates of Shelly Beach seafood pasta. Rosa sat down with us for a moment.

'How is the pasta? Lorenzo never tell me what he puts in.'

'Delicious!' Daphne said, biting into a scallop.

'Lorenzo has refreshed menu for the festival. He's finding new local ingredients – no roadkill or pet rabbits.'

Daphne almost choked on her scallop and Pandora gave her a pat on the back.

'What kind of publicity have you been talking about with slippery Matt, Pandora?' I asked.

'Well, he's just completed a huge TV deal for the girls. The deal's practically set in concrete, so I'm sure he wouldn't mind if I talked about it. He's pulled off the sale of their soon-to-be animated series for international audiences.'

'A TV program for kids about Atticus?'

'That's the one. I think the working title is *Atticus and Friends*. Dimity and Sandy have written the scripts, and Dimity has final say over the animation.'

'That's amazing! Matt's an excellent manager. The girls are lucky to have him working hard for them,' Daphne said.

'I don't need a man to manage me. I've done well by myself, thank you very much!' said Rosa.

Pandora, Daphne and I smiled. Rosa was one woman in Shelly Beach you didn't want to disagree with when she was on fire.

Rosa laughed. 'I bang on tough glass ceiling – make it crack. I don't need to go on golf networking days with the Sea Haven big guys. I can do my own Attila networking, just like my online business course say. Network like Digby and Adrian.'

I didn't have time to offer my affirmation to Rosa before she turned her attention to me. 'You're lucky, Gina, that Alf's putting on his show tonight. I think committee members and locals are getting fed up. Burnt out. Too much festival stuff to worry about and do.'

I looked at Rosa with alarm. She patted my arm again. 'Don't you worry. When yellow marquee and blue marquee go up on Thursday, people will feel happy. Just like when the circus comes to town.'

That was hardly the metaphor I was hoping for.

'Don't you worry!' Rosa said. 'The festival will go clockwise.'

Thankfully my two good friends turned the conversation to lighter matters. Pandora invited Rosa to talk about her old lovers.

'I tell you juicy, fun things,' Rosa whispered, looking around. 'But you girls have to signal' – Rosa put her finger to her mouth – 'like this if you see Lorenzo leave the kitchen.'

We promised.

• Alf's marine PowerPoint show

As Rosa had predicted, Alf had a full house for his PowerPoint show. Alf had a renowned reputation as a self-taught marine biologist and naturalist, knowledge he'd gained over many years.

I could see Terri and her family sitting in the front row. I sent her our secret signal, indicating that I needed to talk to her urgently. I was just starting to think that secret signals were not the communication platform to use with teenagers when Terri appeared at my side.

'You took long enough!'

'You look *so* weird doing that secret signal stuff. Why didn't you text me?'

'Well, since we're apparently done with childish things, I will in the future. Where's Toby?'

'It's his week-on with his mum.'

'How's he going?'

'He's devvo.'

'Excuse me?'

Terri translated. 'Toby's devastated about having to choose which parent he's going to live with full-time. But his mum is letting him stay with us for the festival weekend.'

'Right. I'm going to ask your mother if you can come home with me tonight. I'll make sure you catch the school bus tomorrow morning. I've got something really important I want to talk to you about. Besides, you can give the Dog his tablet before you go to school in the morning.'

I received a cross-eyed look.

'I'm taking it you agree to my proposal? I can see you're not past the childish delivery of cross-eyed looks. You know if you keep doing this there's a good chance you might stay cross-eyed forever.'

No comment.

Joan was extremely happy to be free of a recalcitrant teenage daughter, if only for a short while, to assist me with my recalcitrant non-pill-swallowing Dog. 'Gina, that sounds lovely. We'll go home after the show and pick up Terri's gear, then I'll drop Terri at White Sands.'

I thanked Joan and gave a satisfied smile of accomplishment to Terri. Terri replied with a teenage shrug.

The Dog and I returned to the back of the billiard room. We'd decided that positioning ourselves at the back of the room was a smart tactic in case we needed to make a quick exit. You never know when Violet might turn up with one of her basketed cats.

Amazingly, Bluey and the Dog enjoyed Alf's presentation as much as Shelly Beach locals. Each PowerPoint slide covered a different example of the common marine life found in our small slice of oceanic paradise. Pelicans are the top bird on the Dog's list.

Bluey prefers seagulls because of their ease of herding. The dogs took note to avoid Pacific gulls with their hooked beaks and large wingspan.

Alf's audience left the billiard room with the common names for the shells, seaweed, sea stars and fish of Shelly Beach set in our brains. Alf preaches, 'Once a person puts a name to a plant, bird or sea creature, they gain a new respect for their environment.'

Everyone retired to the front bar for a drink. Matt (post-poker school) and Dimity and Sandy (minus mouse bodysuit) were making a strong pitch to Alf. Matt grinned charmingly. 'How about coming in as advisor on an animated film featuring Atticus in deep water?'

Alf gave his usual agreeable smile. Alf would only take on projects where he could see a clear beginning and end, or projects where he was boss (or joint-boss with Potholer). Wise man. It would have to be a brilliant project to lure him and Beryl away from Shelly Beach.

I pulled Violet aside. 'Did you get on to Scarlett about Anton's shirt? I tried to call her earlier but she wasn't at home.'

'It's sorted, Gina,' Violet said briskly. 'The shirt was with the bed linen, and we're getting it back to Anton tomorrow.'

I smiled in relief. One less thing to worry about. 'And has Anton settled down? Do you need me to do anything? They didn't want to come tonight? I invited them.'

Violet gave me her are-you-mad look. 'Of course Anton wouldn't want to mingle with the locals. Stephanie might – but never Anton.'

'I thought Stephanie wanted to avoid the locals.'

'She's shy, actually. Once she warms up she's not snobby at all. Anyway, Stephanie took Anton to dinner in Sea Haven. She says it's a perfect-storm scenario: a keynote address *and* the upcoming publication of another of Anton's books. Apparently he always loses the plot when one of his novels is due to be published. Did you know he writes one a year and they're always published in the same month?'

'I might have heard that.'

'Evidently he goes crazy when the reviews come out.'

'Really?'

'He's had a lifelong feud with the one reviewer from a big-time New York paper for years. They hate each other.' Violet put a comforting hand on my arm. 'Don't worry, Gina. I'm sure Anton will be okay for his keynote – and he'll do a good job of it. Stephanie will see to that. Go home and get a good night's sleep. Get rid of those dark shadows under your eyes.'

I smiled my mean smile. The Dog and I made our excuses and were waiting at home when Terri plus monstrously heavy backpack (ready for school tomorrow) were deposited at my place. I went to make hot chocolate for supper and Terri followed me into the kitchen. 'Okay. I've waited patiently, Gina. What's the really important stuff you have to tell me?'

I located the Dog's tablets in the cupboard. 'Can you give the Dog his p-i-double-l first?'

Terri gave me her quizzical look.

'I have to spell p-i-double-l because he runs and hides if he hears the word.'

'Right.' Terri grabbed the Dog, placed the pill in the Dog's mouth and gently held his jaws closed until he swallowed. As the Dog scurried away to hide under the bed, Terri turned to me.

'Puh-*lease* tell me your news!'

I took a deep breath. 'Adrian asked me to marry him – again.'

Terri gasped in delight. 'Awesome! And did you say yes?'

'I haven't said anything yet. But he's proposed a non-wedding.'

'A non-wedding?'

'We'd get married at a registry office, but no special bridal suits or dresses, no cake, no flowers, no music . . . and no friends or family.'

'You wouldn't have bridesmaids?'

'No way. Sorry, Terri.'

'You don't think Julia and Barney, and Adrian's daughters and grandchildren would want to be at your wedding?'

'They probably would. But we're only having compulsory witnesses.'

'Why haven't you said yes?'

'Because I'm still recovering from my last marriage. Because I need some independence. Because I'm not sure Adrian has time for a wife. Because I'm not sure if I have time for a *husband*.'

'You'd make time for each other.'

I gave Terri a cross-eyed look.

'What would you wear for your wedding?'

'Probably my smoky plum suit. Or maybe Daphne could source me another suit? Something in a pastel colour.'

Terri was smiling her superior smile.

'You're distracting me on purpose! Now concentrate, Terri. This is important.'

Terri fastened her green eyes on my green eyes.

'The only people who know Adrian has proposed to me again are Adrian, me, the Dog and *you*. Do you understand? You are now caught up in a matter of great secrecy. I don't want anyone else to know until I make up my mind. Once the festival's over.'

'I understand.'

I smiled at my young red-headed friend. 'Right. Let's go to bed. Don't forget to set the alarm so we have plenty of time for a healthy breakfast.'

Terri gave me a big hug. 'I'm really glad Adrian asked you to marry him. And I hope you say yes.'

Bloody hell!

'Do you remember telling me to step outside my comfort zone more often, Gina? Now is the time. Stand on a cliff top and jump!'

'Thank you for your helpful advice, Terri. I'm using the bathroom first.'

From: Adrian <bookstreet@network.com.au>

To: Gina <glaurel@peninsula.com.au>

Subject: The waiting game

I won't pretend I'm not disappointed . . . but I can wait until after the festival for your answer.

Have I ever told you how mesmerising your eyes are?

Missing you.

xx Adrian

Wednesday: Drop in to Pages

The Dog and I were doing our usual check-the-calendar routine. Only two days to go before the festival. Surprisingly, I felt good. The sun was shining and gave every indication it would continue to shine, although the wind was up and the bay a little choppy.

'We should have a relatively quiet day today, Dog. We're going on a walk to see Digby at Pages. He sent me a text but I couldn't understand it. Tomorrow morning the marquees will be arriving, and as Rosa says, the circus will be in town!'

The Dog had no concept of a circus. He stood patiently while I brushed his fur. 'We're not doing a beach walk before we go to Digby's. No sniffing out rotten seabird carcasses. We'll walk back along the beach on the way home.'

When we arrived at the gallery there was no sign of Tiffany.

Digby greeted me with his much-too-familiar hug and usual cheek kiss. Digby's a very slow learner. I still need to work on creating work-colleague distance.

'Your gallery is looking fantastic, Digby!'

'It does look good, doesn't it?' Digby was extremely pleased with himself. After all, he was now a successful owner of a swish must-visit art gallery.

Tiffany appeared, flashed me a smile and dumped a box in front of Digby. She turned, disappeared into the back room and kept returning with more boxes. Digby's 'Can I help?' received a mean smile from the lovely Tiffany. 'Too late!' she said. She turned her calculating charm on to me. 'I've just been to the Sea Haven printers to collect the copies of the Shelly Beach Writers' Group publication, Gina.'

Bloody hell! I looked at the boxes stacked on Digby's polished concrete floor. I'd completely forgotten about the collaborative handbook our writers' group had written and decided to sell at the festival to raise extra funds.

Tiffany slashed one box open and handed us each a copy, examining one herself. 'I'm glad you went for the A format. It's pocket-sized.' She scrutinised the front of the book. 'The cover's brilliant. It will drive sales – and hopefully the content's brilliant too.'

I ignored Tiffany's comment. That handbook was the result of hours of collaboration and negotiation. I remembered a very volatile Shelly Beach Writers' Group meeting (practically a war) over the title for our handbook. *A Novel Dictionary* was the title half our members voted for. *A–Z of Novel-Writing* was the alternate title, which gained the other half of the votes. Against the judgement of a few rational members and outsiders, i.e. Tiffany, a final vote went to having both titles on the cover.

I looked at our dual-titled book cover, composed of multicoloured letters that covered practically every centimetre of space on the white background.

'The cover's worked really well. Alex Dessaix designed it for us.'

'Do I know him?' Digby asked.

'Hel-*lo*?' Tiffany gave Digby one of her wide-eyed stares and pointed to some framed watercolour illustrations hanging on the wall of his gallery. 'Alex did these. They're originals from his picture storybook.' She walked over to a display stand containing Dimity's picture storybooks and located Alex's picture storybook, which was also for sale. She placed a copy of Alex's first book (but hopefully one of many) in Digby's hand.

Digby smiled smoothly. 'Of course! I remember the young man now.'

Tiffany and I exchanged amused looks. We knew Digby didn't remember Alex.

Digby changed topic smoothly. 'I'm thinking our writers' group publication deserves its own launch at the festival.' He turned to Tiffany. 'You wouldn't be able to organise a little launch, would you? Members have put a lot of work into this handbook. It deserves to sell well.'

Tiffany and I exchanged another glance.

'I'll leave it with you two to organise it and make sure it gets plenty of publicity?'

Tiffany and I exchanged glances again. Another of Digby's pass-the-baton moves, and another occasion where he'd receive a good dose of accolade at the end.

No way was I admitting to the in-control Tiffany that I'd completely forgotten about our writers' group publication. It should have been me organising the launch – weeks ago. How could I have forgotten a book the group had written specifically to market at our festival? I'd never even rated it a dot-point on my to-do list.

Note to self: We are all lesser mortals and can stuff up sometimes.

'Tiffany, don't worry about a launch. We'll promote the book via word of mouth. Members can talk to me if they're not happy with that.' I gave Digby a stern look.

'Okay,' said Tiffany. 'I'll keep the bulk of the copies in our storeroom. We'll have copies on sale here, obviously, and I'll see copies are available at every marketable position: meet and greet tables, back of the room sales and so on.'

Note to self: Make sure writer's group handbook is on sale everywhere!

The Dog and I were leaving when Digby called us back. 'A favour to ask, Gina?' Alarm bells started ringing. 'A new colleague in our creative writing faculty has decided to come to the festival. I couldn't put her up at the castle.' Digby gave a tight smile. 'No room at the inn, unfortunately. Adrian mentioned one of his bungalow bookings for the festival had lost its legs so I've sent her there.' Digby checked his watch. 'She said she'd be arriving this afternoon. Thought it'd be a good idea to give her a Shelly Beach meet and greet. You're so much better at doing that sort of thing than I am, Gina.'

I took note again of Digby's cultivated incompetence, which excuses him from stuff he doesn't want to do but allows him to gain credit for the big-picture stuff he does.

'I've got a lot on my plate today . . .' I allowed for a good five seconds of silence to pass, enough to alarm Digby '. . . but I think I can make time to call at Adrian's bungalows this afternoon and see if your colleague has settled in.'

Digby looked relieved. I was sure he knew his limitless hospitality could spin out of control sometimes.

THE CALM BEFORE THE STORM

'What's your colleague's name?'

'Dr Wright. First name starts with an F . . . Fiona, Felicity, Fifi . . .' Digby laughed. 'Got it. *Fenella*. Dr Fenella Wright.'

Bloody hell! It had to be *the* Fenella Wright, the sweet-scary tutor of a writers' workshop I'd been attending when I'd found myself newly dumped and desperate. Did she have a doctorate then? Not that it would have made a difference to me. I wondered if she realised that early days of class are scary no matter how old you are? I was rather rude in a class of perfectly lovely adult novel-writing students. I was probably the student-from-hell she talked about at dinner parties.

Maybe I could avoid meeting her? I did a quick tactical rethink. 'I'm really under the pump at the moment, Digby. I'll do what I can to say hello to your colleague, but I can't promise. We'll probably meet during the festival anyway.'

Digby didn't care. He'd passed his to-do dot-point on to me. He was no doubt (as Violet says) looking for bigger fish to fry. I couldn't help but wonder what had possessed me to spend a night with him. But it was all water under the pier now.

Multi-tasking, Tiffany and I decided to take some boxes of the writer's group multiple-titled handbook to Rosa's to store for the meet and greet table. Two trips by two able-bodied women finished our task. I thanked Tiffany profusely for her help. Thank heavens for competent young women.

Rosa captured me when I returned the storeroom key to her. 'Gina, your King Mouse ex-hubby was just here looking for you. Your mother-in-law was with him, and his beautiful baby boy and a young nanny. He had to leave quickly when his personal trainer came to collect him. She wanted a wheatgrass drink but I told her to get wheatgrass at the Sea Haven health shop. Not a big call for wheatgrasses at my pub. I tell your mother-in-law – beaut-i-ful woman like Gina Lollabrigida – to come back at five o'clock to meet you.'

'Martha's my *ex*-mother-in-law, Rosa.'

'All your ex-family had brunch here. Your ex-mother-in-law said Lorenzo's pasta was better than pasta in Tuscany. It made Lorenzo very happy.'

'Bloody, bloody hell!'

'Don't get upset, Gina. You have a nice ex-family. Be friends with them. Exes can be very useful.'

I looked at Rosa. 'Not *my* exes. Especially not my ex-husband.'

Rosa put her hand on mine. 'Go home. Have a nice walk along the beach with your doggie. Make a cup of strong black coffee. Shower. Use smoky eye make-up. Make yourself look very snappy. Be back here at five to meet your Gina Lollabrigida ex-mother-in-law. Get it over with. You're a new woman now.'

I stared at Rosa, who was actually delivering sensible, useful advice. 'Right! Thank you, Rosa. Come on, Dog. We'll walk back along the beach.' I looked at my watch. 'We have to be back here in three hours. You can have a sleep and . . . and . . . I'll start thinking of scintillating gap-filling conversation for when I meet my former mother-in-law. And while I'm in the spirit of things, I suppose I should apologise for being the student-from-hell in a very helpful tutor's journal-writing workshop. What do you think, Dog?'

No comment.

• Meet and greet Dr Fenella Wright

The weather had done a turnaround by the afternoon. Now there was barely a ripple on blue Shelly Beach bay.

Walking to Adrian's bungalows, I wondered whether I actually needed to confess that I'd been in one of Dr Fenella Wright's journal-writing workshops. Surely she'd have more than one

student-from-hell in her workshops. She'd never remember or recognise me. I'm skinnier, and I have a different hairstyle. In my
former high-flier life I spent buckets of money at a ritzy hair stylist
who regularly tortured my hair, transforming it from a mass of wild
red curls to a helmet of straightened blonde tresses. But I decided
it was better to fess up.

Sweet-scary tutor may not recognise her rude former student
straightaway, but she could later if she keeps bumping into me at
the festival.

Dr Fenella Wright was at the bungalow when we arrived. I did
my confident-and-in-control festival director stuff, and I admitted
I'd been in one of her workshops in a former life. 'It was well over
a year ago. I was an absolute mess.'

My former tutor stared at me. 'I remember you.'

I stretched my lips into a smile and waited for recognition of
my appalling behaviour; my rude, abrupt and loud exits from her
workshops whenever we were asked to share our writing. I'd kept
breaking the golden writing-workshop rule. Students share their
writing. (If other students had duplicated my behaviour, Dr Wright
would have been minus the writing component in her workshops.)

'You had to leave my sessions early,' Fenella Wright continued.
'You were having terrible trouble with your teeth – you were racing
off to get root canal treatment?'

(Lies. Absolute lies.)

I nodded, breathed a sigh of relief and we exchanged a good
writerly chat. Ten minutes later, the Dog and I were on our way
again. Now for stressful meeting no. 2.

• Meet ex-mother-in-law

I concentrated on choosing clothes to meet Martha: the skinny
jeans, obviously – then my cobalt-blue silk shirt, an ink-blue

sweater to wear around my shoulders, pearl-stud earrings and leather loafers. I wanted to create the right balance between practicality and style.

Then I spent time applying discreet but flattering make-up, and fixing my red curls as taught by Bianca. I needed the confidence that comes when a woman knows she's equipped with the right armour for battle.

Rosa greeted me with a whispered compliment as the Dog and I entered the pub. 'You – look – *beaut-i-ful* – Gina!' She pointed to where my ex-mother-in-law was sitting at a table on Rosa's verandah, overlooking Shelly Beach bay.

Martha had been a stunning woman in her youth, and had passed her good looks on to her son, Kenneth. In her new role as a widow of an Italian count, she looked as fantastic as ever.

Martha and I were never great friends. She couldn't see a single fault in her adored son, and the relationship was complicated by the fact she lived with us. My career meant I didn't have time to look after Julia, so Martha rose to the challenge. I trusted her completely when she was caring for Julia. She did an amazing job of bringing up my daughter in my absence, for which I was forever grateful. Once Julia was at university, Martha suddenly left, moving to Tuscany to live with an Italian count. It was very sudden – she just left a note and walked out the door. I knew we probably needed to resolve some stuff. I've never really thanked Martha for all she did for Julia and me.

Martha looked up and waved at me, and the Dog and I went to join her. The Dog did his usual escape under the table.

'Gina. It's lovely to see you.' Martha looked me right in the eye and smiled. 'Will you join me in a glass of wine?'

Amazing. Only a few years and Martha had acquired a seductive Italian accent. She was a smart woman – no doubt she now spoke fluent Italian. 'I'd prefer coffee, Martha. I'll order it from the bar.'

'No, let me.'

I watched my ex-mother-in-law return with two coffees. She was wearing four-inch designer heels, and hadn't spilt one drop of coffee on her way through the tables. Martha always had great poise and balance.

'Rosa is charming, isn't she? She knows you like strong blacks.'

Silence while we sipped our coffee. A sea breeze gently swirled around us. The absolutely gorgeous sea view provided an awesome conversation-stopper, but I knew I had to say something.

'You left so suddenly, Martha. We missed you. And I've never thanked you for all the years you loved and cared for Julia.'

My perfect ex-mother-in-law focused her incredible brown eyes (heightened by expertly applied shimmering eye make-up) on me. She smiled and took my hand. 'And I'm very grateful to you, Gina. You trusted me to care for your daughter – my beautiful Julia. And you've been generous in allowing my boy to have a speedy, trouble-free divorce. It was so important with the baby coming. But then again, you always did take everything in your stride.'

We'd been a very flaky team during my marriage to her son. But I hadn't realised how much it would mean to know that Martha didn't hold any grudges against me.

'I love your makeover,' Martha went on. 'It's amazing how you can discover stylists in the most out-of-the-way places.'

'Thank you, Martha. You look beautiful, as always.'

She smiled acknowledgement regally.

'I caught up with Julia and my adorable Barney last week. It's such a shame Julia's marriage has broken up, but she seems to be doing well. She's looking to buy a property – a house-slash-office?

She wants to run a small accounting business from home until Barney is old enough to go to school.'

Martha sipped her coffee and watched me carefully. I was familiar with these sorts of Martha tests. Question one: Was I up to date with what was happening in my daughter's life? Question two: Had my once flaky mother–daughter relationship been mended?

'Julia's asked me to price some properties for both of us – we're thinking of house-sharing. She's waiting on me to sign the contract for my new job.'

Silence while my ex-mother-in-law assimilated this information. I watched her hands with their beautifully manicured nails position her coffee cup precisely in the saucer. 'That's excellent news! I was hoping you and Julia would be able to get along when Barney was born.' Then a quick segue. 'Dear Rocky – my beloved husband – left most of his capital and investments to his family, but he did bequest me the charming villa in Tuscany. I'm based permanently in Italy now, and thinking of running Italian escapes. Earn a little extra pocket money. You know the type of thing – lovely food, massages and find-yourself time. I've found local help and I've an excellent pizza-and-pasta chef lined up.'

Silence while Martha sipped her coffee. She was different – she'd acquired a glamorous detachment, a buzz and energy she never showed when she was living with us.

'I've told Julia that she and Barney are welcome to come to Tuscany for a vacation anytime.' Martha took another sip of coffee. 'I hear you're doing a brilliant job as director of this charming writers' festival, Gina.'

'Thank you, Martha. Do you know if Kenneth will be around at the festival?' I entertained a vague hope that he might be babysitting son Griffin while Clever Angela went to the sessions.

'Yes, I think so. No doubt he'll catch up with you soon.' Martha finished off her coffee and turned to me, putting one manicured hand on mine. 'Gina, I'm sorry to leave you, but I'm dining with the manager of Sea Haven Resort tonight. He's considering importing Italian beauty products to use in the day spa.' She flashed her charming smile and gave me her business card. 'I'm thinking about taking small groups of writers at the villa. You might be interested in a Tuscan holiday, Gina. Take the occasional writing workshop around the pool. Think about it and email me.'

We exchanged cheek kisses and I watched Martha's elegant figure weave through the tables.

As soon as the Dog and I arrived home I couldn't wait to ring Julia. 'I met your grandmother today.'

'OMG. How did it go?'

'Well, not too badly, actually. I thanked her for looking after you for all those years.'

'That was a really cool thing to do, Mum. She's looking amazing, isn't she?'

'I'd say she's had a lot of work done to maintain her ever-youthful great-grandmother look. She said she'd invited you and Barney to visit her in Tuscany.'

'She did, but we'll have to think about that. You could come too.'

'Martha did suggest I could visit her in Tuscany and take writers' workshops around her pool.'

Julia laughed. 'How are you coping with everything at Shelly Beach?'

'Just. I've nearly let a few things slip under the radar but I think we'll get there. Marquees are arriving tomorrow, along with Adrian. Typical last-minute stuff. Then the festival starts on Friday. I never imagined a small festival could morph into something so huge.'

'You'll be fine, Mum. Ring me if I can help. Love you lots.'

Once we'd hung up, I looked at the Dog. 'Now that was what I call a very satisfying conversation with a much-loved daughter.'

Thursday: Marquee consultation with Alf and Potholer

Alf had texted me last night: *Grabbed 5 a.m. slot for use of sand-raker. Ali detouring on way to job other side of peninsula. Can use tractor headlights if necessary. Potholer and I will help if need be.*

The Dog was as puzzled as I was with my cryptic message. We'd never met a sand-raker. I checked the calendar. We already had a six a.m. meeting pencilled in with Alf and Potholer on the foreshore opposite Piece of Cake to supervise the yellow marquee's arrival. No reason for a plan change.

The Dog was grumpy at having to breakfast at such an ungodly hour – not to mention swallowing his p-i-double-l. I checked for spat-out tablets. None in sight. 'See, it's worth taking your medicine. No itching.'

The Dog ignored me.

'Let's see if the yellow marquee has made touchdown.' As long as a walk along the beach preceded this discovery the Dog was happy.

Yet another beautiful spring morning had landed in Shelly Beach – as forecast via Alf weeks ago. There was scarcely a ripple on the bay. The activity along the sand at six in the morning was equal to the busiest use of an exercise track in an inner-city park (where suits disguised in tracksuits jog their hearts out).

Stephanie Brandt in Lulu Lemon, soothing meditation mantras channelling in her ears via earphones, jogged past and gave us a bare-minimum smile. Daphne and Bluey were doing their oldish-dog walk. (The dogs were annoyed. No time to stop and play. Daphne had to be on time for her yoga on the beach.) Bianca and Pandora jogged past us at a disgustingly fast clip, hardly puffing, beaming smiles on their faces, and Harry and Gary passed not long after – making good jogging pace. Finally Bill Kruger struggled past, pushing young son Hunter with difficulty along the sand. The Dog steered clear of the squirming three-year-old.

We maintained our steady walking pace until we arrived at the foreshore where the yellow marquee was to be erected.

Alf and Potholer were already there, conferring with two workers as they watched a tractor with an attachment (obviously the mysterious sand-raker) being loaded on to a council truck.

'What did you think of the sand, Gina?' Potholer asked.

I paused. This was a tricky Shelly Beach question. What had I missed? I looked at the Dog. Was there any difference in the sand we walked on as we travelled to meet Alf and Potholer? Was it more pristine than usual? I stalled for time.

'Ali and his mate have been here since five,' said Alf. 'The Shelly Beach enviro group doesn't usually approve of using mechanical equipment to clean up the beach – Nature tidies her own tidelines in her own good time, etcetera – but considering the number of people that'll be here for the festival, we got the go-ahead. Doesn't it look good?'

I beamed at my efficient Health and Safety team. 'The beach looks great, guys.'

The Dog knew the Shelly Beach sand hadn't been up to its usual sniffing standard. He'd noticed the absence of decayed birds and the odd dead crab, sea star or stranded fish usually to be found at the tideline among the seaweed.

The council truck drove off, with the sand-raker safely loaded on its trailer. Hot on its heels, the truck with our yellow marquee arrived, along with a team of workers to erect it. Alf, Potholer, and myself conferred with the marquee-assembling team on the correct positioning of our marquee on the foreshore. Then we stood back and watched in awe as the team of workers erected the marquee, and a keynote venue for our festival came to life.

'Awesome!'

I turned around. Terri and Toby with-the-fringe had snuck up behind me.

'Hello, you two. On your way to school?'

Terri gave me a rolled-eye look. She and Toby were both wearing their school uniforms.

'Is everything set for the festival, Gina?' asked Toby.

'Well . . . we have a venue. Now all we need are presenters, sessions and attendees.'

While we were talking, keep-fit festival committee members had gathered to watch our yellow marquee come to life in all its temporary glory.

Not much can upset the equilibrium of Shelly Beach locals, but we were all a little speechless when the yellow marquee stood (hopefully) strong and in its position on the foreshore. It was huge. We went in and clustered in the foyer like mussels on the pier.

Bianca, Pandora, Toby and Terri went with the audiovisual expert who was assembling the bells-and-whistles system that came with the marquee. The remaining committee members took a big-picture view of crowd management for the next three days. The foyer was perfect for our back-of-room sales, plus mixing and mingling. We moved to the main area, with seating for 300.

'We'll have to ask attendees to move to the front when they come in for their sessions,' said Alf.

I made a note. Bill Kruger agreed with this. 'It's hell doing an author event in a huge space, with an audience dotted around like lost sheep on a hill. You feel like you're shouting into the wilderness.'

We nodded. I patted Bill's arm and underlined my note.

Potholer urged members to do the Goldilocks thing and test the fancy plastic seating.

'Bloody hard if you have to sit for too long,' said Alf.

True. Hopefully our session presenters would be so scintillating, attendees would forget their hard seats.

A blast of music and kaleidoscopic flashing lights assaulted our ears and eyes. Our sound system was working. Toby and Josh jumped up on the main stage and did some testing in the microphone and checked out the autocue system.

Josh reported back. 'It's cool, Gina. Not top of the range but it's good.' I breathed a sigh of relief. There was nothing worse than sitting through presentations with electronic malfunctions. Another box ticked. I kept my fingers crossed.

Finally we inspected the temporary male and female rest rooms that were at the side of the marquee. Thumbs-up evaluation from the guys. Daphne, Pandora, Terri and I went on a ladies' rest room inspection. With their cubicles, soap dispensers (amazingly full of soap wash), latest electronic hand dryers and washbasins with glam fittings, they gained our five-star approval.

Committee members and general hangers-on assembled again in the main auditorium. The early spring sun streamed through the faux windows and lit up the interior with natural light. We were impressed. Inspection completed, those who were free voted to retire to Piece of Cake for coffee, tea and muffins.

The Dog thought the yellow marquee looked like a structure from another planet. He prefers uninterrupted views of Shelly Beach bay from the foreshore.

'There's always one or two locals who will disagree with progress in their small town – even if it is only causing a disruption to the community for a very small window of time.' I glared at the Dog.

He watched me cross fingers on both hands.

'I hereby acknowledge I'm keeping my fingers permanently crossed during the entirety of the festival.'

~

Pandora and I pulled the coffees while a beaming Gail made the food. Piece of Cake was buzzing with happy locals. I made sure the Dog was safe and happy with Bluey for company in the Piece of Cake yard, and was enjoying a well-earned cup of coffee when my mobile rang. It is a well known but unwritten rule in Shelly Beach that you never answer your mobile in company – not unless you're on lifesaver duty and are needed to rescue a swimmer in trouble. So I excused myself and walked over to the foreshore to answer my mobile. I soon wished I hadn't.

'Gina – this is Violet.' The normally unflappable Violet sounded shaken. 'I've bad news to tell you. Matt Galinsky died during the night from a massive heart attack.'

Bloody hell! I stared out at the blue rippled sea while I comprehended the startling and sad news.

'Are you okay, Gina?'

'Yes. Yes. Tell me what happened.'

I listened as Violet, in her very matter-of-fact tone, went through her shocking discovery of Matt. 'I'd done the girls' breakfasts and was delivering Matt's. He likes – liked – a breakfast tray at eight o'clock every morning. A good healthy breakfast: juice, fruit compote, muesli, toast and scrambled eggs. He always appreciated the flower I added to his tray.'

I could tell Violet liked Matt; she'd become another victim of his charm.

She continued. 'I knocked and knocked. The eggs were stone cold. Matt was usually up by eight . . . Excuse me, Gina.'

I waited while Violet blew her nose.

'So I used my master key.'

Of course Violet had a master key.

'I knew as soon as I saw Matt in the bed that he was dead. He was lying on his back. His eyes wide open. His mouth was open like one of those clowns you see at the fun fair. I quickly tidied the room.'

'You tidied his room?'

'Yes, and tidied up Matt. I closed his eyes and wiped some residue from the corners of his mouth. I did that for my father when he died of a heart attack. I called the funeral parlour, Zac' – one of Potholer's sons, the constable on duty – 'and the doctor in Sea Haven. I went to tell Dimity and Sandy and brought Dimity back to be with her dad. And then all hell broke loose.'

Bloody hell! 'Are you sure you've done the right thing, Violet? Why did you ring the funeral parlour first and not the ambulance or the doctor? Did you need to involve the police?'

'Have you ever lost a member of your family Gina?'

'My mother died when I was born, and my father when I was fourteen.'

'Did your father die at home?'

'No. In a hospital.'

'My father *and* my husband died of heart attacks at home. I knew Matt was dead. If the ambulance came first the paramedics would have to try to revive him, which would only have been more stressful for Dimity. I called the police and the doctor just to make sure there was an audit trail – nothing suspicious. Zac's got all the paperwork underway. He's a bit of a mess, poor boy. It's the first death he's had to cope with as a constable. Are you okay, Gina?'

'I think so. Are you okay, Violet?'

'Yes.'

'I'll come to Sea Crest straightaway to see Dimity and Sandy, but I don't know what to say.'

'Saying you don't know what to say is exactly the right thing to say. They're both a bit of a mess, but Sandy's a sensible young woman. She's looking after Dimity and is in control at the moment.'

'Right.'

'You'll need to call a committee meeting this afternoon, Gina. We need to keep Matt's death quiet. Shut down talk. Stop salacious news spreading. The death has nothing to do with anyone but Dimity and Sandy.'

'Is that going to be possible?'

'Shelly Beach has done it before. We know how to close ranks.'

Violet gave me a teary-voiced goodbye and hung up. I kept staring out at the blue sea and thinking about Matt's death. I hated to admit it, but I was also thinking about the implications for the festival. I felt like panicking, but that wouldn't help. I had to focus on the festival. I could do it. I would do it.

I took Daphne's recommended ten deep breaths in and out (the exhalations are more important than the inhalations) and went back to Piece of Cake.

'Sorry, folks. An emergency's come up. Can we all meet at Rosa's tonight in the billiard room? Can you tell any committee members I've missed?' I gave Terri and Toby my key to the storeroom at Rosa's where all the children's workshop gear was stored. After school, they and Alex Dessaix would set up all the stuff for the workshops. As quickly as I could, I took my leave.

I noticed Violet's eyes were red-ringed when I arrived at the Sea Crest B&B. She seemed amazingly composed, considering the emotional roller-coaster she'd been on since early this morning.

I patted her arm gently. 'This is terrible. It must have been hard for you, finding Matt.'

'It's sad. Very sad. Especially as Matt was so young to die of a heart attack.' She looked at me. 'I'd start looking for a replacement for Dimity as soon as possible. I'm pretty sure she won't be able to front up for her sessions tomorrow.'

'I guessed. I so hate myself. I know how terrible it is for Dimity losing her father so suddenly . . . but at the same time I'm thinking about our festival beginning with a no-show.'

Violet patted my hand. 'Only natural.'

At that moment Sandy came into the office and gave me a wan smile. I gave her a hug.

'Do you think it's okay to see Dimity?'

Sandy nodded. 'She wants to see you.'

When we arrived at Dimity's room, the young author tried to compose herself between bouts of tears. I gave her a hug.

'I don't know what to say, Dimity. Matt was such a charismatic person. It seems like he'd always been part of Shelly Beach.'

Dimity stifled a sob. 'I'm glad we've had these few years together as a father-and-daughter team.' Then she looked at me meaningfully. 'I'm not sure I can perform tomorrow, Gina.'

'Don't worry, Dimity. It will be fine. Of course you can't perform.'

I left the room, and as I was leaving Sandy indicated she'd be down in a few minutes. 'I need to talk to you about the festival, Gina – just hold on a moment.'

I sat with Violet in the office of Sea Crest. Violet had made tea. No sign of Geraldine or Claude. 'Geraldine's a mess. Claude's not much better. The doctor gave Geraldine a sedative,' Violet explained. We sat and sipped our tea and waited until Sandy reappeared. In my mind I was running through one idea after another: how to create a performance to replace Dimity? One idea after another was being tossed into my mental trash bin.

Violet and I looked up as Sandy entered the room. 'I think I know how we can work out a replacement for Dimity.'

'You can?' The indomitable Sandy was caring for Dimity and salvaging a no-show performance.

'This should be the answer.' Sandy handed me a DVD. 'Matt made this to use at shopping centre gigs to give Dimity a break. It's Dimity singing and dancing against a backdrop. I'm happy to do my Atticus routine in the mouse suit on the stage with the DVD as the background. I think it'll work for your opening presentation.'

I nodded. Relief was flooding into my body. 'I'm sure it will.'

'If Violet looks after Dimity I'll try and get down there today for a run-through. It'll be good if you could have Josh or someone else with techie skills there as well. And wasn't Dimity slotted in to do a workshop with groups of young writers?'

I grimaced. 'We can cover that, Sandy. Don't worry about it.'

'I've got the workshop script Matt wrote for Dimity. If I had a narrator reading it for me, I could mime the instructions as Atticus.'

'That would be *incredible*, Sandy.'

'We might just pull this off.'

We decided on a four o'clock meeting at the yellow marquee. I gave Sandy a big hug before I left. Then I turned to Violet but didn't give her a hug. You never hug Violet – she doesn't like hugs or air kisses. You'd upset her hearing aid. 'What would I do without you, Violet? You managed the situation calmly and with tact. You're a gem.'

'You'd cope just as well.'

• Emergency billiard room meeting

I walked up Shortcut Lane and breathed a sigh of relief as soon as I entered Rosa's beer garden. I mentally ticked a box: the blue marquee was standing strong and firm. I stuck my head inside. It was perfect.

I braced myself, and went to meet the committee members. But first I had to see my young friends Terri and Toby, who were in Rosa's storeroom with Alex Dessaix. The three of them were preparing the materials and equipment for the children's workshops and sorting it all into labelled plastic containers. They looked so happily productive I was reluctant to break the news to them. But it had to be done.

Terri was very distressed. 'It'll be so awful for Dimity.' No doubt Terri was remembering the not-so-long-ago time when her own father died of cancer.

'What's going to happen with Dimity's performances?' asked Toby. I explained Sandy's clever plan. With a sympathetic smile, I excused myself to head to the emergency meeting.

Like most things in life, it wasn't nearly as hard as I'd thought it would be. Committee members were shocked but stalwart. Apart from Pandora. Her face turned white at the news and she burst into tears. After being comforted by Rosa and Daphne, and presented with a cup of tea by Alf, her tears reduced to a sniffle.

'When someone youngish dies suddenly, it really pulls you up, doesn't it?'

I agreed.

'I'll just miss Matt so much. His death makes you realise that you have to live in the moment; there's no guarantee there will be a next day.'

Although she was visibly upset, Pandora could see the importance of keeping Matt's death as quiet as possible. 'They do say bad publicity can be as effective as good publicity, but I don't want to go there. Let's keep this quiet – at least until the festival is over.'

'This is so sad,' said Rosa. 'Matt was such a lovely man.' (Days before Rosa was describing him as 'slippery'.) 'We'll keep Matt's death quiet. Lorenzo and I tell no one. We don't upset the festival.' As the landlady of a pub, Rosa understood completely the necessity to keep confidences confident.

Subdued committee members were cheered by Josh's news. Bianca's husband had met Sandy at the yellow marquee for a run-through earlier that afternoon, and it had worked perfectly. Members were also cheered by Alf's news at the end of the meeting. He confirmed the weather forecast for the next three days. 'Shelly Beach is going to be the hero of the festival, folks. Twenty degrees. Blue skies and white sands.'

Shelly Beach locals returned to the front bar to drink to Matt and to the beginning of our festival. The show would go on.

I was returning Rosa's billiard room to its original purpose when I looked up. Adrian was standing at the door. Uber-cool. Looking tired, but *so* good in his suit, pale green shirt opened at the neck, as usual a designer tie in his pocket. He came over, enveloped me in a wonderful hug and gave me a great kiss. He looked deeply in my eyes. 'Are you all right? Violet told me about Matt.'

I stood tall. 'Yes. Dimity will not be presenting tomorrow, but we're using a DVD and projecting it onto the big screen. Sandy as Atticus is going to do her thing. She's an amazing woman.'

Adrian smiled at me. 'She's not the only one. You didn't need your plans C, D or F?'

'No. Not even a Plan G. But I'm really, really glad you're here.' And I was.

Adrian smiled.

'Come on, Hugo, let's get our talented festival director home. I'll make dinner. Your owner needs a rest.'

The Dog wasn't happy about being called by his former name Hugo, but let it slide.

I went home to a hot bath and a lovely, light meal cooked by a really nice man. Being together but not *always* together is rather nice. They do say that absence makes the heart grow fonder.

The Dog was sulking. He hates sleeping on the day bed.

DAY ONE

Friday: Pirates land

Keeping in mind that the small stuff makes the difference – i.e. the devil is in the detail – I was determined to keep focused, calm, in control and smiling until Schools Day ended.

I'd booked the first use of the bathroom last night and crept out of bed while Adrian was still sleeping. I was feeling much loved. We hadn't said a word about his proposal, and I was grateful. I needed more time.

I decided to get dressed in my pirate gear at home rather than in a cramped cubicle in the yellow marquee's bathroom. I squeezed into the red satin corset and fastened the tattered skirt, pulled on my boots and finally slipped on my jacket with the gold buttons and deep-cuffed sleeves. I looked in the mirror, took Terri's advice and buttoned my jacket.

Adrian was making coffee when I appeared in the kitchen. 'You look spectacular, Gina!' And he gave me a kiss and a hug.

'No smart pirate comments or I'll make you walk the plank. And no – thank you very much – I don't want to spend time with you on a desert island!'

'What can I do to help today?'

'Make sure your Department of Education suits and your speaker are here for the afternoon session. On time!'

I graciously accepted a salute.

'And can I leave the Dog with you? Will you bring him to the yellow marquee before you pick up your suits in Sea Haven? And . . .' I placed the Dog's last tablet on the table. 'Can you please give the Dog his p-i-double-l before you bring him to me? You have to hold his jaws shut until he swallows it.'

I downed my coffee, grabbed some toast, and gave Adrian a quick kiss. I was off. I decided to walk down Beach Road in my pirate gear. What the hell! A pirate walking down Beach Road didn't cause an eye flicker, just a wave from Alf and Potholer, who were closing off Beach Road.

Sandy, aka Atticus, Toby, Josh and Terri were at the yellow marquee to meet me. We did a final quick run-through with the DVD. Flashing lights, bouncy music and happy snappy singing from a 2D Dimity as she appeared larger than life on the huge flat screen. The DVD was working. Hallelujah!

'Everything cool?' Adrian arrived with the Dog under his arm. I nodded. Terri snaffled the Dog up and took him away to dress him in his cute pirate gear. I wasn't sure how he'd go as Ambassador Dog but we'd give it a shot.

Tiffany called in. 'Gina, you look fabulous! I'll see you at lunchtime for Digby's launch. He's picking up more copies of *War and Wool* and collecting the glasses for the red-carpet do. His caterers forgot them.'

I smiled. Two dot-points that I don't need to know about.

Ambassador Dog was returned to me, looking grumpy but piratical. Daphne was putting up a welcome sign directing attendees to the meet and greet table at Rosa's pub. I left the Dog in Daphne's charge.

While Terri and Atticus went off for a very short practice of the workshop presentation, minus our celeb presenter, I whizzed into the ladies' rest room. I tied a red-spotted bandeau around my forehead, and balanced my jaunty tricorn hat on top of my wild curls. I gave my boobs a hitch, and a respectable cleavage emerged from the red satin corset – but I rebuttoned my jacket. Terri had said that my costume had too much attitude, but I've worked very hard this year developing attitude, and I'm not losing it.

Maybe I wouldn't change into my pre-loved corporate suit for Digby's book launch. I'd just unbutton my buccaneer's jacket.

Busloads of school children started to arrive. The Dog and I gave welcoming greetings to bands of small-edition pirates and their piratical teachers.

'I told you the teachers would dress up.' I smirked at the Dog.

The Dog ignored me.

My pirate's apprentices, Terri and Toby, plus friends, joined me to show young students and teachers to their allocated seats in our sumptuous, state-of-the-art marquee. I loved the reaction from our young writers. I was sure they'd never experienced being inside such an awe-inspiring, temporary plastic construction before. We watched our hopefully manageable young pirates flood into the marquee. It seemed like the Pied Piper had rounded up every young writer in our area.

At nine a.m. lights dimmed and teachers shushed their students. I took the stage and did the welcome, and then Dimity Honeysuckle's presentation (minus Dimity) began.

I joined our on-duty committee members standing quietly at the side of the marquee to watch and listen to our opening presentation. We marvelled at the incredible bells and whistles. Atticus's performance actually kept usually twitchy-itchy young students wide-eyed, entertained and engaged. Thank heavens for modern mesmerising technology.

Pandora was teary. 'Everything – the DVD, CDs, video clips, the animated telly series – is all Matt's hard work.' I gave her shoulder a squeeze, passed her a tissue and breathed a huge sigh of relief as our minus-Dimity performance came to a triumphant finale. I handed the Dog to Pandora so I could do a pirate leap on to the stage to direct students and teachers to the foreshore for their scheduled half-hour break.

The young adrenaline-filled pirates and their amazingly cheerful teachers crossed traffic-free Beach Road (thanks to Alf and Potholer) to the foreshore and settled into their school groups to eat their snacks in a setting of blue seas, sky and white sand.

Hopefully the children would run off some steam before they got to the workshops.

Back in the marquee, congratulations were being showered on Atticus, and Josh and Toby who'd manned the tech stuff.

Sandy's head had appeared from her mouse bodysuit. She was pumped. 'The routines worked brilliantly! I'm so relieved. Dimity and I have always worked as a team. I've never done a solo gig.'

There was silence while we thought about Matt and his untimely death. How must Dimity be feeling, grieving for her dad back at Sea Crest B&B?

Violet broke our silence, handing us all a bottle of water. 'You need to replace lost fluids, girls. Anyone else want water?'

I smiled at Sandy. 'I'm so grateful you're covering for Dimity in the workshops.'

'I'm not going to.'

'You're *not*?' My blood pressure soared.

'But Atticus is looking forward to taking the kids' workshops, Gina.'

Right! I'm down that rabbit-hole again. I could now communicate in Alice-in-Wonderland language with a large faux mouse as well as a dog.

• Digby's book launch

We were still talking about Atticus's incredible performance when Digby, looking sartorial in his well-cut suit, arrived with his book launch entourage – his publisher, her PA, a publicity assistant and a mini catering crew of two.

'Ho, ho, ho and a bottle of rum!' I received Digby's too-familiar hug (long enough to inhale deep breaths of his expensive cologne), cheek kisses and a whispered compliment in my ear. 'You look sensational. Come with me while I introduce you to my publishing team.'

Digby was smooth. He introduced me as Shelly Beach's 'brill-i-ant' writers' festival director. Then I was introduced to his 'in-cred-ible' publishing team and his 'a-maz-ing' catering crew.

'Troy and Danielle are doing the champers and nibbles for my launch. Then they'll join the rest of the catering team for my red-carpet cocktails tonight,' Digby explained.

I smiled and shook hands with the entourage before they left to set up for the launch. As he hurried off, Digby called, 'The rest of the catering crew are due to arrive in about two hours' time. If you see them, Gina, can you direct them to the castle?'

Note to self: Tell Digby's catering crew to look for a homestead with a circular drive at the top of McIntosh Hill. A homestead that resembles a castle, if you stretch your imagination and your ego.

Leanne, Digby's publisher, joined me. 'The space you've assigned for the launch is perfect, Gina. Digby suggested we could use Pages Gallery.' Leanne smiled at Digby across the room. 'But it's nicer to hold the launch in an official festival space, to

have the books on display alongside the new curriculum materials when the Department of Education officials and teachers
arrive. We'll transfer Digby's book display to his gallery before we
leave tonight.'

More dot-points zipping off my list, landing on Leanne's. Digby
joined us and I watched as she stroked the arm of Digby's hand-
tailored suit and picked a silver hair from the sleeve of his jacket.
I was just about to excuse myself for the student workshops when
Digby pulled me aside. 'Matt's death is shocking bad luck, Gina.
How are you managing with the festival?'

Typical big-picture Digby. 'Well, Dimity is totalled, but Sandy
is doing a brilliant job of covering for her in the presentations.'

'Talented young woman, Sandy.'

I realised that Digby had probably tried his luck with Sandy.
Not a chance.

I thought of Matt with the chiselled good looks. Maybe if Matt
had settled in Shelly Beach, he would have usurped Digby as
Shelly Beach's no.1 ladies' man.

Leanne called to Digby. 'Come and see the set-up for your book
signing, Digby.'

'Sorry, Gina.' Digby gave my arm a squeeze and my cheek
another kiss. 'Keep up the good work. Have to go.'

• Young pirates workshops

I was starting to panic. Alex Dessaix had been helping with the
techie stuff earlier – and now he'd vanished. I was moving to my
second stage of panic when I noticed Johnny Depp entering the
yellow marquee and striding towards me. Alex, aka a rakish Jack
Sparrow look-alike, was here. Some liberally applied eyeliner and
artful rats' tails completed the look.

I mentally ticked another dot-point.

'Sorry I'm late, Gina. I had to return my mother's sewing machine. Stayed up till three last night sewing my pirate's jacket.'

Of *course* the talented young author–illustrator had to leave us to dash home and return his mother's sewing machine. 'Are you okay working in the blue marquee with your student groups?'

'Not a problem. I'm planning to show the kids how to draw pirate rats. It'll be a ball.'

'Right!' I *so* hated the generational thing where Alex could be completely unfazed at the thought of delivering workshops he *thought* he'd nail, while I was having a seriously serious meltdown at the thought of delivering workshops I'd nailed before.

Terri, Toby and Sandy, aka Atticus, were ready to take their workshop in the yellow marquee. 'It'll work, Gina. Chill.'

I ignored Terri and focused on Atticus.

'Matt's how-to script helps kids create a pirate character so they can create a twelve-page picture storybook. It should be all good.'

I nodded. 'Remember teachers will be close at hand if you need help. You'll be working with your groups over here.' I pointed to a cleared area at the back of the yellow marquee.

'How's Dimity?' asked Toby.

Guilt flooded over me. I stared at Atticus, who was now wearing his head. When someone is wearing a mouse suit it's *so* hard to read their body language.

We strained to hear Atticus's muffled reply. 'Dimity's taking the medication the doctor left for her. Daphne's with her and she'll stay by her side until I get back. Daphne's working out a roster of people to be with Dimity over the festival.'

I smiled. I knew from past experience that Shelly Beach locals were roster-making experts. They love being part of rosters to deliver unrelenting high-quality care (whether you want it or not) to short- or long-term Shelly Beach visitors. It was an unspoken given that no Shelly Beach local carried guilt from not helping (or from killing others with random acts of kindness). Dimity Honeysuckle would be in constant kind and caring hands.

I handed out copies of my workshop timetable, flow chart and map, which I'd laminated. 'Make sure you stick to half-hour sessions and get groups to move in a clockwise rotation to their next workshop station. Everyone is to meet back here at twelve thirty for "sharing time", where the kids will get their goodie bags. Then we can pile them and the teachers in their buses to go back to their schools.'

We could hear the loud voices of excited students assembling at the main entrance of the marquee. I inhaled as much calm as was possible when you were dressed in OTT pirate gear with a mic in your hand and a rumbustious pirate crew ready to follow you on stage.

Atticus was a star turn. Sandy was earning so many elephant stamps it wasn't funny. And Alex came a close second, performing brilliantly in his Johnny Depp role. After our intro, my crew, holding our Jolly Roger flags on high, led our groups away for the workshops. So far, so good.

~

I was just starting to relax when Violet, dressed in a striped T-shirt and pirate headscarf, leapt in front of me. 'Thought you might need a bit of help! The other groups are having a great time.'

I looked at my group of crafty young writers who were energetically rummaging through boxes of recycled materials to make eye-patches, pirate shoe buckles, spy glasses and parrots.

'They're like a pack of rats sorting through rubbish to make a nest,' Violet exclaimed.

I checked to see if my group and teachers had overheard Violet's simile. They hadn't. I allowed her simile to float out to sea and accepted her help gratefully. But I blocked out her answers to young writers' queries: 'No! You can't make a cutlass . . . or a dagger. No! You can't work with a friend and make a cannon. That's a fun thing to do at home when you have more time.'

The knowledge that the festival committee would cease operation at the end of the festival and wouldn't be available to take teacher or parent complaints was comforting. I attended to a request to fasten a cord on a piratical eye-patch.

'You should let the kids do their own stapling, Gina,' said Violet. 'Then again, we'd probably need to have a nurse on duty.'

I smiled in relief as we finished up our activities. Violet called, 'Look lively, ye scurvy dogs! You can't leave a mess like this on the deck!'

As Violet and I watched our group depart, she turned to me. 'I've just had an idea for a new whodunit, Gina. I'm thinking of creating a new detective character.'

'You're not using Red Blaze?' (Red Blaze was Violet's detective character in her published and soon-to-be published whodunits.)

'No. I'm thinking of creating a new cosy amateur sleuth: Mrs Rule, a sixty-something widow who runs a housekeeping service in a small seaside town. She cleans a five-star hotel, three B&Bs and few rental properties. A celebrity guest has died from a heart attack in one of the B&Bs. Mrs Rule thinks it's murder.'

Bloody hell! The next group of young writers arrived and immediately jumped into their piratical craft-making tasks.

'Prefer poker any day,' Violet muttered as she helped children attach foil-covered buckles to their shoes. 'I think the kids have used the wrong glue, Gina. They may have difficulty in removing the buckles when they go home. You might like to mention to their teachers that nail polish remover is a handy glue dissolver. Not sure if I'd use it to get beards off faces. Hot water and soap might be better.'

Bloody hell!

I surveyed my last group of young writers. They *were* enjoying themselves. I kept my eyes on my group while Violet produced a notebook and pencil from her handbag and continued her verbal synopsis of her new whodunit. 'The celebrity guest staying in the B&B could have been working undercover as a spy. Using the pier for his comings and goings. A counter-spy operator could have been sent to finish him off. They could be staying at the same B&B and the counter-spy operator may have been slipping arsenic in his breakfast marmalade. Arsenic is a very quick-acting poison.'

Violet paused to allow her little grey cells to work à la Poirot . . . or was she channelling Miss Marple? 'I'm not sure how long it takes a dose of arsenic to kill someone. I know it has a horrible taste!' Violet scribbled in her notebook, presumably something about checking how long it takes a dose of arsenic to kill someone. 'If you want to kill with arsenic, it's best to feed it to the victim gradually.'

I stapled cord to eye-patches with bloodthirsty vengeance. Note to self: I refuse to allow Violet's fictional sleuthing to throw me.

I watched small pirates duelling with swords they weren't supposed to have made. 'Let's catch up later, Violet, when we have more time. You can run your new whodunit past me again. The plot sounds really interesting.' More like terrifying.

Violet was satisfied with my answer. Now I just had to hope she wouldn't mention it to anyone else. Bloody hell!

At sharing time it was evident young students had had a satisfying piratical experience. Students collected their goodie bags and piled in hordes onto their buses. My pirate crew breathed sighs of relief as we watched the buses drive away.

I looked up and Adrian was shepherding the 'Prof', our after-noon keynote speaker and book-launching professor, with a group of official-looking suits into the yellow marquee foyer. I ticked another two dot-points off my list.

Adrian gave me his special wink and came over to me. 'Work-shops go okay?'

'They went brilliantly. My crew were great with the kids. Vio-let's a bit of a worry, though.'

Adrian gave me his quizzical amused grin. He put a comforting arm around me. 'You can entertain me with Violet stories tonight. I've got to go and meet some of our official guests. Are you busy now?'

'I'm getting something to eat before Digby's launch. And I was going to change.'

'Don't. You look sensational.'

What the hell! I undid my jacket and stood tall. As festival director I was ready to shake hands and meet and greet.

~

I was sitting in Rosa's pub with Terri and Toby, having a quick sandwich, when the door opened and Kenneth walked in. With Angela and baby Griffin in tow.

I took a deep breath. It will make things easier for Julia and Barney if I stop acting like the classic dragon ex-wife. If I can be a reasonable human being, compulsory get-togethers will be tolerable.

Kenneth spotted me and smiled awkwardly. The family made their way over to us.

'Gina, thought I might bump into you here. You know Angela.' Of course I did. Kenneth's former PA – the woman he left me for. 'And this is Griffin.' A cute little boy grinned at me. 'That's an amazing outfit you've got there.'

I sat up a little straighter in my red satin corset and decided not to explain why I was wearing a tricorn hat. I introduced Terri and Toby. One sight of Griffin and the Dog vanished under the table. Faux cheek kisses and hugs were exchanged.

Thank heavens for my young friends. They went into their older-sibling act to divert Griffin. And thank heavens for their intelligent conversation starters about the festival. Between them Terri and Toby kept the conversation bubbling along.

Angela didn't look happy. I felt a pang of pity for her. How long would it take her to realise that Kenneth was a talented bed-hopper? I observed Kenneth deploying his touchy-feely body language with her. I'd seen it before. He was trying to make up for something. Perhaps Kenneth had been drinking too many wheat-grass smoothies with his personal trainer?

The conversation shifted to writing, and the subject of my unpublished novel.

'Angela's always wanted to write.' Devoted husband was smiling at his wife.

Of course she has.

'I've read so many picture books to Griffin. I'm positive I can write one too.'

I assured Angela she could. After a few more minutes of small talk, a friend of Angela's came into the pub and waved from the bar.

'Sorry, Gina, but we arranged to meet my friend for lunch,' Angela explained. Kenneth gave me a condescending smile.

Before she left, Angela took my hand. 'It was lovely to meet you again, Gina. I'm sorry for . . .' Her pretty face creased as she tried to think of how to put it. 'I'm sorry for everything. You've done amazingly well. Amazingly! Shelly Beach is a gorgeous place and I'm sure the festival will be gorgeous too.'

I gave Angela an empathic smile. A comforting thought flashed into my mind: I was so glad I was no longer married to Kenneth.

I watched King Rat ex-husband place his arm around Angela as they walked away. I found myself hoping it would work out for them. I realised I felt no acrimony towards them – nothing but relief to have got the dreaded meeting over and done with.

• Teachers' afternoon session

Digby's book launch and the teachers' afternoon session passed quickly compared to the morning, divided into its agonising half-hour survival sessions full of potential challenges.

Digby's group of suits arrived for his launch and mixed with Adrian's group of suits for the afternoon teachers' session. They made one homogenous collection of authoritative suits – one large shark pool. I was familiar with such pools. The trick to swimming among sharks was to project a calm and assertive image, and keep moving.

All the festival committee members, bar Daphne, arrived for Digby's book launch, and the ambience in our plasticised foyer lightened. We definitely appreciated Digby's small catering crew as they dispensed glasses of champagne and platters of finger sandwiches, accompanied with shiny white smiles.

As I did my best to work the room, Bianca whispered to me, 'Called in to see Dimity. She's pretty much sedated out of it. I said I'd call at Sea Crest later.'

We paused for a moment and thought about Dimity, our sweet and gentle celeb children's author-illustrator-entertainer.

'She's bereft at losing her dad.' Bianca was tearing up. I handed her a tissue. She quietly wiped her tears and had a gentle blow. 'I heard your workshops with the kids were awesome, Gina.'

I smiled and put my arm around my kind-hearted friend. 'Thank you.'

'Attention! Attention, everyone!' Leanne, Digby's publisher, was tapping her champagne glass with her pen, her platinum tones failing to make an impression on the crowd.

'You'd better jump to her rescue, Gina,' Bianca said.

In my best pirate-style I leapt onto the small stage (not sure how I did this), called a halt to networking, and introduced Leanne. She gave a punchy in-the-publishing-moment speech, occasionally directing a very affectionate glance at Digby.

Pandora joined us. 'Do you want to bet that this is the first time she's read this speech?'

'No.'

'Do you want to bet her assistant wrote it?'

'No!'

Next our keynote Prof and book launcher delivered a rather dry ten-minute speech. Thank goodness the champers and nibbles were still circulating. Then Digby, his silver mane in its usual academic ponytail, stepped onto the stage and into the literary limelight. Digby had a long, long list of thank-yous to deliver in his silvery-toned voice.

Adrian had quietly moved through the crowd until he was beside me. Keeping his eyes on Digby, Adrian spoke quietly. 'Let me take you home so you can have a breather before the afternoon session.'

Keeping my eyes on Digby, I whispered back, 'That would be *so* nice.' I mentally ticked Digby's book launch on my to-do list. I gathered up the Dog and we made our subtle escape.

At home, Adrian made me a sandwich and coffee while I changed into my corporate smoky plum suit and heels. The Dog was also glad to be rid of his pirate gear. He was sick of the dressing-up stuff. He believes it's totally unfair to make dogs wear people gear when dogs are already wearing perfectly good all-purpose fur. The Dog grudgingly stood still while I refastened his Ambassador Dog rosette to his collar.

The Dog isn't usually vain, but the thought of being photographed had tempted him to stray from his rule of never wearing adornments of any kind on his collar. The Dog thought it was perfectly cool to break a rule occasionally. Life can be boring sticking to the same rules day in, day out. Especially if the rules are ones you've made for yourself.

When we returned to the yellow marquee, the hype and buzz generated from Digby's book launch had floated out to sea. Teachers had gathered for the afternoon session. I did my festival director thing, introduced Adrian and he took over as moderator, managing the academic panel with diplomacy and flair.

After Adrian wrapped up the session, teachers applauded dutifully, gathered up their goodie bags of pens, notebooks and Department of Education propaganda before emerging in the afternoon sun. Shelly Beach bay sparkled. A soft breeze was creating the smallest of ripples on the water. The Dog and I know the sight of endless blue sea and the scent of ozone in the air can have a miraculous effect on people.

The committee-slash-catering corps distributed coffee, tea and homemade biscuits to help soothe our audience, who still had to attend one final hour-long session.

Violet sidled up to me as I had a quick cup of coffee at one of the stations. 'Waste of time and money giving teachers a new maths curriculum. They're doing a perfectly good job teaching students using the old maths curriculum.'

At least Violet didn't mention Mrs Rule.

- **Teachers' group workshops**

Adrian, Josh and I rearranged the seats for groups, set up white-boards and butcher's paper. At a recent fiery committee meeting, members had finally accepted that you couldn't have a workshop without group decisions being summarised on large sheets of butcher's paper.

When the teachers returned to the yellow marquee Shelly Beach had worked its magic. They were fed and watered, they had Rosa's free-drink vouchers for the final networking session, *and* the weekend was drawing closer. The Dog took delight in the diversion he created as he worked the room. He likes teachers but not students.

The warmth of the afternoon sun seeping into the marquee had a soporific effect. There was a definite lack of inspired or driven discussion about the new maths curriculum. During the session Adrian managed to discreetly brush by me each time we moved past each other. His hands would rest fleetingly on my back, around my waist, on my shoulders. Once he caught a flyaway curl and placed it behind my ear.

Thankfully the workshop wasn't a total sleep-induced haze. There were a few on-target teachers who volunteered to write up their groups' dot-point solutions. Teachers assembled for a quick presentation from each group and the workshop session slid to an early finish. Soon after the same teachers exited the yellow marquee and ambled along the foreshore to Rosa's pub. No dot-point solutions were required from this session.

Adrian met up with the Ambassador Dog and me. He placed a warm arm around my waist. 'You should be feeling really good, Gina. Today has gone so well.'

I sighed contentedly. 'Thank you. But it's not over yet – red-carpet do, gala barbecue and barn dance full steam ahead.'

Adrian smiled. 'Point taken. But hopefully Digby's red-carpet do will kick-start the festival. Add some zest. Matt's death has been a shock for everyone.' He looked at me intently. 'I arranged for Joan to collect you and take you to Digby's. I'm sorry, but I have to look after the suits. One or two are returning to the city but most are staying behind for Digby's function. I think a few are actually booked into our writers' festival.' Adrian gave me a comforting back rub and a kiss on the cheek. 'We may cross paths when I dash home to change – but let's pledge to meet back at White Sands at midnight.'

I received another discreet kiss and the Dog and I watched Adrian stride away.

The Dog won't admit it, but he is loving his role as Ambassador Dog.

• Pre-red-carpet cocktails

When we arrived home Adrian had been and gone. His Italian dinner suit was missing. In its place was a yellow Post-It note. *I'll be looking out for a hot redhead in a black lace dress at Digby's. Don't be late. I love you. A.*

I measured the Dog's dinner allowance of vitamin-packed dog pellets and then took a shower. I'd have preferred a long relaxing bath – a bath where I could soak away the worries of exes turning up on your territory again – but if you have a bath in Shelly Beach you get the guilts. Three-minute showers are the order of the day. Shelly Beach, like the rest of the peninsula, is recovering from a drought, and locals are seriously waterwise.

After my economical shower I started to prepare for Digby's red-carpet do. I looked at the sliver of a dress Daphne had given me hanging in my wardrobe. It was definitely a 'wow' dress. My mobile rang as I stood there and I ran to answer it. It was Pandora.

'I thought you should know, Gina. I just found out that Lee Wang will be at Digby's red-carpet do tonight. It's best to know before you bump into him.'

Bloody hell!

At the thought of Lee, disturbing thoughts filled my mind – of steamy sex in the shower, takeaway Thai curries, indie music and bicycle rides along cliff tops. When I first moved to Shelly Beach Lee had been a regular visitor at Sea View Cottage to borrow books from Adrian's library. Before long, his visits were for more than just books. We had a fling for a few months, but it was never meant to last. He moved to the city, and I stayed in Shelly Beach.

Pandora continued. 'Lee's done very well for himself in the city. Just opened a third noodle bar as part of his chain. Digby invited him tonight.'

'How did you find out?'

'I saw Lee in Rosa's pub. He told me his crime novel is getting published in Hong Kong. The one he started writing when he was working in Rosa's kitchen. He said he was looking forward to see-ing you tonight. Are you okay?'

'I'm fine, Pandora. I'm a little surprised. Thanks for letting me know in advance. I never expected to see Lee again.'

'Don't worry – it'll be fine. Lee's the ultimate cool guy. He won't tell anyone about the good time you both had when he was work-ing in Shelly Beach last year.'

'He better bloody not. Adrian doesn't know about it.'

Pandora was silent for a moment. 'But Adrian wouldn't mind, would he? He was in the UK then. Before you were together.'

True.

～

I was dressed in my bathrobe, halfway through applying my smoky-eye look, when the doorbell rang. The Dog left my side to do his friendly welcoming bark to Terri, and escorted her into the room.

'Aren't you ready yet?'

I ignored her question. 'You look very pretty!'

Terri was pleased with the compliment. 'Daphne found me this awesome dress. It's a bit Jane Eyre-ish.'

'It *is* a gorgeous frock. It's a perfect style for you. That shot-green taffeta looks sensational with your red hair.' Since resuming my natural colouring I could agree with Terri that being a redhead created more than the usual number of fashion challenges.

'Mum asked me to run ahead and tell you she'll be here in twenty minutes. She's having a bad hair day and she couldn't decide what to wear to Digby's do. Well, she can now because I told her to wear the first dress she tried on.'

'It was a smart move by your mother to get you out of her hair while she gets ready.'

I received a rolled-eyed look. 'You'd better get dressed, Gina. I suppose Adrian's already at Digby's.'

I nodded. 'He has to look after official guests.' I paused and looked away. 'But I've decided not to go. I'll text Adrian. He and Digby can do my festival director welcome bit. No one will miss me at the barbecue later. I'll get an early night's sleep and be fit for the next two days of the festival.'

'You're chickening out because Lee Wang's coming to Digby's red-carpet do!' Terri ignored my cross-eyed look. 'Everyone knows you dated Lee last year, Gina. No one cares. Adrian won't care. He was probably dating some gorgeous woman in the UK.'

Then came part two of Terri's perfectly rational argument. 'Anyway, you *have* to come tonight. Toby and I want to hang out with you and Adrian at the barbecue. We don't want to be at the same table as my mum and his dad. They're *so not* cool.'

I made one last stand to withdraw from Digby's red-carpet do. 'My tropical-island-poisonous-plant rash has returned. By the end of the evening I'll look like a freak.'

Terri did a quick medical inspection. 'You won't see the rash when you wear your black lace dress.'

'But I'll be itchy!'

'Take an antihistamine. Just put your dress on. And finish your make-up. It's going to look good. Start practising your speech. And don't forget your shoes!'

Bloody hell!

Under Terri's watchful eye, I finished applying my make-up and slipped into the 'wow' dress. I sprayed Cabouchard perfume (an Adrian gift) in front of Terri and myself to walk through. This was a Daphne tip: walking through a cloud of perfume prevents it from harming expensive dress fabrics.

We checked our reflections. Terri grinned at hers. 'Cool.'

Joan, mother of bossy teenager, beeped the horn of her car. Potential partner-to-be Paul and son Toby were coming separately. Terri gathered up the Dog as I issued a word of caution. 'Watch the Dog doesn't mark your dress.' The Dog was not happy when Terri wrapped an old towel around him. Daphne and I'd decided to leave Bluey and the Dog at Digby's and collect them after the barbecue.

Terri and the Dog settled in the back seat of her mother's car. 'Don't forget your shoes, Gina!'

I went back to the house to collect my silver heels. I wouldn't put them on until I got to Digby's red carpet. Wearing them was like walking on stilts.

I slithered into Joan's car, restricted by the fragile skin-tight skirt of my black lace number. I exchanged looks with Joan, who passed her heels, which also appeared to require walking-on-stilts skill, over the back seat to her daughter. 'Watch the Dog doesn't eat our shoes. And be careful of your dress.'

Terri crossed her eyes.

'Have you got your speech?'

I smiled my thanks across the back seat to Terri. 'It's written in my head.'

Bloody hell! And the festival proper hasn't even begun yet.

• Red-carpet cocktails

Digby's 1850s elegant homestead, aka the castle, was the perfect venue for our festival function. As we drove up McIntosh Hill, Digby's home glowed ahead of us like a Disney fairytale castle.

Alf and Potholer, our festival Health and Safety team, guided Joan so she could park her car in Digby's spacious grounds. I noticed a flash of snappy dinner jackets beneath Alf and Potholer's fluorescent green safety jackets.

'Save us a drink, Gina,' said Potholer. 'We'll be inside as soon as we sort the parking out.'

I promised.

Joan and I scurried barefoot across the manicured lawns while Terri and the Dog walked beside us. We came to a halt at a completely unnecessary this-way-to-the-red-carpet sign. Digby's red carpet was very obvious. It stretched down the garden path and stopped at the imposing floodlit entrance of the castle.

'Isn't it awesome? Tiffany told me she was hiring a red carpet from an event company.' Terri grinned, her eyes alight.

Joan and I, struggling to put on our killer heels, agreed. Tiffany, Digby's soon-to-move-on assistant, had done a brilliant job.

At the entrance of Digby's castle we stepped off the hired red carpet to make space for Pandora. My friend, looking sparkly in a red sequined frock that showcased her great legs, was directing a photographer to take shots of our (lone) big-time international author, Anton Brandt, and wife Stephanie (looking like she stepped from the pages of *Vogue* in a creamy milk chiffon frock), of course accompanied by our host Digby.

Digby gave us a mini wave when the photos were over, and quickly ushered Anton and Stephanie inside his castle. Pandora's photographer turned his attention to taking shots of Digby's guests as they stepped on to the red carpet, capturing a moment-in-time and probably missing the moment-in-time just as quickly. Hardly photographs to last and pass down to future generations – more likely to appear on Facebook.

Pandora joined us once she'd briefed the photographer on the sort of shots she wanted him to take. We'd only been able to grab a few moments of private consolation and girl talk since Matt's death. I doubted whether she'd really come to terms with it yet. But although she might have been feeling like death, she looked brilliant. Pandora knows the transformative value of make-up. Tonight she'd gone for her 'high-end glam' look.

We exchanged air kisses. 'Are you good?' I touched her arm gently.

'I'm good. Keeping busy has helped,' Pandora said. 'Today and tonight were always going to be our major media hits. The party will give us shots for the celebrity pages of mags and city papers. The telly exposure might work too. Great promotion for next year's festival.'

'Are you serious?'

Pandora laughed.

'I'm definitely not going there. Next year? My goal is to get through the following two days without a major glitch.' I looked at

Pandora, suddenly worried. 'I didn't mean to make Matt's death sound like a glitch. I'm sorry. It's a tragedy.'

'It's all right, Gina. I know.'

I was grateful once more for my understanding friend.

'The successful running of this festival is vital for anyone connected with it . . . and for Shelly Beach.'

At that moment Lee Wang appeared on the red carpet. He looked as good as ever: tall, handsome, wearing a slim-cut dinner suit with his dark hair slicked back in a ponytail. I took a deep breath.

Pandora and I exchanged glances. 'Are you cool?' she asked.

'I'm cool.'

Terri, Joan and the Dog, having posed for their shots on the red carpet, joined me inside Digby's castle. I took the Dog's lead and we quietly vanished down the black-and-white tiled passage leading to the kitchen and the outside verandah. Bluey was already settled and the Dog was happy to join him.

I clicked back on the tiles, past the noisy kitchen. I took another deep breath, balanced on my silver heels, and stepped into what was once the ballroom of Digby's homestead and prepared to circulate. I had to admit I was getting used to the limelight in my role as festival director.

Digby's ballroom was overflowing with suits and frocked-up guests determined to have fun. Sparkling wine from our local winery was being served in long-stemmed flutes and the bubbles were having their effect.

Daphne, Shelly Beach's Anna Wintour, joined me. 'Everyone has scrubbed up well.'

I nodded. Josh, aka Shelly Beach pirate, was at the piano playing his cool Coffee Club jazz. Bianca, adoring wife, joined us. 'Isn't Josh talented?'

We agreed. Alf and Potholer entered the ballroom, now resplendent in their black-tie gear and with wives Beryl and Aphrodite on their arms. They worked through the crowd to join us.

The black-tie dress code on the invitations had caused a slight hiccup for the males of Shelly Beach. Daphne was determined the guys should have a taste of glam, even if they never wanted to taste it again. She wove her magic stylist's wand and wrangled tuxes and sharp suits from a Kingston menswear chain in exchange for a sponsor tag in our writers' festival marketing. Result: the guys on our committee now owned tuxes or suits they could keep for weddings and funerals.

Flutes of sparkling in our hands, we surveyed the room. Digby, looking handsome and debonair, was chatting to Anton Brandt and Stephanie. My eyes searched the room for Adrian. I found him looking good in his Italian dinner suit. He was chatting to a group of education guys but signalled he was working his way across the room to be with me. I ignored the flip in my stomach, and signalled back.

'You look beautiful, Madame Director,' he said when he made it close to me. 'That's some dress!' He placed one of my wild curls behind my ear. I didn't think anyone had connected with our connection. They were too busy checking out Leanne, Digby's publisher.

'If the neckline of her dress was any lower, it'd be a belt!' Bianca said in a loud whisper.

Daphne, our style icon, added a more measured comment. 'It's a designer frock. I'd say the woman hasn't gained value per metre of fabric.'

～

After I delivered my welcome-to-the-festival speech to our guests, plus well deserved thank-yous, Digby declared his red-carpet do open. Josh resumed his background piano playing and the noise level created by guests having a good time began to rise again.

I received a subtle kiss on the cheek as Adrian left to network. I did my required welcome circuit to festival guests, ending back with Bianca, Alf, Beryl, Potholer and Aphrodite.

'Has anyone else got butterflies? I've got butterflies and the festival hasn't even started yet – and I'm still feeling awful about Matt Galinsky,' Bianca said.

We all took a few moments to think about Matt and Dimity.

Pandora joined us and pointed to Atticus. 'I've used Sandy in some quirky shots with Anton and Stephanie. We'll never be able to thank that woman enough.'

True. Without Sandy filling the gaps left by Dimity's absence, we'd be in a big hole. We watched Atticus moving round the room, stopping to shake a giant furry paw with bemused guests. It was hard to visualise the cool Sandy we knew actually inside the mouse suit. Maybe she wasn't inside the suit? Note to self: Don't go down that rabbit hole.

Bianca gave the alert. 'Violet's coming over.'

We watched in awe as Violet threaded her way through the crowd. The eccentric cat-loving cosy-crime writer in the cardigan and slippers had vanished.

'Do you like her hairstyle?' Bianca had cut and styled Violet's plaited granny-bun into a glam silver bob. Wearing Daphne's selection of vintage clothes, a silver crepe pantsuit that fitted Violet's slim figure perfectly, she was transformed into a success-ful whodunit author whose published novel is on sale at Pages Gallery.

Bianca added more. 'Violet's unearthed a few Red Blaze novels she'd hidden under the cats' sofa. Apparently her publishers are considering them!'

The Shelly Beach Writers' Festival committee aka Shelly Beach Writers' Group are very familiar with Red Blaze, Violet's detective character. I was *so* hoping Violet didn't start talking about Mrs Rule, and her new (fictional) murder victim.

Bill Kerr, our short-listed author, and wife Deb joined us and broke the awkward silence created by Violet's arrival. By the smile on her face Violet knew we'd been talking about her makeover.

'Congratulations, Violet!' I said, improvising. 'Heard your excellent publishing news. Imagine finding more Red Blaze novels under the cats' sofa.'

Violet brushed my congratulations aside, her eyes gleaming as she took a sip of bubbly. I was hypnotised by the movement of her silver sequinned earrings as she talked. 'This champers is all right but I'd much prefer a G & T.' She refused a choice of mini quiches offered by one of Digby's catering staff. 'Impossible to eat while you're drinking. I imagine the caterers take into account that guests can't eat and drink at the same time. Make a huge profit. Excuse me.' Violet niftily placed her empty flute on a tray as one of Digby's staff went past. 'I'm going to work the room.' She checked a slip of paper she took from her silver sequinned clutch. 'I need to talk to a few guests.'

My alarm bell sounded as I watched Violet's slim and surprisingly stylish figure weave its way through the crowd. Bloody hell! Stay cool, Gina. Violet usually doesn't talk about plot ideas until she has a first draft on paper.

Alarm bells started ringing again as I watched Digby manoeuvre Lee through the crowd towards our group. I fastened a smile on my face, took a deep breath and handed my empty flute to a passing waiter. I glanced through the crowd – no sign of Adrian.

I would have liked him to be by my side. No matter. This was my territory. I could deal with this.

'Hello, Lee!' said Bianca breezily as Lee and Digby joined us. 'I hear things are going very well for you in the city now.'

Lee smiled, handsome as ever. 'Well, my noodle bars are doing well. Just about to open my third.' He made eye contact with me. 'Hello, Gina.'

I gave him my best relaxed smile. 'Hello, Lee.'

Digby jumped into the conversation, and chitchat between Shelly Beach locals and former Shelly Beach denizen Lee Wang was underway.

I excused myself to check on the dogs and slipped away from the group. A gentle touch on my shoulder made me turn around; Lee was behind me. 'Do you mind if I say hello to Hugo, Gina?'

A lame excuse, but what could I say? I knew the Dog wouldn't acknowledge anyone who called him by a name he'd had in a previous life. We hurried down the hall to the verandah. All was quiet in the moonlight. The dogs were asleep. I smiled at the sight of them curled up together. 'A wasted mission, Lee. I'll pass your best on to the Dog.' I made to go, but Lee reached out a hand and stopped me.

'You look fantastic, Gina.' He gently touched a wayward curl. 'Your hair's different.'

'This *is* my own hair.' I laughed nervously. 'Bianca decided I'd outgrown the multi-coloured edgy cut.'

I controlled the urge to scratch my rash. Instead I concentrated on Lee's eyes. Not for the first time I was really, really grateful to the Dog for all the walks I'd been obligated to take with him, and to Daphne for sourcing such an amazing dress to wear tonight.

Lee took a deep breath and squared his broad shoulders in his tailored tux. He looked different from the Lee I met when I first arrived in Shelly Beach – the intelligent, literary-minded young chef who worked at Rosa's. The sharp-minded young man borrowing novels from Adrian's bookshelves. Lee had grown up.

Adrian probably knew that Lee and I had had a short affair. I didn't question Lee's discretion, but I knew most Shelly Beach locals were aware of it. If not while it was happening, then certainly afterwards – when Lee left Shelly Beach, abandoning his bicycle and chef's job at Rosa's. He drove away in his red Porsche (gift from his parents) like a knight on his charger. (Bianca language.)

I gathered and focused on my platonic feelings. 'I read a great review of one of your noodle bars in the paper recently.'

'We've been getting good press.'

'Are you enjoying life in the city?'

'I am. It'd be better if I wasn't so busy. I'd have more time to concentrate on my writing. And I am thinking of resuming my medical studies. Keep the parents happy.' Lee took my left hand and gently traced the veins on it. 'And what about you, Gina?'

I slowly took my left hand from Lee's hold. 'I'm about to make some big changes in my life. I've been offered a great high-profile job with a city firm. Starting in a week or two.'

'Someone said you'd been working at the Sea Haven library. Are you happy to move on?'

'I have been working at the library – part-time, with an offer to go full-time. But I'm ready to move on and get back to the big wide world again.'

'And your writing?'

'The novel's on hold. I've been playing round with ideas for children's storybooks.'

'Sounds good.' Lee smiled and looked at me more closely. 'And is there a man in your life?'

I smiled back. 'Yes, there's a man in my life.' And there was.

Lee took his cue. He was a smart young man. Moving into safer territory, he pulled the festival program from his pocket. 'I've booked to attend sessions over the weekend. Perhaps we could have a coffee together.'

I avoided the impulse to scratch again and concentrated my gaze on Lee. How could I say no?

'Gina!' It was Violet looking like a stylish grey ghost. 'I thought I'd find you here. Daphne said it was your turn to check on the dogs.' Violet, in her new smooth persona as a successful whodunit author, smiled at Lee. 'Well, you two found a quiet place to catch up on old times. Talk about your writing.'

I gave Violet my mind-your-own-business stare.

She completely ignored me. 'Lee, Digby was looking for you. He wanted to introduce you to some publishers from the city.'

I turned my attention to Lee. 'It was lovely to see you again. Great to catch up with your news.' I gave Lee a motherly kiss on the cheek. I felt his arms tighten around me for a moment, and that was that. He left to join Digby.

'Did you enjoy your reunion?' Violet asked with a raised eyebrow.

I bit my tongue and gave Violet an extremely thin smile. I needed to keep her on side. I watched Violet's stylish back as she disappeared down the hall to continue her schmoozing.

My silver heels were tapping a staccato rhythm on the black-and-white tiles of the hall when I saw Adrian coming towards me.

'I've been looking for you. We need to talk for a few minutes.' And Adrian pushed open a door labelled *Pantry* in old-fashioned script. 'We can talk here.'

Inside the pantry I looked at the shelves, holding a few meagre supplies. Once they would have been packed with essential ingredients to last for months: flour, sugar, tea and local preserved products. Maybe a dead body would be lying on the floor if the pantry was the setting for one of Violet's whodunits.

Adrian looked at me closely with his friendly blue eyes. 'Are you all right? Did something happen?'

'I'm fine. I needed to check on the dogs. And I desperately need to have a scratch. I should have taken an antihistamine tablet earlier.'

Adrian began to laugh as I had a satisfying scratch.

'It's not funny!' I carefully wriggled the fragile black lace skirt back into place. 'Okay. What do we need to talk about?' The buzz of conversation floated up the hall. The clatter of food preparation and the sound of voices were coming from the kitchen. 'We'd better keep the door open. It'll look really bad if someone sees us emerging from the pantry.'

Adrian smiled as he wedged the pantry door open with a sack of potatoes. 'Now it looks like we're having a business conference.'

'Don't laugh.' I looked at my watch. 'We have to get everyone on the buses by eight to be at the Shepherds' property for the barbecue and barn dance.'

An annoyingly calm Adrian checked his watch. 'We have at least ten minutes before we start to get people on the buses, Gina.'

And he kissed me. Bloody hell!

Adrian was now holding my face in his hands and looking into my eyes.

'I have to focus! What do we need to talk about?'

'I can't remember.'

'You said it was important.'

Adrian was still gazing at me in the way that makes me go to jelly. 'Did I?' He kissed me again. 'I think I just needed to tell you how absolutely ravishing I find you. Now let's get people on the buses.'

I couldn't help smiling.

'I have to drive our VIP guests to the Shepherds' property, but we can go home together as soon as you're ready to leave the barbecue.'

'I can't go home with you. I'm on the roster to clean the yellow marquee with our Health and Safety team. Pandora's bringing our cleaning gear and we're going to change at the marquee.'

'Not a problem – we'll go to the marquee together, and I'll help you with the cleaning.' He gave me another really good kiss before we left the pantry.

As we walked up the hall together, Adrian said casually, 'I saw Lee Wang leaving just a moment ago. He's a talented and interesting young man. Will he be staying for the festival?'

I went with the Dog's preferred reply when you're thrown a dodgy question. I ignored the question.

• Barbecue and barn dance

Digby announced to the guests, 'The buses are here, folks.'

Networking and mingling came to a halt. The last mouthfuls of bubbly were swallowed and the lights in Digby's castle were dimmed. Guests who'd paid handsomely – or were funded by their respective government departments – made their way to the entrance of the castle. They queued in orderly fashion to board the gratis buses from the Sea Haven bus service to journey to the Shepherds' property, a half-hour's drive away.

Our bus was strangely quiet. Very little chitchat. Committee members were mulling over a successful Day One and preparing for Day Two – our festival proper. Matt's sudden death was still playing on our minds.

I purposefully chose to sit with Violet. No way did I want her to exchange a murder-focused conversation with anyone but me.

I thought she might have dropped off to sleep but I was sadly mistaken.

'Mrs Rule's come to a halt in her investigation. It's disappointing. There was no attempt to secure the murder scene. The local police saw no reason to use their yellow *Do Not Cross* tape in the celebrity room at the B&B.

'Mrs Rule has no access to medical advice to pin down the exact time of the murder. And she has no chance of getting forensics to work on the evidence she collected from the celebrity's room.'

I listened to Violet describe further obstacles in Mrs Rule's detecting path. 'There's no CCTV footage to show people coming to or going from the B&B on the night of the celebrity's murder. But the five-star hotel has CCTV, as do some of the rental properties.'

It was useless feigning sleep. I watched Violet retrieve her iPhone from her silver sequinned clutch. The screen lit up. Her finger moved to the Notes section. She keyed in *Mobile phone missing.*

'The fact the celebrity's mobile phone is missing can either be a red herring or a clue. Haven't decided yet.' Violet keyed in *Female Suspects.* 'It was a bloodless murder. Females usually commit bloodless murders. Lack of bloodstains and splatters in the celebrity's room is a genuine setback for Mrs Rule.'

Bloody hell! Violet continued relaying her whodunit plot.

'The celebrity was a good-looking, sexy guy. He was having flings with several local women during his stay in the seaside town. They'll go on Mrs Rule's list of suspects.'

Fortunately the sight of the flare-edged driveway leading to the Shepherds' barn put a stop to Violet's morbid conversation.

Adrian was waiting when our bus arrived. He put a comforting arm around me and kissed me on the cheek.

'I have to talk to you about Violet,' I said in a low voice. My eyes widened as I glanced around the barn. It looked amazing. 'And I've wasted energy worrying about this function – haven't I?'

'You have.'

'I should have known Digby would never attach his name to a flaky event.'

Bianca joined us. 'Josh is setting up his band. The barn looks gorgeous, doesn't it? It just oozes ambience.'

Our Health and Safety team had done a brilliant job in their alternate role as decorators. The Shepherds' barn made a charming setting, lit with lanterns and decorated with farm equipment and huge branches of indigenous flora. Tables were set with the marked place cards Tiffany had made.

Potholer and sons were manning the barbecue. They looked extremely cool. Dinner jackets and black ties were temporarily abandoned for full chefs' jackets. Seafood entrée choices were already being rolled out.

'Weather's holding up, Gina. Good crop of stars.' Potholer and I stopped to gaze at the huge canopy of stars overhead.

Adrian gave his apologies and left to network. Potholer and I watched him disappear into the well-dressed crowd. This was important networking time for him. The perfect chance to gain funds for our community project.

'You have to have guts to do what Adrian is doing,' mused Potholer. 'It's not easy working a barn full of black ties and frocked-up women, cajoling money for a good cause.'

Alf and Potholer are well aware of the tactics needed to extract donations. They're constantly looking for donations to keep the Shelly Beach lifesavers', footy, cricket, and birdwatchers' clubs afloat.

I stood for a moment and watched the guests as they moved about the room. Anton Brandt was deep in conversation with his

Australian publishing team. I didn't doubt Anton was well aware that networking was vital in moving his novels from the shelf or online. Stephanie was looking unbelievably lovely in her creamy chiffon number. She'd be making sure they attended every function with networking opportunities before they moved on to the big-time writers' festival tour.

I began to move quietly around the room, talking to as many guests as possible. Adrian found me half an hour later. We watched guests gyrating gently on the crowded dance floor. When the tempo changed, Digby cleared an area on the dance floor to do a flamboyant salsa with Leanne, his publisher.

Adrian smiled at me. 'Care to dance?'

We stepped onto the dance floor and snatched a few moments of peace in each other's arms – and it did allow me an occasional unobtrusive scratch as we moved to a slow-tempo number. Then we left to join the line at the barbecues for lamb on the spit, jacket potatoes and salad.

Beryl was in charge of the catering corps providing 150 serves of pavlova and fruit salad. 'It's not rocket science, Gina. One large pavlova serves twelve guests. Divide the number of guests by twelve and you know – with one or two extra pavs for emergencies – how many pavlovas you need to bake.'

She did have trouble sourcing fresh fruit for the fruit salad, though. 'It's not soft-fruit harvest time. We went with cans of fruit and livened it up with frozen berries.'

Note to self: Tell Beryl the dessert is to die for.

Digby had negotiated with local peninsula wineries to provide wine as well as staff to serve the wine. As usual, the Shelly Beach catering corps provided lemonade. 'When life deals you lemons, make lemonade' is a well-applied adage in Shelly Beach.

Digby arranged a classy finale to the night. Josh, aka Shelly

Beach's DJ, played Glen Miller tracks as a tribute to Henry Shepherd. According to Henry's diaries, it was evident that Glen Miller dance music was very close to his heart during his Second World War service. It was amazing how many high-flying guests shed their poise and emerged on the barn dance floor as so-you-think-you-can-dance finalists.

Daphne said she'd take the Dog and I could collect him in the morning. The Dog was pleased – he wanted to go to Daphne's yoga on the beach.

Adrian took our coffee on the balcony and watched the sun come up over Shelly Beach bay. It was amazing how wonderful a good night's sex could make you feel. We sipped our coffee and exchanged our dot-points for the day. Heaven!

Adrian was collecting Anton Brandt and Stephanie and taking them for a buffet breakfast at Digby's castle. 'I'll have Anton and Stephanie back at the yellow marquee in plenty of time for Anton's keynote.'

I was missing the Dog. He liked to watch sunrises too. 'I have to collect the Dog from Daphne.' I checked my Day Two to-do list. 'I'm going to make sure Rosa's cousins haven't drowned anyone on their fishing excursion, and I have to check that the welcome coffee and muffins at the marquee are ready to go.'

'Have I told you that you look fantastic?'

I accepted Adrian's compliment with a smile. I felt I'd embraced my chic potential to its max today. I was wearing my jeans-and-blazer combo from Daphne's treasure trove of fashion, and I'd taken note of her advice: *A blazer dresses up a spring casual look. It avoids the door-to-door salesman look but still achieves a breezy feel.*

'Don't forget you're looking after the yellow marquee sessions after Anton's keynote. I'm looking after the sessions in the blue marquee.'

Adrian smiled and checked the schedule I gave him. He's used to my hands-on approach. I pointed to his schedule. 'Lionel's session should be fine, if a little dry. He's actually finished his novel that's taken four years to write. The rest of the sessions in your marquee have the potential to go pear-shaped. Keep your fingers crossed that Anton Brandt delivers his *Tips for Series Writing* session without a hitch. I'm banking on Stephanie keeping him on track.'

Adrian nodded. 'She will.'

'After lunch Violet's taking her *Writing Cosy Murders* session, and she's doing her book-brain thing when you don't know if she's talking about a plot for her new book or actual real-life stuff.'

I had Adrian's full attention.

'If Violet goes off on a tangent about a celebrity being murdered in a small seaside town – shut her down immediately.'

'I will.'

I received a comforting hug and a really good kiss. 'And don't worry about Dimity's session. Alex Dessaix and Atticus are going to put Plan B into action. Any questions?'

'Not one.'

'There's a book signing at Digby's gallery during the lunch break. Available writers' group members will be signing our *Novel Dictionary*.'

'Good.'

'And there's an invitation-only buffet dinner at the castle tonight. We need to at least do a drop-in there. Beryl's poetry slam . . .' I looked at Adrian. 'We *have* to go to that. It's going to be huge.'

'Understood.'

'Then we need to show our faces at Josh's literary quiz at the pub. And clean the two marquees.'

'Do you want to come home and change when the sessions are over?'

'I'm not sure.'

'I'll put a tie in my pocket in case we can't get home.'

I gave Adrian my rolled-eye look. He watched and waited while I packed a towel, my toiletries, make-up, two chic crush-proof tops in spicy tones, a crush-proof swishy, pale-orange skirt and dangly earrings in my air-stewardess bag. I hesitated over whether to add a pair of comfy peep-toe ink-blue stilettos, but then I packed them too. Pandora says calling stilettos 'comfy' is a paradox. I'd found if I had to concentrate on balancing I didn't worry too much about other stuff.

Adrian promised to leave my air-stewardess case at Rosa's. He was being so cool and understanding, and I *so* hated the fact that he only needed a tie in his pocket to be prepared for any occasion. I watched him store my luggage in his car. He saluted me with his schedule and sent me a kiss as he drove off.

It felt weird walking along the beach without the Dog. I kept looking behind me to make him hurry up. When I arrived at Daphne's yoga on the beach I found the Dog lying close to Bluey. Daphne took a few minutes away from her meditating people to give me a gift: a fabulous long drifty scarf covered in splotches of blue and orange. 'It's the perfect addition to your festival-director look, Gina!'

A quick hug and a thank-you.

The Dog and I waited on the sand while Rosa's fisherman cousins returned with a full boatload of festival attendees, dry and happy. A couple of delighted attendees stopped to show us their catches – glistening snapper.

The Dog and I took a shortcut through the camping section on the foreshore and caught a couple coming back from skinny-dipping in the bay. 'Lost our tent! We know it's near the laundry.' We were happy to point them in the right direction.

Another camping attendee was amazed his tent had stood up all night. 'I had one pole over after I put the tent up.' You can be lucky.

Committee members had decided to meet at Piece of Cake for coffee or breakfast. As we crossed Beach Road I noticed the traffic detour signs were already set up. I wasn't sure I could eat breakfast. My stomach was a churning mess. Bianca had already arrived. Pandora and Sandy in her mouse suit followed soon after, Sandy carrying Atticus's head as usual. 'Impossible to eat when you wear the head!' We understood. Then came more exchanges of group sympathy and concern for Dimity.

Sandy filled us in on Dimity's progress. 'She's feeling a little better. Geraldine's looking after her this morning. Good news, Gina – Dimity's cool to take her session this afternoon. I'll get Atticus to help, and Alex Dessaix will help too.'

'Really? She's okay to do it?' I sighed in relief. My Plan B wouldn't be required after all.

Breakfast orders were served. The only members of the committee to eat a full Shelly Beach breakfast were Alf and Potholer. The rest of us averted our eyes from their plates of runny eggs, bacon, mushies and baked beans and checked our schedules. 'Everyone cool with the dual sessions? If anything goes wrong in the yellow marquee, tell Adrian. I'll be at the blue marquee,' I said.

'The timing's going to be important!' Bianca noted as she ran her finger down her schedule.

She was right. Sessions had to start on time and end on time – otherwise chaos would ensue. There were lots of hugs and kisses and good-luck wishes as the committee members departed to promote Shelly Beach for the next two days as a small piece of paradise for readers and writers. I pinned the Dog's Ambassador Dog rosette to his collar and we walked over to the yellow marquee.

- **Anton Brandt's keynote address**

Coffee and muffin smells greeted us as we entered the spacious foyer of the yellow marquee. Violet was arranging blueberry muffins carefully on a plate. She and friend Scarlett had already set up the coffee, herbal and ordinary tea, orange juice and water. Wearing her health-smart plastic gloves, Violet was sprinkling the muffins with icing sugar and constructing mouth-watering muffin towers. I was *so* hoping Violet was not wearing the health-smart plastic gloves she'd worn to clean up Matt and his room. Don't go there, Gina.

Soon our 300-seat state-of-the-art marquee was practically full with our paid-up writers' festival attendees. The air was filled with the buzz of an enthusiastic audience. I watched Adrian enter the marquee. He sent me his special wink as he assisted Anton and Stephanie on to the stage.

I had goosebumps all over. Shelly Beach *was* going to have a brilliant writers' festival. A writer's festival to remember. A festival that made its mark. I walked on to the stage, shook hands with Anton and Stephanie and gave my official welcome speech. Then I took my seat beside Stephanie.

Adrian gave an entertaining introduction for Anton. Even if our audience had never heard of Anton Brandt, they were suitably impressed with Adrian's intro and showed their approval when Anton Brandt stood up and walked to the podium. He looked very natty in his well-cut suit and Italian shoes. Stephanie too was looking good in a cream designer suit; her pale blonde hair gleamed under the lights. I watched as she elegantly crossed her long legs and fastened her gaze on her celebrity-author husband.

Anton spoke in a commanding voice, reading from his notes on the podium stand and checking every now and then on the yellow marquee's state-of-the-art autocue. He engagingly recounted every would-be writer's dream of how his first novel was found in the slush pile and gained overnight success. He reminded would-be authors that the famous adage, 'Don't give up your day job', was still excellent advice. 'You'll starve to death if you don't get a regular job with regular wages while you're writing "the" novel.'

Anton explained that he wrote his first novel in early morning stints while he was still practising law. He took three hard years to complete it. 'But since 1980 I've been writing a novel a year.'

He talked about yearly deadlines being a spur yet at the same time a distraction – especially when you have to do the publicity circuit for each novel. At this point in his keynote he had the audience in the palm of his hand. Then came the terrifying glitch. I caught it first. He began to repeat what he'd already said.

Just as he was about to launch into the story of how he wrote his first novel, redux, Stephanie jumped up from her seat. Taking measured steps in her elegant heels, she walked calmly over to the confused Anton. She arranged the papers in front of him, pointing to the autocue.

I had my heart in my mouth. I watched Stephanie calmly walking back to her seat as if she were on a models' runway. She sat down again, adjusted her long legs, and placed her hands, adorned with their chickpea-sized flashing diamonds, in her lap. Once more she fastened her gaze on husband Anton.

Anton shuffled his papers and filled the awkward silence with a manly chuckle. And then he took his audience with him as he joked about jetlag and autocue technical malfunctions. Rising to the challenge, he concluded his keynote address on a high to a tumultuous round of applause from his captive audience. My heart was still racing as Adrian and I watched Stephanie and Anton leave the stage. Anton was gripping Stephanie's hand.

I took centre stage again, advising attendees that Anton would be signing copies of his latest novel *Conspicuous Pirates* at Pages Gallery and to follow the directions on their programs to (hopefully) find their complimentary tea and coffee.

Adrian slipped an arm around my waist as the attendees dispersed from the marquee. 'I'm taking Anton and Stephanie back to Crow's Nest after the signing, but I'll be straight back.'

'Is Anton okay?'

'Stephanie's making him have a rest before his next session. That was a very smooth catch-up on her part. Anton can't still have jetlag – he's been in Shelly Beach for over a week.'

I didn't think it was jetlag either, but I couldn't worry about it now. I was trying to put together a Plan B in case Anton didn't make his next session. 'Could you take the *Tips for Series Writing* session if you had to? Or maybe Stephanie could read Anton's notes. Say Anton's got pneumonia.'

'Don't panic. It'll be cool. I'm sure Anton will make it. He's a professional.' Adrian held my waist a little tighter. 'We're off to a good start for your festival, Gina.' And he gave me his special smile. 'I'll catch up with you in the lunch break.'

We'd avoided a potential catastrophe. I was standing there, enveloped in a warm fuzzy feeling from Adrian's comforting words when Violet joined me. 'Well, that was a close shave! Anton can't manage without Stephanie, but Stephanie can manage very well without him.' I gave Violet my keep-your-voice-down glare, and she harrumphed off.

Bloody hell!

- **Blue-marquee morning sessions**

The Dog and I decided to detour up Shortcut Lane to the blue
marquee. I was concentrating on finding my calm zone. Day One
had been a success. Our main keynote event had been a success –
despite potential dodginess. I kept my fingers crossed as I added
aloud, 'Today should go well, don't you think?'

No comment from the Dog. He and Bluey had an interesting
conversation that morning with a bichon frise that was also attending yoga. Evidently the bichon frise's owner had given up his day
job to write a novel, but was barely earning enough money to pay
for dog food. The Dog wondered whether the less-than-successful
owner could write feature articles for a pet magazine and negotiate
payment in cans of dog food.

We caught a glimpse of Violet in the crowd, ducked our heads
and stepped inside Rosa's beer garden. Siobhan O'Reilly, editor,
and April Somers, romance novelist, were preparing to take their
morning sessions. (I quickly checked my program. Not together –
one after the other.) April, aka dental therapist with the toothy
smile, was setting up a back-of-the-room sales table for her novels.

Already seats in the blue marquee were filling. I took a seat
myself and sat in on – and thoroughly enjoyed – Siobhan's excellent session on self-editing: how to edit your manuscript before
you hand it over to an editor. It saves time and money! The Dog
and I stepped into the pub for a breather before April's session
started, only to be met with a flustered Rosa. 'We have a small blop
on the radar, Gina.'

'Blip. What kind of blip, Rosa?'

'Sergio can't cook. His mama wrote his cookbook. And she's
not here.'

'What?'

Against the committee's better judgement, it was agreed that

280

Rosa's sister's son, Sergio Bartelli, the famous international goalie and now cookbook writer, would do a cooking demo and flog his cookbook during the lunchtime break.

From outside the blue marquee I listened to Bianca's voice introducing April Somers, the sound of clapping, and then the confident April launching into her presentation. I checked my watch: spot on with their start. I relaxed enough to be able to concentrate on Rosa's blip.

When I went back to the pub, Rosa was standing with her hot young nephew with lustrous dark curls and a white smile.

'Gina, this is Sergio, my nephew. And this is his book.' She held up a swish-looking cookbook with a grinning Sergio on the cover.

Sergio gave me his white-teeth smile and a firm handshake. 'Sorry about this, Gina. I wanted to cancel, but my manager said no.' Sergio looked over my shoulder as I flipped through the pages of his beautifully designed cookbook. 'We used my mum's recipes.' Sergio shrugged his broad shoulders. 'I've sampled them all, but I don't have time to cook.'

Of course a famous international soccer player wouldn't have time to cook.

'We've got all the ingredients to make vee-ghan burgers,' Rosa said. 'Sergio says he can read from his cookbook, give a commentary, and you can follow his instructions. He and his mama did it like that on morning telly one time. You can do this, Gina.'

I looked at Sergio's team, setting up a glam demo kitchen in Rosa's pub. I needed to get through this lunchtime cooking demo without it ending as a farce.

'Yes, I can do this.' I smiled at Sergio and Rosa.

Sergio clasped my hand with a sigh of relief and Rosa grinned. We started to set out the bowls of ingredients on the table and I studied the 'vee-ghan' burger recipe in the cookbook.

'Watch the flies, Gina!' Rosa was shooing a hungry blowfly away. 'Don't get Sergio's book dirty. It doesn't matter about vee-ghan burgers. People can buy tasty burgers in my pub. But you can't sell a dirty book!'

True. Rosa stopped to give her gorgeous Sergio a big hug and kiss. 'Don't forget to tell people to buy the book, Gina. Get healthy! Kick goals like Sergio.'

Sergio shot me a charming apologetic smile. I could see his minders setting up stacks of books beside a register on a temporary sales table.

And then I heard a huge round of applause to mark the end of April's presentation, and attendees were leaving the blue marquee. Sergio's reputation as an international soccer player was pulling the crowds towards our demo.

Luckily, Terri appeared beside me and I hastily put the Dog in her charge.

'Message from Adrian. The two sessions in the yellow marquee were cool. Anton was cool.'

'Thank heavens for that. Now wish me luck,' I said to Terri as I tied on the brand-embellished apron I was offered by one of Sergio's team.

The charismatic Sergio handed me a bowl of grated carrot and launched into a bravura performance of how to cook vegan burgers when you're not actually cooking them yourself. Showtime!

Fifteen minutes later, Sergio had beautifully plated up a per-fectly cooked vegan burger and took a photogenic bite from it to thundering applause. Rosa hugged me as Sergio headed over to sign books. 'Beaut-i-ful work, Gina! Look! Sergio's selling hun-dreds of books!' Fans were lining up to shell out their hard-earned cash for a signed cookbook by the top international soccer player.

Pandora and her photographer came over. They were rapt – they had great shots of sexy Sergio eating a burger with his adoring fans. 'Sergio's huge, isn't he? His cookbook sales have raced past his kids' soccer book.' Pandora smiled. 'And his billboard promos for designer underpants probably helped too.'

No comment.

• Afternoon session in the blue marquee

I was still flushed with the success of my cooking demo when I bumped into Clever Angela, aka Kenneth's wife no. 2. Angela was excited. She'd just bought a stack of Dimity Honeysuckle's books – probably for her reference and not for young Griffin. 'Gina! Hello. I'm just off to Dimity's session. The festival's jumping, isn't it?'

I was magnanimous. It was nice to see Angela enjoying herself. I gave her my I'm-glad-Kenneth's-married-to-you smile and told her I hoped we'd meet again during the festival. (Lie.) I was taking note of Rosa's advice: you need to keep on friendly terms with your exes.

Next up on the blue marquee schedule, Digby was introducing local short-listed author Bill Kruger for his session and then Bill, local short-listed author, was introducing Digby, memoir writer, for his session. Bill and Digby had been delighted by the idea of presenting each other. In a small town like Shelly Beach everyone has to be prepared to say something nice about something or someone at some time – in public. Alf always followed Western movie star John Wayne's advice when called upon to talk about others in public: 'Talk low, talk slow and don't say too much.'

Bill's presentation went well, and I was preparing myself to sit through Digby's when I realised I needed a break. Digby's entourage – publisher, assistant and publicist – would look after him anyway. They were setting up his notes on the lectern, placing a bottle of boutique sparkling water within his reach – everything short of giving him a pre-presentation massage.

I enjoyed working with Digby as a colleague, and – ignoring one serious Moet-induced misjudgement – I'd happily work with him in the future. Just not right now. I escaped to Rosa's pub, straight into the clutches of Violet, armed with a picnic basket.

'Sometimes that man gets up my nose.' I assumed Violet was referring to Digby. I would presume the feeling was reciprocated. The incorrigible Violet continued, 'I've just finished my session. It went down well. Adrian did a good job for me in his introduction. I've got a thermos of Earl Grey, some cucumber sandwiches and gingernut biscuits – won't you join me? I thought we'd take a breather on the foreshore before we race off for the night's entertainments. There's one or two things I want to run past you, Gina.'

I had an out. 'Sorry, Violet. I have to hang around the blue marquee in case I'm needed.'

Violet was not to be deterred. 'Then we'll have to take a breather on the verandah.' She led me onto Rosa's deck, produced an embroidered cloth from her picnic basket, shook it out and spread it over the nearest table. She set out the cucumber sandwiches and gingersnap biscuits on bakelite picnic plates. Then came the two matching bakelite cups and saucers. She poured our Earl Grey and offered me a wafer-thin cucumber sandwich and a biscuit. I refused the gingersnap. Seeing April, romance novelist and dental therapist, had reminded me I need a dental check-up. A cavity could cause havoc in my carefully controlled budget.

Violet took a small bite of a cucumber sandwich and a sip of her tea. 'I thought you should know Geraldine's letting Matt Galinsky's room to some festival attendees. It shouldn't be a problem. I've used plenty of air-freshener and fumigated Matt's bed, remade it with the rosebud sheets and matching doona. Guests won't have a clue someone died in the bed. I'm sure thousands of hotel and B&B guests all over the globe don't realise they're sleeping in a bed someone has died in at some time.'

As was often the case, Violet's conversation left me speechless.

She shrugged and continued. 'I've been working on a motive, means and opportunity for Mrs Rule. The motive is obviously sex and-slash-or money.'

I winced. Violet was in her book brain again.

'Tom, the Sea Haven police sergeant, told me most murders are committed because of the four Ls.'

'Excuse me?'

'Love, lucre, lust and loathing. The most common cause of murder is love.' Violet took another sip of her tea. 'Mrs Rule found several false passports with the celebrity's photographs on them when she was cleaning out his room. And his laptop has turned up with the hard disk wiped clean. Someone like my friend Scarlett, who's a genius at discovering clues on hard drives, could restore the murder victim's files. Mrs Rule's cagey because she doesn't want the murderer to know she's on to her.'

Bloody hell! I checked my watch. 'Sorry, Violet, we might need to cut this short. I need to change for the buffet dinner.'

'Amazing how the time flies!' Violet methodically packed her picnic basket. An adventurous seagull landed on the railing of the verandah and Violet threw him a remaining soggy cucumber sandwich. She ignored Rosa's *Don't Feed the Seagulls* sign.

'See you tonight at Digby's,' I said to the busily packing whodunit author. Violet didn't hear me. She'd turned her hearing aid off. I glanced at her as I headed back to the blue marquee: a sweet Miss Marple type from an Agatha Christie novel. I'd no doubt by the time Adrian and I fronted up at Digby's buffet dinner, Miss Marple would have flown the coop. The sophisticated crime fiction author with the stylish silver bob would be networking her heart out.

At the entrance of the blue marquee I listened as Bill Kruger thanked Digby for his presentation, then came an enthusiastic round of clapping. The crowd of (hopefully) satisfied readers and writers spilled out from the marquee ready for a night of exciting umbrella-event entertainment – Beryl's poetry slam in the community hall and a literary quiz at Rosa's.

To my great delight, Adrian joined me. He had the Dog with him. 'Everything okay here?'

'It was until Violet turned up.'

Adrian grinned. 'She delivered an entertaining session. Her audience loved it.'

'She didn't talk about an idea she's had for a new book?'

'No. We've enough time to drive you home so you can change for Digby's buffet.'

Thank goodness. 'I need to collect my bag.'

As I picked up my air-stewardess bag in Rosa's storeroom, I found her emptying the contents of her *Complaints* box into the bin. 'One night! Already people complain about noises in bedrooms. Waiting in queues for the bathrooms. What do they expect? If people have noisy sex in bedrooms – not my problem! If people have sex in the shower – not my problem! Just bang on walls and doors. Hurry guests up!'

I collected my bag from her storeroom and made a quick exit.

• Buffet dinner

Attendees had travelled up McIntosh Hill to Digby's castle to continue partying. Digby's smiling caterers were back again, serving hungry guests from tantalising platters of seafood and salads.

Adrian went to talk to Digby while I joined committee members, who had settled to enjoy the invitation-only 'fork' buffet. Bianca was impressed. 'Digby's incredibly generous.'

Pandora gave us her raised eyebrow look. 'This isn't Digby's doing.' She looked around the room. 'This function is sponsored by Dimity's UK publishers.'

We checked out Digby's ballroom. The Singing Bird branding jumped out at us from the tasteful signs and banners and a smiling PR assistant was manning a table selling Dimity's picture storybooks.

'Tiffany put a heap of work into getting this function happening. If Digby had outlaid any of his cash, you can guarantee our distinguished local self-promoter would have let us know about it. And have retained invoices and receipts to give to his tax consultant.'

I could see Bianca storing promotional know-how in her smart young brain. I quickly surveyed the room. It contained a collection of people I didn't want to meet – but would have to meet – and be polite to. I caught a glimpse of handsome Lee in the crowd. I would definitely avoid talking to him again. Maybe in twenty years' time? Clever Angela and King Rat ex-husband were chatting to Dimity's publishers. Probably making contacts for Angela's unwritten children's picture storybooks.

I waved to Dr Fenella Wright, my former tutor. I was *so* glad she only remembered me as someone with terrible root-canal trouble.

I checked my watch. Only fifteen minutes left before I had to head off to Beryl's poetry slam. I caught a glimpse of Violet in another stylish outfit. Definitely another to avoid. Adrian appeared next to me with a flute of champagne.

'I'm going to circulate quickly before the poetry slam.'

Adrian gave me a quick kiss. 'No problem. Meet you at Digby's entrance in fifteen.'

And he did.

's poetry slam

removed my ink-blue peep-toe stilettos to limp across the sandy foreshore with Adrian to the community hall. It was bulging at the seams with poets. Adrian was staggered by the numbers. We met Alf at the door, oozing pride as he gazed at his long-time partner. 'Look at the woman. She's amazing.'

Beryl, Shelly Beach's newly blossomed poet, waved to us. I ticked off a dot-point in my head. Up until a few days ago Beryl was in meltdown, thinking no one would come to her poetry slam. Writers' group members (mostly novel writers, not the best or most enthusiastic poets in the world) had been pushed into writing poems on a sea theme for Beryl. We'd promised to read them at the poetry slam in case no one turned up. Looking at the packed hall, I felt nothing but intense relief at not having to read my tragic poem about a seagull. Maybe I could write a picture storybook about a seagull instead?

Alf brought us up to speed. 'There are so many poets willing to read their poems Beryl's decided to pull names out of a hat. It's all the advertising on the blog that's done it.'

I noticed Violet was sitting in the front row. How did she get here before us? She'd probably written a poem about murder and mayhem in a small seaside town.

After listening to one or two poems performed, we moved on to check on Josh's literary quiz at Rosa's. Josh's umbrella event hasn't caused me one sleepless night. I concurred with Bianca's opinion of her hubby: 'You never have to worry about an event when Josh's in charge. He's awesome at crowd control. It's his teachery thing.'

True. Rosa's pub was rocking off its foundations when we arrived. Josh's band Ellipsis played mostly mainstream rock with indie touches. They left hard rock behind (Rosa couldn't stand the noise). Ellipsis was playing to a packed dance floor of partying festival attendees.

Bianca waved to us to join her. She too had left Digby's buffet early, and was sitting at the table reserved for the band. 'I caught the end of the literary quiz. You should have been here. It was like the Battle of the Titans. There were three main tables competing for prizes – only bottles of wine, but it was like they were competing for a trip to Europe.'

Not surprising. Most 'fun' competitive events in Shelly Beach end up as do-or-die battles.

'The two tables over there,' Bianca pointed discreetly, are publishing industry guys, and the table over there . . .' Bianca pointed in the other direction, 'is Digby's academic mates.'

Siobhan, Bill's much-loved editor, came over to say hello. She'd been on one of the publishing industry tables. 'Gina! We won. Beat Piers' table!'

I hugged the gutsy young woman. 'Congratulations!'

Siobhan took a sip of her wine. 'Would you believe he's already hooked up with another editor? He's left his editor-in-training at the B&B. Not surprisingly, really.' Siobhan laughed. 'After all, she didn't know the difference between "your" and "you're". Hopefully this editor-*out*-of-training will be able to help Piers with his grammar issues.'

Adrian looked confused. I whispered, 'I'll fill you in later.'

'Sorry, Gina, must dash,' continued Siobhan. 'Isn't Alex Dessaix a talented guy? I'm thinking I can do some agenting for him. Catch up with you tomorrow when I do my second session.'

We watched Siobhan, well on the road to recovery from broken-heart syndrome, emerging from the cold ashes of a burnt-out relationship (Bianca language), weave her way across the pub to her young author–illustrator looking rakish and handsome.

drian had been talking to Potholer earlier and had some good
ws. 'We're excused from cleaning duty. Digby's catering crew is
doing it. Digby's covering their wages!'

'Excellent!'

'And what time are you meeting your new boss tomorrow?'

Bloody hell! I did a quick mental flick through Sunday's crowded
schedule. 'I'm meeting Rod Lidner after the festival has wrapped.
At Rosa's pub at six. We're going to work out a starting date.'

'You've done a brilliant job today. Now, let me take you home . . .'

DAY THREE

I quickly quietened the alarm. We left Adrian sleeping and the
Dog and I crept onto the balcony. 'Life's made up of decisions and
accidents, Dog. Today is a decision day.'

The Dog was well aware of decisions and accidents. You made
a decision: you decided to run away. You dug and dug and dug a
hole under the fence. You scrambled under the fence. The road to
freedom stretched before you. Then came the accident. You ran
straight into the arms of a council dog catcher.

'I *so* need today to go well. I don't want my new boss to turn up
and get sucked into chaotic Day Three vibes. Rod Lidner should
inhale the vibes of a boutique writers' festival that leaves partic-
ipants and residents of a small seaside town feeling elated and
happy. And that gives me the kudos required to make an attractive
salary package an irresistible salary package.'

No comment.

'I admit one bad day does not a career break, but I'd prefer to
finish the festival on a high note.'

The Dog agreed. Since he's known about our move to the city,
he's been checking out a new career in advertising. According to
his research, advertising companies are looking for dogs that can

sit. It didn't matter if you had one ear that wouldn't stand up or one ear that wouldn't hang down, uneven teeth, a crooked tail – you were in demand if you could sit.

The Dog has a talent for sitting.

I quietly checked my wow-the-festival wardrobe for the last time. I went with a jeans-and-blazer combo again – this time the inky-blue blazer with an apricot shirt and espadrilles. My feet were killing me. I added a stand-out element – a (fake) sapphire bracelet. (According to Daphne, one great element could lift an outfit.) I quietly packed a plunging jersey number in purple in my air-stewardess luggage just in case. I planned to leave the case with Rosa on the off-chance something disastrous happened to my jeans-and-blazer combo before I met my new boss. I added a pair of new-season lizard-skin heels that an impulse buyer had abandoned at Daphne's shop before the new season began.

Adrian was still asleep. Last night we'd agreed he shouldn't attend the Breakfast with the Birds session. I needed him to hold the fort at the festival. I left a reminder note on his pillow and then stuck similar notes throughout the house.

Good morning, Adrian!
1. *Can you check if the marquee cleaning went okay?*
2. *Make sure your discussion panel members get to the yellow marquee on time.*
3. *I'll be at Piece of Cake before the first session for a cup of coffee.*
4. *You snore adorably.*

I set my three alarm clocks to allow Adrian plenty of time for breakfast and to get ready. We crept out of the house.

Shelly Beach's white sand was packed with seagulls.

Standing-room only. Evidently the seagulls' satnav had sent out an alert: cold chips in Shelly Beach. The Dog did his usual stuff – chasing after the seagulls until they took off into the blue sky or settled on the waves. He returned exhausted. Too many gulls to chase for one small dog.

We weaved our way through the sleeping campers' tents on the foreshore to the yellow marquee. I left the Dog with Daphne and my bag with Rosa, and boarded the Breakfast with the Birds bus waiting outside the yellow marquee. An hour later Adrian met me outside Piece of Cake with a smile and a kiss. He handed the Dog over.

'How was Breakfast with the Birds?'

'Alf and his birdo club gave an entertaining yet informative talk about our endangered hooded plovers. Thankfully, no one fell down the back beach cliff.'

'You'll be pleased to hear both marquees are immaculate and ready for Day Three. Rosa's put your air-stewardess bag in the bathroom with the *Out of Order* sign. She said not to get a fright but there's a shark in the bath. If you need a shower she's left you a clean towel.'

'A shark!'

'It's dead. Her cousins are keeping it fresh so their fishing clients can have photos of themselves with it.'

'Tell me these photos aren't happening today?'

'No. After the festival.'

'Stop smiling.'

Adrian gave me another kiss on the cheek. 'I'm off to collect our VIPs for the panel discussion. Keep your fingers crossed . . . Digby's lined up one of his professorial colleagues for the panel. This prof's got the cachet but he's very long-winded.'

Aren't they all? Adrian could look after his long-winded prof.

I did a quick check of my make-up, calmed my hair and walked inside Piece of Cake for a strong cup of coffee. Wrong move. Violet beckoned me over to her window seat.

Her notebook was open in front of her. 'Last night I did some what-if thinking, Gina. While she's been cleaning, Mrs Rule's become very chatty with the fourth wife of a wealthy man in the five-star hotel. What if the fourth wife murders the celebrity in the B&B? The fourth wife and the celebrity have shady pasts. Mrs Rule's been checking them out on the internet.'

Bloody hell! I sipped my coffee and checked my watch. Would I leave or would I stay? Better to stay. 'You need evidence, Violet.'

'Mrs Rule has evidence, uncontaminated evidence. She wore her health-smart gloves when she collected it. She's kept it in a large plastic bag under the cats' sofa.'

I took another sip of coffee and concentrated on not worrying.

'Mrs Rule has a glass with a lipstick imprint that matches the fourth wife's high-end lipstick brand, a glass containing a residue of sleeping pills, and a pillow, with DNA evidence to prove it was used to suffocate the murder victim.' Violet gave me her sharpest-knife-in-the drawer look. 'What do you think about that for a plot?'

'You need a motive, Violet. Your plot won't work without a motive.'

Violet narrowed her eyes. 'I've got a motive. The fourth wife and the celebrity both knew each other when the celebrity was a band manager and the fourth wife was a model. The fourth wife got involved in the sex, alcohol and drugs scene. She left the country. Reinvented herself. Fate has it they both meet in the small seaside town. The celebrity blackmails the fourth wife. He's threatening to blow her luxurious lifestyle out the water. So she murders him.'

I finished my coffee. 'I have to meet our discussion panel guests. I think your plot needs a lot of work to make it credible for your readers.' I gathered up the Dog from under the table and we bolted.

'I feel like I'm starring in my own reality-TV show . . . and everyone knows reality shows are not really real.'

The Dog disagreed. He knew *Bondi Vet* was real.

I ignored the Dog. 'Violet is my constant challenge. I can hear the judges saying, "You have one day to go! Your time is starting now! Can you do it?"'

- **Morning-session discussion panel**

I did my final intro as festival director. Adrian handled the panel on *The Future of the Book* with his usual charm and skill. He kept the discussion moving when it got stuck in a bottleneck due to the professor's rambling explanations. I ticked a dot-point on my shrinking to-do list.

After the panel the Dog and I took a breather with Alf. We stood outside the yellow marquee in the spring morning sunshine and gazed at the dazzling bay. Alf was happy. 'Breakfast with the Birds went well.'

'It did.'

'That prof took a long time to deliver a little info.'

'He did.'

'Unresolved issues between your publishing folks on the panel, Gina. Never got a chance to ask if audio-book sales are included in the standard book contract.'

Alf, Potholer and sons were into 'reading' novels as audio books – 'Breaks the boredom on long trips.' They'd formed a truckies' book club. In my soon-to-be abandoned role as Sea Haven Library's acquisitions officer, they'd kept me on my toes with their reading list demands. Potholer's latest choice had been *Wind in the Willows*. 'Into comfort reading at the moment, Gina,' he'd said.

'Mr Toad's a bit like you, actually. Taking people on a mad ride and everyone loving it.'

Alf thought it would take a while before e-books outsold hard copy. 'I can't see folks reading e-books on the beach. Sand's a worry if it gets in electronic stuff.'

True.

Alf went to check on the waste bins and the portable loos on the foreshore, and to look at his lifesavers' roster. The Dog and I hurried off to the blue marquee.

Lionel's session on spec fic was in full swing. Bianca was on duty at our meet and greet table. 'Gina!' she whispered. 'I've just sold one of our festival mugs to that gorgeous guy. He's gone to buy a second Anton Brandt novel at Pages Gallery. Wants to get it signed.'

We watched a thirty-something guy, tanned and with tatts, walking away with his complimentary Shelly Beach goodie bag and a mug.

'He's the saddest man I've ever met,' Bianca said. 'He never reads – or writes.'

'And he's at our festival?'

'He's been married for fourteen years but he just got his divorce papers last week. His wife and two kids have moved interstate. He found his wife's Shelly Beach Writers' Festival ticket when he was cleaning up on Friday and made a spur-of-the-moment decision to come. He liked Anton Brandt's keynote speech. Hadn't read a novel since he was at school but he bought one of Anton's books and read it last night. Now he's coming to Anton's session in the blue marquee. Thinks he might write a novel.'

I left Bianca listening to another attendee's story and went to see if Rosa had sparkling water, 'preferably imported'. Stephanie wanted it for Anton's session. I kept thinking about the non-reader who'd happened on our festival by accident – and could be our next big-name bestselling novelist.

From the moment Anton began his session in the blue marquee, it was evident he was in control. According to Stephanie, Anton was happier with a smaller, more intimate audience to charm with his tips for writing a crime series. And Stephanie was at his side with a bottle of imported mineral water.

I mentally ran down my to-do list. Only the afternoon sessions to get through, the raffle to draw and my festival director role would be over. With a bit of luck I'd survive long enough to meet my new boss and sign my contract. I was trying to shut down my inner voice, which kept repeating a snippet of conversation I'd overheard in Rosa's: 'My working life is ruled by key performance indicators, measurable outcomes and parking tickets.'

Ouch!

The Dog and I saw Violet in the distance and we ducked for cover.

• Bonnets and Ruffles meeting

In the Shelly Beach community hall, Geraldine, guest speaker for Bianca's Bonnets and Ruffles meeting, was efficiently connecting leads from her laptop to the digital screen projector. Bianca joined the Dog and me. 'Thanks for coming, Gina.' She dropped her voice. 'Geraldine wanted to cancel after Matt Galinsky's death. She's still weepy. Having a guest die in her B&B must have been terrible.'

I wondered whether he was more than just a guest, perhaps.

Bianca dashed off to welcome arriving Austenite members. Then she was back at my side with a cup of tea for me. 'We decided to go with tea. Jane always drank tea in gorgeous cups with saucers.'

I checked my watch as Geraldine finished the last of her set-up.

I felt like Alice's white rabbit – perpetually rushing and always late for my next appointment.

'Don't you wish you lived in the Regency period and could wear those gorgeous floaty empire-line dresses and cute little jackets, Gina?' Bianca continued. 'The corsetless dresses must have been a breeze to wear. Very airy.'

I agreed. Geraldine had her opening slide on the screen, and began her talk. Once I could see that she was, in appearance at least, her usual charming and in-control self, I sneaked out of the hall. I was running very, very late for Bill's book signing.

• **Oyster shucking at Pages**

Pages Gallery was packed. Alf and Potholer, looking cool in white shirts, bow ties and chef's aprons, were shucking individual oysters for guests at the swanky temporary oyster bar. They'd not long ago branched into the oyster-shucking business and quite liked it. In fact they'd trialled their new business at one of our festival committee meetings. 'You need a special oyster knife,' Alf had explained. 'You have to feel for the little muscle where the two shells meet, make your incision there, and the oyster will open like magic. You give the oyster in its shell to guests and watch it slide down their throats.'

I noted a smiling and relaxed short-listed author Bill and wife Deb working as a neat team at the sales table. Deb was taking payment for Bill's novels, and handing them to Bill to sign.

Sandy was standing near the oyster bar, minus Atticus.

'How's Dimity doing? Is she okay for the last session today?'

'She's fine for the session, Gina – she'll rest after today. Her mum is flying out and will be here for Matt's funeral. She's coming with us on Dimity's national tour. Our Australian publicist is going to take over the organisation. It looks like everything will be cool.'

I smiled in relief. Thank goodness for Sandy.

Once the launch looked like finishing up, I found Rosa in the pub. 'Can you reserve a window table for me at six, Rosa? On the verandah please. I'm meeting my new boss.'

'Is he a guy with hair that looks like he's put a finger in an electric socket? He already spoke to me about a table.'

'Rod Lidner?'

'That was him. He thinks Shelly Beach is a lovely place to live. He was off to look at some land.'

'Shelly Place *is* a lovely place to live. Did you tell him it's full of crazy people?'

'You are crazy person too, Gina.'

I smiled my mean smile. 'Thank you, Rosa!'

I found myself a quiet corner in the pub and sat for a few moments to contemplate my meeting with Rod Lidner. In the background I could hear Violet's voice on the mic in the blue marquee, giving her second session. If Violet talked about her new cosy whodunit, I didn't care. In two hours the festival would be over. And as Pandora always said, bad publicity could be as good as good publicity.

I didn't know how long I'd been sitting there when Pandora and Bianca found me.

'Want some company?' Pandora asked. She was carrying a cup of strong black coffee for me. I offered her a grateful smile.

'Digby wants us to fill out evaluation forms for the festival,' Bianca said. 'I'm stuck. Do you think forty or fifty is classified as middle-aged? I suppose it depends whether you die at eighty or a hundred.'

'It could.' I sipped my coffee.

'How do you define middle-class?'

'No idea.' I watched Bianca fill in her evaluation form in her tiny handwriting.

'Would you estimate our writers' festival attendance was seventy-five per cent middle-class, middle-aged women? Maybe fifty per cent?'

'No idea.'

'Why do you think there are more middle-class, middle-aged women at the festival?'

Pandora stood up abruptly. 'Sorry. Have to dash off to Piece of Cake. There's a backload of dishes that this soon-to-be middle-aged and middle-class female offered to do for the writers' festival.' She gave a tight smile and left.

Bianca's eyes widened. 'I hope I haven't upset Pandora. She shouldn't be upset. She's only forty-ish.'

I didn't say a word.

'You and Pandora are my heroes, Gina. I want to be just like you when I'm your age . . . in about twenty-five years' time.'

'Thank you, Bianca. That's sweet.'

• Draw the raffle

'Squeezed in like sardines!' Beryl said. I smiled back at her. Rosa's foyer was crammed with festival attendees who'd turned up to see if their lucky ticket was drawn from the hat – or Rosa's plastic bucket in this case. The very last dot-point on my to-do list.

The committee had voted for informality to conclude our writers' festival. No standing ovation, cheers, stomping, balloons or fireworks. And no long tedious thank-you speeches. Our small committee had more important things to do – like packing up and cleaning up.

Amid flowers, applause and cheers, I pulled the winning raffle ticket from Rosa's plastic bucket. A shriek from the back of the room alerted us to our winner – a very excited emerging writer (who'd never won anything in her life). She was delighted to accept our booklover's hamper brimming over with beauty and wellness products (and choc body sauce), plus heaps of donated novels from publishers connected with the festival. Sustenance on her novel-writing journey.

The crowd dispersed quickly to finish the festival with drinks and frivolity.

I checked the time. Time for a quick freshen-up; time to re-armour. I called to Rosa as I passed her at the bar, 'Taking a shower!'

'Watch out for the shark!'

- **Contract signing**

The Dog and I sat on Rosa's verandah watching the sunset. It was receiving admiring 'oohs' and 'aahs' from attendees who'd chosen to have their last drink on the white Shelly Beach sand. We all gazed at the pink-and-yellow sky.

'I can't believe the festival is over, Dog. I'm looking forward to a new start. You'll be pleased to know I've made up my mind on all scores.'

No comment.

Our fifteen-minute breather had passed. Rosa came out to the verandah with a glass of sauv blanc. 'Your Mr Lidner is here. I'll tell him where to find you.' She winked. 'Wine is compliments of the house.'

I smiled at her gratefully.

Rod stepped onto the deck and greeted me with a handshake. 'Gina, lovely to see you again.' He sat down with a glass of wine and a heap of real estate brochures. He looked strangely out of place without a fluorescent-lit boardroom setting. 'Brilliant place you live in here.'

'I know.'

'I've been looking at real estate prices. There are some bargain properties and land for sale.'

If he was buying for himself, I didn't mind. But I didn't want to hear any of that greed-is-good city property developer mentality, buying up heaps of Shelly Beach land at bargain prices in order to resell at top prices. 'It takes forever – hours, almost a day – to get to the city. Absolute hell commuting from Shelly Beach. Public transport ranges from infrequent to non-existent. And the drive is just as bad.'

Rod pushed the real estate brochures aside and took my contract from his briefcase. 'Well, down to business then. You've directed a killer festival, Gina. Congratulations.'

'I've had a great team to work with.'

'And I'm pleased to say that I can definitely offer you the bonus salary package that I mentioned. The smooth organisation of the festival has clearly shown how capable you are. Now, when would you be ready to start?'

I looked at Rod and took a deep breath. 'I'm sorry, Rod. Thank you, but I can't sign the contract.'

He looked momentarily flabbergasted and then a knowing look came over his face. 'You've been headhunted, haven't you? How much have they offered? We can up our offer.'

'No, it's not that. I've decided to stay in Shelly Beach.'

Rod looked at me and got the message. 'Are you absolutely sure?'

'I'm absolutely sure.'

He put my unsigned contract back in his briefcase. 'It's a shame. You would have been an excellent addition to our team.'

'I'm *so* sorry to have brought you here for nothing.'

'Don't worry about it.' Rod was keen to leave. 'It was an opportunity to check out Sea Haven Resort as a conference venue anyway. We have a number of other strong applicants we can reinterview.'

Of course they had a shortlist of applicants ready to call on. Rod and I shook hands again. He gave me his business card. 'Give us a call if you ever decide to move to the city. And good luck.' He gave a professional smile and left. I watched Rod exit the pub, and collected the Dog from under the table as I shakily gathered my thoughts. Rosa beckoned me to the bar, her eyes glinting. 'You're not taking the job, are you?'

'No. I'm staying in Shelly Beach.'

'Ha! Smart woman.'

'Don't tell anyone, Rosa. You're the first to know.'

'I keep my mouth shut, Gina. Don't forget to collect your baggages from the bathroom. And don't forget shark.'

'Thank you, Rosa.'

I didn't know whether I was surprised or relieved – or both. I'd made the decision to stay in Shelly Beach long before meeting with Rod. I realised I didn't want to enter the rat race, and I didn't want to move to the city. I'd miss the shouts from across Beach Road, the daily exchange of weatherspeak and local goss. How could I survive without the on-tap advice (admittedly sometimes dodgy), given whether you need it or not? And I could never survive without the friendships I share in Shelly Beach.

I took off my lizard-skin heels. I trundled my air-stewardess bag behind me as the Dog and I walked along the beach track. The yellow marquee had vanished – dismantled and on the back of a truck. All that remained was a large expanse of flattened foreshore grass, and Shelly Beach once more has an uninterrupted view of the bay. We watched the truck back onto Beach Road and head off to the city.

The Dog was happy. He'd stay with me in Shelly Beach after all. But not if the cat moves in. 'I'm sure Princess is happy to stay with the Jenkins family. She likes surveying customers from the front window.' I smiled. 'I can't wait to tell Adrian we're staying.'

The Dog looked at me with his beady eyes.

'All right. Yes. And I can't wait to tell him that I've decided to accept his proposal.'

We stopped in our tracks. Adrian was walking towards us along the track. 'Signed your contract?'

'No. I'm staying in Shelly Beach.'

Adrian smiled at me, and I smiled back. Adrian would probably deny it but I had a feeling he'd known all along that I wouldn't leave Shelly Beach – no matter how tempting my new job offer was.

'Good choice,' he said. 'Everything good?'

'Yes . . . Everything's good.'

Adrian looked at me intensely. It was his look that makes me go to jelly. 'Gina, you need to make a decision about committing to me. Yes or no?'

I smiled and took a deep breath. I was ready to jump off that cliff. 'Yes. Our relationship is on.'

Adrian took both my hands in his and gave me another of his special, intense looks. 'I'm very pleased,' he said quietly. 'Now we need to find a date for a no-fuss wedding.'

He checked his watch. 'I've a few suits I need to catch before they leave Shelly Beach. Can we meet in an hour?'

'Not sure I can make it by then.' I was mentally starting a new to-do list and adding dot-points. 'I have to find Terri and tell her about our decision. Her family are helping with the clean-up. I need to call Julia and tell her. You'll need to tell your daughters. And I need to send an email tomorrow confirming I'm happy to take the new position at the Sea Haven library.'

'Right . . .' Adrian smiled wryly.

'And I need to talk to Dimity and Sandy.'

Adrian raised an eyebrow. 'You'll need another of your dot-points.'

'Really?'

'You'll need to catch up with Violet and Scarlett. Don't let them near Dimity and Sandy. They're considering going into the funeral industry – they have a friend who can make customised cardboard coffins. Very environmentally friendly. You can have anything you think of printed on the coffins.'

'Bloody hell!'

'Violet hasn't spoken to you about it yet?'

'No! I'm avoiding her. She keeps trying to run her final modus operandi for her whodunit past me.'

Adrian smiled and kissed me softly on the cheek. 'Let's meet at White Sands at midnight. Have your diary opened and ready.' He held me close. 'I'm not letting you escape, Gina, but you won't get far in Shelly Beach.'

The Dog and I watched Adrian as he set off down the beach track. I called after him. 'Don't forget. We're not making public comments yet!'

Adrian turned. Saluted and sent me a kiss.

ACKNOWLEDGEMENTS

I would like to thank the following people:
My supportive agent Lyn Amy, my amazingly
optimistic publisher Belinda Byrne and the team
at Penguin. My micro-managing editor,
Arwen Summers, who again lived and breathed
Shelly Beach with me and made sure all the
festival presenters made their sessions on
time. Brilliant cover designer Al Colpoys,
whose beautiful artwork is so Shelly Beach.

My husband, my loving, walking, talking
thesaurus and dictionary. Our big beautiful family
(especially Tammy) who were again always
available to listen to tales from Shelly Beach.
(And in remembrance of Sally, an amazing
kelpie who provided research for this book.
We will never forget you.
Happy ferretting, Sally!)

ALSO BY JUNE LOVES

the Shelly Beach Writers' Group

What do you do when your husband dumps you for his PA, your company goes broke and your nearly published novel is cancelled?

Gina, a barely 50-something corporate high-flier, is counting her losses when a chance meeting throws a sea change her way. A job as a house/dog-sitter – albeit in a minus one-star leaky cottage in windswept Shelly Beach – seems the perfect opportunity to relax and regroup. But Gina hasn't counted on the locals, and soon finds herself reluctantly convening the writers' group, babysitting, baking, seal-watching, bicycling…and perhaps even falling in love.

With a cast of unforgettable characters, *The Shelly Beach Writers' Group* is an irresistible story of reinvention.